To £1

# A Very English

# Revolution

# A Very English Revolution

## By

## S. G. Norris

Mirador Publishing
http://www.miradorpublishing.co.uk

First Published in Great Britain 2011 by Mirador Publishing

Copyright © 2011 by S.G. Norris

Second edition: 2011

A copy of this work is available though the British Library.

ISBN : 978-1-908200-08-2

Mirador Publishing
Mirador
Wearne Lane
Langport
Somerset
TA10 9HB

# Prologue

## 1981

Events can have an impact way beyond their significance, way beyond the scope of the time. Not in a butterfly flaps its wings kind of way but more like a ghost that returns to haunt.

Joe Barker and Jenny Henderson, two sixteen year olds in love could never have known that such a trivial thing, something or nothing at the time, would seal their fate many years later.

It happened on an early September evening as they huddled together seeking warmth from each other on a cold concrete floor. The heat of the day had disappeared along with the light and even with a blanket they still felt a chill.

'We have to go soon. My dad will go mad if I'm not back before eight,' Jenny said clinging to Joe. She was frustrated that her father insisted on her coming back when it went dark.

'I don't want to go home yet, it's only early,' he replied.

Joe huddled as close as he could and kissed her again.

'Don't start again Joe. I really will have to go soon,' she said pushing him away, she loved his amorous advances but her mood had darkened now with the realisation of the time.

He relented and turned off the tape deck, as he got up. The sound of Led Zeppelin 'All of my love' stopped playing and suddenly all they could hear was silence.

Joe packed his rucksack, the silence becoming more eerie as his unease returned. He really didn't like the place though he'd been coming with his mates for years.

There had never been anything rational behind the fear, but the place created feelings in him that returned in regular nightmares. It was a ruined set of concrete buildings that was all, but Joe sometimes felt he could create fear out of anything if he thought about it enough.

He knew nothing about these buildings other than they were on some scrub land between the main Carlton council estate and the new spreading estate of Belter along Toll Lane. The buildings had no roofs and there was no access to them other than walking across the scrubland. Joe reckoned loads of people hung out there because there were always piss stains, cans of lager and cigarette butts. Fortunately in the early evenings they appeared to be the only ones around.

There were seven or eight different rooms and he and Jenny had spent a lot of time there in the last few weeks. Even though he didn't like the place he didn't know anywhere else they could go where no one would see them. They'd found a relatively clean spot and made the most of their time alone, talking endlessly and listening to music on the tape recorder.

They didn't speak as they got everything together, knowing that they both hated the feeling of being apart. Finally Joe put his hand in hers and they set off. It was then that the silence was pierced with a sound of voices and an indescribable shuffling noise. They both stood perfectly still looking at each other not knowing what to think. The noise of the voices seemed to lower and the shuffling now changed to a metallic clattering.

'Someone's out there,' Jenny said, holding on to Joe's arm.

'It's ok. It's nearly dark now no one will see us,' Joe said, trying to sound more confident than he was. The sound continued. It was a repeated soulless clanging of metal and it echoed horrifically around the concrete walks. The darkness and the unpleasant smells seemed to worsen as Joe's senses tensed with the growing fear. It sounded as if somebody was banging an object repeatedly but he couldn't identify it.

His nightmares about this place raced back to him now as he tried to fathom the sounds and listen to the voices. Those nights where he imagined being made to walk across a tightrope from one of these walls to the other, an open fire burned away underneath, made his fear more real.

'Joe, we have to go Joe, my dad is really going to kill me, and I should be back by now.'

Jenny was panicking and it was spreading to him as well. They'd never seen anybody here before and they didn't want to change that right now.

He looked out of the old doorway and could make out the shape of two boys, digging a few metres away. That was the sound. It was the spades crashing into the solid stony ground, scraping as they shovelled the loose soil and gravel. It was obvious that they were not adults just by the shape and size of them. He couldn't see who they were because the light was too bad. He could just make out the shapes against the orange glow from street lights of the estate far behind them. What were they digging? What could they possibly be doing?

'Quick, let's go out the other way, we can take the long way round,' Joe suggested.

They made their way back through the smelly corridor trying to avoid making too much noise. They got to the back doorway and ran out across the field towards the estate. They didn't stop to look around.

As they arrived at the passage, taking them back into the new estate, they ran straight into the one person they didn't expect to see. The furious face they saw was that of Father Peters, a Catholic Priest from St Margaret's. For a moment they felt the relief of seeing someone they knew, that was until his anger registered with them.

'What are you two doing here?' he barked at them, 'I'll tell your parents I saw you.'

Jenny started to cry. The whole situation had overwhelmed her and seeing Peters was the last straw. Peters was a priest, but Joe had long been scared of him as he constantly took a hard line in church, especially with the kids. They'd met many different priests over the years and he was probably the worst of them, nothing like the ones in the Bible group, they attended together, who tried to be cool with the kids. Jenny's parents came from the same school of Christian nastiness as Father Peters and he knew Jenny was in big trouble. Peters would tell her parents about seeing them out here.

They ran off home that night. Joe stayed with Jenny until they got to the end of her street, before going home himself. He didn't know it then, but it would be the last time Joe saw Jenny Henderson. He soon forgot that last evening together, a casualty of the transience typical of many people's teenage years. The consequences would not become clear until nearly thirty years later.

# Part 1

# Foundations

*'Our character is what we do when we think no one is looking'*
**H Jackson Brown (Jnr)**

# CHAPTER ONE

**October 2009**

*Tuesday*

Trying to stay out of view, behind the wall, she thought she was going to collapse with fear. Her hands and body were shaking in unison. She could just about see what was happening through the railings, but didn't dare look for fear he'd see her. She hadn't expected to get so close to him. Fortunately his back was turned as he stood in the alley and she was out of his sight line. She really didn't want to imagine the consequences if he found her there.

From where she stood, she could hear every word anyway, and that was enough to tell her what she needed to know. It appeared he wasn't shy about letting the world know how he liked to play the game.

'I've seen you three times this week Akhbal, you and your mates,' he said firmly to the young Asian youth,' three times, and every time you've been at it.'

'It wasn't me officer, I swear, and my name's Yousuf, not Akhbal. You got the wrong guy,' the young Asian pleaded. As she took a glance again she could see his face and the fear in his eyes. With good reason, she thought, spotting the extended truncheon pinning his body to the wall.

'Do you think I give a fuck what your name is? You swap and change your names more often than the stupid pyjamas that you wear every day. I'm going to call you Akhbal, so I know just who you are. And I don't forget faces, I'm good at remembering which one of you shits I saw doing your dirty little business. So don't tell me it wasn't you.'

'I swear…'

The punch in his gut told him that denying anything wasn't going to get him anywhere.

'Let's get this straight, you're mine now. Say anything more and my Constable here is going to break your arm so you'll have to wipe your arse with the same hand you dip your chapattis with.'

She hadn't paid much attention to the constable with him, having come to check out the sergeant, but interestingly the constable didn't look nearly as up for this bullying as his sergeant was.

'I'm the law around here, not your Ayatollah at the Mosque. You report to me. I've got a few more spies around Old Street, so I'll know if you're lying to me.'

She couldn't hear anymore as a bus pulled up in the lay-by near where she stood. A few seconds later, she saw the youth appear, running quickly away down Old Street. The sergeant must have decided to use some discretion as people got off the bus. She decided to move herself, she didn't want to be seen when he came out.

As she stepped across the top of the alley using the cover of the bus passengers, she glanced over to where the sergeant had stood. Again his back was to her but this time she looked straight into the fearful eyes of the constable. He saw her but didn't acknowledge it. He was too focussed on the tyranny of abuse coming from his sergeant. She couldn't make it out but she could see finger pointing and hear him shouting. Whatever the young lad had done, the sergeant wasn't happy.

She continued on, pretending it wasn't of interest to her. Once past the end of the Old Street she got back to her car, leaving the estate as quickly as possible. She'd seen enough of Sergeant Mark Davies to know exactly how he operated.


The soldier stepped off the bus, happy to walk the last few hundred metres up the steep hill to his home. It had been a long slog back from barracks and he was pleased to be back among his own in Dewsbury. Even with his heavy pack, the walk up the hill was a pleasure, his mind filled with the face of his mother and the smells of her kitchen.

The lads in the battalion were good to him and he was one hundred per cent part of the team. For all that, he remained different from them in so many ways, the most significant being that parts of his background had far more in common with those they were fighting, than those he fought with.

It was a problem when he first joined up, there was no denying that, everyone, including the officers, were suspicious of his motives. That meant proving himself, much more than anyone else, that he was fit to be there and was on the same side. People would ask him at home and in the job, why he'd joined up. It didn't make sense. Yet it did to him. He was British and didn't have great job prospects in the civilian world just like many of the other white guys who signed up, so why not? He'd learnt a trade, it gave him self-respect and self determination, and it gave him a far more defined life than he found on the streets of West Yorkshire.

Round here, they'd accuse him of killing fellow Muslims, but he knew and he believed they knew as well, that the Taliban were a million miles away from Muslims in England. The enemy he fought was closer to an ignorant savage than a twenty-first century Muslim and if they didn't understand that then didn't deserve any respect from him. Their hatred of British institutions was far more to do with their own crap lives than any empathy with the Afghan people.

He turned, as he heard a passing car pull up behind him. His legs were taken from him, before he could see who it was. He cursed himself as he realised that coming home, he'd taken his eye off the ball. He'd switched off. Bundled to the ground, face down, he could hear shouting and feel kicks landing on him.

'That uniform don't belong on you,' he could just make out.

The next moment he was lifted off the ground and into the back of a van. As the doors slammed and the van drove him away, the thought that raced through his mind wasn't fear; it was anger that for six months he'd dodged bombs and shells in Afghanistan only to find his death in his home town.

A few hours later, Rachel Lancaster had recovered from the excitement of her encounter with Mark Davies in Beckton. She sat in the reception of the Courtyard Hotel ten miles away, thinking about what to do next.

The Hotel was the perfect anti-dote to the stress of earlier. She was only supposed to have gone down to Beckton on the off chance he would be there and within minutes she had not only found him, but had seen what he was capable of.

Her research on Mark Davies over recent weeks, had given her a rough idea of the way he worked but that was nothing compared to the reality of watching it happen. Although of no practical use to her, it at least made it clear in her own mind that this guy deserved all that was coming to him.

She was a researcher for Stockton's Solicitors in the centre of Leeds. Her job was to look into defendants or plaintiffs of relevant cases and provide information, good or bad, for the solicitors to deal with. Davies was the target of a number of police complaints that Stockton's were handling, although so far it seemed that he'd managed to dodge any serious action, due to a lack of reliable witnesses.

Her task was to find more usable evidence, link various cases and find connections that would make witness evidence less important.

She had come to the hotel as planned that afternoon. Normally it was quite a boring job but today she was glad of the quiet time to recover and rethink what she would do now.

Working on her laptop, she downed a couple of coffees, whilst waiting for the occupants of room 115 to leave.

Rachel knew already what was going on, so it didn't matter that she was working on something else. She was just being thorough by clocking the times of the regular Tuesday afternoon meeting between Mr Jack Purnell and an associate Colin Stewart.

Jack Purnell was the owner of Purnell's Motor Superstore, a chain of car supermarkets across the North. Purnell had a reputation for selling car finance to people who couldn't possibly afford to pay; selling cars with known faults and not upholding warranties on numerous technicalities. Of course, this was not a shock in the world of Used Car Sales. However this wasn't a back-street-nobody but a major chain of showrooms.

A number of people over the years had challenged the statements that Purnell's cowboy sales team had made, especially those about low interest rates and forgetting to mention early settlement penalties. Her boss, Anna Stockton, chief executive of Stockton's, had decided to take on Purnell's on a more strategic basis rather than just pursuing the numerous small claims that had come in. Small claims were expensive to pursue, tied up in small print and resulted in little reward for the firm or for the complainant. Rachel had managed to canvas a number of customers of Purnell's through a complaints website she'd set up and had paid a visit to each of them. Now they had a much more substantial case for illegal sales techniques and even fraud.

In the same way as she was doing with Mark Davies, she had to build a profile on the individual and find ways to win legitimately or not, as the case might be.

Rachel had started to follow Jack Purnell a few weeks ago, as part of her normal approach to investigation, and tracked him here, to this hotel. She enjoyed her job, partly because she was good at it, and partly because she took great satisfaction in uncovering the secrets that unpleasant members of the community would rather others didn't know.

The key to her success was not just her nosy nature, but the fact that no one took much notice of her. Rachel was distinctly average in everyway. She could stand out when she dropped her hair and put on the right make up, but mostly it served her well to be anonymous. Her long, jet-black hair was always tied up and her eye make-up minimal making her brown eyes indistinct. She contented herself with people underestimating her interest.

'Do you want another coffee, Rachel?' Julie the receptionist asked.

'It's ok thanks, I think I've had enough,' Rachel replied.

'If you want to get off, I can text when he goes...you look a bit tired today.'

'If you wouldn't mind, that would be great.'

She was a bit tired but she would have stuck it out. Julie was fairly useful though and it helped to keep her on side, and made her think she was part of the game. Julie was bright, bubbly and loved to gossip. Rachel had got chatting to her on her regular visits to the hotel and they'd become good friends, at least to the extent that Rachel could plug her for information. She much preferred to be doing the asking, rather than the telling, priding herself on people knowing little about her.

'Maybe we should go out one night, have a girl's night,' Julie suggested as Rachel closed up her laptop. 'We could have a proper chat about you know who and this place.'

'That would be nice, although I can't do it this week. Haven't you got that new boyfriend to entertain at the moment?' Rachel asked, not wanting to tell Julie that she had a date lined up.

'No, I dumped him. Bastard had gone back to seeing his old one, but neglected to share it with me.'

Rachel was tempted to drill her for more information but decided the opportunity to leave was more compelling. She said her goodbyes as Julie returned to the desk. She packed the laptop away and got her stuff together.

She thought about the new date tomorrow and promised herself that she would try not to be so pushy with this one. She was naturally curious and never held back in asking questions, which got up the nose of a few people, even if it often served its purpose in finding out whether they were any good early on. In her mid-thirties, she found it frustrating that it was quite hard to meet decent blokes. She received plenty of offers, especially at the pubs where she sang with her band. Music was a link to her past that few knew about. She kept up the singing out of passion for the music she'd grown up with, and liked the contrast to her professional life. It was all the more fun knowing it was no longer about being in the lime light.

Rarely at gigs did she meet men she considered her type, so instead tended to meet them through agencies where she could find out quite a lot about them before meeting.

That was one of the things about Purnell she found interesting. How did he find his liaisons? Was there an Agency for this kind of thing? She presumed yes as there seemed to be one for any kind of fetish or requirement these days. Rachel would have liked to have found out more about this but it required hacking skills which she didn't have.

Rachel didn't find her information by hacking, as was the modern trend with private investigation, mainly because she didn't know how. She saw herself as a traditional legwork girl. She had contacts who could hack but she used them only as a last resort as the information was largely unusable. She preferred traditional routes and had great success using public sources and asking the right questions of the right people.

She headed out the front door, waving to Julie, her mind ticking over the lengths people would go to pursue their desires. She wondered how Purnell ensured discretion; the risk of getting caught would have been enormous. Perhaps the risk was countered when it was equally dangerous to both parties. In this case Stewart was the Reverend Colin Stewart Vicar of St Hilda's Anglican Church in Haddington over the far side of Pontefract. He had a wife which she supposed was why the secrecy was required. Being gay wasn't exactly encouraged in the church these days but it was hardly breaking news either. A gay affair though, for a married vicar, wouldn't have played well at all. Over the last few weeks she'd built a catalogue of these meetings, Stewart not being the only one, who appeared.

According to Julie, Purnell's meetings had been happening as long as she'd worked there, which was about a year. Another way Purnell had ensured discretion by using another ID whilst there. He registered as Pete Devlin and arrogantly put the account through the business. Quite a clever touch, she thought, wondering if Pete Devlin, one of his sales staff, knew what his name was being used for.

This kind of information wasn't the sort of thing Stockton's would use in court, but it was a useful tool in negotiating an out of court settlement when there was little substance in a case. The firm's name was nowhere near any communication about the blackmail, and her boss would never know any details, but she would win the case one way or another. Although, she was aware that she was creating her own morality, Rachel was satisfied that she only did it when the people she was targeting were not playing fair either.

She arrived at her beloved Black RX8. As she fumbled in her bag for the key the breeze across the car park picked up. She felt the chill through her thin suit. Rachel carried on fumbling. Her mind was still jumping between Purnell and Davies, and she wasn't concentrating on what she was doing. Rachel reached down to the bottom of her bag and managed to find the key. As she brought it out she carelessly pulled out one of her notebooks and dropped it on the floor. It blew under the front of the car and she had to quickly run round the front to catch it. She picked up the notebook and looked around to see if anyone had seen her scrambling around. It was funny, she thought, how it was instinctive to do that even in the mildest of situations.

As she got in the car, she looked again at the black four wheel drive across the car park. It was a Lexus she noted and then it struck her in that 'déjà vu' kind of way that she'd seen a similar car before, maybe even the same one, not here, but in the car park near the office. The windows were blacked out so she couldn't see if anyone was inside.

Once in the car she turned on the engine and jumped in shock at the music blasting out. She hadn't realised how on edge she was. She'd been playing Red Hot Chilli Peppers Greatest Hits and Anthony Kiedis was screaming to 'Give it away now'. She turned it down to a more reasonable level.

The engine screamed as she put the car into gear. She loved the sound and the pull of speed as she shot out of the space. It made her smile every time.

She looked over at the Lexus as she left the car park. It couldn't be the same car, she thought as she pulled out of the car park and sped away.

# CHAPTER TWO

*Wednesday*

The rain poured as Joe Barker always remembered in Manchester. The landscape remained unchanged driving up the hill along the M62, a journey that for so many years had been the route home, now felt like a journey into a different time.

Joe pulled off the motorway and drove into Carlton. The first thing he noticed was a bright purple light advertising one his favourite old pubs as a Balti house. It was fifteen years since he'd been to Carlton and it felt like a very different place. He'd left the area when he went to university, but he'd finally stopped coming back when his parents retired to Spain in 1994. He hadn't maintained any contact with friends he knew back then. He'd moved on and so had his life.

He headed into the centre of Carlton, observing the buildings he remembered and the things that were new or no longer there. He noticed the old precinct had disappeared and was now replaced by a gym. He eventually pulled up outside St Margaret's church. The car park was busy so he drove past the entrance and found a space in the next street past the church. The streets appeared so much smaller and the corners tighter than he ever remembered them.

The hint of nostalgia as he acknowledged those things he recognised and those that were no longer was not usual for him. He'd always been someone who didn't dwell on the past with a natural optimism and positive outlook on himself.

Joe made his way down to the car park and could see people hanging round in the church entrance. As he got closer he tried to catch their faces to see if he recognised anyone. Twenty years on he was not sure whether they'd immediately recognise him either. He found it a little embarrassing seeing people who had last seen him as a foolish teenager, but then if he felt like that, so would the others.

Thinking about what had brought him back here, caused Joe to catch the lump in his throat.

It had started with a simple email.

The shock of what had happened since that mail stopped him in his tracks every time he thought about it. It wasn't just what had happened here that caused him pain. His own very real past, never too far away, had resurfaced again. This frustrated him a little as it countered his positive instinct to keep control of his mind. Professional and personal curiosity had ensured that he came in the end.

Joe had almost deleted the email, assuming it was junk.

The mail had come into his inbox at the internet news agency '24Seven' where he was a journalist, but the address label just said Jenny with the title "Please read me". It could have been any Jenny, and he certainly had not thought it could have been from Jenny Henderson.

He'd read the message intrigued. Often he would receive mails from anonymous sources, most were rubbish but some led to his best stories. He immediately knew that this wasn't just a story but a chance to open a chapter on his life that he didn't even know had been hidden from him.

Joe,

I can't say much, too much has happened already. Remember that last night together in '81. I think I know what happened.

Can you come back to Bury? I think we may have witnessed something we weren't supposed to see. Be careful this is really dangerous.

Jen x

Joe hadn't thought about that night for so many years. They'd been so scared running home that last night together, not worrying about what they'd seen but caring more about getting home safely. He'd decided to stay away for a few days after walking her back, assuming she'd be in trouble and a boyfriend calling round for her was not going to help matters. A few days later when she didn't appear at the Bible Group meeting, they attended together, Joe had gone round to see her. He found the house empty, no sign of anybody living there. It was the eighties, well before the age of mobile phones and email. He didn't know where she'd gone and he had no way of contacting her.

A life time later, he received this email. It contained a link which clicked on. It opened a story in the Evening News from two weeks earlier. It talked about the discovery of a body buried on a building plot in Belter. The land was being prepared by the builder before foundation work began. The body had not yet been identified. The immediate response from the police was to connect the body that had clearly been dead for many years, with the ruined concrete buildings that had been a storage facility before the war.

Joe thought back and couldn't believe that this was the same thing he and Jenny had witnessed. He remembered those boys they'd seen digging something. It made sense in an obvious way, after all, what else would they have been doing? But on the other hand, why were two boys burying a body? He felt stupid that all he'd cared about at the time was how much trouble Jenny was in, and had never considered that they were witnessing a crime.

The story went on to say that although the body had been in the ground many years, forensic evidence indicated that the body could not have been in the ground for more than thirty or forty years. Police said that they were examining the body and the site for further forensic evidence but confirmed that information received so far indicated suspicious circumstances. Police were appealing for anyone who may have information to contact them.

He'd replied to Jenny's email asking questions about whether she'd been to the police with what they'd seen that night. Her reply, a day later, had merely said that she'd been to the police and they took her statement. They'd laughed at her when she mentioned seeing Father Peters and didn't take her seriously. Joe had forgotten totally about Father Peters. Why did Jenny mention that? He supposed she'd just been thorough in telling the police everything.

The last line of the mail had been the scariest part of it and the last thing she ever said to him.

Joe, this is serious, things are happening to me. I think some one is trying to frighten me. I have to talk to you about this. Please come.

Joe had decided to head back up North at the end of the week. He'd tried to email her again but she didn't reply. He had to admit to a certain excitement hearing from Jenny again. He'd liked her as kid and the fact that she'd contacted him now, meant that she hadn't forgotten him. This flattered his ego a little.

Before heading back north to Manchester from his North London base he'd decided to do some homework finding out as much as he could about the body and what Jenny could have found.

Joe had researched local newspapers to find more information on the story but nothing new came up. When Jenny didn't reply to his mails, he did a bit more digging on her life. He found her quite easily on 'Friendsreunited' and found her married name there; Bowes. She'd married a Russell Bowes in 1993 according to the profile, but at some point they must have moved back round to Bury. It didn't take too long afterwards to find an address and phone number.

The phone call had stunned him completely. Her younger sister Sarah answered the call, informing him that Jenny had been killed in a car accident. She'd missed a bend on the back road from Burnley. The car had turned over and Jenny was killed instantly. There was no one else involved and no one knew how a careful driver like Jenny could possibly have come off the road like that.

The hearse pulled into the church and Sarah Brownlee saw the crowd standing outside. She'd managed to hold herself together so far but the sight of all Jenny's friends made her catch herself again. Surely she'd done all the crying she could? She pressed down her overcoat and black dress, playing with her long blond hair trying to relax before she had to meet everyone.

She looked at all the old faces, sheltering under the umbrellas. There was only eighteen months between her and Jenny so whilst she'd always had her own friends she was also very familiar with Jenny's.

Pete Hillman, Andrew Collins, Joe Barker, Janine Dixon, Louise Buckley, those were the names she could remember. They all looked so much older of course but some of the faces had not changed that much. There were a few others who she recognised, but her memory for names was blank. Probably the last time she'd seen them was at Jenny's wedding and she would have to bluff her way through the inevitable small talk that would come.

The car stopped and the undertaker opened the door. Russ and Sarah's Mum and Dad stepped out of the first row of seats. Sarah climbed out of the back with Jenny's two teenage daughters Beth and Holly. She didn't dare look at them even though she was supposed to look after them for Russ. They just looked totally stunned.

How does a child cope with the pain of losing their mother in such a sudden way? The answer was etched in the faces of Beth and Holly and it broke Sarah's heart to see it.

Once out of the car she immediately went to Russ and grabbed his arm perhaps for her own support as much as his. Russ and Jenny had been married for so many years and had been so close. She put aside her own slightly negative feelings about Russ and comforted him for Jenny's sake. She never could understand his obsession with being a good catholic family at the expense of bringing up well rounded children. But she knew Jenny had been devoted to him and she respected that. Russ and the kids would need all the support they could get from her, and she had to put aside her own feelings about him.

Her stomach rumbled. She hadn't eaten anything substantial for days, her faddy diets forgotten with the grief of the last few days.

She acknowledged a few faces as she went in but mostly she managed to avoid eye contact. She fought to hold herself together and ignore her stomach-ache. Sarah's husband, Connor, joined her in the church with their fourteen year old daughter Jane. She was relieved not to be with him in the car as he was driving her mad at the moment. He constantly complained that she didn't pay enough attention and that Jane was going astray. Over the years the pressure of Connor's job as a lawyer working, for the prosecution service, had turned him into an obnoxious presence at home. She'd managed to build a life for herself without him, so now whilst living in the same house, she could keep him very much at arms length. Sarah only really went anywhere with him on such family occasions where she couldn't avoid it. He even complained about taking time off work to come to the funeral. Sarah was grateful that Jane was fully aware of their differences and stood between them, the whole time.

Feeling absolutely dreadful and lonely, Sarah couldn't believe her sister was dead, and the one person who should have helped her through this, her husband, was a total waste of space.


The Stockton's office in central Leeds was a grand Victorian building typical of Leeds. It was not large but it had a great position within the exclusive area of the city centre around Westgate. Legal firms, small finance companies, accountants with high revenues, were the only businesses able to afford the expensive rents in the area. This area was a world away from the shopping streets and gave Leeds the reputation as being a good city for business outside London.

Walking through the exclusive buildings a person would have been forgiven for thinking they'd been transported out of Yorkshire into a side street of Mayfair. That was until they stumbled on the International Pool and the concrete monolith that was the Inner Ring Road. These sixties design disasters were perfect examples of the massive under investment in infrastructure and facilities in the city.

Anna Stockton was already at her desk when Rachel wandered in.

'Hi Rach, how are you?' Anna asked.

'Ok I think. I need coffee though,' Rachel said, taking her coat off, '…let me drop my bag on my desk a sec.'

'Sure, get your coffee and come sit down. I've something I want to talk to you about.'

Rachel went into her office, dropped her bag down as usual and switched on her computer. Whilst the computer warmed up she went to get her morning coffee from the machine in the kitchen wishing she'd gone to the café at the end of the street, where the coffee was just as she liked it. She thought about moaning to Anna about the quality of the machine again but decided that she was probably bored of hearing it by now.

Coffee in place and note book in hand she went to knock on Anna's door, who waved her in.

Rachel had always admired Anna; she was such a robust driven woman and often wondered whether she would have liked to have been that way. Rachel was much happier out of the limelight these days but Anna loved it. She was quite short and full figured which might have reduced the confidence of many women but she used every ounce of it in her personality. She was a success at so many things and was able to command the support and attention of everyone around.

'How are things in here?' Rachel asked her.

'Really busy actually, I had some issues with James over at the garden centres yesterday so I had to make some calls this morning. There were some problems with the delivery of a new set of pots that were damaged. I had to make some threatening phone calls, to get them to pick them up.'

As well as being the Chief Executive of Stockton's solicitors Anna also owned a number of garden centres in the Yorkshire area. James, her partner, was the manager of the business. Most of the time she left it to him to run them, but sometimes it was useful for her to add weight with her legal weaponry when various disputes came to light.

'So, what have you got for me today?' asked Rachel.

'You're going to love this one,' Anna said passing her a file.

'Sounds promising,' Rachel said, wondering what Anna's tease was all about.

John Pilkington was the name on the front.

'In summary, it's an unfair dismissal case. Dave will take the case but I need you do some homework on this guy. Find out what there is to know. I want to go into it with our eyes open.'

Dave Millington was one of the company's most experienced Solicitors and Rachel didn't mind working with him. He was as cynical and questioning as she was.

'What's the story then? From the sound of your voice I can tell that this is not just an unfair dismissal?'

'You're not wrong there,' she laughed and then explained what had happened. 'John Pilkington was HR Manager for North Leeds General Hospital. He was sacked last week for being a member of a political party.'

'I didn't know that wasn't permitted.'

'In normal circumstances that would be right, but, not if they are a member of the BFB.'

The BFB, Rachel knew, was the Britain for British Party, a newly formed party trying to bring together a number of nationalist groups with one stronger heading.

'What?' Rachel was stunned, 'we can't take this case, and I'd say they were probably right to boot him out.'

'Firstly, before we all go off on one, I got the same reaction from Dave. We don't judge our clients. If people have a valid case, and they can pay, we take it on. This is why I want you on the task. I want you to look into him and his history. The official reason given was that his political views made him unable to treat all job applicants equally. As the hospital was a public body they didn't think his position was tenable. His defence is that he's done nothing in his role to say that his membership of the party has caused an issue. Also there's no specific rule about political party membership.'

Rachel opened her mouth to jump in but Anna continued.

'I want you to dig up anything on him which would either substantiate his claim or would undermine it. Quite frankly, if you find the latter I'd be more than happy because we could then drop the whole thing.'

'Now you put it like that, I think I might enjoy this one.'

'I thought you might.'

Rachel smiled, and asked if there was anything else. As there was nothing more she went back to her desk to work out how she was going to expose Pilkington as the lying racist pig she already had him down for. Anna would probably chastise her for prejudging the case but racism and BFB membership clearly went together as far as she was concerned.

Unlocking her computer screen she saw her unread email list before her. Top of the list was a mail forwarded from one of the solicitors working on Purnell. Apparently another complaint had come in from the canvassing site. She opened it and read the details. A young woman from Dewsbury was complaining that she'd been back to the garage with a total of six separate faults over the three months she'd owned her new two year old Peugeot 206. The service manager had informed her that any new faults would have to be paid for by her as the warranty expired when more than five complaints had been dealt with. Rachel laughed at the concept of a warranty that expired the worse a car got. The solicitor asked her to check the details and see if it added anything new to the case.

She suspected the email wouldn't add much to an already large list of complaints, but she filed it anyway.

Rachel went back to the Pilkington file. She looked into the summary of what had happened. It seemed his membership of the BFB had come to light when he'd told a girlfriend about it, thinking she was on his wavelength. She obviously wasn't and had apparently reacted quite badly to the news. The girlfriend was a staff nurse on a medical ward at the hospital and immediately reported him to the Director of Nursing. According to her statement, which she'd made openly, Pilkington had threatened that if she didn't drop the complaint and say it was a joke then she'd suddenly find life very difficult. She didn't know quite what he'd meant by that but she knew that he kept some very dubious company and the threat was meant maliciously. So she'd tried to remove her complaint.

By this time though, it was too late. Once management had the details they interviewed him formally and dismissed him with immediate affect. He hadn't denied his membership when asked; he had just said that it made no difference to his job. How naive would they have to be, to believe that being a member of a racist organisation didn't make you a racist at work? He'd said that they should check out his recruitment and dismissal record and they could see that he'd always been fair. She intended to do that and she intended to find out the unofficial story of what he was like. The place to start was with the staff around the hospital and close colleagues in his office. Find out whether people were surprised or not by the scandal.

She picked the phone up and called her friend Jane, a radiologist at the hospital. There was a chance Jane may have heard about it and Rachel could get some gossip from her.

She chatted for a moment and managed to get a lunch time chat in the hospital coffee bar to catch up. Pleased with her start she went back to the Purnell case.


The funeral reception was at Russ and Jenny's Bowes house about a mile away, up through the estate. Joe Barker decided to go there, partly to pay his respects but he really wanted to talk to Jenny's sister Sarah and perhaps Russ to find out more about what

Jenny was trying to tell him. He would pick his moment wisely; he wasn't totally insensitive, but just wanted to know if they'd talk to him sometime. His journalistic instinct was itching at him to find out more.

Outside the church he'd got talking to Andy Collins and Janine Dixon. They'd all been friends in their school days.

'So, what are you doing now?' Andy asked him, breaking the ice with typical small talk.

'I've been a journalist for as many years as I can remember, currently work for a news agency now, based in London. I'm not exactly freelance but I get paid for finding and submitting stories. I can make more money that way. Worked on a few newspapers over the years, but this seemed to be a good idea. I get a desk, I get my own by-line and I get paid on results.'

'I suppose you must be confident in your ability,' Janine said.

'I suppose so yeah, you have to know what is going to sell and what isn't. I do have the back up that if the Agency doesn't want the story then I can sell it on direct, to a newspaper.'

'What about you, Andy?'

'I stayed around here really, 'he said, 'sad to say I even did a stint of teaching at our old place. Although, I'm not there now, working up in Salford, deputy head.' From his expression Joe thought Andy was embarrassed at his seemingly limited migration from home.

'Nothing wrong with that,' Janine said, 'I stayed round here and I've been more than happy. It's not the best place in the world but it's not that bad either. I've married three times and had four kids, all a bit of a rollercoaster but can't complain really.'

Joe remembered Janine was always a bit of a cuckoo, never quite satisfied with one relationship, moving on quickly to the next. He had a two-week-something of a relationship with her before he went to university, but it was clear that it wasn't serious as they both simultaneously found out they'd being seeing other people.

They chatted on, catching up on their family history until Andy hit Joe with the question he always dreaded.

'What about you Joe are you married; any kids?'

'I was married, but I'm afraid she died some time ago,' Joe said ready with his reply. He found he could talk about it quite unemotionally these days, simply for the reason that the feeling of loss never really went away. Talking about it didn't make it worse or better and in the end, like life, it was something you just had to get on with and do.

'Oh God, that's terrible. I am so sorry,' Andy said.

Joe felt the need to rescue Andy from his obvious guilt at asking the question.

'It's ok, Andy, it was a perfectly innocent question,' Joe half smiled to relieve the embarrassment.

'It was all very sudden and a long time ago.'

'It was terrible about Jenny though wasn't it? I still can't believe it,' Janine pulled the conversation back to the reason they were all there which took the focus off Joe, to his relief.

'Had anyone seen her recently?' Andy asked.

'I did,' another voice joined them. It was Heather Adams. 'Her kids went to St Margaret's, the same as mine.'

'Hi Heather, gosh I didn't recognise you,' Janine said.

Joe hadn't realised it was Heather, he remembered her as a skinny eighteen year old when he left for university. She was now enormous and unrecognisable.

'I suppose I've changed a bit since then,' Heather answered, revelling in the self deprecating understatement, 'it's what child birth can do to you.'

'What was she like these days?' Andy asked, trying to move the subject on to less embarrassing topics.

'She only came back round here a few years ago. I hadn't seen her for years. She told me her husband Russ had got a job at Bury council so they moved back round here. I can't imagine what it must be like for Beth and Holly.'

'Did you speak to her a lot?' Andy asked her. Joe smiled. Andy was asking all the questions he wanted to ask, he just needed to listen.

'My Denise and their Holly go to the Guide troop at the church. We had things in common but to be honest we didn't talk much. She never hung around really with the other mothers. I got the impression Russ wanted her home, so she never stayed and talked. Tell you what though; Jenny and Russ were big noises at the church. Russ was well into his religion. I thought we had all left that behind years ago.'

Joe remembered at the service that the priest, for once, sounded like he knew her well and talked glowingly of her as a model mother and wife. He was obviously a new guy here, Father Peters having been shipped out long ago or most probably dead now. He definitely had not been sorry to see that the old bastard wasn't still here.

The small talk went on for a while, but really Joe wanted to move on and talk to Russ or Sarah. He looked around to see Russ had gone into the hall, talking intently to a large guy in an expensive looking suit, he certainly looked a class above some of the people here. Joe made his excuses to the others and followed after him.

Sarah Brownlee was holding herself together quite well. In truth she was numb and although everyone had nothing but nice things to say to her, she couldn't take on board their words. She had the weight of her own grief to deal with and other people's nice words and cherished memories were just adding more wood to an already burning fire. The words were just consumed, without ever filling the gaping hole she felt inside.

She had talked to so many people. The numbness had ensured she wouldn't remember what they said to her, or even what she said to them. It didn't matter. This was a day she just had to get through.

Sarah went to the kitchen, to bring out some more sandwiches. She could see Russ in the hallway talking to people. He seemed to be doing the exact same thing as her, smiling, talking but not really present in the conversation. He was just feeling his own pain.

Joe Barker was talking to him now. One of Russ's friends was stood with them but she didn't know who he was. He didn't seem to be involved in the conversation. She remembered that Joe had called her last week looking for Jenny. She never asked him why and supposed now that the news of Jenny's death had changed everything. She watched Joe for a minute and allowed herself a moment of indulgence. Joe was still a nice looking guy. He was tall, slim, full head of curly boyish hair and a clear glint in his eye. It made her think about what might have been if he and Jenny had remained an item. In a second the moment of indulgence was taken away as the escapist thoughts slipped away and her mind was back on the day. She couldn't imagine how long it would be before every time she had a positive thought it wouldn't be countered by the sadness of Jenny not being able to share in it.

She could see that Russ appeared not to be enjoying the conversation with Joe. He was asking him something but Russ was either not able to answer or looked upset at the question. She decided to go over and intervene.

'Hi Joe, how are you?' she quickly asked. Russ immediately took the opportunity to turn away, back to his friend who perhaps was a more sympathetic, less intrusive, ear.

'Hello, are you Jenny's sister?' Russ's friend asked, ignoring Russ for a moment and before Joe could say anything, 'I'm so sorry for your loss.'

Sarah noted the strange accent, seeming to have a touch of American but not quite there.

'Thank you for your kind words,' she replied politely, 'did you know Jenny?'

'Sorry, yes. I knew Jenny and Russ from university,' he replied. The accent sounded a little strange.

'Sarah this is William Hunter, a long time friend of ours,' Russ explained.

The small talk continued for a moment as she tried to make eye contact with Joe. Eventually they managed to edge away from Russ and this other guy, with Russ's assistance.

'Hi, I'm sorry about that,' Joe said sounding a little embarrassed, 'that felt a tad awkward,' he smiled, and then his face became more serious breaking the spell, 'it must have been such a shock for you.'

'Thanks Joe. I still can't believe it really,' she said pulling him further away from Russ's earshot, '…do you smoke by any chance?'

'No. Why?' he asked.

'Back in a minute,' she said as she dashed into the living room.

Ten seconds later, she returned, and beckoned him out the back through the kitchen.

'Been trying to give these up for years, but I was desperate for one today,' she said, hiding them both out of view, behind the garage. 'Russ and Connor, my husband, will go mad if they see me, but they can both sod off today.'

'Feel like a naughty school boy,' Joe said, as he watched her desperately puffing away as the rain poured down.

Sarah cracked a smile, something she hadn't done for days.

'Jenny always liked you, you know? Even when we moved away from Bury she still talked about you.'

'Thanks, that nice to know. I always liked her as well. I have to tell you I was a bit upset when you all moved away.'

'Yes, it was a bit of a shock to us as well. Father just told us that he had a new job in Stockport. He was an administrator back then, not sure what he did really, but we just had to go, you know.'

'Yes I'm sure you did, I suppose that was life then.'

'What were you talking to Russ about? He seemed a bit upset?'

'Perhaps it's best not to mention, it's clear that I upset Russ mentioning it. I don't want to cause a problem for anyone,' Joe said, now seemingly regretting whatever it was he got into with Russ.

'Now you've got to tell me. You've pricked my interest. What were you talking about Joe?'

'You always were more vocal than your sister, even at fifteen years old,' Joe said teasing her, 'oh I'm sorry,' he immediately stopped himself, 'sorry I'm being insensitive again.'

'It's ok,' Sarah replied, wishing he would get on with it, 'I don't want you to stand on eggshells with me, I'm not suddenly going to forget about the things Jenny and I had in common and the many differences we had.'

'If you're sure,' he said scratching his head nervously, 'Jenny sent me an email two weeks ago, asking me to come back to Bury to talk to her. She said something was frightening her, and I wondered if she'd talked to you or Russ about this. Russ didn't like me asking about it.'

Sarah thought for a minute, she was surprised by what Joe had said. She'd expected him to be saying something inappropriate about his relationship with Jenny. She didn't expect this bombshell.

'Got a mint or anything chewy?' she asked as she stubbed out the cigarette and threw it on the roof, 'don't want to smell when I have to do all that polite kissing later on.'

As they returned to the kitchen, she stopped him.

'First how did Jenny know how to find you? Second, why did she come to you? What would you have to do with it?'

Joe explained about the email and the story. He explained that she somehow had found his newspaper email address. He didn't know how she'd even known where he worked.

'Ok, so something that happened nearly thirty years ago was scaring Jenny? Is that what you're saying?' Sarah asked, not really needing a reply. It was clear from Joe's face.

'Well, she certainly didn't say anything about this to me. I'm not sure what to think. Did she go to the police about it?'

'She said that they didn't take her too seriously,' Joe replied, 'look we should go in, it's pouring down.'

'Ok, we can't talk about this here, and Russ is certainly not going to be fit to discuss it. Are you staying here tonight? Maybe we can discuss this properly away from here.'

Sarah had to admit she was intrigued and it lifted her out of her cloud. Perhaps she had something to focus on now.

'I was going to get a room tonight, and maybe do a bit of digging tomorrow. Do you want to join me?'

Once they'd stepped inside, Sarah took his phone number. She said she would call him when she'd thought about it. She knew already she would. It wasn't just that she wanted to find out more, she found herself liking Joe Barker and some time in his company felt like a tonic she could really do with right now.

# CHAPTER THREE

There was the usual noise in Leeds Civic Hall as the council meeting finished. The councillors poured out into the hall and mobile phones began to ring with messages and emails. Colleagues and partners would review the outcome of the debates that had just been completed. It was always an exciting time as councillors were usually at their most engaged. Some were angry that the debate hadn't gone their way, others excited with success, reliving their moment of glory.

Patrick Barclay was particularly pleased today. Fifty Years old and a successful local businessman running a computer parts supply industry. He'd sold the business a few years ago and devoted his life to working for the party and the council. For a long time he'd been the lone voice of nationalism in Leeds but the continual deterioration in race-relations in the city and low price housing estates dominated by immigrants had led to a surge in the vote. The formation of the new BFB party Britain for British, an amalgamation of all nationalist interests into one flag-waving entity had given the movement a new focus and energy.

The model had been the Scottish Nationalists. He didn't particularly like their anti-English agenda but he admired their success as a respected national party, which may be accused of many anti-English sentiments but was never seen as inherently racist. That was a real achievement and one that his party needed to learn from if they wanted to win mass support. He'd been a nationalist councillor for five years and was leader of the Yorkshire branch of the party. Since the last round of council elections the surge in support had brought the agenda much more their way. They had become the party the media loved to hate but could not ignore. Support for their message was everywhere as it poured out of the mouths of so many from the housing estates of Yorkshire.

He and Lucy Sayers, his fellow BFB councillor, were not loved by anyone in the council as nationalists but they didn't have a problem with that. They used it to their advantage and wore the jeers like a badge of honour. They enjoyed disrupting votes with their radical views and proposals. Even where issues were non race-related, when they were dealing with the most pragmatic of issues, they would turn it back to a nationalist argument.

Lucy was the star of the show again today and he couldn't help but admire her. In the six months since she'd won her council seat she'd become the villain and star of the council chamber. She was a good looking woman, with her slim athletic figure honed by regular running and gym work. She was thirty three years old married with two kids, and effectively out of bounds to everyone, including him. Her figure was only the start of it. She was smart, eloquent and outspoken. She could run rings round most of the old die-hard councillors and the big mouth wannabes who filled the chamber. He was convinced she was absolute dynamite and would become the poster girl of the BFB.

The BFB, almost by default, was a male dominated organisation. It was opinionated, often bigoted and uncompromising; all typical male traits. He knew this was its strength as well as its downfall. The BFB's honest, outspoken views were attractive to many of its supporters because they felt they were hearing what people instinctively believed. The problem was that the nature of these antagonistic views was they were often directed equally towards women. Whilst this often amused the party faithful, it was outdated and never going to win many female fans, who shared the same nationalist views. The whole point of the BFB was that it could brand itself as a modern political party able to win votes not just as a nationalist force but with an agenda for business and community. To do that, they had to shut up the bigots and racists and work on a more sophisticated inclusive level.

This was where Lucy was a dream. She came to the party from a traditional working class family, voting labour all their lives. She'd been to university and managed to work her way up to a senior executive job in the council social services department. Lucy had done reasonably well for herself but she didn't see it that way. She believed she'd had to fight to succeed against positive discrimination. She'd experienced discrimination against her in favour of ethnic minorities but also in support of her on one occasion, being promoted to increase the number of women in management. As far as Lucy was concerned, this undermined her ability.

This had frustrated her career but it was nothing compared to the hatred that she fought to suppress each day from a tragedy that happened ten years ago. This had built such distrust and anti-Asian feeling in her that she continually had to check herself to make sure she didn't become overly emotional and fanatical. She wanted to use her anger to motivate and lead the debate, not invoke sympathy and a feeling of need.

It had occurred back in 1999 when an uninsured, unlicensed Pakistani father had fallen asleep at the wheel of his fifteen year old Toyota Previa driving along the M62 back from a family wedding in Lancashire. He'd swerved out of control as he woke briefly and slammed into the side of Lucy's parent's Peugeot 206 as it passed them. The collision had caused the Peugeot to swerve into the central reservation and killed both of Lucy's parents. The Previa had turned over due to a blow out killing the driver's mother and three of the five children with no seatbelts in the back. The husband and wife survived. The police had led her to believe that the driver was negligent and was unaware of the rules of the road.

Although the incident had occurred ten years previously she had never got over it and every day it fired her passion for believing that these people had no right to be in this country. The blatant disregard for the laws of the country she saw as widespread in the ethnic communities and the constant weakening of the status of white hard working people in their own country was not acceptable.

There were plenty of nationalist supporters who could quote more extreme examples of being victims at the expense of minority interests. However the difference with Lucy was her ability to rise above rhetoric and drive the point home. Her good looks would get her through any door, particularly the media's, but once she was in that room, including the male dominated BFB meetings, she could electrify everyone in the place. She managed to use her anger to generate a passion and almost evangelical response from people. This served to inspire and astonish in equal measures.

'Who was that?' Patrick asked Lucy as she finished her call.

'Andrew,' she said referring to Andrew Bebbington the American academic working with the party in Yorkshire,' they are wanting to know if I might be interested to stand in the bi-election now that Makerfield's heart gave us an opportunity.'

'Yes, that was rather lucky, him dying like that. They did say they were thinking of putting you forward.' Patrick didn't want to say it was he who suggested Lucy to the party leadership.

'Why won't you stand?' she asked.

'Because I won't win, simple as that, I know that appeal for someone like me isn't going to sit well among the masses. Whereas you; you've got that something that will appeal across the board…you know what I mean don't you?'

'You mean I've got nice legs,' she laughed at him.

'That as well, it can't be denied,' Patrick smiled,'…will you do it?'

'I'll think about it,' she replied, '…apparently the party want to really go strong on this one. They see this as a chance to break through.'

'Well, it is. This seat has always been a Tory/Labour marginal. Normally with the current political climate it would switch back to Tory. This is our chance to steal the disillusioned masses onto our agenda. It is definitely a good opportunity.'

'We'll see,' she replied, with a smile.

Patrick could tell she enjoyed the attention and there was no doubt she'd go for it.

'Are you going to join us for a drink at The Printers tonight?' Patrick asked, referring to the bar where the party often met up.

'No, not tonight, I'm going to hit the gym. I've got some shit I need to work through. I'll go home then, spend some time with Pete and the kids. I've been spending too much time out and about recently, better show my face at home. I'll mention to them about me standing. '

Saying their goodbyes, she wandered off out of the front entrance. As she did, numerous eyes, both male and female, followed her through the door.

One pair of eyes belonged to Alex Thompson, who watched as Lucy Sayers walked out of the front entrance onto Millennium Square. He quickly tried to catch up with her so he could get her on her own.

'Mrs Sayers. Hello Mrs Sayers,' he said loudly as he tried to get in front of her.

She turned to him with a look that said who the hell are you?

'Alex Thompson, West Yorkshire Courier. I wondered if I could do an interview with you, a feature piece. What do you think?' The words came out before he even realised what he'd said. He'd wanted to get her attention and this was the first thing that jumped into his head. He felt a touch of panic at the same time knowing that as a base-level reporter he didn't have any authority to do it.

Although Lucy at least responded she was not impressed.

'What? …Another Courier campaign to discredit the BFB, putting words in our mouths, accusing us of anything and everything? No chance,' she said.

'No I don't mean that. I want it to be about you, your background, how you got to where you are now? What the BFB means to you now? A chance for you to put your viewpoint,' he said, sounding rather desperate. If he could get the interview then it was a good start. His editor wouldn't be happy with him but he would also know that Sayers was a great story. He was sure that he'd go for it one way or another.

Sayers was right though. The Courier had gone to town on the BFB and tried to ruin them with campaign after campaign working against them. They considered the BFB a smokescreen for the racism smouldering away across the towns and cities of Northern England.

'How old are you?' she said looking him up and down. He figured his gelled hair and his youthful twenty seven year old looks were not doing him any favours at that moment.

'What does that matter? You should be concerned with whether I can write a decent piece or not,' he said boldly.

'You best go back to doing the garden party beat,' she said turning away from him, making her lack of interest obvious.

On the back foot now, he had to do something.

'Who is else is giving you any decent write ups? I don't see much going your way in print right now.'

Lucy stopped and thought for a second.

'So a positive feature, a chance to present my point of view, no twisting of words or using it against me?' she asked.

'Of course I'll have to give the article balance, I'm not going to write your campaign literature for you.'

'I'll have to clear it with the party first. You got a card?'

He quickly handed her one.

'Call me if you want to do it.'

She didn't reply and just walked off. He knew he'd tempted her and he was sure she'd agree. He just needed to talk to his boss now and see what he'd say. He was going to look a mighty fool if he said no.


It was eight o'clock and Rachel sat in an Indian restaurant out on the Leeds ring road. She liked this place. It was reasonably good quality without being too expensive, and it was certainly well above the post pub crawl vindaloo, chips and lager outfits on most high streets.

She was waiting for a blind date, called Alan. She'd met him from one of the dating sites she used and as usual had done her homework, chatting online to him and asking plenty of questions. He seemed ok, fairly straightforward with no obvious hang ups. He was a forty year old divorcee with two kids, a bit older than her, that didn't matter.

She only had two rules for first meetings, no sex on the first date and no married men. She didn't particularly have a problem with married men, as such, especially for a quick fling. The main problem was that they were usually not particularly flexible and they were never available for more than a night, plus they were more interested in what time they had to get away, than relaxing with her.

Alan was due at eight, she'd arrived early giving her a chance to check her phone for messages and mail after her long day of chasing information.

After the morning in the office, she'd gone to meet her friend, Jane, at the hospital. They'd had a sandwich and a coffee together and caught up about Pilkington, the unfair dismissal case. Jane had asked around about him in her department and checked with some of the nurses she knew on the wards. Jane herself didn't know him, but she'd heard about the sacking as it had gone round the hospital. No one had known the official reason but there was plenty of gossip around, everyone assuming it was a sexual indiscretion. His reputation as a ladies' man was well known, even though he had a regular girlfriend who worked on the ward as a nurse. The ironic thing about his regular girlfriend was that she was a local white girl, because the girls he was normally associated with were all foreign. He was seen with Asian, Black, Polish, Philippino, anything but English girls. It was like it was a mission to have work through all the ethnic groups. Rachel had thought this odd but not particularly concerning. At the same time it was hardly material for the HR Manager of the year award.

Later in the office Dave Millington, the solicitor handling Pilkington's case informed Rachel, he was coming in. To avoid being seen she disappeared into a closed office, so she could discreetly follow him out and see where he went.

Rachel had expected him to have come in by car, so she was anticipating a problem if he didn't go to the same car park as she had. As it was, he just walked into the centre. He walked along The Headrow to Briggate and then into the Kings Arms in one of the back alleys. She hadn't followed him in because she didn't want to be too obvious. She knew this pub was not particularly a shopper's bar and was much more likely to be filled with men rather than women. She had to have a reason to go in. She waited fifteen minutes, pulled a shopping bag out of her hand bag and then put a book she had into it.

She walked in to the bar, asking the large disinterested girl behind the bar, if she bought a coke, could she use the ladies. The girl nodded and took a pound off her. Rachel then quickly took her bag and walked towards the ladies toilet. As she walked across the bar she took the opportunity to see what Pilkington was doing. He'd taken his coat off now but kept his Leeds United scarf on for some reason. It looked stupid, as he stood in his shirt, with sleeves rolled up, tattoos showing. The two other blokes with him were both typical of the kind she would have expected to find in a bar at four in the afternoon. All bulging tattooed muscles and beer belly. The names Bill and Ben came to mind, two brain-dead bruisers who looked as if nothing could shift them from the bar. If there was an earthquake outside, they would be in there complaining that that their beer was spilt. Pilkington had his back to her and didn't turn round. Bill bruiser number one watched her as she walked past but took no real interest. He turned away from her like her presence was not worthy of his attention.

As she made her way back out, she heard a voice, which although desperate to ignore, she knew she couldn't.

'I know you, don't I…I've seen you at Stockton's.'

She turned round to see John Pilkington smiling at her as he approached. He must have seen her there on a previous visit, when she hadn't known what he was there for.

'Err, yes,' she replied, nervously.

'Dave Millington handling a case for me, unfair dismissal at the hospital,' he said as he stood right in front of her…'What do you reckon my chances are?'

Crap, she thought, if you don't dump that scarf.

'Sorry I don't know about that case, but Dave's a good solicitor, he'll do a good job,' she replied, hoping that was enough. He was friendly enough, but she felt undressed by him. She'd opened her coat as she'd gone to the toilet and was aware her chest was exposed albeit under a white blouse. She wrapped her coat round her again as if to close of his view, sure that he'd taken a good old look.

Fortunately he let it go at that and she got out of there straightaway. He didn't seem to think she was following him anyway, and was happy to return to his mates. She then called Dave Millington and asked for a case update. Dave spent the first ten minutes complaining bitterly about the arrogance of the guy, and being dumped with the case. It seemed Pilkington thought that he'd been targeted for being racist when they had no evidence of that. He figured that political correctness had taken over at the hospital and it was a board level plan that they wanted to increase the number of minorities working at the hospital to balance out the community. Pilkington believed they sacked him because he didn't present the right image for their workforce plan but they had no actual evidence that he'd done anything wrong.

In his defence, Pilkington had been right, according to Dave. The hospital had not presented any evidence of poor practice or performance. They just said his position was untenable given the diversity intentions of the hospital.

Rachel decided that she needed to find out more about him. The likelihood was that he presented a professional image to all around him but underneath was manipulative and clever. It was clear from what Dave had said that he was quite shrewd in his operation. He could not possibly be on side with the hospitals equal-opportunities policy and be a member of the BFB.

She'd already learnt a few things that didn't fit about him. One was his dating of the non-English or non-white women. There was something quite sadistic about that. The second was that he was clearly a creep. She could still feel his eyes on her from earlier. The other was Bill and Ben, the brain-dead men from the Kings Arms. They certainly were not the regular company of your average middle management professional.

She was hoping for a message from Jane, telling her one of Pilkington's supposed girlfriends would speak to her, but there was nothing.

Rachel ordered a drink of white wine from the waiter and picked up the menu to pass the time until Alan was due to arrive. She regretted bringing the car, one drink of wine was fine, but that would mean she probably would want another. On the contrary, though, sobriety wasn't a bad idea for a first date.

Five minutes later Alan walked in. She spotted him straightaway from the photograph. He was reasonably attractive in smart jeans and collared black T-Shirt. Whilst he didn't exactly look like he worked out, he wasn't carrying any excess baggage. He had good hair, short and dark. She hadn't got a great look at him before but, at least he wasn't one of those who used someone else's photo to impress and then looked more like the back end of a donkey. She waved him over and reached out her hand.

'Hi, it's Rachel isn't it,' he said nervously, 'you look nice.'

'Thank you,' she accepted his flattery but felt she didn't really look that nice. She'd gone through about four or five different choices of what to wear and hadn't been happy with any of them. She'd settled for a low cut black t-shirt showing off her chest, and blue jeans. It was a safety first option, not too boring but not too outrageous either.

They went through routine nervous small talk until they were more relaxed. Once they'd ordered food the conversation became more purposeful.

'I know you said what you did in your emails but I don't think I understood it.'

Rachel was pleased to find her vague description had the right effect, she didn't like to say too much about the type of research she did, and never about the lengths she would go to in finding answers.

'I just do a lot of admin checking at a legal firm in town, quite boring really. It's the sort of thing that needs to be done but nobody ever wants to. Fortunately I quite enjoy it.'

'It must be quite enjoyable working at a solicitor's office; you must see all sorts of things?' Alan enquired.

'Not that exciting at all to be honest, most of it's boringly legalistic and if there's any excitement, I don't see it stuck in the back office,' she replied.

Her modest tone was meant to put him off any more interest in the job, and just in case he wasn't finished she moved the conversation on to him.

'Tell me about working in the council planning office. Do you go out around town doing assessments or are you more in the office?'

'I suppose I enjoy it. I go to see a lot of planned developments, review them and then pass a report to the boss. He decides whether it gets a green light or not.'

'It must be quite controversial your job?' she asked, 'people are always complaining about planning decisions.'

'Yes and people are always complaining about lawyers as well,' he replied smiling.

'Fair enough,' she replied, 'I can't argue with that.'

'Enough talk of work, you said in our email exchange that you were a singer. Tell me about that.'

'It's nothing spectacular. I play guitar and sing, mostly folkie, easy listening kind of stuff. I have a couple of guys with me, Mark on drums and Tom on piano. '

'I see…and you're not involved with either of them?' Alan asked.

Rachel spotted the digging tactic. He was definitely on the wrong wavelength there.

'Err no…I don't think so, 'she laughed, 'Mark and Tom have far too much interest in each other to be worried about me.'

'Ah,' he said clearly caught out, his face turning a bright shade of pink. He tried to rescue his dignity with another question. 'Where do you play? Maybe I should come and check you out.'

'I haven't got any dates coming up, I took a break for a little while, but maybe I'll do some stuff at Christmas. Usually I get a set at a couple of bars in town who like to put live music on.'

Rachel, pleased she had control of the conversation, decided to be more direct. There was a whole life time of things she could talk about with her years in a full scale rock band, and her stupid husband at the time, but she'd save that for a later date.

'So how many women have you been with off this site?'

'You're the first,' he replied not looking her in the eye.

'I don't believe that for a second,' Rachel scoffed, 'they all say that. Its ok, you know, you can be honest with me. I know the game here. We don't all come to this as vestal virgins.'

'Well ok,' he said nervously, 'I've had a couple of dates, but they didn't really work out.'

'Why? What was wrong with them?' Rachel said sharply. She started to think about the next question and then held herself back. She quite liked this guy and decided she should lighten the tone a bit.

'Sorry that sounded like an interrogation, I was just curious…what do you like in a girl, and did they just not live up to it?'

'You don't miss a trick do you,' he said with a half smile.

'Did you tell them you weren't interested before or after the sex?' She apologised immediately having jumped in with the question without even letting him speak

'I must sound like a right bitch,' she said, but of course he was too polite to even facetiously agree.

'I don't think I ever had anyone cut through the shit like that before, I like that. Your questions don't worry me; it just means we get to the point a bit quicker.'

Rachel looked at him hearing the words but she got the distinct impression that he definitely was worried by her questions. But that wasn't a problem. It gave him a certain charm that she could wind him up a bit.

The conversation progressed in much the same way. At the end of the evening she'd quite enjoyed it. Reflecting on the conversation, she still knew relatively little about him. Like her, he'd fobbed off much chat about his history although she knew enough to know that he was worthy of a further meeting. She hadn't seen any rough edges so far. She'd be a bit more direct next time and perhaps she might get to find out what the tattoo was on the left side of his chest. The final point in his favour was that he paid the bill, which she always liked to see. It wasn't that she wouldn't pay her share; it just showed he wasn't tight.

She left the restaurant smiling, forgetting all about work and Pilkington. Alan had ignited a pleasant and warm fire inside her. The glow stayed with her as she considered switching her IPOD playlist in the Mazda to something more moody. She selected her romantic playlist as David Gray's ballad "This Years Love" came on. Perfect, she thought as she pulled out of the car park, singing along. She felt so relaxed that she was unaware of the black Lexus at the back of the car park pulling out behind her.

# CHAPTER FOUR

*Thursday*

'Did you know they announced the details of the by-election this morning?' Anna asked Rachel as she sat with her for their normal morning meeting.

'No, to be honest I've given up listening to the news on the radio in the morning. It just depresses me. I'll put up with the headlines but I think for the most part I'm happy to bury my head in the sand, whilst the world gets on with itself.'

Rachel took a drink of her coffee generally happy with the world. She'd come in still on a high from the evening before, surprising herself that she felt so positive about Alan. That definitely was not her.

'Anyway, what's the story?' Rachel asked, focussing on what Anna was saying.

'You remember David Makerfield the local MP who died last month? Well, they have announced the date for the by-election.'

'So?' Rachel said, sounding unconcerned. She knew David Makerfield had been the MP for Leeds North but beyond that he didn't mean anything to her. 'No big deal is it? Let's face it, one politician leaves a void, then some two-faced wannabe of whatever flavour suits at the time will just replace him…Did you know him or something?'

'I met him once or twice. He was a nice enough guy, but you're right. He was nothing special and the likelihood is that he'll be replaced with someone equally unspectacular. Unless? –'

Anna stopped mid-sentence staring at Rachel, with that familiar look meaning I'm going to say something you won't like but I'm really excited about it.

'Unless what?' Rachel asked, playing along with the charade.

'You know you and I have worked together for a long time and I really value your opinion?' she said.

'Get on with it…I know you're dying to tell me.'

'I'm thinking of standing. What do you think?'

'Come off it, no way,' that was not what she thought she was going to say at all, '…Look, I'm not saying you would be bad at it, but hell you have a business to run for starters. You're not even a member of a political party.'

It never ceased to amaze Rachel, the frequency that Anna would come up with new challenges and how she would always drag her into it. For a long time now she'd been the person closest to Anna. She'd been lucky to get the job working for Anna back when she'd returned to Leeds after walking out on her band and marriage, both at the same time. Her life had been a mess, but fortunately she'd known Anna through a mutual friend. Anna had been persuaded to let her do some legwork on cases as none of the others in the office had been keen to do it. Rachel had taken to the work and quickly fitted in. Their relationship as two forthright women could have been disastrous but actually Anna enjoyed Rachel's passion and used it to full advantage. Rachel always saw herself as self sufficient but in Anna she had someone she could admire for her self-determination and drive, as well as someone to work off.

'I'd stand as an independent. I was listening to the latest bun fight in parliament on the news and I just thought it was ridiculous. Politics has become a game of power and postulating. It's no longer about real people and real issues. It's just point scoring on a macro scale. I decided that it was about time that normal people stood up to be counted.'

'I'm not saying you would be bad, in fact you would be brilliant. But who is going to vote for you? Everyone votes for parties these days, not individuals. You'll get eaten alive by the spin doctors,' Rachel countered.

Watching Anna talking excitedly about her plans was fun but she knew it was likely to be folly. Rachel figured she should bring her down to earth. Perhaps Anna sensed what she was thinking as she began to speak before Rachel could say anything.

'To be honest I haven't talked about it to James, and I know I haven't thought it through. I'm just convinced that the existing system is not working and becoming more and more detached from reality. Something has to change, and I think that people like me should be doing this stuff, not egomaniacs. You know what I mean?'

Rachel decided that saying nothing was the best response.

'Don't look at me like that. We need level-headed, experienced normal people in jobs that they are qualified to do. We should look at it like a national business and appoint the best people for the job with clear goals to achieve.'

Rachel continued with her silence, a sly smile growing on her face.

'Ok I can see that I need to work on my presentation. I certainly haven't convinced you,' Anna said smiling back.

'Have you got any real work to talk about, or are we going to be living in Anna's little bubble all morning?' Rachel asked.

'I've sent you some stuff on the car rental case, if you can have a look at that; otherwise I suppose you've plenty to be getting on with.'

Thankfully Anna didn't have much to add to her workload. The car rental case was coming to a close so hopefully that wasn't too much. It was all about a Car Rental firm pursuing a couple of Asian renters for false insurance claims. They'd dodged prosecution so far, using false names, and claiming they didn't understand the agreements. It was a frustrating tactic, but now with solicitors on the firm from the same community they were finding it easier to cut throughout the smokescreen of language.

'So what will you do about this, when it comes to the Stockton Revolution?' Rachel asked, teasingly as she got up to leave the room.

'Cheeky sod…by the way, how did the date go last night? I guess by the smile on your face that he was a winner.'

'You know how it goes, first date and all that. But yes he was ok. Worth a second look anyway, a lot better than some I've come across that's for sure. And he made with the cash, so can't complain really.'

'Sounds like love to me.'

Rachel blushed and left the office, refusing to talk about it further. That was all she needed, Anna teasing her about a relationship, she didn't have that much interest in herself.

She sat down to look through her latest case work and see where she was up to. Firstly she wanted to collate the photographs and log of Purnell's hotel visits. Probably she now had enough evidence to prove his indiscretions although she didn't really enjoy exposing personal secrets and dalliances. She enjoyed the research process but she took no pleasure in providing tabloid fodder. People like Purnell had enough contacts and friends in the right places, plus the money to defend any legal cases. With the evidence she had she could certainly make life difficult for him and likely ruin his marriage and reputation. That would be a pain he would probably prefer to pay to avoid and faced with such pressure he might chose the expensive medicine of an out-of-court settlement.

The next case was Pilkington and his BFB membership. She found it difficult to have any sympathy with this idiot even though he was a paying customer of Stockton's. Consequently she decided that her mission was to make Anna drop the case and expose him for the fool he was. The rumours around the hospital it seemed had nothing to do with his job. Nobody had guessed his BFB sympathies. She parked that whilst she waited for Jane to call her hopefully with a meeting with one of his ex's.

Following on from the BFB and Pilkington there was also her other victim to be. Mark Davies, Police Sergeant and full time racist bully. He was effectively performing his own personal brand of ethnic cleansing, arresting Asians, Blacks, any other race that Davies felt didn't belong on his streets. The police officers under his charge were expected to follow his lead and even though some of them complained about him, he still managed to continue his own concerted race war. In her mind it didn't seem to matter to the police that he was a racist, that complaints made against him were never substantiated because the person complaining was usually isolated by the rest of the team. Effectively they were bullied into suppression and quickly moved out. The links to the BFB, however, would be very damaging because this was strictly forbidden by the police establishment. So in reality a police officer could get away with being a racist as long as he didn't belong to a racist organisation.

As usual, in order to do her investigation she did her reading and digging in documents and paperwork, but also she followed him. That had nearly exposed her investigation when she almost ran into him on Tuesday harassing an Asian youth. At least that had confirmed some of her suspicions about him. The real coup from Tuesday was seeing him bully one of his team. Now she had a description of one of the officers who had a problem with Davies she might get him to provide information or maybe even stand against him. That was a long shot but worth a try.

Her first call was to Jane at the hospital to see whether she'd got hold any of the nurses who knew Pilkington. The department receptionist answered and called Jane over.

The five minute conversation was useful as she now had the name of a Polish nurse, Patrycja Wladek, who she knew was involved with him. Jane would get her to call Rachel.

Rachel continued with her agenda, wondering if this Polish girl would prove helpful. She hoped so; otherwise she didn't see any way Pilkington would lose his tribunal.


Once again the nostalgia was working through Joe as he walked through the centre of Bury having finished at the Police Station. He planned to have lunch at the Old Heart in the town square. He remembered the many pleasurable hours he'd spent in there, before and after the age of eighteen sampling the various beers on offer and then attempting to get into the limited night clubs of Bury. Those were the days when he tried to look cool for the girls in dodgy night clubs and probably failed miserably. In the end he'd been too much of a good boy to attract the girls. He developed his persona of being the guy in the background, not involved in what was happening and sprouting drunken rhetoric and silliness to anyone still around to listen, providing a sound basis for a career in journalism.

Bury didn't seem that much different from his days around the town, probably because in the late seventies and eighties the centre had gone through such a major transformation with the bus and metro interchange and the inner ring road.

The contrast of concrete precincts and traditional Victorian brick buildings was all around with perhaps the town hall and the indoor market providing the only things to stand out as distinctive to Bury.

The visit to the police station in Bolton Street hadn't gone well. Joe had decided that he should go and explain what he knew about the body on the waste ground, on the pretext he was doing his civic duty, although really he was keen to know who Jenny had spoken to. He'd been told to wait in the reception for half an hour whilst a large constable came out, with a face only a mother could love. He introduced himself as P.C. Robbins, speaking with the minimum of courtesy and didn't seem particularly interested in Joe. When Robbins learnt that Joe was a journalist, even the minimal courtesy dwindled as he became hostile and suspicious about his motives. Joe made a mental note next time to say he was a teacher or something, as he normally did. For a change he'd tried to play this one straight given his involvement in the story and it had got him nowhere.

Eventually frustrated with Robbins, Joe asked the officer if he was going to take his statement or not, because if he wasn't then he had better things to be doing. As if in acceptance of the inevitable the officer went out and returned a moment later with a statement form and completed it.

Once Robbins had dismissed him, Joe had taken the short walk from the police station to the pub. He gave some thought to understanding what Jenny was talking about in her emails, and more to the point, what she so scared of. There was a body which was obviously what he and Jenny had seen, and then Peters had frightened the life out of them. Over the years Joe wondered whether the myth of Peters' scary demeanour had become exaggerated and this story just perpetuated the myth. As kids a lot of people were pretty scary but that didn't make them bad.

The thought of Peters' heavy handed religious demeanour and Jenny's devotion to the church over the years instinctively felt like a connection to Joe.

Sarah Brownlee turned up at half twelve and Joe found himself quite excited to see her. That had taken him a bit by surprise as he felt he hadn't taken much notice of her yesterday. Meeting so many people at the funeral, he hadn't thought too much about her. Sarah had just been Jenny's sister and she was a way to finding more information, although he had guiltily noted her smart tall figure in that black dress. He'd asked to meet her again today without thinking much about it and was a little bit surprised that she'd called him last night to make arrangements.

Here she was now in a T-shirt, denim jacket and jeans looking really good. She was tall, certainly not skinny thin, but definitely attractive, much more so than the slightly plump motherly looking picture he'd seen of Jenny at the funeral. Even with those sharp blue eyes it appeared Jenny had lost whatever Joe had seen in her. Sarah had aged quite the better with those same eyes as Jenny and shoulder length blonde hair.

Joe asked her if she wanted a drink and something to eat. They both ordered the soup and a roll, and he politely enquired as to how she was feeling after the funeral.

'Fine I suppose, not much more I can say really. How was the hotel last night?' Sarah asked.

'Ok, fairly typical. Nothing special that's for sure.' Joe replied.

He'd stayed at the City Inn hotel on Rochdale Road. Bury wasn't known for its cosmopolitan choice of hotels and this seemed to be the only decent one around.

'I went for a drink with Andy Collins last night,' he went on to say.

'Oh how was that? I don't know Andy that well. He seems like a nice enough guy.'

'It was ok. Not much to say really. We chatted about the old times…what we have been doing and all that but nothing to get excited about.'

'I think you're a bit unimpressed with us locals up here, never quite doing as well as you in the big smoke,' she said with a coy look.

'That's not true, it's just a bit different, coming back after all this time,' he replied embarrassed she would read his mind.

'It's ok, I'm only teasing you...we can all be a bit snobby sometimes.'

The soup came and they started to tuck in.

Sarah seemed to lean back and think for a moment before speaking.

'So Joe, pardon me for asking, but are you married? I noticed you came up on your own.'

Sarah asked the same question as had been asked the day before and he answered it the same way, just hoping the ghost of his wife didn't scare her off.

'Oh gosh, sorry for asking,' Sarah said with clear regret.

Joe rescued her from it with a smile and encouragement in his face that told her it was ok.

'Yesterday must have been all the more terrible for you? Can I ask what happened? Sorry if this is painful, you don't have to answer if you don't want to... God that sounded awkward I'm really sorry.'

Sarah was clearly a little nervous with her mind working faster than her tact could censure.

'It's ok,' Joe replied rescuing her again, 'I'm used to it, and no it's not easy to talk about. But it happened and it doesn't change anything. She died in a fire in our home. I've no idea what caused it, whether it was deliberate or not. It was an electrical fault apparently, but I didn't think there was anything abnormal in our electrics at the time. I was away that night and it was only when I received a call early in the morning that I knew anything about it.'

He decided not to say anymore, as tears began welling in Sarah's eyes. Her nervousness had been replaced with the raw grief of yesterday returning.

'I'm so sorry, that's terrible,' she said.

'It was a long time ago now, don't worry about it,' he said, 'it's not a pleasant thing of course, but I've moved on in my own mind, I have to otherwise it just drags you down. I've had a few girlfriends since but they never worked out, perhaps the ghost of Liza, that was her name, hadn't quite left me then.'

'Has she now?' Sarah asked intently and then it appeared immediately regretting the question, 'sorry that was unfair.'

'I think so,' he said, nodding a little as if to encourage her, 'I think so.'

They both returned to soup, whilst thinking of the next thing to say.

'Do you want my roll?' Sarah said, 'I'm not that hungry at the moment... haven't been for days. Works wonders for my diet, this grief business.

She cracked a weak smile.

'Diet, you?' he said, 'you're really slim...I can't see why you need to diet.'

'Weight doesn't keep off on its own, you know?' she joked, 'but thanks for the thought?'

Joe took the roll anyway ignoring the fact that his flattery had gone over her head. He was never one to miss out on an extra portion.

'Let's talk about Jenny,' he said, in between mouthfuls, '...I guess that's why we're here.'

Sarah smiled in acknowledgement and then surprised him.

'So do you think that Jenny being frightened of something or someone was connected to her accident?' she asked, 'it's the obvious question, isn't it?

Joe didn't answer immediately not wanting to stop her now that she'd relaxed a little, so she went on.

'I'll take silence as some degree of you thinking the same,' looking him in the eye, she pushed him further, '...well do you think that? Is that why you're still here digging around?'

'Let's go with what you said for a moment,' he said, 'and no, for your information, I hadn't really voiced that connection to myself. As far as I was aware it was an accident. Do you know something I don't?'

'No, but it's one big coincidence. Even if, you look at an indirect connection between the two things, if she was frightened maybe she wasn't thinking straight when she crashed.'

'In that case, they are not really linked. One may have caused the other, but that doesn't mean they are linked.'

'Andy said that Father Peters left the parish, years ago, do you know what happened to him?'

'Oh yeah, he died ages ago, my dad went to his funeral, although I can't think why, miserable old sod didn't deserve any sympathy. He might have been a Catholic Priest but if he's sat in Heaven, I'm going for the other place.'

'I agree totally, at least we know it's got nothing to do with him, whoever was tormenting Jenny.'

Changing the subject Sarah asked another question.

'Did you go to the Police this morning?' she asked.

Joe explained what had happened and about the charming Officer Robbins.

'He sounds like a right charmer, doesn't he? You wonder why we have all the problems with the police when that's the sort of recruit we get these days.'

'So, what's next then?' Sarah asked him.

'Good question,' Joe sat back for a moment, 'here's what we know. We know twenty eight years ago somebody buried a body on that scrubland. A mean old local priest either was a witness to it or potentially knew something about it. That same mean old priest is dead and buried long ago. Your sister discovered something about what happened that night. She is now gone.'

'Do we know who the body is likely to be? The newspaper said something about a teenage boy,' Sarah said.

'Yes well that's all that is known from what I've seen. They haven't been able to find any missing persons in the immediate area fitting that description. I guess identify the body and you probably have a good idea who the killer or killers are.'

'Surely there was a missing person hunt at the time, a teenage boy can't just go missing and no-one be looking for them,' Joe was about to jump in, when she held her hand up.

'It's ok, it was a stupid statement. Teenage boys disappear all the time. Most runaways must come into that category and it's unlikely that the police will have suspected anything other than that without any evidence to the contrary.'

'You can see now why it was easy to get away with,' Joe said glibly.

'This is a nightmare. What can we do?'

'The first thing I think is to look for a missing person. That should be something practical we can do. And maybe you can talk to Russ and see if he has anything to tell you. He may talk to you. He certainly didn't want to talk to me.'

'Ok I guess so. How are you going to find the missing person?'

'I suppose what I'd usually do with something like this. Go up to central library and go through newspapers at the time. We can see what the internet has to say on the matter. We should be able to produce a shortlist.'

'I suppose it's a start. Are you still going to be here tonight?'

'Why do you fancy meeting for dinner?' he smiled. Again he'd said it without thinking, not sure he expected her to agree.

'Are you sure?' she asked seriously.

He could see she was wary of wading into scary waters and then her expression changed probably wanting to play it light.

'Are you going to treat me to a lovely meal at the Hotel? How could a girl resist?'

Joe laughed.

'Look I don't want to cause a problem with your husband or anything; he's welcome to come along as well.'

'Don't go spoiling it by inviting him along,' she said quickly, '…sorry that came out a bit wrong. Connor and I don't have what you call a close relationship, to be honest he does his thing and I do mine. That doesn't mean that I'm going off here, there and everywhere with anyone I meet, but it does mean I make my own decisions about who I go out with and where I go. He does the same and as long as he doesn't bring it to my door, I'm past caring. I hope that doesn't sound too callous.'

'No, no,' he replied, 'I'm not judging anybody. I just didn't want to cause any embarrassment,' he knew not to comment on other peoples marital arrangements.

'I'll see you tonight then, if I haven't scared you off with this idea that I'm a desperate married woman.'

'No, no, of course not,' he said wondering or perhaps hoping she was in fact a desperate married woman. He was already looking forward to her coming that night.

They got their stuff together, preparing to leave. They liked each other it seemed but didn't quite know whether, to kiss, hug or just shake hands. So they did nothing in that very English way and left separately.


The metro pulled out of Bury station, part of the Manchester tram network. Sarah Brownlee found a seat to herself and got comfortable. In the few minutes since she'd left Joe she'd thought about nothing else other than whether there could really be a link between Jenny's accident and all this history.

She had never been a great believer in conspiracy stories, particularly the convoluted way in which storytellers adapted the facts to meet the rhetoric. As anyone who has read widely and viewed the world with a healthy dose of cynicism knew, conspiracies could be conjured up all too easily and she had to consider whether she was falling for the same thing here.

Something was not right however and that was clear in Sarah's mind. Whether they were clutching at straws or not, it made no difference, she still felt the need to try to find out more and get at what really happened to Jenny.

Her thoughts drifted back to the afternoon ahead. She would return home to prepare dinner for Jane. She had no idea if Connor would be home, as he frequently ate dinner in Manchester before returning. She didn't really care anymore. She'd lost interest in what he did with his time and his career. As long as he paid the mortgage and put money in the joint bank account he could pretty much do as he liked. She'd taken to staying in the spare room and was more than happy to continue with this arrangement. Although they'd never discussed it, divorce and formal separation seemed to be an expensive and difficult process that neither of them felt was worth the effort.

She suspected at some point one of them would seek a good enough reason to leave and that would be it. Perhaps once Jane was at university the pretence of staying together for the family would no longer hold together the very un-sticky glue that existed between them.

Living a separate life within the same house had turned her fairly insular and anti-social. She'd taken pleasure in Jane's needs so that was ok, and for all intents and purposes family life continued on as normal. It was more her social life that suffered and certainly her perception of herself as a sexual being. For years now she'd considered ways to rediscover herself as a living breathing woman especially now she'd begun her forties, but nothing really came off as real life threw so many practical obstacles in her way, something as simple as picking her daughter up from school. Having no need of a job due to the good money that Connor earned she didn't even have that as an outlet.

Bringing her thoughts back to the present, Sarah cursed herself for indulging in momentary fantasies whilst her sister was still not cold in the ground.

Thinking about the last time she saw Jenny, Sarah was trying to consider whether she'd behaved differently, or had said anything that would have given her a clue to follow. She remembered that they'd been at their mother's on the Saturday afternoon three weeks before now. The Saturday afternoon get-together with her mother and sister was a family ritual which none of the men in the family had been involved in or interested in either. They often repeated the same conversations each week and even the same arguments, but it never mattered. It was just a comfortable ritual for each of them.

Jenny had seemed normal to Sarah, there was nothing she'd said recently that could have been considered to be unusual. She complained about some of Russ's obsessive ways with continually encouraging Beth and Holly to be more involved in the church. Jenny preferred to leave them to work their way through the teenage years with her at a safe supporting distance rather than telling them what to do. Russ was the opposite and wanted to know and control everything they did. Jenny had told him that you couldn't do that with teenage girls, privacy and independence was vital to them as they grew up. It was like his attitude to Jenny herself though. He wanted to control everyone around him and he used the bible as his rule book.

The body on the scrubland had come up in conversation, but it had been more as a claim to fame, as if to say she was the one who saw it being put there rather than any concern about who it was. At that time Jenny mustn't have seen any danger in it as she was quite dismissive of it.

Then it came back to her what Jenny had said that day. Her complaint about Russ was that he'd got involved in a new religious organisation that she wasn't keen on

They were a new political group, some sort of Christian alliance that was all about strengthening the traditional Christian faiths in the UK. Apparently from what Jenny told Sarah it was a response to the growing imported religions and the church felt the need to re-assert itself. Jenny had become concerned about the tone and the motives of this group. She'd heard of these groups in the US and they often turned out to be quite fundamentalist, male dominated and with racism at the heart. Russ had assured her it was nothing like that; it was just what it said. He also said that there were numerous black, Asian and eastern European Christians and therefore was inclusive by default. Jenny had said that she'd been searching on the internet about them and didn't like Russ being involved.

Jenny had stayed with the church over the years, probably because of Russ' influence, whilst Sarah had long since not given a care about it. She saw Russ's attitude to Beth and Holly pretty much the same way her father had been with Jenny and her. That was probably why Jenny had been resistant to Russ's heavy handling of them. Once she'd gone to University, Sarah had decided that sex, drink and boys were far more fun and quickly moved on from her previous life at home. Sarah also had a serious accident on the back of a mate's motorbike and realised in the rather painful recovery process that life was about what you made it and not what someone else determined for you. No amount of church attendance and praying was going to change any of it.

Having met Russ at college Jenny seemed to stay in the same mode as the one she'd grown up with. Sarah had argued many times with her father about it in the early days and certainly he'd plenty to say, but a truce had been drawn at some point and everyone had got on reasonably well as long as the church wasn't discussed.

Sarah was broken out of her daydreaming as she approached her stop. She got up from her seat and set off towards home. As soon she was away from the station, she began to think about smoking again. Her stomach had settled down following the soup but her smoking craving had returned, particularly after she sneaked one at the funeral. It was only the fact that she didn't have any and Joe clearly didn't smoke, that had stopped her going outside for one, after they'd eaten. As she walked past the shops, she fought the urge to go into the newsagents and buy a packet, so instead turned her mind to thinking about Joe Barker again.

Goose pimples of embarrassment prickled her skin when she remembered putting her foot in it about his late wife, but how was she to know. Anyway, it appeared they both now had a connection, even if it was the sudden death of someone close to them. He definitely had a certain charm about him. He wasn't overtly good looking, but his full head of dark hair meant he looked a lot younger, and although he wasn't much taller than her, he had a strong presence. He made her feel safe and relaxed, and that was a feeling she craved right now, even more than a cigarette. Maybe, there was something good to come out of this, and whilst she may be way ahead of the situation, she felt she wanted to get to know him. There was definitely more to find out about Jenny's fears but was it so terrible to use the opportunity to spend more time with Joe Barker as well?

Traffic was crazy as usual as Anna Stockton tried to make her way out of the city. The city loop road, designed to enable smooth progression of traffic, was clogged with the usual mixture of daytime transport of every shape and size. In her experience Anna found the buses to be the worst hazard blocking up numerous lanes. However, Anna had the least room to complain as she ploughed her way through Leeds in her Audi Q7. Still she felt impatient and didn't feel like being rational or empathic.

The news came on the radio, grabbing her attention with a shocking report. A Muslim soldier in the British Army had been badly injured in a horrific attack. He'd been returning home for leave of absence in Dewsbury, West Yorkshire and had been attacked as he made his way home. The soldier had been set fire to after a severe beating, but apparently had managed to stop the flames. The police were appealing for witnesses but as yet none had come forward. The soldier was said to be in a stable condition in hospital but not yet able to speak to anyone.

Anna shrugged coldly at the news. She could never get her head around the cruelty and inhumanity of people. The newsreader moved on to mention the Leeds by-election and she again listened intently. The news reader was reciting poll results which put Labour lower than the BFB in the polls, such was the unpopularity of the government. The Conservatives were leading the poll but it was felt that the vote was wide open with no clear winner. It seemed the government was destined to lose. Who the masses wanted to replace them was unclear and whilst the Conservatives were in the lead they still couldn't count on majority support.

Anna sighed. There was no one who she could see herself voting for. Had things got this bad? New Labour had done their best to ruin the country over the last few years when they could have done things so much better; it was definitely time for a change.

But Anna believed, as did many others, that changing the party of government would not change the way the country was run. There were still the civil servants and the media circus pulling the strings. The system encouraged dishonesty and popularism. Governments tried to be all things to all people and there was no doubt that you cannot keep all of the people happy all of the time. They had to be honest about why they did something and stand or fall by it. That was what politics was supposed to be about. Too many times people moved their position in reaction to public or media opinion rather than showing the leadership to determine it.

This was the soap-box in her own mind and it made her angry that so few people seemed to see this. The media was obsessed with the soap opera element of politics and little about the real effect of policies.

Could she really do it? Was she brave enough to put her head above the parapet to be shot at? How would she deal with that horrific assault on the soldier?

Rachel laughed at her and probably many others would too. She didn't say she'd be bad at it, she just figured she was mad for doing it. But she had never been a shrinking violet and perhaps she should at least see what other people thought about it. Anyway, to stand she had to provide ten signatures so they at least would have to think she was worth it.

She continued out of Leeds through the leafy suburbs of North Leeds, continuing to debate with herself whether she really should consider this, but much as in one breath she doubted the whole thing, excitement grew in her that it was something she could do. The slow progress of traffic through Headingley gave her more time to think until eventually she found her way out past the ring road, making faster progress out into the countryside.

Anna arrived home at six thirty making the firm decision to talk to James about it properly that night.

# CHAPTER FIVE

Her head was spinning with smoke as it her filled her lungs and wound its way into her body. Sarah Brownlee sat with the window open so the air could blow through and the smell didn't linger. Knowing Connor would complain didn't matter, she needed this tonight. Passing the supermarket on Heywood Road following her disastrous visit to Russ's house, she pulled over, went in, and came out with a box of *20 Embassy Number1* and a pack of extra strong mints. She proceeded to light up, without a single hesitant thought. Her hands shook as she held the first one, but began to relax as the nicotine did its job. Her face was still flush with emotion, but she at least was beginning to calm down, unable to believe that Russ could speak to her with such spite and bitterness in her sister's house.

Sarah was used to Russ and she acknowledged that they didn't see eye-to- eye on many things, particularly the church. Sarah's increasing passiveness about religion was a bad influence on Jenny. In his mind, anytime Jenny had questioned Russ or their way of life, he'd blamed Sarah. She had to be very careful what she said when he was around. Russ was obsessive and controlling and probably felt that Sarah was something he couldn't restrain in the same way. For all this she respected his presence and relationship with Jenny. He was part of her life and she liked that he was protective and involved in his family, something that she couldn't say the same of Connor, her own husband.

This subtext to their relationship festered under the surface but rarely reared its head. Instead, they maintained a comfortable existence. Whenever Sarah visited, Russ would go out of the room or sit with his books, but he never stopped Jenny seeing her and didn't get involved in their conversations.

Tonight, however had been completely different.

She'd called round and everything had been polite. She'd chatted to the girls who were tearful and very uncommunicative. In the end they'd gone up to their rooms.

That left just her and Russ across the kitchen table, faced with each other. The twenty or so years they'd known each other, the arguments, silences, irritations and pain of the loss of Jenny were laid bare across that table. It was the first time she could remember that she'd had a one to one conversation with him and those latent emotions and frustrations made the atmosphere unbearable. He looked very anxious staring continually at the cup which he held intently in his hands.

Russ told her that he was coping ok, but it was clear he was not. Typically Sarah was the one to say something to break the mood. She asked if there was anything she could do but didn't get any response. The cloud still remained.

She'd been avoiding the question she wanted to ask, but she couldn't avoid it any longer. She needed to know and this atmosphere of silence was dragging her down.

'Was Jenny worried about anything before the accident?'

It sounded an innocent enough question but Sarah might as well have pulled out a stick of dynamite, it would have had less impact

At first he didn't say anything. He just stared at his cup as before, the intensity visibly growing.

Then he erupted. It was if all the tension in the room had come together in that moment, sucked into a black hole and the resulting explosive verbal assault was unrestrained and vicious.

'It's you isn't it? You poisoned her mind. I knew I should never have let her see you. You put all sorts of ideas in her head. You always were a heathen bitch, trying to make her think that it was alright that people killed their own babies or themselves or didn't believe in God. You made her doubt herself and doubt me. Well, you can get out of this house now and never come back. You're not going to poison Beth and Holly like you did Jenny. It's your fault she's dead.'

Sarah couldn't believe the venom and anger coming from him.

'Russ, I'm Jenny's sister, you can't say that to me. I just asked if she was worried about something,' Sarah replied desperately.

'Yes, just like that Joe Barker yesterday. You know she'd been talking to him about that body, making her believe that it was something to do with the church. It's the likes of you and him that made her think that and you had no right to.'

'Russ, I never discussed it with her.'

'You didn't need to, did you? She would never have had such ungodly thoughts before you filled her head full of vile. You may as well have killed her just as much as putting a gun to her head.'

'How dare you say that to me?' Sarah was in tears now, still unable to believe what was happening. '…that's my sister. I'd never harm her.'

'Yes, well you did. Otherwise where was she going on that day? She had no good reason to be out on the moors that day. It's your fault. Go! Get out. I don't want to see your evil face here again.'

'Russ, no! Don't do this. I don't know where she was going. It was nothing to do with me,' the tears were flooding down her face now as she grabbed her bag and backed up towards the back door, '…I just wanted to help,' she said as a final attempt to appeal to him.

'Get Out! Don't come back,' he said pushing her out the door.

She got back to her car and cried for what seemed forever. As she pulled herself together, drying her eyes, anger began to take over. She replayed each accusation in her mind trying to understand and rationalise, but it seemed to make her worse. It was the fact that Russ had accused her of poisoning her sister's mind. It was the fact that he'd banned her from seeing her nieces. She couldn't believe the stupid obsessive fool would do this to her.

Stopping for the cigarette had given her an extra few minutes to calm down, but now as she got herself together to meet Joe at the hotel, she was conscious that she stank of smoke and a mouthful of mints wasn't going to change that.

She was quite early given the short time at Russ's, so she ran into the ladies to freshen up. She washed her tear stained face and sprayed perfume hoping to get rid of the stale smell. She almost regretted having the car because now she needed a very big glass of wine. Tonight, all her vices were fighting for prominence.

Fifteen minutes later she was in the bar feeling slightly calmer. She called Joe and told him she was already there if he wanted to join her.

She ordered a glass of coke in the meantime and tried to forget about the red wine she really would have preferred.

By the time she sat down again Joe came in. She got up and gave him a hug. His arms reached around her and she almost started crying again. She needed that comfort and had not realised quite how much.

'I wasn't expecting so much of a welcome,' Joe said, smiling as they let each other go.

'I'm sorry,' she said, 'I didn't really mean to do that. I guess I just needed it. Thank you. I hope I didn't embarrass you.'

'No problem, don't worry about it. I know this is a difficult time for you.'

'It's not just that,' Sarah went on to explain what happened and how angry she felt.

'I can't believe it. That guy is certainly paranoid, that's for sure,' he replied.

'Anyway, that's enough of that. I guess I'm not going to get much joy from Russ in the near future. Maybe he'll come round when he gets over Jenny a bit more.'

Sarah leant back and relaxed a little, noting once again how he made her feel. Realising she was thinking and not saying anything she quickly jumped back to the conversation.

'What happened with you today? Sorry I forgot to ask with all my worries.'

'Don't worry about that, your issues were far more important than mine,' he gave her a sympathetic smile again.

'Stop it!' she said laughing now, 'you'll set me off again.'

'The afternoon didn't quite go as planned,' he said, raising his eyebrows to her suggesting to Sarah there was another surprise on the way,' my car was stolen.'

'God no...where from?' she asked, 'not from the Police Station?'

'Almost, but it was gone from the street outside where I parked it.'

'What was it? I mean what type of car?' she cursed her nervousness telling herself to slow down.

'It was a ten year old BMW, serves me right for having a highly desirable, highly nickable car,' he laughed. It appeared that he wasn't too stressed about it.

'Did you report it?' she asked.

'Yes I walked straight back in, and the desk sergeant recognised me from earlier. He didn't exactly laugh in my face but you could tell that the moment he walked in the back office he was going to have a good chuckle with his mates.'

'Typical,' she said, 'so what can you do now?'

'Good question, I don't expect to see my car again. I'll have to head home on the train and see about the insurance. I can survive in London without a car, it's no problem really. It's just the pain of the insurance process and finding a replacement. I'll have to go back to London in the morning,'

Sarah's heart dropped to hear him talk of going home already. She'd just got used to him being around in the last two days. She stopped herself, feeling stupid, they'd only just met and there was nothing holding them together.

As if sensing her thoughts, Joe said, 'I'll come back up you know and we can keep in touch about this. There's definitely something going on here that is not right.'

'Talking of which...' Sarah just remembered, 'I did remember something that Jenny said. She had an argument with Russ about a group that he'd joined. She called it a Christian Alliance but she didn't tell me the proper name of it. She told me she was concerned about Russ getting involved in something like that and she'd been looking into them on the Net.'

Sarah explained some of the brief concerns Jenny had raised about these groups.

'I've heard of a few alliances like this. What makes this one so worrying?'

'I don't know to be honest,' Sarah replied, 'she never got the chance to tell me much at the time. She told me at a time when other things were happening at my mothers. Of course I never got the chance again.'

She tripped up over her own emotionally charged words

'Jenny gave me the impression that it was about reasserting the authority of the Christian churches in the UK. People are continuing to turn away from the traditional churches either into religious apathy or into more trendy new age religions. Also the rise of Islam in the UK and the increasing influence it has in councils and government is something they need to resist. Russ joined on recommendation from a friend.'

'That sounds like a typical Christian alliance. Usually they come to nothing, although if it comes from the US then maybe it is a bit more hardcore,' Joe said looking puzzled, 'she didn't say the name of them?'

'No, but I guess Google may provide the answer.'

'Let me just nip and get my laptop. You don't mind waiting a minute?' he asked her, 'should I get you a drink?'

'You know, I think I will have a glass of wine. I could get a taxi back, and come back for the car tomorrow. I think I deserve a drink,' she said with a smile. Once again she found herself totally relaxed in his company. Being with him was giving her just the lift she needed to take her out of the cloud.

Five minutes later Joe was back with his laptop and the waitress had brought over a bottle of red and two glasses. Joe poured a glass for each of them.

'To Jenny,' he said as they clicked glasses.

'To Jenny,' Sarah added, 'a wonderful sister.'

'Let's see what we can find,' he said opening the laptop and finding the internet. It didn't take long to find what he was looking for.

'There it is. The British Christian Alliance - BCA. A new Alliance, it seems they have a website and a write up on some online Christian news site. Nothing mainstream which is probably why no-one has heard of them.'

'That didn't take long', Sarah said, 'it's crazy how much is going on that you don't hear about. There seems to be a group for everything these days. What does it say?'

'It says it's an Alliance of common aims across Christian religions in the UK. The purpose is to create a more powerful pressure group to assert the basic principles of British Christian life. It lists heterosexual marriage as the only stable model for family life, anti-gay marriage, church as the centre of the community, anti-abortion, anti-stem cell research, etc. Here's a new one I haven't heard before, voluntary treatment for correction of sexual deviance. It states that Christianity is the one true religion of the UK and that whilst it has respect for other faiths, the BCA believes that the UK needs to stand by its traditions.'

'That is a fairly big claim, isn't it? Let's face it they can't even agree which Christian faith is the right one, never mind argue about any other faiths.'

'Since when have religious groups needed any basis for rationale when making claims…have your read the bible recently?' Joe laughed, and it even brought her to a giggle, something she really didn't think she could do an hour ago.

'Oh God, Joe,' she said, 'thank you for making me laugh, I really needed this.'

'I'm glad,' he said and then returning to his laptop, 'I have to say this lot don't seem that scary to me.'

'Is there anything more to know?' Sarah asked.

'That's interesting…they have a program of activities coming up, over the next few weeks. The first is in London this weekend,' Joe thought for a moment, '…I might pay one of those a visit. They are holding a big family day publicity event in a Victoria Park. It'd be good to see what they were about.'

'Do you think the BCA could be connected to what happened to Jenny?' Sarah asked.

'Who knows? I mean they appear to be a harmless bunch of the misguided. I'll go anyway; there's always a story in some of their extreme claims. It's my job after all to sniff out this kind of thing and you never know I might find something of real use to us.'

Sarah leant back to take a drink, reflecting on what they'd discussed. Joe jumped back with another idea.

'I've had another thought,' Joe said, 'she used an email address to mail me and it was an anonymous address. Usually people use that when they don't want the receiver to have any reference to who they really are. She may have used it to do the digging. Maybe we can guess her password and get into it. '

'That seems a bit nosey. God, it's like looking at someone's diary.'

'I know, but how else are we going to find out what she was doing,' he explained, 'do you have any idea what she would have used as a password?'

'No idea but I suppose we can have a go. Not sure where to start though,' Sarah replied, '…still feel like I'm intruding. You can tell you're a journalist, all this poking around?'

Joe found the mail address in outlook.

'I'm wondering what she might use for passwords, I don't think she'd use Russ or the kids, too obvious. Did she have pets? Many people use that. Favourite TV programmes… something easy to remember.'

'She had a cat called Percy.'

'Ok let's try that with a number "Percy1".'

The password was rejected.

'Let's try it with her year of birth, 1964.'

Nothing again. Joe tried it with and without capitals and variations with the numbers. This time he got a locked email error. Another thought came to him as he saw the forgotten password message.

'Did she have a regular email address? Something she would use for household stuff, photographs or things like that,' she probably used that as a reference for this email address. They always ask you for an alternative email address when you set these things up. People tend to use less secure passwords on that sort of thing as they don't think people are that interested in it.'

'Sounds like you might have done this before,' Sarah said, with a sly smile.

'Let me think for a moment…something like jenny.bowes1964, I think it was on hotmail. Let's try that with percy64 or something like that.'

It took three attempts and he was in.

'We're in, and there it is; the forgotten password mail. The password is…. you're not going to believe this,' Joe's jaw dropped in amazement as he read it, 'I think your sister was definitely a bit pissed off. The password is "'1evilbastard".'

'God, I hope that's not Russ she's referring too. I'd never have believed that of her.'

Joe quickly went back to the email address and logged in. Disappointingly there were only a few emails. The first of the mails appeared to be from the BCA. It was a website registration confirmation, plus two copies of the email newsletter. There was also a site registration email from some sort of justice website. There were no details on it, so Joe read the others. There were a few spam mails. Then of course there were Joe's emails to her. He looked again at the SPAM. One of which had been opened.

It invitingly said 'Something You Should Know' and the contact was 'A Friend'. Jenny had opened this perhaps not realising it was SPAM. Joe opened it expecting some content on Viagra pills or penis expansion that he always received in his spam mail. The message wasn't quite what he was expecting and was probably the source of Jenny's fears.

*Some things in life are best left undiscovered, and I'd suggest you take this advice.*

*Just in case you're about to hit the delete button then let me just put you in no doubt that I know exactly what you've been looking at and who you've been talking to, Mrs Jennifer Bowes. Let sleeping dogs lie, or should I say sleeping bodies. Do I need to spell it out further?*

*Consider this a friendly warning, please ensure you heed it.*

He looked at the sender's email address, but it was equally unidentifiable.

'I think we are beginning to see why she was scared,' he said showing it to Sarah, 'I wonder where that came from.'

He went back to the mail on justice and followed the embedded site link.

Sarah tried to follow what was Joe was doing as he seemed to be jumping around the screen so much.

The site required him to enter an email address, which he thought was odd. Clearly the site owner wanted to know who was looking at it. He entered Jenny's address and her email password. It opened in a new window.

The page welcomed the user to the only major website dedicated to detailing cases where defendants had got away with heinous crimes. It wasn't about traditional miscarriages of justice where people were incorrectly convicted, but the opposite. It detailed evidence where it believed that people who had been clearly guilty had got away with it, whether through a clever defence, incompetent prosecution or just plain lies, the site was there to document and expose these cases. There were a number of case histories catalogued as murder, fraud, abuse, rape. There was quite a lot to go through here and Joe thought it might take some time to find what Jenny was looking for.

'I wonder if she stumbled on something here,' Sarah said.

'Maybe, all of this is quite interesting when you put it together. A twenty eight year old murder, a website dedicated to exposing murderers and rapists, and a bunch of misguided religious fanatics.'

'I guess you could add potentially Jenny's murder made to look like an accident,' Sarah added, 'but it's all a bit of a stretch isn't it? I know Jenny was worried about something, but it does seem silly to believe all of this could be happening.'

'I agree, but we haven't got any other explanation so far. It might be wise to be a bit careful here, until we work out something more innocent. Jenny walked into something and we should avoid the same mistake. Whoever owns this site is keeping a log of email addresses. There maybe a logical reason but it could be a warning flag to him, in which case, if this site is connected to Jenny's death we've just rang a big warning bell.'

'How do you mean?' Sarah asked.

'A supposedly dead person has just logged onto the site,' Joe answered blackly.

'Shit, that sounds a bit sinister.'

Realising he was scaring her; Joe decided to back track a bit.

'Let's not allow our imagination to run too far,' he said, 'we don't even know if Jenny's death was connected to this. We need to find out the possibilities…What have the police told you about it? As the sister they should have given you some information.'

'They just said there was no one else involved and the police investigation team were trying to determine how it happened. So far the investigation is inconclusive.'

'When did you last hear from them?'

'Five days after the accident when they released the body,' she answered.

'Maybe you should go back and see them, ask some more questions. Perhaps even let them take you to the crash site. See what you think yourself. As the sister they should humour you. I guess this is obvious but make sure you don't involve Russ. We don't know how much he knows but clearly he is not going to welcome any more intrusion from you at the moment.'

'Too right there.'

'I'll go back to London tomorrow and see what else I can find out about these sites.'

Joe closed his laptop and they carried on talking. Sarah thought about asking him more about Liza but she didn't want to sound intrusive or more likely she didn't want it to ruin the mood between them.    She decided to leave it and just hope there was another opportunity for her to talk to him.

As she went out to get her taxi Sarah gave Joe another hug and kissed him lightly.

'Thank you,' she said.

'Why? What have I done?' he asked stupidly.

'I just needed this; I needed something to believe in. Be careful and please come back soon. You will come back won't you?'

'Yes, of course,' he said. He didn't say anymore about whether he'd be back to see her or just to follow up the story. The question was left in the air for the moment, and perhaps she already knew the answer from his smile. As Sarah turned away, her domestic situation came back to her. It was like leaving a warm house and putting on a cold soggy raincoat. The dull reality of her life ruined any warm feeling the night had given her.

She dashed off into the taxi, before the tears came again.

# CHAPTER SIX

*Friday*

Alex Thompson settled himself down with a large coffee in the reception at the Marriot Hotel. He'd agreed to meet Lucy at a neutral venue to make life easier for both of them.

His editor had been furious with him for going for this interview with the BFB never mind whether it was their new darling or not. He didn't want anything in his paper that encouraged nationalism and bigotry. The Courier had family and traditional values at their core, and the BFB were not compatible as far as he was concerned. He'd persuaded him in the end, firstly explaining the extent of the coup he had, she was after all going to be the new prospective Member of Parliament for North Leeds, but secondly he'd convinced him that as long as the article was balanced and his questioning good, then the arguments themselves would provide their own inevitable conclusions. In the end his editor conceded that if he didn't like it, he didn't have to print it.

Having conceded to let the article go ahead, he gave Alex a long lecture about how he needed to be more incisive and challenging. The only other consideration had been a photographer who he'd arranged for after the interview.

Meeting Lucy Sayers again came as a shock to him. Her blonde hair, determined manner and sharp eyes immediately pulled him in. She wore a grey business suit with skirt and black tights. She looked so formal that she was almost as sternly, coldly conservative as the women's institute, but then her presence, her eyes, her broad smile, drew him in like a moth to a flame. As she sat down, she unbuttoned her suit jacket, revealing a smart white blouse, with a button undone just across her medium breasts, showing a hint of her white bra underneath. It was such an intimate view, that he didn't want say anything about fastening it, as that would indicate he'd been looking. He forced his eyes onto her face not even daring to let them slip further to her legs.

They hadn't exchanged a word and he was already under her spell. At least he was aware of it, which might stop him slipping from an interrogative interview into a cosy chat in the pub.

He arranged for her to have a coffee and clicked on his recorder.

'I'm taking a big risk with you, you know that?' she asked him, setting the agenda straight away.

As she spoke, she brushed herself down appearing to want to neaten her appearance and then pushed some loose hair back over her left ear. She must have been unaware of the unfastened button as she didn't do anything with it.

'I guess I am too,' Alex replied, trying to focus on what he was doing and not her appearance. 'Should we be honest about those risks so we both have our cards on the table…clear the air if you like?'

'Ok, fair enough, good way to begin,' she paused for a second, considering her choice of words, '…alright, here's my risk. This is a carpet bagging exercise. You're looking for cheap quotes that you can twist to make me out to be a mad Nazi bitch.'

Alex was surprised by her candour. He took a second to register that it was a deliberate tactic and he shouldn't react. He should just answer in his own straightforward manner.

'Here's my risk. My editor will sack me, because I go back with a party political broadcast on behalf of the BFB. I have to be seen to challenge you on the issues you raise. I have to give balance and brevity to the controversial issues that your party stands for; otherwise we both come out of this with nothing. I will have no career and you'll not have an article in the paper.'

'That's fair. We both understand where we are coming from. I like that. Shall we start?'

'Oh first, can I confirm you're definitely going to be the BFB nomination for this seat, you weren't sure when we spoke last?' Alex asked.

'Yes I've decided to stand,' she said, 'the party are in full support of me.'

'Congratulations,' Alex said, really excited to know his gamble had worked. He would have the first story on her.

He started with the easy stuff, partly to give his article some back story, but partly because it was useful to get over how nervous he was.

Once that was out of the way, he got to the core of the interview.

'Why do you think people are scared of nationalist parties like yours and automatically assume you're racist?'

Lucy leant forward and with her left hand, pulled her hair forward and then pushed it back over her ear. It seemed to be something she did when thinking or was it a nervous thing? He liked the idea that she might be nervous, but her voice didn't show it as she spoke again.

'I can't tell you what other people think and why they make assumptions but I can speculate. I think it's because people use it as a defence against the argument we are making. To play the race card is to ignore the issue that is being debated. It sweeps it under the carpet until it festers out another day. If you don't deal with an issue head on, then it will always be shrouded and never solved. It's left to people like us, who are straight talkers, to raise those issues and I think people get scared when they hear such honest views.'

She took a drink of coffee. Alex let her continue sensing there was more to come.

'I can't deny that the party of the past has attracted some undesirables, but every group in the country has always had trouble with militant members. Remember labour in the eighties with the Clause Four brigade? Even the Tory's have the Young Tory's, a bunch of rich kids with far too much to say. So I don't think we are any different. All political causes attract over enthusiastic activists.'

'But you have to agree that you've had your fair share of the worst of them: National Front etc.'

'That was a long time ago.'

'Are you the smiling face of fascism or racism?' Alex followed up without a pause in an attempt to throw her off track.

'Ok which one am I? Fascist or Racist? Do you understand the difference?' she replied, showing she was more than equal to his tactic. She had an off-the-cuff answer which probably showed it wasn't the first time it had been asked. There was no nervous hair movement this time. He was going to say something but Lucy ignored him. She had plenty of ammunition saved up for this topic.

'I'm not going to get into an intellectual argument over what this is about because it doesn't need one,' she said, '…people can sling these labels on me and my colleagues all day because it doesn't matter. As I stated above, it's easier to put labels on us than it is to deal with what we have to say. We are about protecting this country, what it stands for. Protecting what the people in the war fought for; continuing the British way of life in Britain.'

Alex jumped in again, trying to plug the grandstanding speech.

'And what is the British way of life you refer to? Is that not just a chocolate box view of a world that doesn't exist any more?'

'Of course the world is changing, but the way it's changing is frightening people. We are made to feel guilty for challenging every time one of our well established rights disappear in this country. We are made to feel guilty every time we complain about money spent on something that's for the good of people who curse us and rob us rather than appreciate the hospitality and generosity this country has given them.'

'You're referring to the debate the other day in the council chamber?'

'Yes, that's an example of favouring a population which despises and resents our way of life. If you want to see blatant racism, go and listen to one of their sermons. We are not just whites or non-believers. We are infidels. Why can't we complain about them saying that?'

'As far as I can see there's no law saying that you can't?'

'Don't be naive, the race relations act and the religious hatred act, forbid us to raise these issues; in case we incite religious hatred and upset them. In my view they're the ones upsetting us. We're doing the same things we've done for centuries, which is welcome other cultures into our country, we just ask that they abide by our laws and way of life. It's clear that this isn't happening any more. Political correctness has removed our ability to defend ourselves. We can't challenge them on their behaviours because we're being racist and insensitive. So what happens; they take advantage and start abusing our good nature and are turning it back on us now. Then everywhere sees us as a soft touch and the numbers become overwhelming. We've opened the door too wide and now we need to shut it. We need to get Britain back to the strong country it was and then see whether we've space for more immigrants.'

Alex felt he wasn't going to get much further with the political argument so he moved on to her. He kept watching her to see when her hand would seek out the hair over her ear, but she seemed to do less of it as she spoke more confidently. Trying to focus on the questions and look for her nervousness was confusing him so he tried to put it out of his mind.

'What do you bring to the debate that the party didn't have before?'

Lucy appeared relieved to get off the defensive and onto something more positive for her.

'Hopefully I'm a bit better looking than some of my predecessors,' she said with a nervous giggle 'but I hope you can see that I'm a lot more than just a pretty face.'

As she spoke, she definitely moved her hand to her hair again, as well as leaning forward and crossing her legs. It was interesting to Alex how unused to this she was, perhaps she wasn't quite as hard nosed as she liked to portray. He tried not to think about it, but he couldn't help liking her more for it.

Lucy continued talking when Alex didn't jump in with a question.

'I think it's good to hear a woman presenting these views that have so often been presented by men. Nationalism was always seen as the domain of men rather than women and consequently it was easy for the mainstream to put down these arguments to selfish white males who want everything their own way. I hope to broaden the appeal to all, male and female, and show them that the BFB is an honest, modern, intelligent, political force that deserves to be given consideration. Whether they choose to vote for us is their choice, but at least listen to what we have to say.'

'What drives you to be so passionately anti-everything; you seem to be so angry in some ways, almost bitter that these people are taking something away from you.'

'We are not anti-everything, we are for Britain and its people.'

'You've just given me a whole list of things you don't like. That sounds pretty negative to me. Can you give me one positive inclusive policy that you have?'

'Look, I can give you positive, and our party has many policies to rebuild Britain's cities and make them strong again, investing in cheap, quality housing, re-establishing our economic self sufficiency. But, this can only be done if we face up to the issues stopping us, and that's the fact that our doors are open to all and sundry to come and claim their piece of territory.'

'What about the EU? Do you think leaving the EU, as your party suggests, is a wise idea? The economic impact would be enormous.'

'The economic impact would be massive, but in fact a positive one. This country could concentrate on itself instead of pumping billions of pounds into Europe with little or no benefit to the UK economy. We could use that money to invest in Britain and British jobs.'

'That sounds like a very naïve and outdated political viewpoint. Almost every economist around would say that Britain needs to be in Europe.'

'I don't see globalisation and global trade doing much for this country except killing off our manufacturing industries and making this country the debt ridden mess it is.'

'Do you think you can win this bi-election?' Alex asked directly.

'Yes, look at the opinion polls, the electorate are fed up with being dominated by the main parties who are not in touch with the people. Listen to folk on the streets and you'll know that they agree with us.'

'You mean the white English population?'

'I mean all British people who see what is happening to the fabric of this country,' Lucy replied firmly.

At this point Alex was wondering where to go with the interview so he was pleased to be rescued by Cassie, his photographer. She came over after spotting them. He asked Lucy if she was happy to finish off and have the photos taken.

She seemed as relieved as Alex to get to the end. The hour had gone quickly and it had been exhausting for both of them.

Lucy posed for the photos, seeming to enjoy the attention. He noticed the button had been done up, and wondered if she spotted it herself or Cassie had said something.

Alex thought that if this campaign succeeded then she was going to be everywhere. The tabloids would love her. She then got up saying she had to go. Alex thanked her for her time.

'If you want to hear more, and listen to other points of view, we've a march in City Square on Sunday. You will see then perhaps that the BFB is a broad church with many different points of view. You will also see the family friendly nature we have. If you get there early enough, ask for me, I might be able to get you to chat with some of the others directly.'

With that she left. He was pleased with himself that he'd achieved a degree of comfort with Lucy Sayers, that she was open to more exposure. He wondered whether his editor would agree; whether he was incisive enough. Maybe he'd been too easy on her.


Leaving the hotel, Lucy decided to walk up through the city, rather than take a taxi. It was cold but she fancied the walk. She hadn't had time for a run in the last couple of days so was happy to take exercise where she could.

She crossed Boar Lane and walked up the hill and through the precinct, thinking about how the interview had gone.

Alex had fallen for the button trick easily. She'd used it before in interviews and liked the idea that it put men off their stride. He was a good interviewer though and had kept his focus. That wasn't a problem as she needed him to be a good challenging outlet for her, but she just liked the idea that she was in control.

She'd been a bit nervous; she was, after all, still getting used to the role, but she enjoyed the attention and was looking forward to the challenges ahead. She knew she had to work on her style and presentation and get rid of her nervous twitches. Alex was a nice introduction, but there would be a lot tougher bridges to cross with what they had planned over the next few weeks.

Surprisingly, though, she did find that she quite liked him. He could do to lose the blond highlights in his messy gelled hair, but she figured that was an age thing. He probably thought he looked cool with his mates on the pull. He was intelligent and polite, which was more than most men around, including many in her party. To top it all, he was a good looking, tall and broad shouldered with an innocent twinkle in his eyes.

I could make mince-meat of him was her final thought as she heard the familiar ring-tone of her phone in her handbag.

# CHAPTER SEVEN

In front of the mirror wasn't the best place to be standing this morning, but he thought he ought to make an effort to look smart. Not that it seemed to do any good; another job interview, another rejection was all that ever seemed to happen. He hated the mirror, looking crap and dated with its seventies pink frame against the green tiled bathroom wall, although that was just his mother's bad taste. The real problem was the image it showed him. With the exception of those occasional braver moments, he avoided having to face up to who he really was.

Everyday he told himself that he'd overcome it, he should be proud of who he was, proud of his family and his background, and he believed it. That was never an issue, but he just found it harder each day to live with the consequences, especially as the eyes of others continued to judge him.

Today was a typical example of the torture he felt. He'd turn up for an interview that the job centre had found for him. That was fine, he wanted to work, wanted to show everyone that he could succeed like them, hold his head up high and finally fit in.

If he had a job he could show Alice that he was the real thing and they had a future together. He could prove to her that she didn't have to worry, the baby would be ok, they could be a family and no one would bother them. They could have a house, a car, a big TV, lots of his mates round for parties. He could look his parents in the eye and tell them how well he'd done.

His dream was a simple one, but a dream it remained whilst every time he appeared at an interview he could see that suspicion, that sneer from those across the table, 'could we trust someone like that, do we know much about him?' he could imagine them saying.

So, as always, a few days later came the rejection letter - *Unfortunately you were unsuccessful on this occasion* - He had the qualifications, he wasn't stupid, he just wanted the chance to prove himself.

Until then his real life continued in secret. There was the outward pretence of bravado with his mates, dealing here, dealing there. Always a scam to make some money and he went with it …he had to. Inside he was sure that he was different and he wanted to find a way to show it but everyday Alice pushed him away and everyday he didn't get that job he took a step closer to becoming more like his mates. He didn't tell anyone about Alice and the baby, he couldn't do that. Half of them would have cursed him with their horror at what he'd done; the other half would have laughed at his stupidity and the mess he'd made for himself. He didn't need anyone to tell him that, he knew it already, but he loved her and knew it was right for him. But even Alice rejected him.

'I can manage with my single parent benefit,' Alice had said, 'come back when you can do something for your daughter.'

If only it was that simple, desire and effort were not a problem, everything else was.

The boys were talking today about the rally on Sunday. The newspaper had said they would be up there waving their flags and running their banners, telling everyone how bad things were for them. They were going along, they said, to make sure they were heard, bit of bother...bit of a laugh. They wanted to know if he was up for it. He said yes, but he wasn't. He didn't care about rallies or politics. He just cared about his dream and someone giving him a chance. But he'd go anyway, keep in with the boys. He'd make sure he could get some cash from their deals, their little jobs. It was just enough to keep him going when the benefit ran out.

Feeling a moment of bravery return, he lifted his eyes to check out his face, check his shirt was done up right and the tie was straight.

'Today,' he said to the mirror, 'Qamar, you're going to get this job, and you're going to prove to everyone that you can do it.'


Once again Rachel Lancaster found herself in the hospital cafeteria for lunch. This time she was meeting Patrycja Wladek, the Polish nurse who had been out with John Pilkington. She was hoping to get some real insight into what Pilkington was all about.

Jane had managed to arrange the meeting for her, and told her to look for a striking small blonde girl in the coffee bar at one.

When she arrived it couldn't have been more obvious who Patrycja was if she'd had a Polish flag in her hand.

'Hello,' Rachel asked her straightaway, 'are you Patrycja?'

'Yes, are you Rachel? Everyone calls me Pat,' she replied smiling and seemingly relaxed. She wondered how much Jane had told her of what this was about.

'You sound very English. Have you been here a long time?'

She laughed at her.

'God if I had a penny for every time somebody said that to me I'd be seriously rich by now. In truth I'm as English as you are; I'm third generation Polish, living here. I have a Polish name because my parents are Polish. I've lived here all of my life and to be honest so have my parents. My grandparents came from Poland after the war…my parents were very young then. So I grew up here. Obviously I visit Poland regularly and I speak Polish fluently and am more than happy with my dual history.'

'I'm sorry,' Rachel said, 'I've known Polish people all my life but because everyone talks about the influx of people from Eastern Europe in the last few years, everyone forgets that there were many here already, well and truly part of society.'

'Anyway, what did you want to talk to me about? Jane said something about you being a researcher from a legal firm looking into John Pilkington?' Pat asked her.

'Yes, well that's mostly right,' Rachel had rehearsed this part, trying not to give away her interest in this. She wanted to explain it positively, because if Pilkington figured she was just trying to dig up dirt on him then Anna would go mad with her. She didn't want this case, but she didn't want the firm to drop the ball and lose credibility either. Mostly the risk here was that anything she said to Pat would get back to Pilkington if in fact they were still close.

'Yes I'm looking into John Pilkington. I'm trying to get more background information on his personality so my firm can present a broader case in court,' Rachel explained trying to present an open and honest demeanour.

'Then this is going to be a short conversation. I haven't got anything good to say about John Pilkington so if that's what you're looking for then you'll have to look elsewhere,' Pat started to stand up and take her drink with her.

'Please don't rush off, I didn't mean to scare you off,' Rachel said, panicking, 'it seems you're not on good terms with him?'

'Whatever led you to believe that? Did Jane tell you that?'

'Actually Jane didn't tell me anything other than she knew that you had been out with him.'

'Ok, I see. Well take it from me, I'm no friend of that bigoted bastard and I don't mind who gets to hear about it. I'm so glad he lost his job. He deserves everything he gets.'

Pat was clearly pissed off and Rachel was excited to have found precisely what she'd hoped for. She was relieved to be able to explain more honestly why she'd come.

'That's a bit cynical isn't it? You mean you're happy to take the case as long as you can win it?' Pat asked in response.

'You misunderstand me. Our firm prides itself on not judging its clients. We take on cases based on breaches of the law, not on whether we think our clients are model citizens or not. We have to appear to be about legal representation, not judging peoples' lifestyles. It's the same with Pilkington. We can defend him because we believe he's been unfairly dismissed according to the law. It doesn't mean that we have to like him or even disagree with the sentiments of the board that sacked him. Our role is to see that he is given a fair decision and if not, seek the compensation he is entitled to.'

'To be honest, I'm not sure I care what your motives are. It doesn't change my opinion of him. He is an ignorant racist bastard and I'm happy to say the same to anybody who asks me.'

'Thanks for your honesty. I really do appreciate it. If you don't mind me asking, what happened with him? Did he do something?'

'I went out with him. That was my first mistake. I'd seen him around and I knew he'd been out with some of the girls. I came across him on a recruitment training course. He was teaching us diversity and interview techniques. I admit he charmed and flattered me and I fell for it.'

'What? ... Pilkington teaching diversity... that's hilarious,' Rachel laughed.

'I know... I know, and I couldn't believe it either when I found out more about him. We went for dinner at the Chinese in the centre. At first I thought he was just being charming and taking a genuine interest in me. But every time I changed the subject he kept pulling it back to the same thing; my Polish origins. He kept asking me why I'd come here. Was it really that bad in Poland that I needed to live here? I tried to explain to him that I was born and bred here, as were my parents but he didn't seem interested in listening. Even after we got past that, he nagged me about whether I preferred English or Polish guys. I told him it didn't matter to me. I went for people on personality and charm, not on where they came from. He wasn't having it though.'

Rachel listened whilst Pat explained how much Pilkington had upset her. This was so much what she wanted to hear.

'What did you do?' Rachel asked.

'I told him I was leaving and that if he couldn't treat me as a proper person then I was not prepared to spend anymore time with him. He was supposed to be a HR Manager, someone who could talk to and handle people. That was maybe what he did at work but all he'd done was intimidate me, and I told him that. The top and bottom of it was he didn't like being told this. I don't suppose he was going to jump for joy, but his reaction was really scary. He went off on one. He was ranting about me being a frigid bitch who hated English guys. He said I was happy to take their money, their jobs and everything on offer but as soon as it came to delivering and respecting an English guy then I'd drop them like a stone. He said I should go back to Poland where I belonged, in the ghetto, with all the other leeches from that part of the world.

'Did he turn violent?'

'Not as such, I thought at one point he might do but I was ahead of him and got out of the way. It was a scary moment though,' Pat replied.

'Did you complain about him?' Rachel asked.

'No, no way,' she answered clearly, 'he was the HR manager of the hospital. Who could I complain to? It was his word against mine. No, I didn't mind putting it about that he was a twat but I wasn't going to lodge a formal complaint or else I could have been out of a job myself. So I talked to friends and put it down to experience.'

Pat looked round nervously to see if anyone else was listening, and then leant forward to Rachel.

'Oh, and I hated that scarf he always wore,' she jumped in before Rachel could ask anything.

'You mean the Leeds United one?' Rachel asked, recalling him wearing it the other day.

'No, he wasn't allowed to wear that at work, although I'm sure he would have done if he could; he always wore it when he was out. At work he wore a small, scarf tucked under the collar of his shirt, but it always looked odd. On one of our more intimate occasions, which I try not to think about, I did get to see what was underneath and I asked him about it.'

Rachel's interest rose again

'It was a horrible scar running from the back of his ear, round onto his collar bone. I can see why he wore the scarf as it was really unsightly. He said it was from a cycling accident when he was a kid, but I'm a nurse and I think it was more recent than that. The stitch marks were still too clear for it to have happened a long time ago.'

'What's your theory then?'

'Someone attacked him, probably with a bottle if you look at the shape of the scar and it was likely a woman because I definitely felt like lamping him one. Claiming it was an accident as a kid is an easy way of dodging too many questions especially from a potential girlfriend.'

Rachel couldn't believe it. A violent past, hints of racial intolerance and abuse of women, this guy was definitely flawed. His professional pretence at work must have been an extremely thin veneer over a nasty underbelly. If this came out it would tear apart his reputation at the hospital and would lose him the case. She was hoping to find a crack in his armour but this was a gaping hole. None of this was real evidence, as such, but it did fit into a picture of the real person. She wondered if it didn't work in court whether a newspaper campaign might be the answer. She knew just the person who could help her with that.

She let Pat go and thanked her for her time. She then picked up her mobile and called Alex Thompson at the West Yorkshire Courier.


Alex's phone rang disturbing his relaxing late-lunch in the coffee bar on Briggate. He was writing the transcript of his Lucy Sayers interview. He'd take it to his editor later to go over the content and the timing. With the rally coming up on Sunday the timing could be very useful.

'Hi Rachel,' he said, 'I haven't heard from you in a little while.'

'Hi Alex,' she said, 'what colour's the hair today?'

'You're so funny.'

Yes I know, have you missed me?' she continued

'Of course, I wonder how I can get through the day when I don't hear from you.'

'You still two-timing me with that girl from reception?'

'Yep, still seeing Tina…when I get time off for good behaviour, that is,' he replied, 'have you got something useful for me, or did you just call to hear my voice?'

'Ha, you wish. Ok firstly, as usual this didn't come from me right?'

'Sounds good already.'

'Did you hear about the HR Manager at the North Leeds Hospital getting the sack?'

'No, I didn't. Tell me more.'

Rachel went on to tell him the story and about her conversation with Pat.

'Now that's funny,' he said at the end, 'what a weirdo.'

'I think it's worse than that. If he was a straightforward weirdo then we'd know where we stood. But he isn't. He is a guy who can present a professional persona and play the game, but underneath he is manipulative and obsessive… a real Jekyll and Hyde.'

'I'll have a think about it and talk to my editor. We have to be careful what we say. I could go and get a statement from the hospital about the dismissal. That is a story in itself, but the Pat stuff is really hard to print. I'll probably have to go a bit deeper on that one.'

'I thought you could probably do better than me. So go on, I get the impression you're not taken with the idea.'

'Yes, this is a bit more complicated. I've just gone with a big profile on the BFB bi-election nominee Lucy Sayers. She' would be seriously pissed off with me if we put this one in next to her interview.'

'Alex, no… you can't do that. I know she's a big change for the BFB, but I can't believe she's anything other than a typical fascist in a skirt.'

'Rachel I'm not sure that's fair, she's forthright in her views alright, but she's articulate and very convincing. She's going to be big.'

'And yeah, she looks good in a bikini as well. I'm surprised you haven't gone for a glamour spread on page three as well. This is not the stuff of the courier.'

'We are independent remember. We have to present all sides. I'll see what I can do… I take it you're looking to undermine his case. That's why you're dropping it in my lap?'

'Of course I couldn't possibly answer that. This story could have come from anywhere in the hospital so it doesn't have to tie back to Stockton's. That's all I care about.'

Alex put the phone down, and thought about the call. This was good stuff and his editor would like it. It was a good local story and another chance to present the BFB in a negative light.

But did it really do that? Or did it just play into the BFB's hands? After all didn't it make the establishment out to be over protective of minorities again? This was exactly what Lucy Sayers had been saying. There wasn't that much to go on anyway. The gossip stuff was unprintable unless he substantiated more of that rumour. Maybe if he could talk to a few more of the nurses at the hospital he could find evidence of his violence and abuse going a lot further.

# CHAPTER EIGHT

The train was quiet in the early afternoon so Joe Barker had been able to spread his laptop and notebooks around him. It had been an interesting if not a sad few days in Manchester. He loved being back home, seeing the same old streets and the places of his youth as well as seeing old friends and reliving stories. He'd enjoyed meeting Sarah and spending time with her but he was unsure how to deal with that. She was married and didn't say much about her home life, but it was clear to him that things were not good. She'd enjoyed her time with him, he was sure of that and Joe definitely wanted to see her again. The problem was that he didn't think it was a good idea to get involved with someone who was married, especially when she had a teenage daughter.

For all the nice thoughts about Sarah, the trip had still been quite difficult with what happened to Jenny cutting through everything. He had also had his car nicked and was pissed off about that too.

It would be good to get back to North London, where his life was now, even though this whole trip had turned his mind back to a time he thought had long since disappeared.

He'd had his new flat for a while now since the accident with his wife. Due to losing everything as well as Liza in the fire, the contents were new. Nothing from his past, not even an old photograph remained. It was heartbreaking at the time but enormously refreshing in retrospect. No clutter and no nostalgia, just new and sterile. A few years later and it was just the same again, except now the music and books were more recent. This was his life now. Manchester had long left him and he was part and parcel of London culture, five minutes walk from the underground, five minutes from restaurants of every cuisine imaginable, a shop on every street, the theatre and the arts just a tube ride away.

This whole business had reignited his interest in being back in Manchester though. It gave him a boost that he didn't realise was missing, his old and new life merging into one.

Then there was Jenny. Judging by the photographs at the funeral, he didn't think he would have found the old cute Jenny of his youth. Maybe, though, under the large frame hidden in Russ's shadow the old Jenny was still there. He'd seen small signs of it in the chats with Sarah and the digging in her files. Perhaps she was rebelling in her own innocent way. The question of what she'd been doing up to her death still remained intriguing and he was convinced there was a story. There was little to know in terms of facts but it would be good to try and retrace her steps and discover what she found. Maybe it was linked to her death, maybe it wasn't. If Sarah managed to get something more from the police then perhaps that would give them a lead.

The advantage of not having his car meant he could do some work on the train. After checking his emails and updating himself on the latest news he tucked into the research he wanted to do.

He started with the BCA. He would attend the rally tomorrow in London but first he wanted to know everything there was to know about this group. He would then try to get an interview with one of the chiefs. He suspected that getting an interview with these people wouldn't be too difficult. It appeared that they were looking for publicity.

Digging around on the site, he found the chairman's statement.

James Garrity, Catholic Bishop of East Lancashire.

*'Welcome to the British Christian Alliance. For many centuries the Christian faiths have sought to find differences between themselves. This has created rifts, anger and bitterness. Very rarely have we worked together as friends and allies. The BCA is an attempt to reverse this process here in England. It is not a new religion and it does not undermine any of the faiths represented here. It is, though, an opportunity to concentrate on the beliefs we hold in common so that we can provide a more powerful representation of the true traditions of the Christian Faith in the UK. The map of this country is changing. The number of people attending church has become unsustainable in some cases. More and more, people are finding their answers to the questions of life on the television and through the media. Not through us. Minds have been turned away by the more attractive temptations presented through celebrity and greed. We have to find a way to turn this tide.*

*In addition, we are faced with the other great threat of the increasing power of Islamic culture in the UK. It's now the fastest growing religion and will continue to grow in influence. We don't seek to question Islam, but more to reassert our voice as the religion of this land..*

*So join us and help to rebuild the great traditions of these magnificent Islands. Help to stop the immigration of evil and the fight the culture of greed, selfishness and apathy through the love of God.'*

One phrase stood out above all others in there, "The immigration of evil". If that wasn't a loaded comment then he had never heard one. He wondered whether the bishop had really meant to say that as strongly as it came across. In his mind there was only one interpretation to read into it.

The site went on to list the central council which represented a number of churches. These were Church of England, Scotland, Welsh Presbyterian, Baptists Catholic, and Methodists. There were some other smaller churches listed but he hadn't heard of them. The curious thing he thought was that none of these board members represented the top layer of their churches. There were no arch bishops or the like. Did that mean that their involvement in this group was not sanctioned at the highest level? That was definitely one issue to look into further.

The site went on to explain some of the principles they shared, much as he and Sarah had seen the other day. Again it was nothing out of the ordinary for a Christian campaign, but nevertheless there were always more extreme views hanging around the moderate ones. He made notes on various aspects of the site and checked out plans for the rallies, which was probably the best way to find the real truth.

There was nothing more to be learned so he moved onto the other site he'd found. It was headed Justice for Victims. He was careful not to use Jenny's email this time. He constructed his own on Hotmail account and logged in.

He began to search through the categories. It was clear from the cases listed this was mainly of American interest but there were one or two for the UK, which he read. Nothing jumped out at him as something that would have interested Jenny or indicated how she would have come across the site. It was not somewhere she would have known to look at unless directed, so she must have done a search and this site had come up. He thought back to what Sarah had said, Jenny was concerned about Russ and the BCA, she'd even called someone an evil bastard with that password. Finally there was the connection to the body which he'd almost forgotten about.

So, what had she being searching for? Unsolved murders or crimes related to the church perhaps. This was all very vague and the only possible church link he could think of was Father Peters. So he tried to retrace her steps and do the same.

He ran a search on Father Michael Peters. There was surprisingly quite a lot of links listed. He had a number of church biographies written about him. There was an obituary in a Catholic newspaper from 1999 when he died at aged seventy three. What caught Joe's attention was that there were a number of newspaper articles and websites referring to court cases where he'd been involved, even as far as Ireland. On the third page he found the link, Justice for Victims. He needed to follow the link onto the page he wanted, which he clicked. Once again it asked him for an email address. As he was already logged in on another session, he closed that down and re-logged in again.

The link took him directly to a case under the category "Other".

The case was one Joe thought he'd heard of, but he knew there were also a few similar ones. The case dating back to 1992 was from the small town of Maltshaw in the East Lancashire moors. A priest, Peter Doohan, had been accused of abusing a number of Altar Boys in his care. It was alleged that he had, on a number of separate occasions, asked them to perform sexual acts on him, which the boys had described separately in detail. The case had fallen down on a lack of material evidence and representations by colleagues in the Priesthood. The key witness statements that had swung the jury were from Father Peters plus some other Altar Boys who had been under his care in previous parishes. Peters, was described as a senior priest in the local region, spoke glowingly of Doohan's record of achievement particularly the work he'd done for children's charities in Africa. To say he behaved in this manner was considered ridiculous and he could only feel sorry for the children who made this evil accusation. He'd clearly blamed the parents for believing the misguided tales of young boys and for pursuing such an unfounded story in the hope of compensation. He'd told the court that he'd pray for the families in the hope they would find the forgiveness of God.

The article indicated that the testimony was delivered very powerfully and the priest had the whole court in his hands. This didn't surprise Joe. He would never forget the doom-laden power of his sermons in St Margaret's. The guy could certainly hold an audience. He imagined if the Altar Boys' testimonies matched the priest's wrath then the prosecution had no where to go with it.

The family were distraught by the jury's not guilty verdict and had tried to get together a case in the civil courts but they didn't have the money or the support and eventually they let it go.

So reading between the lines, the Church had stood against the families and faced them down. Chief, among those defending Doohan's honour, had been Peters, the nasty old bastard. Not only was he a religious bully, well known for terrorising kids in his own church, but he had gone out of his way to cover for a paedophile. This was incredible.

Joe closed this article and then looked down the list to see if there was anything else.

He found it quickly. 1996 Stoke on Trent.

A priest, Father O'Mahon, accused of abuse, was said to have been found drunk with his hand up the skirt of a twelve year old girl who he'd asked over to discuss her confirmation. He was discovered by his curate, who had entered the Priest's chambers that evening.

It went on to explain that the case rested on whether the curate, David McDonald, had been telling the truth or not, as the girl was too frightened by the whole experience to speak about it. The family refused to let her be a witness and had moved out of the area.

That left the evidence of the curate, and the church turned on him and vilified him. They told of his bitterness at being rejected for a move to a new parish as he didn't enjoy working with Father O'Mahon. Father O'Mahon had indicated, via his colleagues, that McDonald was lazy and had a poor reputation. Again, another glowing witness statement was presented by Father Michael Peters of Carlton, Manchester. The case never made it to court due to lack of evidence.

Now Joe knew what Jenny had found on this site. She was looking into Peters' activities and she believed that he was covering things up, some kind of religious fixer.

It definitely wasn't Peters who scared her, he was long dead. So someone else had something to lose by uncovering Peters' history. Were they involved in the body in the field or were they one of the people that Peters covered for? This was serious, but he had no real place to go. He still had no real facts, just the very bad smell of conspiracy.

He thought back to that night in 1981 with Jenny. Who were the lads he'd seen and who was the body? So far the police had said very little about it.

There were so many questions and lots of loose ends. Jenny had been thinking the same, he was sure about that. He knew he was on the right track. He just needed to be careful not to trigger the same panic button that Jenny must have.

# CHAPTER NINE

Patrick Barclay felt confident that Sunday was going to be a good day. They had a great line up for the BFB rally, plenty of publicity and hopefully Lucy's profile in the Courier would attract a new generation of interest.

Looking round the table, he was happy to see that he now had a team of professionals and not amateurs. He now had people who understood what it would take to get power. He could go to the National Executive meetings with his head held high, confident that the Yorkshire region had one of the fastest growing memberships and that party funds were swelling.

The meeting was to plan the rally on Sunday. He'd chatted with the party leader, Kevin Inkerman, that morning and checked he was still coming up from London. Patrick had agreed the line up with him and was hoping to go through the details with the team. Just prior to the meeting he'd been to see the Assistant Chief Constable to discuss security.

Around the table he had the party workforce. Lucy Sayers was to his left, the new attractive and forceful, face of the party. Next to her was John Pilkington. Having lost his job, Patrick had been able to take him on as a full time employee at the BFB, responsible for PR and communication issues. Beside him was Diane Kettering the office Manager and then John Murphy and Declan Collins councillors from the other BFB stronghold in Halifax.

On the other side he had his backers, the backbone of the party philosophy. Firstly, there was Andrew Bebbington who provided a large amount of party funding. He was a very controversial figure for the party to take on but his money and connections were useful. Bebbington was an American Professor from Bible-Belt America living on a farm estate in North Yorkshire; he'd left the US after finding he'd made too many black enemies following his outspoken views on their inability to live a civilised Christian life. He'd found Yorkshire a perfect place to restart his political career again. Next was David Bleasby who was proprietor and editor of the right wing Northern political magazine 'Brass Tacks'. The magazine was well known for its forthright articles on the state of the economy and immigration issues. Finally there was James Worthing, celebrity chef and outspoken hunting campaigner. He regularly wrote articles on the government's surrender to Europe and blamed Europe and

Immigration for the singular failure of the British way of live, from hunting, farming, fishing to imported mass production and globalisation.

'The first item on the agenda is to confirm that Lucy will be our candidate for the bi-election. This has been discussed by the party leadership and I'm looking at each of you to support me in wishing Lucy every success with this. We believe she is our best chance to win this seat.

There were a few murmurs and nods round the room.

Andrew Bebbington, the American academic spoke first.

'Excellent news, just what we were hoping would happen.'

Patrick noticed Andrew's eyes flash quickly around the room but came to a perfectly timed halt with Lucy's. He wondered about a connection there for a second but then quickly moved on to checking who was not meeting his own eyes; perhaps any hidden dissenters in the room. He knew a few didn't agree with the direction the party had moved in and definitely didn't agree with Patrick's management.

Nobody said anything other than to agree with Andrew so he moved on.

'Lucy, how did your interview go with the Courier?' Patrick asked, 'will we get a good write up or will it be the usual whitewash?'

'If I read Alex Thompson's eyes right, I'm pretty sure he was sold,' she said instinctively leaning forward and pushing her hair over her ear. 'He tried not to be, but he was. He probably won't admit it to anyone, but like many of these liberal types; when faced with the facts it's hard to deny we are right. He had the right questions and arguments but the more he asked the less he seemed willing to challenge. Oh, he liked my legs, judging by the number of times he took a peek. So I reckon he'll write something good for us. We will have to see what his editor does though. That's where the real decision will be made.'

'One can hardly blame him for admiring your legs, my dear.'

Lucy looked over the table to see the sickly smile of David Bleasby.

'Let's hope he got the right message from you,' he continued.

Lucy stared and said nothing.

'Ok, thanks Lucy. Is he going to print tomorrow?' Patrick knew very well that Bleasby didn't like Lucy. He appeared to be living in 1950 where women knew their place. Bleasby was definitely old school Yorkshire, straightforward and arrogant. However, he was useful, not least because of his magazine and the funds it brought in.

'It should be in tomorrow,' Lucy said.

Patrick got back to the agenda.

'Let's move on to discuss Sunday. I've managed to arrange a little surprise. I invited Dutch writer and film maker Kirsten de Wink.'

From the reaction around the room, Patrick thought he must have actually started speaking in Dutch as nobody had a clue who he meant.

'I can see by looking at some of your ignorant blank faces that you have no idea who she is. '

Andrew Bebbington spoke up.

'I know her. She's the Muslim film maker right? She made a whole series of films on the evils of the Quran.'

'I don't get it, Muslim, slagging off the Quran. She sounds pretty confused to me,' Lucy said, looking back to her notepad appearing to dismiss this as pointless.

'Actually she is not confused. Born a Muslim in Morocco, she came to the Netherlands as a child and married a Dutch guy. Family and friends disowned her because she turned away from her heritage and married outside of her faith. This led her to dump Islam and her old life. She then started to write about her past and the outdated, fairly nasty suppression of women in Muslim communities, both in the Netherlands and Africa. Her films and writings have caused her to become a hate figure to all Muslims and a heroine to the Dutch right wing.'

Nobody around the table said anything, not sure how to digest this. Patrick went on... 'The big story for us, is that an ex-Muslim black woman speaking on our Nationalist stage will show that we are not about race or religion, but about protecting our national way of life. She's appeared at many nationalist rallies as long as they have a non-race discrimination constitution. Now that we are the BFB and will allow anyone to join as long as they are British resident with a British passport then she would have no problem speaking at our rally.'

'Won't having a black woman on the stage cause a problem with some of our more traditional support? I mean she's hardly rank and file British,' Bleasby asked.

'Look, we've got to realise that we cannot win any battles in this country until we can get into the mainstream of British politics. We cannot do that if we continue to have perceived racism in our core values. We have to make people believe this is about Britain and not race. If that loses some of our support from the Boot Boys at The Printers, then maybe it's not a bad thing.'

'I think you're going soft and so is this party,' Bleasby said, 'I happen to think it is about race. If this country didn't have any Muslims or blacks it would be a better place

'Yes well, you better get a reality check soon because as long as you keep saying that, then we can continue to have our party meetings in the back room of a pub instead of the offices of Downing street.'

'Patrick is right,' Andrew said defending Patrick's broad stance, 'no matter what we each think of her, as long as we talk in those terms we wont get anywhere. She's a big coup for us in terms of widening our appeal. You can ask anyone who is non-Muslim whether they welcome the words she'll speak and probably ninety percent of them will say yes. If that means a few more listen to what we have to say then I think we will be pretty successful.'

'Thank you Andrew that is exactly the point.'

The debate had come to an end so Patrick moved on.

'Ok, next item …election media. John your item I think.'

'Yes thanks Patrick,' John Pilkington spoke up, 'I'll be working with Patrick on our key messages for the leaflet. This is a rough draft although not yet in colour. Should give you an idea,' he said as he passed it around, 'you will see a few choice pictures based around the Union Jack, some photos of the Olympics, a selection of family shots with a few token black faces, some rural meadows, flowers and finally some of Leeds and the town hall. Thanks to James I got these shots of his farm and some of the animals.'

'Looks a bit poncy to me,' said David Bleasby again, 'I can understand the family values message and all that but this looks more like an advert for the Yorkshire Show than it does for a serious election campaign.'

'To be honest David this is exactly what we want,' John said, 'we want to appear as if we represent what is good about this country, in a positive way. We don't want to appear as the bad boys anymore but a party that takes tough decisions with the intention of making Britain great again. It's quite simple if you think about it.'

David Bleasby grunted again and Patrick saw his anger at being patronised by John. Patrick gave John a look which told him he ought to soften this.

'Sorry David, I didn't mean to sound disrespectful,' John said trying to be apologetic, 'do you know what I'm getting at?'

'I know perfectly well what you're getting at, but let me be clear. I've been around this business for a lot longer than you have and I know what people think. You lot want to dress us up in a skirt and stick a flower in our pockets to make us look like we are modern and forward thinking, but in reality out there on the streets, people don't give a fuck about that. They are good northern people and they don't like what they see. They just want rid of immigrants stealing their jobs and driving down wages. All they care about is whether they have enough money to get pissed on a Friday night with their mates. You give people too much credit for thinking about stuff like this and if you ask me, you might win over a few liberals, but you'll lose more hardcore support. If they want flowers and pretty pictures they'll vote for the Vicars Tea Party at the fucking conservative club.'

'Ok David, we get what you saying,' Patrick intervened, 'we are not trying to lose anyone's vote, just win a few more.'

'Look I know I'm old school here, but don't forget that I warned you about this.' the magazine editor said. 'And wearing that football scarf, isn't going to win any prizes with the liberal elite either,' he said, turning to John Pilkington.'

'Let's not start getting too personal,' Patrick said, holding his hands up in a peaceful gesture.

John Pilkington ignored the comment and resumed his agenda.

'The point is, I want comments on this today so I can get it printed tomorrow ready for Sunday. Once this is out there we all need to be on message about it. Everyone ok with that?'

The meeting went on working through the document and onto other issues of the day. After another hour they retired to The Printers pub across the road where they regularly finished their meetings informally. The large England flag over the door gave a clue to the landlord's sympathies and the team were more than welcome.

Patrick approached John Pilkington at the bar. He ordered a glass of coke for himself and a pint for John.

'Are you happy with this new job in the party? Sorry I can't pay you what you were on before.'

'I wasn't paid that much anyway,' John laughed, 'you know I told you I was thinking of appealing? Well I've decided to go ahead. Stockton's think I have a case. What do you think?'

Patrick thought for a moment.

'Of course I think you have a right to get your job back. Shame though, I was getting used to the idea of having some full time help on the team.'

Lucy, standing behind Patrick, entered the conversation.

'Do you think you have a chance to win the case, realistically?'

'Probably not, but maybe there's a pay off due,' he replied, 'still don't think they were right of course but I'd take the compensation. Why, are you thinking about the publicity?'

'God you sound like some waster from the council estate chasing compensation,' Lucy said, with a superior look.

'It's not like that,' John said in protest, 'I'm defending a principle and I lost my job over a principle that we all share, you're supposed to be on my side.'

'Ok children,' Patrick intervened, 'John's right. We should defend him. They had no right to sack him for being a member of our party and we should make what we can of it. It can't do us any harm. I mean on the basis of facts there shouldn't be anything to worry about, unless you've got something that you haven't told anyone?' he said looking straight at John.

'No, of course not,' said John, staring straight back at Patrick, 'you're right, they had no right to sack me and I'm not going to let those twats get away with it.'

Lucy Sayers looked at John Pilkington sure that he was a lying bastard and Patrick didn't have a clue about him. He was intelligent right enough and he could certainly play the part but Lucy felt she knew a guy when she looked him in the eyes. Lucy only saw one thing in John Pilkington's eyes and that was pure porn. She was damn sure that Pilkington had secrets and she reckoned he was up for shagging anything that moved. How the hell he'd got anywhere in that HR job she had no idea, whilst he could put a suit on to look like a managing director, he was pure Leeds United boot boy underneath, especially with that grotty scarf round his neck.

The phone, vibrating in her bag, interrupted her thoughts. She reached in and answered it turning away from Patrick and John at the bar.

'Are you on your way yet?' The voice on the end of the phone said.

'I will be, in five minutes. I'm just showing my face.'

'Good, we don't want anybody to get the wrong idea.'

'I'll be there in twenty minutes, make sure the champagne is cold.' She ended the call trying not to give away the smile inside. She was looking forward to the rest of her evening.

'So, do you fancy her or not?' Rachel asked Dave Millington as they sat in the Halters Arms not ten minutes' walk from The Printers, but a world away in style, atmosphere and clientele. This was the regular Friday evening retreat for those wanting to savour the last hour of freedom from the chores of domesticity. Tonight there were only four of them who'd made it from Stockton's; Dave Millington the solicitor dealing with John Pilkington, Caroline Owens the legal secretary manager and Tony Abbott from accounts.

Rachel had known for weeks that Dave liked the girl working in the bar, Chrissie, but he hadn't asked her out. He thought she was a bit out of his league so he'd bottled it. That didn't stop him using any excuse he could to nip in the bar for a drink each day to catch a few minutes with her.

'Look, I'm not going to ask her when you lot are here am I?' he said, as usual loving the attention of the crowd whilst pretending not to.

'Why not, we don't mind, we can watch? We get little enough fun in life as it is,' said Caroline encouraging Rachel to continue the game.

At this point Chrissie came over with the last round of drinks ordered. Rachel decided it was time to deal with the situation.

'Chrissie, can I ask you something?' she said with a straight face.

'Of course…what?' Chrissie asked.

'Do you have a boyfriend at the moment?'

She could see Dave almost crying with embarrassment behind her as his head hid behind Caroline's shoulder. Tony and Caroline were staring in amazement at how once again Rachel had put a big mixing spoon right in the middle of the pot, happily twisting it round and round.

'Sort of,' Chrissie replied.

'What does that mean? You're getting married tomorrow? Or you've been out, shagged a couple of times and now you don't know where you stand?'

Chrissie's face went pink with embarrassment as she registered what Rachel had asked her.

'Rachel you can't say that,' Tony said giggling with laughter and shock at the same time, 'God you never stop do you?'

Rachel went on relentless.

'Sorry, was that a bit personal? Well, you know what I mean don't you?'

'I suppose so,' Chrissie replied relaxing a little and deciding to laugh along with them a bit, 'I've been seeing this guy but he is a bit useless to be honest.'

'Ok then, that's perfect,' Rachel said delighted that this was now her crowning moment, 'because my mate Dave here would like your phone number, and whilst he ain't the greatest oil painting, given his nice salary as a solicitor he could easily pay for a decent dinner at the Bar and Grill round the corner. So what have you got to lose?'

'Rachel, no,' came the cry from behind Caroline.

Chrissie just laughed, 'I knew it,' she said as she looked at Dave still hidden behind Caroline, his embarrassment shrinking him visibly. She turned back to Rachel.

'Tell Dave to come and talk to me himself when he can lift himself from off the floor, and we can discuss it,' she then ran off quickly seeking the refuge of the bar.

'That's the last we will see of her tonight,' Tony said, 'she won't come serving us again.'

'You can come out now Dave. See how simple that was?' Rachel said, 'now you could have saved all that pain and embarrassment if you had just dealt with it yourself. My work here is done I think,'

'You're a fucking bitch, Rachel Lancaster,' he said still recovering from the pain of it, 'I will get you back for this one day.'

'In your dreams, Dave, in your dreams,' she collected her bags together, 'time for me to go. There's a bottle in Tesco's with my name on it and if I don't get there soon it may have gone to a new owner.'

She left them all, still revelling in Dave's embarrassment. She enjoyed the moment and she enjoyed that nobody believed she would do it. They would be talking about it for days to come. So Dave would get his date, what was the harm in that?

She walked round the corner to her car, pleased to see the traffic had died down a bit. She figured the drive home shouldn't be too bad.

Pulling off the motorway for the last mile home was almost a disappointment. It was not that she didn't want to get home, but she just loved the opportunity to put her foot down on the M1 as she sped the small amount of miles to the junction north of Garforth.

Her RX8 loved to be revved and subject to dodging police on the way round, Rachel loved to play with the rev counter as she sped through the full gear range. By the time she was home she had often got the shit of the day out of her system and she could easily relax.

The merriment of earlier had gone from her mind as she popped into the supermarket.

Arriving home at eight, she pulled up outside her recently built two bedroom townhouse. The house was small but it suited her.

Tonight would be a quiet night in, just what she needed after a busy week.

Home was a refuge away from the day-to-day crap of work and the advantage of living alone was that you didn't have to share it. Rachel had a decent social life especially when she was singing, and she was already thinking about booking some dates before the end of the year. It was a good time of year to get some extra cash in and the atmosphere was often more fun.

Her mind drifted onto tomorrow knowing she was due to go out again with Alan. He'd contacted her today and she'd happily agreed to a second date having spent a bit of time in the last few days finding out more about him. Rachel now knew where he lived, that he was married before, didn't have kids of his own, but often went round to see his sister's kids after work. She also knew that he definitely worked at the Council Planning Office and drank at the Bulls Head in Westwood not far from where he lived.

The information had been relatively easy to find out so that was good. Having difficulty was always a sign of secrets. She could now look forward to the date knowing he was at least who he said he was. Maybe if it went well she'd invite him back. As she walked to her front door her mind was focussed very much on the following evening.

She opened the door and immediately knew something was not right. Her mood changed as her instinct kicked in. The front door opened into the lounge so she quickly would be able see what it was. She tensed up as she flicked on the light switch. Immediately Rachel saw what was wrong.

All across the wall above the sofa, written in bright red paint standing out against her plain lemon wall were the words.

ARE YOU SCARED YET?

She might not have been before but she was now.

Rachel looked around the room for evidence of anything else, not sure what to do. Should she just leave and call the police or investigate further herself? She decided that she couldn't sense anyone here so she would do an initial search. This was her house and she didn't want to be intimidated. Tentatively stepping through the lounge she pushed open the kitchen door.

The familiar door creak made her jump, but she relaxed a little when she found nothing there. She could feel her exaggerated heartbeat, which told her she must be scared and that perhaps she should let someone else do this.

Continuing to argue with herself over how mad this was, she made her way upstairs. Each door she opened was like a trap door releasing a screaming madman, and although it felt like an anti-climax to find nothing to match her fear, she told herself that this was a good thing.

Within a few minutes Rachel had confirmed there was nobody in the house. She breathed again, happier to be back in control. Picking up the phone, she called the Police.

'Perhaps you have done something to upset someone, Ms Lancaster,' said Police Constable Simon Eccles of West Yorkshire Police.

Rachel said nothing, still continuing to stare at the writing on the wall.

There had been no sign of a break in, so somebody had used a key. She'd had chance to think about it some more and there was no getting away from the fact that this was personal. The copper may not have articulated it well, but he wasn't wrong. She'd pissed someone off, but who?

'Yes, I probably have' she said finally to the officer.

The other constable, a woman, who had introduced herself as Deborah Smith, was out the back checking for signs of a break in.

'Who do you work for?' he asked.

'Stockton's Solicitors in the City,' she replied flatly, knowing what was coming. He'd already been quite sarcastic with her but now he knew she worked for a legal firm she expected it to get worse.

'I see. Yes I've heard of them, 'he said seemingly unimpressed, 'what do you do for them?'

'I'm a researcher,' she said being deliberately vague.

'So, I imagine somebody didn't like you doing research on them. What do you think Ms Lancaster?' He paused for a minute and then continued with his innuendo... 'Stockton's handled some pretty damning complaint cases against the police, didn't they?'

'Yes, but what has that got to do with anything?' she asked, starting to get seriously pissed off with this guy, 'are you saying that I deserve this because my firm handled some police complaints?'

'No need to be so defensive, Ms Lancaster. I was merely commenting on your company. It's not too much of a stretch to believe that some of the people you mix with in your circles may not appreciate the research you do. Surely you can agree with that?'

'Yes. But you can say the same of the police couldn't you? You go digging into some undesirable corners of people's lives. It doesn't mean you deserve people doing this to you, does it?' Rachel answered, barely able to contain her anger.

'Fair enough,' he replied, not really caring much about her protests

Perhaps it would be helpful if we could go through your client list and see if there's anything to suggest who might want to do this to you.'

'Absolutely not,' she answered sternly.

He smiled, clearly anticipating that reply. He said it to wind her up more, she was sure.

'I'm afraid my firm's client list is confidential and it's impossible for me to share any details with the police. I'll review it myself and if I find anything suspicious I'll be sure to let you know.'

'Perhaps you should do that, Ms Lancaster. After all, we can't very well help you unless you give us more to go on.'

His colleague came in, reporting back that she hadn't found anything out the back. They left, saying that they would be in touch if they found anything. Rachel thought that unlikely. The worst was the way that Eccles turned round to her as he walked out of the door. The way he said, 'Take care, Ms Lancaster,' with such intent to scare that she felt a knife had been put between her shoulders.

Up to now she'd managed to wander in and out of people's lives without any consequences, but apparently that wasn't working anymore. The only conclusion was that someone knew who she was and what she'd been doing. If only, she knew who it was so she could do something about it.

With the police gone she was back on her own. She locked the door feeling very alone.

# CHAPTER TEN

*Saturday*

It was hard for Sarah to believe she was so close to the urban conurbation that was Greater Manchester. Out here on the moors she felt she could have been anywhere but a city. The drizzly rain and mist that had set in began to feel like it would never move on, making an atmosphere of misery a commanding feature.

Down by the roadside in the valley the darkness was worse. It was the mid morning but it felt like the shroud of night. Except night out here was total darkness and nothing else. Sarah was relieved she didn't need to be here then. The legends of Pendle witches and dark deeds belonged to this area and it was not hard to see why.

Sarah stood watching the trees on the hillside ahead of her, buffeting in the wind and squally showers. The leaves had long since given up the ghost leaving only the silhouette against the olive shades of green and brown coating the moorland. She was sure in the summer this area could be bright, refreshing and colourful but at the moment she couldn't see how. Cars raced by, from one town to the next, never stopping to engage with the landscape, perhaps escaping from the tragedy masked by the hills.

She was on the A591 Burnley road visiting the site of Jenny's accident. It was not a spectacular or particularly dangerous section of road, but the whole place gave Sarah the creeps. It was a high speed bend probably taken at forty or fifty miles an hour by most cars in good conditions. There was a small hedge but no trees, so visibility was good. In fact, it looked much like a lot of bends and stretches of road along this route.

Here was where it happened. This was where Jenny died. It was hard to grasp that she'd gone through her last moments in this unfortunate depressing place. Sarah hoped Jenny had not lived long that day, thinking of the pain and desperation that could not have escaped her on this horrible road.

Sarah had been driven here by Sergeant Peter James, from the accident investigation team. She'd managed to get an appointment to see him this morning and he'd agreed to go through his preliminary findings with her before passing them to the coroner. Sarah appreciated his honesty but at times found the details hard to take. The wreckage and damage an accident like this caused were so shocking that she wondered how it was possible to get behind the wheel of a car ever again, once you had seen it.

After going over the details in the station and looking at the wreck that was Jenny's car, a Mondeo Estate, he'd taken her to the scene. At each point he generously asked if she was ok to do this, and she told him that she was fine. She had to be brave and face the reality of what happened if she was going to learn the truth.

Jenny appeared to have approached the bend in question from the North, so she must have been returning home. It would have been light at around three forty in the afternoon. Conditions were good and therefore more than likely she had a good view of the road ahead. The Police could not calculate the speed she was driving at because she didn't brake. This indicated as much as anything else that she didn't see whatever it was and had no chance to react. The officer explained that the car had turned over before it left the road. It then rolled over the barrier on the other side and down a steep bank before coming to rest on its wheels again. He believed it turned once on the road and twice down the banking.

'What made the car roll?' Sarah asked him.

'We don't know, but we are sure it wasn't another car and it wasn't an animal. There's no evidence of any collision or dead animal. It could have been a rock or an object in the road but there's no sign of anything.'

'So you don't know why the car turned over?'

'No, I'm afraid not. It could have been a wheel collapsing, but it's unusual that it would have happened so instantly. Unfortunately the car is so damaged from the number of rolls that it's very hard to be precise about what was caused at what stage.'

'Where did the roll start?' Sarah asked, 'do you know?'

He took her to the point the car first rolled and she could see some vague markings on the road where his team had taken their measurements. He then took her to the place, where based on the first roll, the incident must have occurred.

'You see there's nothing to indicate any issue here.'

Sarah looked around and it seemed the most obvious thing but James hadn't mentioned it.

'What about this farm track here, could anything have been coming out from there?'

'We looked into it, but most likely if that had happened she would either have braked, swerved or there would be collision evidence. So we think it unlikely it happened this way. To make the car roll, the collision would need to be on the ground at the wheels to lift it up.'

'Ah I see, so it was more likely a rock or something that she hit hard?'

'Maybe, but there's no evidence of that either.'

'Could somebody have removed the rock, to cover up their involvement in what happened? I mean if they had placed it there by accident and my sister hit it, then surely they might want to cover up their involvement.'

'I'm sorry to say that there's no evidence for this, and we are in the area of guesswork now. Besides your sister would probably have seen it and swerved. To cause something this big it must have been very obvious.'

Sarah thought yes, but maybe it was placed at the very last minute so she didn't see it? She didn't know how it could be done but it was possible that somebody had planted an object in the road which caused Jenny's car to flip.

'But you can't say it didn't happen?' Sarah pushed the Sergeant.

'It's unlikely as I've explained, and there were no witnesses. My only conclusion is there was a fault on the car and it very sadly caused your sister's death. I cannot say anything more. I'm so very sorry.'

'Last question,' she asked, ignoring his sympathy, 'where does the track go?'

'Just down to the farm and then I think you can then take another track into Sunnyside village.'

'Thanks,' she said finally, 'thanks for showing me.'

They returned to his car and drove back to the station. Sarah sat in the car thinking about what the officer said. It would be easy for her to walk away from this and take the police's line on it, that this was a tragic accident. Accident was the way it looked and accident was the way it was meant to look, but knowing Jenny and knowing the fears she had, Sarah was convinced more than ever that this was manufactured. Whoever did this meant to kill Jenny and she could now see how it could have been done.


Joe Barker figured the BCA rally was less a Rally and more a village fete. It was so low key. It was held in Victoria Park in East London near Mile End. He could understand why the numbers were relatively low because it was a fair excursion out to that area if you were not local.

He'd taken the walk from the underground station, passing through estates of converted warehouses in the area. An area transformed from its working class history. Many such areas had new money injected into them from the demand for a step on the housing ladder. This had positive and negative results. Initially new money increased generally wealth and jobs in the area but reduced the cheap housing stock. Many could no longer afford to live in the areas they had grown up in. This created a negative undercurrent in its otherwise successful multi-cultural society.

Race related violence consequently still existed in the city but for most it was a land of opportunity regardless of background. Jobs were always available if you could afford the commuting and housing costs. Many would argue that London only succeeded due to foreign workers. A large number of public sector and key worker professions had difficulty recruiting due to low salaries relative to the cost of living. It was much easier to get a job in London then probably anywhere else in the country.

It was always easy to look for success and integration where wealth and opportunity were plentiful and that was perhaps the real contrast with the North. Jobs and wealth were spread more thinly; differences and conflicts would more easily surface as social problems increased.

The sight of the park brought Joe's mind back to business. He hadn't been too sure what to expect at the fair, but it appeared to be the same as any other of this type of thing, the focus was just on God and not on cars, or homes, or whatever else people went to the fairs for.

There were a number of merchandise stores selling various religious trinkets. Food wagons were also taking the opportunity to sell cheap junk food to anyone caring to hand over cash. Finally there were some charity tents, covering the full range from overseas aid to child protection. Everybody wanted the punters cash.

Joe spotted an information tent which provided T-Shirts, badges, caps and leaflets. There was also a membership form with a £10 fee. This would support the Alliance in expanding the organisation and raising its profile. He picked up what information he could without handing over cash.

Walking through the tents he then found the main stage. It wasn't exactly a stage, more a wagon with a fold down side. It seemed to provide enough room for a Christian rock band to bang out their easy-on-the-ear pop tunes. They were inviting the small number of watchers to praise the Lord, raising their hands in the way a gospel choir would with none of the presence and none of the effect. Full marks for trying though, he thought.

By the stage area was the VIP tent, where the main speakers appeared to be hanging out. He'd called the offices yesterday and asked for the possibility to meet a senior member today. They asked him to leave his name and if he came to the tent they would see what they could do.

He walked in and found the first person he could to introduce himself. As it happened, he got to the right person straight away. He was a middle aged man in smart trousers, open shirt with a round-necked blue jumper. He couldn't have looked more village tea party if he tried.

'My name is Anthony Harrison, Alliance spokesman. How can I help you?'

Joe introduced himself and asked if he could do an interview with him or one of the other senior members, explaining that he had phoned ahead yesterday.

Harrison agreed and said that he had no problem with that. They had nothing to hide from the press. He even candidly said to him, that he was a little disappointed that not a lot more had turned up. Invites were sent out to all the nationals.

They went to sit on the chairs outside one of the coffee vans.

Joe took out his tape recorder and asked a few questions about the day and what they intended to achieve. After a few minutes of background he decided it was time to up the aggression and put some pressure on this guy. He wanted to get under his skin and find some real answers.

'Why does the Alliance not have the backing of senior members of the various churches?'

'What make's you think they haven't?' Harrison asked deflecting Joe's question back on him.

'Because I rang a few head offices asking for comment on the Alliance. Every time I asked I was refused an interview. Given I don't see any senior members quoted on your literature, it follows, that this was not something sanctioned at that level. Doesn't this just make the Alliance a talking shop with no real power?'

'You have a point, but it's not quite as negative as you make out. There are certain ecclesiastical issues you see. Whilst they may wish to support the Alliance in spirit and for the churches to work together in an informal way, they could not support such a formal partnership.'

'I don't understand, why not?' Joe pushed. Harrison seemed quite open to talking which made it easier, maybe there really was nothing to hide here.

'I think you're looking too deeply. Formal arrangements between the Christian religions have been a tricky situation for many years now. Trying to push through detailed doctrinal compromises through boards and committees can take years. The Anglican and the Catholic Church have such a broad range of philosophies within them, even trying to get internal changes passed often fails. Think about the controversy over women priests. Informal partnerships however have worked quite well. We thought it easier to proceed on this basis with private funding rather than waste many years working through complex understandings and getting nowhere.'

'Talking of funding then, how are you funded?'

'Simply by donations. We are registered as club or society and that way we can ask for subscriptions and membership. Our accounts and membership can be viewed publicly. Only we haven't been in place that long as yet so those details haven't been formally published.'

'Do you have any major donations, are you prepared to disclose those benefactors?'

'No I'm afraid not. We will publish accounts as we are required to do by law, but donations are given in confidence and we wouldn't wish to compromise people's privacy.'

Joe realised that line of questioning wasn't going anywhere so he moved on. He might get some of his colleagues to do some digging on the membership and donations. There were ways to find that information, even if not all of them were legal.

'Who are the people speaking today?' he asked….'some of the themes of the Alliance seem very similar to doctrines presented by the BFB. This talk of returning the British tradition of Christian worship seems a very nationalist type of argument.'

'I don't know how you draw that conclusion. We do not comment on immigration or other religions. We are simply trying to reassert the Christian faith in a country that has become apathetic towards us. They take Christianity for granted and we feel if people don't start waking up and recognise that we need their support, then one day they may wake up to find we are gone or reduced to a minority ourselves. A church needs vocal and financial support in order to survive.'

'Do we need Christianity in this country? Is it possible that the country could cope perfectly well without it?'

'What a ridiculous question. The country is bound to the traditions of Christianity and has been for centuries, in its constitution and in its people. The country would descend into anarchy if there was no church to provide a moral backbone. It would simply not survive.'

'Many other countries survive without religion written into their constitution. Surely people have a choice as to what they want to believe?'

'Yes, but that's not what you're asking. You're suggesting that our belief in Christian values for this country is racism, which is the most ridiculous thing I've ever heard. You only have to look at the make up of our churches to see that we are very multi-racial.'

'Perhaps, but I don't see many Asian faces,' Joe said.

'That is not a religious issue but much more about geographic and cultural origins. And we are going way beyond the realms of this interview about the Alliance. I'm absolutely insulted by your insinuation that this is a racist organisation.'

Joe could see the anger rising as he spoke.

'I will just say this. This country is the heart of everything. If we do not strengthen the Christian church here, particularly Anglican churches, then the whole framework of the religion will start to collapse into factions and cults and the country into moral chaos. So your type of secular language and negative tone will only serve to encourage that state of affairs. I won't sit here and discuss it with you any longer.'

At this point he stood up and left.

Joe wasn't sure how he felt about this. He'd hit a nerve with this guy which was always a sign of getting to the truth but he also hadn't really learnt much either. Perhaps he was looking for something that wasn't there. He could see the point of what they were trying to do. It made sense for them to want to protect their own way of life. He just had a negative feeling about their attitude and possibly that said more about him.

Joe was bored already of the place and was about to give up on the whole thing when his phone rang.

He was pleased to see on the display it was Sarah. She asked him where he was.

'I'm at the BCA rally and to be honest it's immensely boring, although I'm not sure I expected a rave as such. What about you? Did you talk to the Police?'

'Actually that's why I was ringing. I've just got back from the crash site.'

'God, Sarah that must have been horrific for you.'

'Yes it was. Anyway I think I had to do it and I understand a lot more about what happened. The Police are sure something went wrong on the car and you can see there's no evidence to suggest otherwise, but…..Joe I think it's possible something else happened.'

Sarah explained her theory and how it could have worked.

'I can see what you're saying, but it had to be a very purposeful mechanism and very quick to be able to do that. You're saying that somebody waited for Jenny's car to come down the road, quickly placed a large object in front of the car wheel and then withdrew it, before making an escape down the farm track.'

'If you think of some of those hydraulic hammers they use for banging in metal stakes. Something like that would be pretty powerful.'

'Yes, and extremely noisy,' Joe said, not really sure about it.

'I don't know, I guess it would have to be something fairly portable,' Sarah said, sounding to have lost confidence in her theory, 'I don't really know what they'd have used; I just think it's possible.'

'Ok, fair enough. There's little more we can do about that until the Coroner's hearing and see what the final conclusions are. Sounds like the Police are not looking at it any deeper. How is everything else?' he asked.

'I suppose I'm ok. Having this to look at has been a help. Did you learn anything?'

He gave her a quick rundown of the information he'd found and his day with the BCA.

'Joe, this is a bit of a minefield, isn't it. There seem to be so many possibilities and angles but we don't really know anything do we? This could all be a fairy story.'

'Yes you're right, but I think some aspects are clear. Jenny was scared and that email was proof. It's also clear that she was looking at the behaviour of our friend Father Peters. Whether the BCA have anything to do with it, I don't know. It could just be a red herring. But something is not right about the Peters thing. Would somebody really go to that length to cover up a story about a dead priest?'

'So the BCA was a waste of time then?' Sarah asked.

'Probably, they don't having anything particularly new or threatening to say, they are just scared that their safe and secure little world might be falling apart.'

'I think I know that feeling,' Sarah said flatly, 'what do we do now? Are you coming back North sometime soon?'

'Actually that's a good question. I'm coincidently heading to Leeds tomorrow to attend the BFB march. There's always a good story to be had there, which I can submit that regardless of this whole thing. I'll go up to Leeds in the morning and then nip over to Manchester in the evening. It would be nice to see you if you would like. I'll give you a call depending on what time I arrive.'

Once again, the suggestion had popped into his head without planning it. He didn't need to go to Manchester but the conversation and the slightly flirtatious thoughts in his head led him to ask her. Sarah seemed happy to accept.

'Thanks Joe. Call me please. And be careful in Leeds. Those marches can be pretty nasty affairs.'

'I think you may be right. If it's not the BFB it will be the anti-brigade. They definitely have always got something to contribute to these occasions. I'm going to take my camera with me and get some good shots.'

They said their goodbyes and Joe left the park. He'd had his fill of religion for one day.

As she drew her finger round the large tattoo on his chest she wondered what it meant. Alan had told her but she didn't quite get it. It was a White Heart, which Alan had said he liked when he'd been in the tattoo shop that day. He'd always wanted to get something done and this was a bit different. It was certainly very pretty and well done, but didn't make any sense.

Rachel hadn't been the only one checking out tattoos. She had a few dotted around her body that only a privileged few got to see. There was a black horse on her shoulder which had been the name of her first group, even before her ex was on the scene. She had never really had much of a love for horses but the name and image had meant a lot at the time. She also had a flower above the left side of her naval, by her jewelled belly button, which she'd enjoyed showing off with the flat stomach of her twenties. Finally she had a few patterns dotted across her feet. She liked her tattoos but she was also glad she hadn't gone mad getting lots done as a kid. She really wouldn't have been happy to look at herself now with a body full of artwork.

'Another glass of wine?' he asked pouring himself one from the chilled bottle.

'No thanks, I've had enough…my head will be spinning soon.'

Alan had picked her up earlier and he'd driven. They had gone to a country pub out towards Wetherby. She'd had a couple of glasses with dinner so was well ahead of him on the alcohol consumption scale.

She hadn't told Alan about the message on the wall and had spent the day cleaning it up with a fresh coat of paint. She wasn't exactly sure why she didn't tell him, but she felt at the moment, that she didn't want to seem vulnerable and in need of a protector. She wanted to deal with a boyfriend as an equal not as a dependant. If things went on like this then maybe she would need to say more.

It had been a pleasant evening and she'd become more comfortable with Alan, which had resulted in her inviting him for coffee and a whole lot more.

It hadn't taken too long for chat to turn to kissing, and kissing to result in clothes coming off, followed by her inviting him up to her bedroom.

She didn't want to say anything, but the sex hadn't been that fantastic, but that was often the case with the first date. It was all very exciting but he hadn't touched her in the places she liked and it left her with something wanting. Maybe she would have to educate him a bit if this was going to be a regular thing. She liked her own pleasure from relationships otherwise what was the point?

'I think there's more to that tattoo than you're telling me,' she asked teasing him.

'There isn't really,' he replied quickly, 'I was quite superficial in those days, there wasn't much to choose from and I just wanted to pick something I hadn't seen before.'

'What were you thinking when you were in the shop?' she asked continuing to run her hands over his smooth chest, 'was there some girlfriend with you telling you what you should do?'

He laughed, 'Don't you think I was capable of making my own decision?'

'Men are always incapable in my opinion and always need the guidance of a woman when it comes to making a decision.'

'Typical woman,' he said, 'anyway if you want to know my thought process, I'm a Yorkshire man so I thought about a white rose, but I didn't want a rose, too girly, so this was the next best thing. Do you like it?'

'Well yes it's nice, and certainly different,' she replied.

'Tell me about your days in Black Horse,' he said, 'were you really a rock and roll type?'

Rachel rarely talked about those days. It was almost as if it wasn't her life now, something she'd read in a book. Somehow the mess that it became was intensely personal and she didn't feel the need to share that pain with anyone else. She decided to give Alan enough to satisfy the question but nothing more for now, at least until she knew him better.

'Black Horse was just a phase, all guitars and noise really. It was just because we hated eighties disco pop and wanted to play something different but we were never a great act. We drank a lot, did the drugs thing, partied all night but we didn't have any money for anything too outrageous. We had to pay for any damage and were barely able to afford our instruments in the first place.'

'So what happened to the band?'

'It fell apart after I left. There was no band without me, even if I say so myself. I was the only one with any talent,' she explained.

'Oh nice, I didn't realise you were so talented. Did it really end with you leaving?' he asked.

Rachel gave a false titter ignoring his joke.

'I left because I was picked up by another group who spotted me at the gig, they asked if I'd sing for them, and that's when I got into it seriously.'

'That's where you met your ex-husband?' he asked, 'what was he like?'

'He was a prat and so was I. He was self-obsessed and dominated everything. I got bored of him in the end. Look, can we not talk about this, I'm really not in the mood for it,' she said.

'Ok, I was just curious, it all fascinates me, life in a rock band,' he said.

'Trust me there's nothing fascinating about it,' she replied deciding she'd talked enough about her past, 'tell me about your ex-wife now then and pass me another glass, I suddenly feel the need for it.'

He leant over and filled her glass, kissing her as she smiled at him. She was much happier when she was asking the questions.

# CHAPTER ELEVEN

*Sunday*

Alex looked out over the mass of people in City Square. There must have been over a thousand hanging around, plus a couple of hundred police in their bright green vests. He knew also there were horses and riot shields round the corner in case of trouble.

The march had travelled down from the Town Hall and had been allowed to congregate in City Square for an hour of speeches. Each street off Park Row had been barricaded to stop the anticipated anti-BFB protesters getting near the march.

Alex had turned up to city square in the morning at around ten, well before the march started, his plan being to get good access to the party officials. He'd caught site of Lucy Sayers with some others preparing for the day. Everyone was in place early as it would have been hard to get anywhere near the site once the march began at noon.

Lucy had spotted him and invited him into the porta-cabin they were using for a production office. She introduced him to Patrick Barclay and some of the other party officials from across Yorkshire. He also recognised David Bleasby and James Worthing from the TV. Next he was introduced to John Pilkington. This was the guy that Rachel had mentioned the other day. Coincidently Alex realised he already knew him. Well, he didn't know him as such, but he was a member of the Leeds United supporters club and had seen his face there. In fact he may have even seen him at the game the day before but that might just be him finding a connection that wasn't there. He hadn't got round to doing much with the story Rachel had given him as he'd been so busy preparing for today, but the guy seemed alright to him. Football fans could be a mixed bunch anyway so the fact that he saw him regularly at Leeds didn't mean anything.

'I've seen you at Leeds,' Pilkington said, instantly confirming Alex's guess.

'I thought I recognised you,' Alex said, '...were you there yesterday? God, we were awful.'

'Season ticket holder me, always have been, always will be,' he said bragging about his partisan interest, 'we were ok, I think, just a crap referee.'

Alex thought he must have been watching a different game because in his opinion even the most biased supporter would have been aware of the lifeless performance.

They talked some more about the game and life in the lower divisions, at least agreeing on one thing, that Leeds needed to be promoted to bring the city back to life again.

He saw over John's shoulder that Lucy was trying to get his attention again. It was clear from her body language that she was not the slightest bit interested in football or what John Pilkington had to say.

'Nice article,' Lucy said to him pulling him away from John.

'It wasn't meant to be nice,' Alex said, 'maybe I didn't give you a hard enough time.'

'Oh, your questions were good enough. It's just I had all the right answers. Anyway, feel free to stay and listen to the speakers from here. Consider it a reward for a balanced article. We don't get too many of those around here.'

So he'd hung around and watched everything that was going on. His editor had gone to town on a lot of what he'd written, but Alex had won a few battles with him by using Lucy's very strong argument that by just dismissing the BFB as racist thugs didn't lessen some of the very real issues that people on the streets were talking about as long as he'd countered each of the claims made by Lucy Sayers with statements from other parties, the editor let it through.

As the main march had made its way into City Square he saw all the banners and heard the chants of various groups. The fact that the crowd carried banners was not a surprise but some of the outright racism was quite a shock. There were a lot of Union Jacks and England Flags. "No More Immigration", "England for English", "Islam is murder", was common on placards. "Bring our boys home" was another theme. These were the tasteful ones. They were plenty of others that were not so subtle with some blatant racist ones and more than once he watched police barge their way in and remove placards such as "Pakis go home", "Ban the Muslim Murderers".

The chants, more like the ones he heard at Elland Road watching the football, covered much the same ground. The crowd as expected was mainly white male, of all ages, with the odd woman dotted about. There were even some kids but fortunately not too many young ones. He figured this might have been quite a scary place for a young child. This crowd definitely was not the middle class family-friendly audience that Lucy suggested would be here if you went by the general clothing, language and attitude of the crowd.

Alex wondered whether the more sophisticated tone the BFB wanted to present would be lost on this crowd.

He even suggested this to Lucy who pointed to the TV cameras. That was where they were looking for an audience. The crowd was just noisy window dressing.

Patrick Barclay was first on stage and introduced what was to happen. He spoke for ten minutes mainly aimed at getting some interest in the speakers and away from the endless chanting. It felt very hostile out there and he wondered if the party officials had underestimated the situation. Alex was also very aware that the Police were holding back a number of Anti-BFB protests, some from Muslim groups and others from the Anti-Fascist League just a few hundred metres away.

After Patrick Barclay's introduction the first speaker was Kevin Inkerman the BFB party leader who had come up to Leeds from London. He spoke for twenty minutes on the aims of the new party to be confident in speaking honestly about the state the country was in. He told them they had no need to resort to tactics of the street anymore. They had no longer any need to hide in pubs and behind their flags. The facts would speak for themselves. He then reeled off some selective statistics to demonstrate how the facts would back up their arguments. He urged people to stick to the facts and eventually people would have to listen. His final statement was that the truth was obvious to all, and it was time the country faced it.

This had won a large amount of cheers from the crowd.

Lucy was next on, presenting herself as the new candidate for the party. There were a lot of cheers and Alex could distinctly see a few of the crowd seeing her as a bit of sport. Some shouts of, '*Show us your tits*' came across loud and clear. Lucy ignored this and was as forthright as usual.

The crowd soon went quiet and listened as she talked about the values of the party, the support of her own family, and the promise of a future Britain that looked like the Britain of old. She talked about investment in British engineering and British innovation to reinvigorate the brands that made Britain great and would be the envy of the world. As for 'Free Trade' she suggested that if Britain wanted to subsidise its own great industries in times of trouble then that was a matter for Britain and not anyone else. That received more popular cheers. She referred to the imported organised crime which came with immigrants that the police found impossible to contain. This all had to stop so Britain could return to the family values and honest endeavour it was known for. She played to the crowd and milked the cheers.

After a few minutes of detail the crowd appeared to get bored again and Lucy decided enough was enough and finished off to a good cheer again.

Alex watched her step down from the stage. She looked a bit shell-shocked as the others congratulated her on a good effort. She'd conceded to Alex earlier that she had never done anything like that before and it had been a scary experience for her. Alex thought that given the audience she had, she'd done well enough

The next person on stage was Kirsten de Wink. Barclay had tried to sell her as an Ex-Muslim who understood the frustrations of the resident population's attempt to retain their traditions. It was an attempt to show different ways of looking at nationalism.

It was clear right from the start that this was lost on the crowd. At first it was quiet and there was much muttering, once again the sexist shouts produced some merriment in the boorish crowd. Then a few bottles were thrown, and some chants of "boring". The situation was getting worse as the offensive chanting grew, telling her she should go back where she came from.

This energised the police who were trying to calm things down. At the left side of the stage the police line broke where a number of the noisiest elements had been. The crowd in this area started lashing out at the police lines and immediately the police took hold of people and attempted to restrain them. The press, directly in front of the stage, ran round to that area and camera flashes were going off all over. Alex knew there was likely more than one photographer from the Courier in the press pack.

The bottle throwing got worse and de Wink ran off the stage. She'd had enough and she was angry. She turned on Patrick Barclay saying, she hadn't come here to be treated like this. Barclay immediately tried to appeal for calm. The chanting now was growing with constant repeating of 'En-ger-land, En-ger-land'.

The crowd noise was horrendous, becoming increasingly aggressive. There was a growing fear in the porta-cabin that they had no control over this situation.

There were random outbreaks of fighting all over the square and police were struggling to cope. People were beginning to panic and were looking for a way out. He could see the riot police and horses advancing from the side of the Queens hotel. They opened an escape route down under the station towards Granary Wharf and the peaceful, frightened elements of the crowd were desperately seeking that as a way out.

A senior police officer, whose name Alex didn't hear, took to the stage and asked the crowd to disperse in the way suggested. It was clear the event was over and it was now an exercise in dispersing the crowd in the safest way as possible.

Alex left the porta-cabin and made his way towards the action on the left side of the stage. The fighting now was all out and it seemed to centre on a group of leather-clad men in their twenties with scarves up around their faces. There was no doubt about it. This lot had come for a fight with the police and loved it. At this point, with the broken police lines, the worst thing possible happened. The anti-BFB protesters somehow got through the Police lines and run down Wellington Street to get to where the fighting was taking place.

They dived into the mob and started their own pitched battles. Alex couldn't believe what he was seeing. There was now mayhem with two groups intent on kicking hell out of each other and any police officer who got in their way. They had clearly been looking for a way in with their own mob and had found it. He couldn't imagine when Leeds had last seen scenes like this for anything other than a football match.

Alex made his way down through the group trying to get out. He was hit by a police baton, but managed to keep his footing. He flashed his press card and the officer let him go. Blood ran down the side of his face as he ran on. He tripped and fell over the kerb and panicked as people started trampling over him. People were falling over him. Every time he tried to stand up, another foot knocked him down.

Hands lifted him under his armpits and pulled him upright again. The entrance to Aire Street was in sight so he ran that way managing to escape through the masses. As he was running he looked round to see the face of the person who had rescued him. His press tag swinging round his neck as he followed.

Alex allowed the guy to catch up and thanked him.

The guy reached his hand out to shake it, 'Joe Barker,' he said

'Alex Thompson, good to meet you,' Alex said with a big ironic smile on his face.


Three hours later that afternoon, Rachel Lancaster sat in her Mazda outside the Printers Arms in South Leeds. She wasn't sure why she'd stayed so long but she had the feeling that there was more to happen today and keeping an eye on the movements of certain BFB elements may prove useful.

She'd been at the rally and had fortunately managed to keep away from the main areas of trouble. She'd stood on the station approach with a good view of the speakers away from the bulk of the crowd. There were still shoppers milling around in these areas, going to and from the station, but the stage and the speakers were still visible. She'd enjoyed the spectacle of pretence from the speakers defending themselves as reasonable non racists at the same time spouting ignorant racist drivel. Her good mood of the morning after a nice night with Alan last night dissolved as she watched the depressing narrow-minded anger get worse. The treatment of the Dutch woman was just sickening.

As the trouble started she at first thought about running, but staying in the shelter of the station access had kept her out of the main movement of people. She'd been able to watch the general panic and charging of the mobs from a safe distance.

As the crowd had been dispersed she found a way to stay around. She was a woman on her own, so the police had ignored her. She was able to see the BFB leadership escape back towards Boar lane as the square was cleared and followed Patrick Barclay, Kevin Inkerman, Lucy Sayers, John Pilkington, the black Dutch woman and numerous others walking down Boar Lane with a police escort. They seemed to pile into two minibuses which must have been quickly organised by the police to get them out.

Once they had gone she went back round to the Car Park near Stockton's and collected her car. She decided on a whim to go down to the Printers as she knew that many of them liked to drink there. She reckoned there would be a post mortem on this one and she wouldn't mind being a fly on the wall.

An hour later she was sat outside watching them all turn up separately. Barclay came with Kevin Inkerman, the party leader she'd seen before. Lucy Sayers arrived fifteen minutes later with a guy she didn't know. She wondered if it was her husband. There were various other suits who must have been from the party. The black Dutch woman was nowhere to be seen which Rachel assumed meant she must have disappeared away from this lot as fast as she could get away. Rachel guessed that she wouldn't be turning up at any more BFB rallies.

Finally the scarf wearing Pilkington turned up in a taxi looking more like he was off to the match, with the two big guys she remembered as Bill and Ben, who she'd seen with him earlier in the week. Fortunately they didn't look her way.

She longed to know what was going on in the bar, what was being said. There was a lot of cheering and noise but she couldn't make out anything. She couldn't go inside, Pilkington would definitely recognise her.

She decided after a while that this was getting her nowhere and it was time to go home. She noted the time was four O'clock.

Rachel started the car and looked in her rear view mirror as she was about to move. Seeing a police car coming down the street behind her, she waited for it to pass. The car pulled into a space outside the pub and thinking this was interesting she changed her mind and decided not to leave. She killed her engine and turned out the lights watching two police officers get out of the car.

She wondered if there had been a complaint, there was certainly plenty of noise inside. But there had been no evidence of violence and trouble and the only people outside had stepped out for a smoke.

It then all became perfectly clear as she recognised the driver of the police car. Of course it was Sergeant Mark Davies. As he got out of the car she saw a woman come out and speak to him. It appeared to be Lucy Sayers. Rachel noted down the time she'd seen them. If anyone had any doubt about his involvement with the BFB then it was there for all to see. He was reporting in.

Rachel took a quick photograph on her phone, her instinct telling her this might be significant. She hoped she wouldn't be seen. Once she was sure she wouldn't be noticed Rachel pulled off in the car more disillusioned than ever, unaware of the real significance of what she'd just witnessed.

At the same time, across town, the traffic light changed to green as a stolen Vectra pulled along Hardman Street through the middle of Beckton. Kevin Markham and Paul Evans sat in the front of the car smoking in silence; they had not even put the radio on. Both wore dark plain caps. They didn't want people to see or notice them. They were just faceless people in a faceless car.

'Are we going to do this or what?' Kev turned to Paul.

'Course yeah! Defo!' Paul confirmed trying to look confident as he drove, but Kev could see that he wasn't happy.

'You scared?' Kev asked him.

'A bit, never done anything like this before, you know.'

'Course not mate, that's why we are doing it, big man. We are going to do som'at no one else 'as ever done. We are going to be the first and we're going to wake this country up into a storm to know that us white guys are not going to be messed with. So be brave, toughen up like your mate Kev and we are going to do good shit today, right?'

'Right, yeah I'm with you bruv,' Paul replied feeling more confident and beating the steering wheel, 'this is going to be big.'

'Stay cool. Turn right down here.'

Paul turned the car right in to Old Street, conducting the perfect right hand turn manoeuvre for a twenty one year old male. His driving instructor would have been proud of him...that would be if he'd had one, or if he passed any kind of test. Where Paul and Kev came from driving tests were not required, insurance and ownership were never a consideration.

'There it is. Fucking massive it is,' Kev talked about it almost in awe.

'Leave it there in front,' he commanded

Paul pulled the car up at the side of road, neatly again, designed not to attract any attention. They both calmly got out and left the car. Paul was desperate to run but he knew, just like his driving he had to stay calm and make sure nobody noticed them.

They walked back to Parkman Street and briskly made their way to the bus stop. As planned a Blue Mondeo waited in the bus lay-by with a black man decked out in a dark jacket and plain cap. Kev jumped in the front and Paul in the back.

'Well done, Dom,' Kev said smiling at his mate, 'ok let's do it,' he pulled out a small mobile phone purchased yesterday and programmed in with a particular number, 'ready?'

'Do it, for fucks sake,' Paul screamed at him.

Kev pressed the call button. At first nothing happened...then they heard what they'd come for.

The noise tore through the street, one hundred times louder than anything they could have heard before. Everything around them stopped in that second, as people attempted to grasp what it was. Even in the Mondeo where they knew the cause, they were struck dumb for a moment. They looked at each other for a reaction, but could only see a weird smile of satisfaction. Did they really just do this? Excitement and adrenalin coursed through them, no thought for the horror they'd delivered to the street.

The car pulled away from the bus stop into the now chaotic scenes of people running towards Old Street. At the same time people were running out of the street, covered in brick dust, plaster dust and in many cases dripping with blood. Kev removed the SIM card from the phone, wiped the handset clean and threw it into middle of the road, satisfied to see a car going the opposite direction drive over it. The phone was smashed beyond recognition.

The car continued along the road and away from the sirens, panic and devastation that surrounded the Old Street Mosque. It was a Mosque that had formed the heart of the Beckton Muslim community for 40 years.

# Part 2

# Propaganda

*"There's nothing so absurd that if you repeat it often enough, people will believe it."*
**- William James**

# CHAPTER TWELVE

## 2 Weeks Later

*Tuesday*

Stepping off the bus, he caught the bruise on his back on the door, making him pause until his body let the pain recede. After a second or so he was able to move again and continue walking. It had been like that for days but there was nothing to be done, it would get better in time. His mates laughed at him as they all compared their wounds, badges of honour, they said. Qamar ignored them, who did they think they were - martyrs? They were just nobodies like him.

His life had been bad before but it was even worse now. Even when he was on the bus people looked at him, seeing if he was trouble, whether he was going to do anything, who was he going to meet? Qamar could feel their eyes on every move he made. His dream seemed so much further away these days, the pain of the police baton across his back, a message that he was on the outside.

He hated that copper who hit him. He didn't know him and would probably never see him again, but just remembered seeing his face as he happily lashed out at everyone he could reach. The pleasure of his job was apparent as he efficiently swung his baton, striking the target. The copper knew nothing about any of them, yet he was still happy to hit anyone who happened to have a darker shade of skin than he did.

Qamar had been in the wrong place again as always was his luck these days. Some of the boys loved the aggro, thinking they could fight the oppressor, start the Islamic revolution here in Leeds. He hated that talk. He was a Muslim just like them, and everyone knew that battling, bombing and looting had nothing to do with religion and everything to do with revenge and power. If they were honest about that at least then he could see it. Everyone was furious about the mosque bombing especially as Qamar knew a few of the dead and injured, everyone round here did. He got all that and he'd gone along with them once again to keep in with them, intending to stay out of it and watch from the sidelines. He couldn't deny the entertainment, watching the coppers run, but hated it when it got malicious, when someone got isolated and then they all dived in. That was vicious and unnecessary. Trying to keep to the sidelines though was his mistake, he didn't realise how quickly it spread and how indiscriminate the police were in handing out punishment. He didn't see any one of these coppers caring two shits about finding who had bombed their mosque, they were too happy to be "Paki-bashing".

The job rejection at the car dealership two weeks earlier had been his last interview, now it didn't seem as if he was going to get anything. He would have to help his mates out in the next couple of weeks just to get by. Probably shifting some drugs round the estate or doing another car smash for them. He hated that as well, just made him feel as bad about himself as those on the bus.

He was getting more frustrated and angry each day as he listened to everyone on the TV and the estate talking about what people wanted and what they should do. No one spoke for him; no one would tell him how he could get a job when everyone thought he was just another crazy terrorist. Ok, he knew not everyone thought like that, but he could see that mistrust in their eyes, that something that told them he wasn't worth the gamble. Now he wouldn't even get the interview, one look at his name would see them throwing the application in the bin.

He walked round the corner to the top of his street, some of his mates were milling around. He guessed his next assignment was coming. Frustrated with everything, he walked over to find out what they had.


Leeds was suffering, there was no doubt. The bombing of Old Street Mosque had triggered substantial violence and rioting unprecedented in the UK. The media were camped in various parts of Leeds waiting for the next wave of action, and most days were rewarded sufficiently to want to extend their stay.

The city was not exactly in chaos, normal life continued. It was just that the everyday routine had an undercurrent of fear and mistrust. Fear created by not knowing where the violence would spring up next. Mistrust stemmed from not knowing who to believe as claim and counter claim escalated.

At the centre of everything were the police who not only had to manage the investigation into the bombing, but limit and try to bring the violence to a halt. Five people had been killed that day with numerous people receiving minor injuries. The police had not made any arrests or identified the two youths who had been seen leaving the area. They believed that these youths were not acting alone and that the bomb was orchestrated by some sort of terrorist organisation.

There had been no claims of responsibility but there had certainly been many denials. Every anti- Muslim or right wing group had been forced to deny it, but still added their own *told-you-so* message at every opportunity.

It was impossible to know what the true intention of the bomber was, but a fair guess would have been something akin to what ensued. Muslim youths were on the streets of every city protesting, rioting and causing general mischief wherever they could. Numerous other gangs, black and white were happy to give the Muslim youths the fight they were looking for. The battle over Old Street Mosque was in name only as the escalation was much more to do with retribution from the last attack. Curfews were now in place in many areas, but the police couldn't monitor every part of the city so the violence just moved. With sophisticated online networking sites, getting information on where and when something was going to happen was quite easy, and allowed them to keep well ahead of the police.

The BFB had born the brunt of much of the political warfare following the bad press from the rally in City Square. The surprise factor over the period was that support for the BFB increased rather than the expected loss. Forced with nothing to lose they had gone on the attack against their political opposites blaming their ambiguous policies for the state the country was in. The aggression and the brutal honesty in the message had appealed to many people who saw the continuation of violence by Muslim rioters as way out of proportion to any justified response to the bombing. Growing in confidence, with Lucy Sayers as commander-in-chief, the party had stepped up their rhetoric leading to further accusations from other parties that they were making things worse, not better.

At some point people expected the trouble would fade out but so far it hadn't. The violence had spread nationally but not yet to the same extent as West Yorkshire and particularly Leeds.

For the last two weeks daily press conferences were held by various members of the community sitting with the Senior Police Officials and investigating officers. The purpose was to communicate progress on the ongoing investigations both into the Mosque Bombing and instigators of the riots. It was also an opportunity for various community leaders to call for calm and reiterate that violence would not solve anything.

Sitting, listening at the back, at today's press conference were Joe Barker and Alex Thompson. Joe had made regular trips to Leeds since the rally and the mosque bombing. As with the other media representatives, the continual cycle of activity provided a constant supply of stories to fill the twenty-four hour schedules. Joe had sold on his own stories and photographs numerous times, whereas Alex had made the most of his own dramatic story from the BFB rally, being rewarded with writing the daily diary of updates on the aftermath.

Since that day Joe and Alex had become friends meeting up on a few occasions sharing research and rumours.

The conference was wrapping up again after the day's speeches. Today's messages of peace came from the Chief Constable and the Chairman of the National Muslim Council. He was pleading for patience with the police investigation and for Muslims and people of all denominations to enjoy a day of reconciliation. The idea was that those that created fear and hate in the country could be shouted down by others who preached love and friendship for all, but Joe thought the likelihood of that happening was somewhere between no hope and no chance.

The attendees headed back out into the street and started turning to colleagues to discuss writing up their notes and feeding back to their offices. Alex headed over to Joe and asked if he'd time for a pint.

'Yeah of course, got to get the train after that, going to see Sarah tonight,' Joe replied.

'Cool,' Joe said, as the both of them set off walking into the centre, passing through the market and onto Boar Lane.

'So how is Sarah? 'Alex asked as they were walking.

'Ok I think,' Joe paused before completing his answer, '…she's still getting over her sister's death and she's happy to have me as a distraction but I guess she has some issues to work through.'

'Do you think the husband's sussed you yet?' Alex asked, 'could get quite tricky then.'

'I hope not, well not yet anyway, we are trying to be discreet, but who knows what's going on with him, Sarah doesn't even know herself.'

As they arrived in the bar, Alex ordered a bitter for both of them.

'So you ok, drinking this proper Yorkshire beer? I know you Lancastrian types start getting a bit loopy when you get a few miles from the land of Boddingtons.'

'Actually that would be funny, if Boddingtons was actually made in Manchester these days. With the land of globalisation God knows where it comes from now. The 'Cream of Manchester' is now a car park. You're lucky that you still get beer made in Leeds these days.'

They sat down with their beer ready to put the world to rights.

'So is it love then? I mean it's a big thing for you, from what you told me about your wife?' Alex said.

'Love...far too old and cynical for that' he replied, laughing to hide his real feelings, '...I do like her though, but we both have so much baggage it could quite easily go wrong. For the moment it's best to just enjoy it for what it is. At least I don't have to feel guilty about her upsetting her husband as I reckon he probably has something going on himself.'

'I know this is a bit heavy, and tell me to mind my own, if you like, but how does it work in your head with the ghost of your wife hanging around?'

'Well I could tell you to sod off for being an insensitive bastard, but I guess I'll save that for another time,' Joe laughed at him lightening the tension in the question, 'the simple answer is that you get on with it. Grief and sadness are such negative emotions and in the end can destroy you. I'm just not that sort of person and you have to get on with it. Sometimes you think you're being a bit cold but what's the alternative? I know for sure that wouldn't have been what Liza wanted. I still think about her, still remember certain things but mostly it has become a blur, not that different from other relationships in the past. She was just a special person and it was a privilege to know her, but that doesn't mean I shouldn't live my life.'

'Ah that was quite touching,' Alex smiled at him, 'you'll have me in tears in a minute.'

Joe laughed covering up the hidden emotion of what he said. Throughout everything he'd done as he told Alex, got on with it and tried to live his life. But underneath all the bravado he was annoyed a little with himself that he sometimes couldn't remember what it was like to be with her on a day-to-day basis, and that he remembered the bad times as much as the good. He felt she'd deserved better than that from him. That was the feeling that haunted him more than anything else, he was just not honouring her as much as her memory deserved.

'Enough about me...tell me how is it going with Tina?' Joe asked happy to deflect attention on to Alex's girlfriend.

'She's cool, but a bit pissed off with me. As you know I've been putting in the hours since this story broke and I haven't seen much of her. In fact I can't be too long here, got to get my lines written and take her out tonight, otherwise I'm in trouble again.'

'Haven't I heard that one before?' Joe said happy to know he was not the only one balancing work and life.

'What do you make of today's bulletin then?' Alex asked as they settled down into bench chairs.

'It isn't getting any better that's for sure. I think the police have lost the plot and I wonder whether this will eventually stop because everyone will get bored rather than because of any initiative by the police. These things have a habit of petering out in the end.'

'There speaks the man of experience,' Alex loved to wind Joe up about his age and his *seen it all before* monologues.

'Hey, you can't knock experience. When it comes down to it most people like an easy life, and that's what will stop this. They may not have liked the lifestyle they had before but they'll soon get fed up of the daily pressure of fighting, running and dodging other gangs as well as the police. Apathy will be the winner in the end.'

'I hope you're right, because I don't see it that way. I think this is something a lot uglier than we've seen before.'

'Are you still in with Lucy Sayers?' Joe asked.

'What do you mean *in* with her? Cheeky sod,' Alex said in mock defence, 'if you mean am I still having regular contact with her to get the inside line on the BFB, then you're spot on.'

'If you say so, I think I was right the first time. In fact I do believe that's why Tina is pissed off with you, spending too much time with your nose up Lucy Sayers's skirt.'

'Ah I see it now, you're jealous. I'm getting access to information you can't get,' Alex replied.

'Let's get this straight, just because you've got fancy for a Nazi bitch with high heels, don't bring me in on your little fetish.'

'You really reckon she's a Nazi?' Alex asked.

'They all are aren't they? They dress it up in some flowery words, wrap a flag around it and call it the politics of the man of the street. But they forget the man in the street often doesn't give two shits about politics as long as there's a regular supply of beer on tap,' Joe had always been unforgiving about what he saw as blatant racism dressed up as politics of the people. He believed individuals were not instinctively racist but were simply looking after their own; it was just easy to define those who were different from them in racist terms. However politicians turned that message on its head and used it for their own agenda, playing to the ignorance of the masses.

Alex went on with his defence of Lucy Sayers.

'I don't think she's as bad as you make out. I think she has some forthright views which many people will not agree with, but don't underestimate her. She's going places and I reckon if the BFB fell apart around her, she'd still be standing and would be the one leading the troops to form a new party. I think she's big news and unless somebody uncovers some serious dirt on her, then she'll find her way to Westminster with a long trail of folk following behind her.'

'I heard about an independent standing in the bi-election, Anna Stockton. What's her campaign about?' Joe asked.

'I don't think she has any specific issue, her speeches are all about changing politics into less party soap opera and more into people like her with business expertise and real life experience to take on the challenges of the country. She believes the party system is failing the country.'

'She's probably right, except for the fact that they all turn into politicians once they get a sniff of Westminster... So, how are the riots going to affect the outcome?'

'God you've got a cynical head today haven't you?' Alex said, 'I'm not sure how to read the effects of the riot. The Muslims will all vote labour because they have one of their own standing and the rest of the masses will vote Tory or BFB depending on how disaffected they are with life I guess. Those of above average intelligence will either use the 'None of the above' option and stay at home or vote the Tories a nice landslide. The support across the BFB and Labour is polarised already and I don't see that changing.'

Joe emptied the last of his beer and looked at his watch. Alex did the same. It was time to go.

Five miles away in the more sedate suburban environment of Garforth, Rachel Lancaster sat having a similar conversation with Lee Potter in the Wellington pub, off the bypass. He was a twenty-year-old uniformed constable, who in the lottery of first time assignments in the force had the misfortune to be assigned to Sergeant Mark Davies's team. She met Lee in Garforth as it was way off his normal territory. He had been the officer who Rachel had witnessed getting a tongue lashing from Davies when he'd challenged his harassment of an Asian in Beckton.

She liked to use The Wellington for meetings like this, because it was quiet, with most people eating. This meant no loud jukebox and they could talk easily. It also had many dark corners so it wasn't obvious to anybody looking into the pub who was there.

Rachel had managed to find Lee by getting close enough to find out his PC number, and then ringing the station stating that she'd really like to speak to officer 343 who had been so helpful when her bag had been snatched. In all the excitement she hadn't taken his name but she did remember his number. The desk sergeant had forwarded her message and she received a call from Lee, who was somewhat confused. He hadn't recalled such an incident.

As soon as Lee called, she'd blurted out her prepared story so she could get him to talk to her. She'd thought about making up a story where he'd be intrigued enough to come to her. Something that would be in his interest to know, but in truth she couldn't convince herself of a story, never mind him. So she decided to take a big gamble and go for a more honest and direct route.

'Hi Lee,' she'd said, 'I know you don't know me, but I know who you are; I also know which Sergeant you're working with and I've a good idea of what you think of him. You seem a good guy Lee, and therefore I'm asking for your help and we may be able to help each other. I intend to expose your Sergeant for his behaviour and ensure that he and his bully-boy mates lose their jobs. If you don't want to go down with him then I suggest you might want to talk to me.'

Of course he'd reacted badly at first and told her to leave him alone. It was only after her waiting outside the station on two occasions and convincing him that she wasn't a reporter that he finally agreed to see her.

Since then he'd met her three times and had not only talked to her but in fact had off-loaded completely about the pressure he felt as a young officer, trying to do a good job but being constantly pushed from pillar to post by the top brass who all seemed to have their own agenda.

He was told that he should always report and question the action of other officers through management so that any problems were dealt with internally to give the force chance to put things right. The reality was very different from the book. He'd tried to complain about Davies on two separate occasions but had been told that he should not be seen to be complaining too much as a young officer. It would not win him any friends. The first complaint resulted in him being stuck up against the lockers in the Locker Room and threatened by Davies. The second time, when he went back to complain about the threats, he was told that if he wanted to survive in the force then he had to learn to shut up. That resulted in another session with Davies in the locker room but this time in public with the rest of the team watching for extra humiliation.

He hadn't dared to say anything again and the rest of them wouldn't talk to him at all. Rachel was more than happy to listen to his complaints, and to hear him confirm all her previous suspicions about what was happening in Davies's squad.

He'd given Rachel numerous examples of how illegal searches had been done and potential planting of evidence such as dope on suspects as they were searched. Davies wasn't even interested in arresting them. That would mean responsibility and paperwork, and increase the potential for complaints about his actions. No, all he wanted was leverage. Something he could use against them. That way he could run the streets under his own control. He warned them to stay out of his way, he didn't want anything happening on his patch and if they didn't like it; he would make it his business to make their life hell.

For this reason the local youths had no trust in the police force and they knew if they complained then Davies would make more trouble for them. He was a bully of the worst type, sadistic and spiteful, but worst of all he was getting away with it. His superiors either were not aware of what he was really doing or turned a blind eye on the basis that the crime rate in his area had fallen, where in others they had risen. His form of community policing was working and no one wanted to ask too many questions.

'So, what's going on now, with all these riots lingering on?' Rachel asked Lee after he'd sat down with his usual pint of Carlsberg.

'At the moment we are trying to just throw bodies at it. We've got teams coming in from all the rural places out in Yorkshire and the like, not used to city coppering. They are coming in and loving it on overtime. They don't often get much scrapping where they are, so this is like a holiday at the seaside.'

'What about Davies? …Where is he?'

'He is in charge of the curfew squad, which is like handing over the asylum to the chief loony. I'm telling you that guy has his own rules which make sense to no one but him. Still, no one dare cross him.'

'Don't the coppers from other forces question him?' Rachel asked.

'That's the thing, he's a clever bastard. First of all he uses local knowledge as his badge of honour. His first line is always that he knows this place like the back of his hand. He knows the people and he knows how what they respond to.'

'Clearly that idea is a bit of myth, given the escalation.'

'No, he talks a good fight. They listen to him and once they see him talking to a few of the locals the way he does, they won't question him or challenge him. His tough manner gains him respect and they believe the bullshit he spouts.'

'They can't all agree with him, can they?'

'Maybe some do, maybe most of them don't care. As I said before a lot of them enjoy this stuff. As a copper you spend so much time being restrained by procedure and red tape that you're scared to do anything. When they are faced with this kind of rioting and public disorder, they feel that the restraints are off and they can march round in a group able to arrest and beat up anyone they feel like. They see this as a proportionate response to the violence around and to a certain extent they are right.'

Rachel's eyebrows rose in surprise at what Lee was saying. He went on to explain himself... 'Look, I'm not soft and I'm not a Liberal either, I don't particularly believe that they have any more right to be here than Davies. I just don't think that the way to do it is to beat the shit out of any guy who has got a bit more of a suntan than me. The world is full of chancers, regardless of race and colour and most people will take opportunities where they come. These people saw an opportunity and took it. It's our job to deal with crimes and uphold the law the same whether they fall out of the arse end of a council estate or inner city Baghdad. The only way to earn respect from people is to treat everyone the same. Davies picks and chooses his causes and plays his own band of politics. Really he is just a thug in a uniform. Trouble is someone gave him a brain as well which makes him a tad more dangerous than the average boot boy from round here.'

'You're quite a bright guy for a young lad' Rachel said flattering him.

'Yeah well, some things are easy to see when you're faced with a twat like Davies. Anyway, I have to go in a min. This is the first night off I've had in a week and no offence but you're bit old for me.'

'Cheeky sod, I'm not that much older than you.'

'Enough though eh!' Lee said laughing, 'anyway what are you going to do about him? All this stuff I'm giving you has got to be worth something.'

'You're right, this stuff is pretty good. I'm going to need something a bit more factual though. So far, what you've given me could be misconstrued or denied. I probably need something on tape, what do you think? You would always remain anonymous; you just have to get close to him.'

'Fuck Rachel, that's a big ask. He would kill me no problem, if he sussed that out, and his mates would join in as well; they'd kick the shit out of me.'

'If you're clever with it no one will know it was you. Here are a microphone and a recorder,' she said as she handed him the small gadget with a trailing wire and a microphone the size of a small headphone. It's small and no one will notice it. You can hide the microphone behind your lapel. If you're in a crowd or close enough to him to hear him speak, the mike will pick it up. He won't know if it's you or anyone else who is around at the time. If you do this then we are sure to get him.'

'He'll know it's me though. I'm still a dead man.'

'Look he might think he does, but remember he is paranoid as well. You can't be the only one who doesn't agree with him and he knows that. That's why he is so hard-faced. The only way to keep his team loyal is to scare the shit out of them. So he may suspect you but equally he would look at any of the others who he thinks might let him down,' Rachel knew she was chancing her arm here but she needed something more substantial than what she was getting.

'What will you do with it?' Lee asked her after considering it for a moment.

'Probably take the story to the Courier, I've some contacts there. And then I'll use it as leverage in a number of claims for wrongful arrest or mistreatment against the West Yorkshire Police where he's been at the centre of those operations. A good tape recording would nail him to the wall.'

'If he finds out that you've done this, I reckon he'll come for you. I agree we have to do something, but a guy like Davies won't let something like this go,' Lee wasn't giving in that easily.

She thought about telling him about the attack on her house, and her suspicion that maybe it was Davies who did it, but decided it wouldn't help. Lee got up to leave, which closed the discussion.

Rachel finished her drink thinking about what she was really going to be able to do with the information and what Davies would do if he knew she was behind it. The one thing she could do was make sure he was chief suspect if anything did happen.


A chink of glasses, a sip of wine and the relaxed aftermath of love-making were enough for Sarah and Joe to forget everything that was happening. Sarah had picked Joe up from Manchester earlier on, and they'd driven back to the hotel in Bury via the Off Licence. When they arrived in the room, the wine had almost been forgotten as other things had taken priority.

'I wonder what Jenny would think about this,' Sarah said.

Joe laughed.

'I haven't really thought about it. You knew her better than me, you tell me?'

'You know what I really think?' Sarah said, with the hint of sly conspiracy growing in her smile. 'I think she would be jealous.'

'You can't say that, she was happily married with Russ. She wouldn't even have looked at me.'

'Oh, yes she would. I'm sure of that. She always liked you and knowing what I know about you now she couldn't possibly have thought any differently, regardless of Russ. I'm not being nasty. I just think you would have turned her head like you did all those years ago.'

Her smile wavered as she thought more about her sister.

'I wouldn't have gone for you if she were here you know. I'd have seen you as Jenny's. I kind of still do in some ways, but I know she would have approved so I don't feel guilty about it.'

'I was never really Jenny's though either,' he said.

'I know, sorry, didn't mean to upset you.'

'That's ok, I didn't mean it to sound like that,' Joe said reassuring her, he didn't want Liza to be an issue anymore with any further relationships he had.

'Tell me about her, what was she like?' Sarah asked sitting up to drink her wine.

'Are you sure you want to know?' he asked.

'No not really, I suppose I'm a little jealous of the relationship she had with you, but I guess if I knew more about her then I'd understand you all the better.'

'What can I say? She was very beautiful, surprisingly tall for an Asian girl. She was the kindest, most generous person I ever knew. She saw the good in everyone and she put up with a lot of frustration and silliness from me when I was starting out. '

'Was her family ok with you?' she asked.

'Not at first, they didn't like her having a relationship with a non-Muslim, but in the end they respected their daughter's wishes, which she told me was quite brave for a Muslim family. Like most strict societies these things are not really about faith, but more about what is expected, what the neighbours would think.'

'Sounds interesting,' Sarah said.

'Look, I know you want to know more about her, and I don't want to make her disappear as such, but you're not her and she's not you. Whatever we do, will be about us and nobody else, so let's talk about something else.'

'I'm sorry, just one last question and I promise I'll shut up,' she said. Joe could see something was eating at her.

'I didn't ask you this before and I didn't want to push it, but I really would like to understand this about you, especially because of Jane. Why didn't you have kids?'

Joe didn't say anything for a moment. He climbed out of the bed and took a drink from his glass.

'I've put my foot in it again haven't I,' Sarah immediately said, 'don't worry about it; you don't have to tell me.'

He sat back down on the bed again next to her.

'It's ok, it's just a bit hard for me, and this thing with Jenny has brought a lot back. I know it's hard for you as well,' Joe was filling up with emotion and he turned away from Sarah as he didn't want her to pick up on how much it was affecting him.

'I never told anybody this before as I just couldn't come to terms with it at the time, but she was ten weeks pregnant when she died,' as he said it he couldn't hold back the emotion. Tears flowed down his cheek and even the rescue of the wine couldn't stop them.

Sarah leant over and hugged him. She told him how sorry she was, holding onto him for dear life. She cried with him for a long time while emotion drained from them.

He apologised for the emotional response and went to bathroom to wipe his face.

When he returned, they said nothing but sat sipping from their glasses, staying with their own thoughts, trying to find where to pick up from again.

'Have the police said anything more to you about Jenny?' Joe asked breaking the silence.

'No,' Sarah said, 'I think the coroner's report was the end of it. Unless I try to appeal against the verdict or we find some concrete evidence, it will remain as misadventure.'

'What do you think happened, really?' he asked

'To be honest Joe I don't know what to think, and as time goes on I think we are just chasing shadows. We are looking for explanations that are not there. I mean yes, I saw a way that Jenny's accident could have been caused, but it was purely speculation. That traffic officer certainly wasn't going to entertain anything like that. And this BCA stuff, it's all a bit Famous Five isn't it?'

'You're right, there are some facts we don't know but something was going on. Remember all that cover up about Peters? All those abuse cases he was involved in? There's a story there to be told and somebody didn't like her looking into it.'

'Still doesn't tell us much about Jenny though does it?'

'I did find some things about the BCA. Remember I told you about Fletch back at the Agency, the back office computer geek?' Joe said, referring to Chris Fletcher, who everyone knew as Fletch...'He does a lot of the operations' work on the site and the servers. I told you that he also is quite a useful hacker. The management don't know about it and would sack him if they knew what he did or if anything was traced back to the Agency. However, most of the Journos know what he can do and as long as we look after him from our commissions then he does some extra-curricula digging for us. He got the memberships list, which was unremarkable in itself. I found seven thousand or so listed members, which doesn't seem a right lot to me for an organisation that can put on three major rallies across the country. If each subscriber pays the twenty-five pound annual fee, that makes an income of about £170,000. Running an operation with five full-time staff, plus all the PR/marketing costs doesn't add up to me. There was only five thousand left at the end of each year. That means that someone is flying under the radar here. Someone funded that rally and the future ones. It couldn't have been done just with the subscribers. There isn't enough money there.'

'So can you find out who paid for those rallies?'

'Yep, that's what we are doing now? I'm waiting on a call from Fletch, soon as he susses it.'

'What are you going to do now you're back up in Bury?'

'You mean other than entertain you?' he said teasingly, 'I intend to follow up more on the riots, make some calls, just generally doing my job.'

Sarah reached over to the bedside table and looked at her watch.

'I'll have to go soon. You know I can't be out too late.'

'I reckon you've got a little while yet,' Joe reached over and kissed her as they disappeared under the covers again.


A not too dissimilar scene was occurring forty-five miles away in a Premier Inn near the top of the M62 at Ainley Top. The hotel had been prepaid for the night, as usual, which was the advantage to Andrew Bebbington. This was the kind of place where nobody took any notice of who came in and it was possible to check out at anytime without having to return to reception. As everything was prepaid in cash, if he only used the room for a couple of hours, nobody was any the wiser.

So they satisfied themselves with a basic clean room and the dank purple and white décor the chain favoured. Whilst the décor didn't quite match the lifestyle they were used to, the expensive champagne and chocolates went some way to recreating an atmosphere they could enjoy along side the passionate sex.

At least that was how Bebbington saw it. Lucy herself had a very different opinion. The sex wasn't bad but the exclusive access to Bebbington and his friends was what Lucy really cherished. The more she understood politics and the way the world worked, the more she found herself wanting away from the miserable, small-minded attitudes of Northern England. She wanted to move in the circles of *real* power and *real* money. She saw Bebbington as her way into that.

Lucy knew that Bebbington saw her as a play-thing. He loved Lucy, and may even had understood what Lucy's real motivation was, but whilst her beautiful long legs were spread wide open he was not going to take too much time to think about things. He would take his chances.

Tonight, after the obligatory sex, they had more important things to discuss.

'Are we ready for the second wave?' Bebbington asked.

'Yes, as far as I know, it's all done. I told you before I'm not getting involved in the details, trying to keep as far away from it as possible,' Lucy replied.

'Excellent.'

'Are you sure this is the right step? It could cause a mass panic.'

'Lucy, we talked about this. It's the only way people will wake up and realise what has happened to their country.'

'Yes, but will there be anything left to rule?'

'You know there are many people interested in protecting the future of this country. We just need to play our roles, and it will all work out. This country will be back to its magnificent best, with the right people running it.'

'I love it when you talk dirty,' she said pouring another glass of champagne down her throat.

# CHAPTER THIRTEEN

*Wednesday*

At her desk on Wednesday morning, Rachel Lancaster was catching up with her work and speculating on what she would do with the day.

Anna Stockton popped her head around the door with a short polite knock.

'Busy?' she asked.

'No, come in,' Rachel replied, 'just thinking about our ongoing stuff.'

She updated Anna on the latest with Mark Davies and persuading Lee to wear a wire.

'Brilliant…well done. I'm impressed... never doubted you. Do you think he can handle it?'

'I've no doubt he can handle it, he is a bright lad. I think he's learnt a lot being on Davies' shift. He's learnt how to keep his head down, being the secret revolutionary. I just hope he doesn't make a mistake. He could get in serious trouble for it. He knows that working through official channels will do nothing, so this is the only way to get him out.'

'If he gets the tape, we can start to think about presenting all this to the Chief Constable. Maybe they will take us seriously this time.' Anna said seemingly wanting to move on to other things…. 'John Pilkington has dropped his appeal, by the way.'

'Blimey,' Rachel said, 'why? …I know Alex put out that story out about him, but he kept the gossip stuff out of it. He did hint at some controversy but nothing like the real story and not enough to scare him off. In fact, most people seemed to think he was right judging by what I read.'

'You know how open-minded some of our electorate are?' Anna said smiling, 'he said that he's moved on now, bigger fish to fry and he wants to focus on that. He did say that whilst he didn't want to fight for his job, this wouldn't be the last to be said on the matter. The BFB have now added to their manifesto that membership of a political party cannot preclude you from a job.'

'I'm glad we don't have to go to court behind him, that's for sure, but I think we will keep the file open on him for now. I've a feeling we may yet feel the wrath of Pilkington here as well. I don't think he felt we were one-hundred percent behind him.'

'Next point is Purnell,' Anna said, referring to the car dealership they were pursuing multiple claims against.

'Ok, what about him? Tell me he's paid out all the claims and he's joined the priesthood after he gave his last confession?' Rachel replied.

'If only… he's not giving in at all and wants to go court.'

'Doesn't he think we've enough with the weight of claims against him?' Rachel asked. She was a little surprised that Purnell would want to defend them, it was a lot of trouble to go to, but then she figured guys like Purnell would do so just for the principle of not losing.

'His solicitor has written advising me that they refute every single claim and are happy to defend each one if need be.'

'That's not good,' Rachel replied, 'that could be really expensive for us and high risk.'

'Exactly,' her boss said as she stared at Rachel, 'so…'

'I hear you,' Rachel said, understanding what Anna had left hanging in the air.

She couldn't do any more to ensure Purnell would settle the claim out of court and she wouldn't want to risk losing in court. These cases were always tricky and a good lawyer could tear the whole thing apart. With Rachel's experience and talent for the underhand, she could work on persuading Purnell to settle or become tabloid fodder. She had to decide whether to leak this out to a newspaper who might want it, the Courier was not right for this kind of thing, or whether the internet would be the best option.

'Anyway,' Anna said coyly, breaking into Rachel's thoughts 'talking about the election.'

'I didn't know we were,' Rachel said laughing at her.

'It seems we have a full list of candidates now.' Anna placed a list on Rachel's desk. 'There are ten names here.'

'You want me to find out everything and anything on this lot?'

'You read my mind.'

'Funny how that happens. I think I've been working here too long. Is it definitely going ahead? I thought there was some suggestion that it might not with all the trouble.'

'Yes, I think they believe delaying the by-election will extend the period of unease and they want to get it done and out of the way.'

'You mean the government want rid of this by-election before they go into a general election year.'

'Gosh Rachel, you're such a cynic.'

'I know, and proud of it.'

'I just want to know what I'm dealing with in terms of personalities. Other than the obvious party machinery I mean.'

'Yes, I know exactly what you mean, abusing my talents. It's a good job I like you,' Rachel laughed, 'so how is it looking in the polls for you? It's early days I know but do you not think you're putting in a lot of effort for no reward?'

'You may be right. But I can live with that. I just feel I'd like to make a point. So far I don't think I've even registered on anyone's radar. But I intend to change that this week. The other point is that the parties are all busy blaming each other for the violence and no one is taking any lead of the situation.'

'And you are?'

'Are you coming over all Jeremy Paxman on me now?' Anna laughed at Rachel, 'it's ok. I can take it, I'll have to get used to that. Anyway they all carry the weight of party machinery but I can say what I like. It's much easier for me to get off the fence.'

'Yes but you don't have the weaponry either.'

'I have you though. That's far more effective than their party spin machines.'

'Flattery will get you absolutely nowhere,' Rachel said smiling.

'Ha, of course it will. It works every time,' Anna snapped back. 'By the way, I wouldn't mind your help with some radio interviews this week. I need to start raising my profile and getting some votes.'

'Excuse me, I don't recall a new contract and job title for Campaign Manager appearing on my desk.'

'I'll put you on the list for knighthood when I'm in the corridors of power.'

Anna walked to the office door with Rachel, 'dream on boss, dream on. You will be back here in two weeks with your tail between your legs.'

Rachel couldn't believe Anna's blind optimism. As she turned to the candidate list in front of her, she imagined that Anna would get the kicking of her life.


Across the Pennines, in Bury, Sarah Brownlee had just returned from taking her daughter, Jane, to school. Normally Jane would walk but she'd been late this morning and Sarah had to hurry her out of the door. Finally she agreed to get the car out and take her.

She put the kettle on and out of habit flicked on the TV in the kitchen for some background noise. Breakfast TV was just finishing and the headlines came on. She hardly paid attention to the predictable headlines as she poured the boiling water into the teapot and sliced some bread for toast. The news referred to another death in Afghanistan, another piece of climate change science in advance of the conference in Copenhagen. It was followed by the latest revelation in the MP's expenses scandal, claiming they were being hard done by with this virtual public stoning. Finally there was the gossip on whether the latest expulsion from the X factor was the right one. Sarah wondered if anyone really cared, and then she thought, clearly some did, as people appeared much happier to argue about this then anything really serious going on in the world.

As she buttered her toast and poured the tea, the programme moved to the local North West news.

*'A body found on wasteland in the Carlton area has been identified as Adrian Cullen, who went missing in 1981 in Preston. Forensic experts have confirmed via D.N.A. that the body was a match to a stored sample.. Police are appealing for information on the boy and have offered no explanation as to how he came to be in Carlton. Police stated they were able to identify the body as a boy from an apparently unconnected area due to forward thinking parents. The mother had kept the boy's belongings over the years, never having the heart to throw them out. In the early days of D.N.A. technology she had seen a chance to identify her son and asked for a sample to be stored.'*

Sarah immediately dug out her phone and found she already had two text messages from Joe, asking her if she'd seen the news, and secondly to ring her as soon as possible.

She was about to call Joe when the door bell rang.

'Shit,' she said, 'why is everything happening at once?'

She ran to the front door with her phone still in her hand. She opened the door with not a moment's thought as to who would be coming round. Her head was still spinning with the news.

'Russ,' was all she could say as she stared at her brother-in-law. It was more of a question than a statement.

He marched past without saying a word.

She closed the door and followed him into the kitchen.

'Do you want a drink or anything, the kettle has just boiled?' she asked trying to be polite but still he didn't say anything. He seemed to be trying to find the words.

'The police came to see me this morning. It was about that body on the estate,' he appeared preoccupied and nervous.

Sarah wondered where this was going.

'Why would they come to you to talk about this?'

'They wanted to know what Jenny knew about it.'

'What do you mean?' she asked.

'Apparently Jenny talked to them about witnessing something a long time ago.'

'She told about that?'

'Yes of course she did. Jenny told me everything.'

Sarah was thinking that she knew for a fact that Jenny most definitely did not tell him everything.

'She told me she'd seen something and that she thought she knew what it was, but I told her not to get involved.'

'OK, so she obviously went to the police. What did she tell them?'

'That's why I'm here, what do you know?'

'Me? … I don't know anything?' Sarah said, not wanting to get into this with Russ, 'how would I know?'

'You came to me the other week, asking about what Jenny was up to so you definitely know something. She must have told you,' his initial nervousness had turned to anger. 'Tell me… I looked a right fool in front of the police, not knowing what was going on with my own wife.'

'I told you already what I knew when I came to see you, so don't come round here accusing me of things. You refused to discuss it with me.'

Sarah's patience had worn thin and before he could protest she went on the attack.

'I told you then Russ what I knew, which was that Jenny was looking into something and she was scared, but you told me to butt out. So no, I don't know anything and if you're going to continue to throw this shit at me then you can go. You made me out to be the evil bitch sister and banned me from seeing my nieces. Well, you can just go, Russ. Come back when you can hold a civilised conversation.'

Much as she didn't want Russ to get to her, as she screamed the words out, tears inevitably came. Russ had hit a raw nerve with his accusation and she hated how easily he could get to her.

He looked like he might stay and argue but like Sarah, he knew it was pointless and left without another word. Sarah slammed the door shut and collapsed on the floor sobbing.

'I was beginning to get worried. Where have you been?' Joe demanded when Sarah eventually answered the phone.'

'I'm sorry,' she said, still tearful, 'it's just been an awful morning.'

'What happened?' Joe asked, 'are you ok?'

Sarah explained what had happened with Russ coming round.

'You must think me a weepy little girl. I seem to be always crying. I'm not normally this bad, I just don't where it's all coming from,' she said trying to talk herself round again.

Joe didn't mind, he was well aware of how much of an emotional time this was for Sarah and that it wouldn't take much, never mind an idiot brother-in-law to set her off.

'Anyway,' she said, 'did you see the news this morning? That's why Russ came round.'

'Yes that's why I was ringing you. I was in the hotel writing up my notes and heard it on the news. What do you think?'

'To be honest I haven't had a chance to react. Russ kind of stole the moment when he burst in,' Sarah said, now able to talk about it rationally, 'what do you think about it?'

'The interesting thing is that the boy came from a different area. But we thought this must have been case as they would have got there earlier if he was local.'

'What does it tell us, though?' Sarah asked.

'Not much really, but we do have a name now and that means we can start to dig deeper. Do you fancy a trip to Preston?' Joe asked her.

'When do you want to go? I have to be back for Jane this afternoon,' Sarah asked.

'Ok I suppose it will have to be tomorrow, but we need to get going on this. We want to get to the parents and find out about this kid. We find them and we find out what happened.'

'Do we need to go the police? Surely they will want to speak to you?'

'I haven't heard from them yet, but I guess if they have been to see Russ then I'll probably be on their list for today,' Joe said.

'Perhaps we should go down together today, get it over with.'

'Are you sure you want to go there, it's not exactly a pleasant experience?' Joe asked.

'I want to hear this directly from the police. She's my sister and I think they'll say more if I'm there.'

'Ok but we don't talk about all this BCA stuff and the website. It's all just speculation for now and we don't want to make trouble for ourselves.'

'Do you want me to come round and pick you up? When should I come?' Sarah asked.

'Great, pick me up at eleven.'

# CHAPTER FOURTEEN

John Pilkington parked his car in The Light car park and walked up the stairs into the shopping centre. He liked The Light; it was the sort of place that put Leeds on the map. It was housed in the old Leeds Permanent Building Society offices. When it disappeared from the banking world the classic building dominating the Headrow was left empty and useless. For a while a hotel chain took over but didn't have the money to really invest in the building.

Five years ago in one of the rare good decisions that Leeds City Council made, it was agreed that the core of the building could be turned into a cinema and high spec shopping complex. This had been a great success and was one of the most popular spots in the city, particularly for young people, with its modern café style restaurants and designer stores. It gave John the sense of what Leeds could achieve if it didn't let itself get distracted by the small minded lefties who dominated the council. There was still plenty to be pissed off about as the local brands disappeared, to be replaced by foreign ones. In some cases names remained, like Yorkshire Bank, but that was only there to convince the people of Yorkshire that they still had an interest in them, but in fact the company was no more Yorkshire than the Bank of America. It was owned and financed by a multi-national corporation whose only interest in Yorkshire was to exploit the brand to its maximum with Yorkshire residents.

For a change the weather wasn't too bad as he wandered along the road. It was cool but the sun had made an appearance and the wind had dropped, putting John in a relatively optimistic mood. Returning from the printers with the new election leaflet, he was quite impressed with himself. He lit a cigarette, glad of the five minute walk that would allow him to finish it without having to rush.

He moved out onto the Headrow towards the BFB office at the far end of Briggate. Once again his mind drifted to the changing face of Leeds. The old Lewis's department store had now become a supermarket. Another iconic brand of the North lost to conglomerates taking over the world.

As he walked passed the steady crowds he made a point of studying the faces he saw. It was clear to anybody who had walked these streets, for as many years as he had, the colour of skin was distinctly different and the actual propensity to hear English voices had reduced unbelievably given that this was a high street in the heart of Yorkshire. He noticed this every time he walked the streets and became increasingly angered and obsessed by it. This was the proof, should anyone need it, to show how immigration was ruining the identity of the country and could only get worse. It wasn't just about Black and Asian. They had long since dominated the landscape, but it was the Polish, Spanish, French and even Russian voices that could be heard interspersed with Leeds accents. John couldn't imagine they were here as tourists.

Then people like him were punished for defending the rights of local people. Even his beloved Leeds United seemed to have dwindled which was symptomatic of the weakening Leeds profile. The town had lost its confidence and this was because it had lost its identity.

Lost in his angry world he didn't see a young Asian girl in front of him and she banged into him. He was about to apologise and then stopped as her headscarf registered with him. He just turned away and said nothing. At least it wasn't a full burka he thought but then, the husband would be there with her, not letting her out of his sight. He didn't have any respect for women who covered their head like this. He turned to look at her again from behind and noted her tight jeans. Shame he thought, she's got a really nice arse. If she took all that stuff off with a bit of make up, there was a pretty hot chick waiting to come out.

Smiling to himself, he walked on. His mind had now moved on from the frustrations of the British way of life to fancying an Asian girl. He had to admit that for all his disgust of the headscarf and the religion, he would just once love to fuck one of them. He saw it as an exciting challenge and the height of sexual achievement. He was well aware that he didn't think like other blokes but he didn't care. In fact he was quite proud of his own fetish. Everyone has their thing he figured, this one is mine. You never know, he thought as his fantasy drifted on, I might convince the bitch to drop her stupid religion and hang out with some real men.

Arriving at the office at the end of Briggate, just before the exit for the inner ring road, he decided he should concentrate on being professional. Get his mind on the job and out of his own self styled sexual gutter.

He walked up the stairs, and noted pleasantly the union jack adorning the stair-well. It was like coming home to a welcoming committee as he tapped in the security code. Diane was sat at her desk, and said hi to him without looking up. She didn't like him, but he didn't care. Since he'd started working full time for the party she'd sulked. All of her sway with Patrick had gone as he now looked to him to do all the important stuff. Diane was relegated to doing the mail and making the tea. John figured that was perfectly fine with him, it was all she was good for.

He took off his jacket and loosened his scarf, feeling over-warm having to wear it inside even though the alternative of people seeing his scar was worse. Diane spoke to him before he sat down.

'Don't get too comfy, Patrick wants to see you.'

'Now?' John asked, not sure whether he was expected to jump to attention or not.

'Yes, he said as soon as you come in. I think that means now,' she said with a dry sarcastic tone.

John ignored her but he really would have preferred to slap the sarcastic smile right off her face. He knocked on Patrick's door. 'John, come in,' Patrick said

John entered the small office and sat opposite Patrick. They talked for a few minutes about the trivialities of the morning until Patrick finally got to the point.

'You're not going to pursue this appeal?'

'We talked about it last week and I agreed with you that we could achieve much more with a good newspaper campaign against them. After all, we can say what we like about the Health Authority. They can't sue us for it. Like you said, if we went to appeal and lost, we would be completely on the defensive. This way we can grab the moral high ground and embarrass the hospital with its narrow-minded policies.'

'OK good, glad you're seeing it my way,' Patrick said, nodding.

'Lucy has got me an interview with Alex Thompson at the courier. She says he'll give us a fair bite of the cherry.'

'That's one place to start, but can we not get on TV with this? Use your imagination. We want to get this message out far and wide. Come on John, if you're going to be full-time here I really want you out there pushing this kind of message. We want attention. Look what Lucy is doing, her face is already the talk of this campaign and I want you supporting her every step of the way. We've a real chance if we get these two weeks right.'

John groaned inside at the sound of Lucy Sayers name. He reckoned Patrick was obsessed with her, probably obsessed with getting in her pants. Did he have to compare everything he did to what Lucy was doing? She was good, fair enough, but he didn't want to be second choice to her in everything just because he was on the sniff.

'The polls are looking good I hear,' he said changing the subject, 'which is a bit of a surprise after the rally and the bombing.'

'Yes well, it seems with some good politics, and Lucy's style, we can happily still show our faces around town. So ring up every media outlet you can; find who will let you put your face out there and let's get the message going.'

'Fine,' he replied, 'I can do that, but what theme do we go with; the failure of equal opportunities or the political correctness mess that is ruining the country?'

'To be honest I like both, you just need to intermingle them. Let's work on a press release which you can follow up in your interview. We can word it strongly and get some ambitious claims in there. It doesn't matter how true they are, we want attention and we won't get anywhere if the message isn't strong enough.'

'Right I get it, we go with the idea that ethics and positive discrimination of hospitals and public sector organisations are favouring non-white and non British candidates an attempt to balance the racial mix in the hospital. This kind of unequal treatment is blocking the opportunities and potential of the local population who have always been and would continue to be, more than capable of staffing and running their own hospital.'

'That's the idea but let's make it snappier, and I want a nice headline to get the point over.'

'Ok, I'm on it.' John left Patrick's office and returned to his desk. Was this easier than doing HR, he thought to himself. He certainly had never done anything like this. He began to realise the pressure of expectation on him. Patrick expected him to do everything in his power to ensure that Lucy won that election. With everything else that was going on, this was going to be the biggest job of his life.


In contrast to the sunshine in Leeds, the weather and mood in Bury was far from cheerful that afternoon. Rain showers promised in the weather forecast that morning, had arrived and the walk or run from the car to the Police Station had made the whole experience that bit more stressful.

The police were more welcoming than Joe's last visit but not much. Joe and Sarah weren't kept waiting for long and were even offered a cup of machine tea. They were invited into an interview room and seen this time by Detective Inspector Adrian Hutchinson, the detective in charge of the case and his Sergeant, Rebecca Timms, who was most likely there to play good cop as she seemed to be the only one smiling. At first they were again suspicious of Joe's motives for turning up at the police station, but once Joe got to tell his story, their interest changed. This time when he dropped in the religious connection with Peters there was a definite pricking of ears and sideways glances.

Trying to keep control of the conversation they asked three or four times about whether Joe and Sarah had heard the dead boy's name before, trying to catch them out. As they didn't know him at that time, it was fairly easy to shrug off the question.

'What made you come back to Manchester now, Mr Barker?' The Sergeant asked, changing the subject. This was a bit tricky to handle so Joe tried to keep the answer very factual. They didn't want to start theorising with their suspicions about what Jenny knew as it might jeopardise their credibility with the Police.

'It's what I said to you before,' Sarah jumped in, and Joe was happy to let her take some of the questions, 'my sister was with Joe when it happened. She emailed Joe recently saying that she wanted to talk to him about it.'

'Do you have a copy of that email?' Sergeant Timms asked again.

'No, I'm afraid not. It was a personal email account and I deleted it by accident,' Joe lied outright, but he didn't intend sharing it with the police. This would disrupt one of the major sources of information they had. …'it wasn't that useful anyway. It just said that she wanted to talk to me. I replied but she wouldn't tell me anything. She just asked if I could go to Manchester when I had chance. Then I tracked down her phone number and tried to call her, I got Sarah instead.'

'She'd passed away earlier that week,' Sarah added.

'When did your sister die?' Timms asked again, making a note of Sarah's answer.

There was a pause and Joe started talking again trying to keep things moving.

'When I came up here for the funeral Sarah and I discussed it and of course we followed it on the news. Hence we came to see you to share what we knew.'

'Are you sure you've shared everything with us, Mr Barker?' Hutchinson asked, this time staring intently, 'I get the impression there's something you're not sharing with us.'

'No, absolutely, you know what I know,' Joe said flatly. Hutchinson didn't take his eyes of Joe for a moment as he assessed whether he believed him.

Noting that the two of them were running out of questions to ask, Sarah decided to do what she'd come here to, which was to ask some questions of her own.

'Have you found any connection between the church and the boy?' she asked.

'Why do you ask that?' Timms asked.

'Well, if you take the leap that Joe's sighting of Father Peters that night was connected to the body, then there could be some religious connection to the boy,' Sarah replied.

'What about you?' Hutchinson asked looking at Joe, 'were you involved in the church, an altar boy or something of the like? You obviously knew Father Peters and he knew you.'

'I was in a young Christian Group but I didn't do any of the altar boy stuff. I had been attending St Margaret's for years so everyone in the church knew Father Peters and he definitely knew everyone in the regular congregation. My parents wouldn't let me do the altar, they said I was too young in my early teens and I didn't want to do it as I got older.'

'So, you had no connection with the deceased then?' Hutchinson asked.

'No I didn't, I already told you,' Joe said getting tired of the tone.

'The boy was an altar boy wasn't he?' Sarah jumped in, realising where the police were going with this, 'that's why you were asking if Joe was one. You think that the link between Peters and the boy is because he was an altar boy?'

Joe looked at Sarah impressed with the leap she'd made. She smiled back grateful for the encouragement.

Immediately Inspector Hutchinson put his hand up to stop her getting ahead of herself.

'It's clear that this is a possible connection but we don't know anything for certain. We don't want to speculate and therefore I'd ask that you keep this information under your hat,' he was looking pointedly at Joe, 'if you publish anything about it I will simply deny it and then your story would be lost. It is too early to say whether this is significant or not. For the moment let's just say it is a line of enquiry.'

They saw they were not going to get anywhere but at least had learnt something about the case. The Inspector thanked them for coming in and asked them to let him know if they thought of anything else. He then repeated his subtle threat about putting anything in print at this stage. Joe ignored the tone having heard it numerous times before and was more than happy to step out of the oppressive room.

'Let's go get a drink,' he said to Sarah, who seemed more than happy to oblige, 'ever thought about becoming a journalist?'


Alex looked around the small room in the back of the Old Bull Inn on Wakefield Road. About twenty people in were there. There was a regular music slot on Wednesdays and he knew Rachel had played here before, although it was unlikely that anyone came here to listen specifically to her.

He'd been a bit confused when he arrived and saw the line up, no sign of Rachel Lancaster. He hadn't realised she used an alias. When he saw Juliette Black on the board outside he thought Rachel must have changed her plans and almost didn't recognise her when he first came in, she looked so different. He noted her black dress, sheer tights and heavy make up with bright red lipstick. Her long dark hair was down and she looked extremely sexy and passionate. It was a side of Rachel he hadn't seen before and couldn't help be drawn into the whole thing. He had never connected her with her rock and roll past before but now he could see the whole thing before him.

He discreetly got a drink and took a seat in the corner to enjoy the show.

As she worked through her songs and got to the last one, Alex looked around the room thinking how many would come and see her again. He was sure he would.

She was coming to the end of the set but not one person in the room was doing anything other than staring mesmerised at Rachel. She was singing the Alanis Morrisette song, "The Uninvited". He hadn't heard the song in a while and had forgotten the haunting sound. He could hear the pianist with the slow, piercing, chime-like sound of the keys, which seemed to echo. Rachel's voice floated in the room like a swirl of cigarette smoke lingering and spreading steadily enveloping each person. The notes rose and fell, sometimes aggressively, piercing the room, other times gently, melting in the air. It was almost the perfect environment to hear a voice like that as the acoustics of the small room added to the effect. She had an amazing voice and the song choice seemed to suit her just fine.

She played a few different kinds of songs starting with a version of "The Butterfly Collector" from The Jam. He had only ever heard the song a couple of times and wouldn't have known what it was if she hadn't told everyone as she finished. It sounded great though and he definitely needed to check out the words. She played a couple of songs, he hadn't heard of before but then that was no surprise as he wasn't the greatest music listener. He did recognise the Elbow song The Everthere, as he had the album on repeat a few years back.

After she'd finished her set and had taken her applause, she came over to the bar and kissed the guy he had seen sat there. That must be Alan, her boyfriend, Alex thought although he hadn't met him before. He walked over to them.

'Hi Alex, I was just going to come and say hello. I saw you back there,' Rachel said, smiling as she leant over and kissed Alex on the cheek, 'this is Alan, by the way.'

Alex shook Alan's hand as Rachel introduced him.

'That was quite a set and voice Juliette,' Alex said emphasising her stage name, 'I'm impressed and I love the look. That totally threw me. How come you don't do it seriously?'

'Thank you Alex, always nice to get a compliment.' She was glowing with the attention, 'been there, done that I suppose. I like doing this because I can do it on my own terms. It might have been an exercise in chasing money and fame when I was young, but I never got the fame and my ex-husband screwed me on the money. What did you think?' Rachel asked turning to Alan who so far had said nothing.

'Speechless. That was incredible,' Alan said with an awestruck look on his face, 'were one or two of those your own songs or were they all covers? I've never heard them before.'

'Have you not seen her before?' Alex asked Alan before Rachel could reply.

'No, no. This is my first time. She didn't let me come before.'

'Ha ha, liar,' she laughed, 'I haven't done a gig for a while, been too busy, I was a bit rusty I think. There were some of my own, ones that are mine and I have all the rights too, but I don't like to make too much of my own stuff. For a start not too many people know them and I like to play stuff people might identify with a bit. Also building a singing career is behind me now. I'm not aiming for commercial success and the pressure of keeping a record company happy is just not worth it. The ones I play are just very personal to me and I enjoy singing them.'

'I see,' Alex said, 'if that was rusty, I'd love to see when you're on top form.'

'Anyway, what are you doing here?' Rachel asked Alex, as Alan ordered some fresh drinks for each of them.

'I knew you said you would be here when we spoke the other day and I wanted to ask you something. I had a free night so here I am,' Alex said shrugging his shoulders, 'I guess I also thought I'd see whether you were any good or not. I was quite impressed with Juliette Black anyway.'

Rachel laughed relaxing with Alex's joke, 'Yes well I like to keep things very separate, makes life so much easier. Where is Tina? I thought she would be here with you?'

'She had a better offer,' he said flippantly, 'actually she's working. I'm going to pick her up later on.'

'Has she forgiven you yet? Are you getting laid regularly again?' she asked enjoying touching a nerve with him.

'For your information, she's forgiven me, and things are fine thank you very much.'

'Enough frivolity,' she said, 'what was it you wanted to talk to me about?'

Before she answered, a guy passing the bar interrupted to compliment Rachel on her set. She smiled gratefully enjoying the attention. She could tell he wanted to ask more but looking at Alan and Alex he decided that this wasn't the time and moved on.

Alex laughed as Alan passed each of them a drink.

'They love you it seems…not like you to crave the attention.'

He noticed Alan didn't seem quite so happy sharing her with the audience, pulling a face as the guy leant over her.

'It's one thing getting the attention in this place, but once I'm out of here then it's Rachel you'll see and not Juliette.'

'Too right, too right, think I prefer Juliette though,' he said admiring her sharp black dress. He watched her take a drink of wine and leave a large red lipstick stain on the glass contrasting wonderfully with the clear white wine.

'Anyway, come on get to the point, what was it you wanted?' she asked him again.

Alex shuffled uncomfortably, his eyes quickly shifting to Alan, hinting that he wanted to talk to her alone.

'It's ok,' Alan said picking up on the vibes, 'I'm off to the loo anyway.'

'Sorry about that,' he said as Alan was out of earshot, 'I didn't want to be untactful.'

'It's ok. He's cool,' Rachel said reassuring him.

'I got a call from John Pilkington. He gave me a press release and a story for tomorrow's paper.'

'What? I thought he'd dropped his appeal?' Rachel said, suddenly very curious.

'It seems he dropped it so he can use it as a political campaign message.'

'Did he say that?' she asked.

'No. I just read between the lines of the press release. Think about it, if he'd won his appeal he would have got his job back or a pay off, a non-event with the possibility of a non-disclosure agreement. This way, he gets to plead hard-done-by due to the political correctness of the authorities. He can say what he likes and they can't touch him.'

'And you're going to print it?' Rachel asked becoming very pissed off with what she was hearing. She realised that she may have won in the short term with him dropping the case, but, she'd been naïve to believe that he wouldn't have a broader agenda.

'Should be able to, I will give it due balance of course and I've got a quote from the hospital although that doesn't state much other than general rhetoric about being an equal opportunities employer and reflecting the local community. I was just wondering if you had anything more substantial than those rumours you gave me? No one I spoke to wanted to put their names out there, so I couldn't print even an insinuation without him suing the arse of me.'

'I can have a word again with Pat, but I don't expect to get much,' she tried not to be pissed off with Alex but she was frustrated by not being able to get the message across about what this guy was really like.

'It's fucking wrong that this guy should be able to say what he likes in the paper and no one can challenge the smug bastard. Anyway, it will be another few ticks in the box for your mate Lucy Sayers. I thought you would be up for that,' Rachel said with a condescending look.

'Yeah right. You keep going on about this, it's getting boring now Rachel. Anyway, as I've said numerous times before, she's not my mate, and I'm not on anyone's side. We will find a way to expose Pilkington. It may take a bit of hard cash, but we will find a way to wipe that smile of his face. What will your boss Anna have to say about it? I'll give her a quote if she likes?'

'I think she's got an interview booked with one of your hacks. She's only just kicked off her campaign. I think she's just starting to understand how much work she's going to have to do on her own publicity if she's going to do anything serious in this election.'

Alan came back to the bar with a look that said; 'can I join in?'

'Its ok love, we are done now I think,' Rachel said looking at Alex for confirmation.

'Sure, sorry about that. I'm going to get off soon anyway.'

They chatted some more and Alex left a few minutes later feeling that he'd worn out his welcome. This Alan guy seemed ok although he gave Alex a few dirty looks as if to say, this is my night. He couldn't really blame him as Alex knew he'd kind of interrupted things. Rachel appeared happy enough with him and it was good to see her smiling. His thoughts moved on to Tina and whether she would be in a good mood when he picked her up. He could do without the hassle tonight.

# CHAPTER FIFTEEN

*Thursday*

'Whose idea was this anyway? I'm sure people have got better things to do than sit here and listen to me'. Anna took a sip of her coffee as she waited outside the studio door. They had come to a pre-arranged interview at the BBC Radio Leeds studio. She had a slot on the breakfast show and it was her first big chance to get her message across.

'It seems, whatever you think about what you're saying, people want to listen,' Rachel answered, 'let's go back over our notes again.'

'Come on, there's not one thing that I've said that someone else hasn't thought,' she went on ignoring Rachel.

She knew Rachel was a bit frustrated with her, judging by the disapproving looks that said I told you so. Up until now, Anna had been full steam ahead for this campaign and all of a sudden faced with this radio interview she'd become self-conscious and nervous.

'Remember, that's exactly why people like you. Because you're saying what they think.'

'You look tired,' Anna said, suddenly changing the subject, 'good night last night?'

Rachel suddenly looked embarrassed.

'The gig was great thanks, nice to get back into it again,' she said 'got another one on Friday as well.'

'I didn't mean that and you know it,' Anna said enjoying the distraction for a moment. Rachel was really blushing now which wasn't like her at all. Anna loved that she could still get her on the back foot.

The program producer popped her head out of the door and waved at her.

'Go for it girl,' Rachel said as Anna stood up nervously and disappeared into the studio.

This was her first time in a radio studio. She could see the presenter Adam Parker talking away into the microphone seemingly conducting an interview with someone not in the room. The assistant put her into a chair and gave her some headphones. On her left side another desk was occupied by a young guy and as Adam finished the interview, the young guy started speaking… apparently the traffic presenter.

It was incredibly dynamic, slick and remarkably professional. This amused her slightly. She rarely listened to local radio as most of the time it sounded like a bunch of amateurs trying desperately to find something interesting to fill up the vast space of twenty-four hour talk radio.

The producer whispered that she was on after the travel and to just speak into the mike when she was introduced.

'And now we turn to Anna Stockton. Independent Candidate in the Leeds North by-election. Welcome Anna.'

'Err, hi Adam,' she quickly tried to recover herself, she'd been so busy listening to the travel and watching the movement in the room, she hadn't quite been ready for her cue.

'Anna why are you standing in this election, surely as independent candidate you haven't got much of a chance?' Adam asked nodding at her that this was her cue now.

'I'm standing in the election as an ordinary Joe.' She swallowed, trying to calm down and remember Rachel's coaching… 'Politicians and politics in this country are a joke. People have lost interest because they cannot tell a blatant lie from a spin story, another set of statistics or a government policy. None of them speak the truth, they are just general messages designed to impress somewhere called middle England and worded just cleverly enough so the opposition cannot pick holes in it. That may be successful or maybe not, but it doesn't make any difference because the other lot will just revert back to the same message they've been rolling out for years. It doesn't matter who is saying it, they are just the same and people have stopped listening.'

'Why do you think they will listen to you?' he said making his first challenge. This was ideal for her as she loved this kind of debate

'They may not and indeed that is their choice. However, I felt it was time for someone who wasn't a politician by breed and who can say what an ordinary person thinks about the issues of the day. I've no party to keep happy; I'm not seeking overall power. I just want the opportunity to voice an opinion that is honest, straightforward and not covered in flowery rhetoric designed to confuse people.'

'Ok then, this is your chance to tell people what your message is. Why should the people of Leeds vote for you?' Adam nodded at her again to take her cue.

Anna paused for a second wanting to get this right.

'I believe that the party system currently in place is flawed. For reasons I've already explained, the system actually encourages dishonesty in the name of protecting power. This means that the real story of what is happening is lost and the tactics for dealing with the issues are compromised by party doctrine. It is clear to anyone with their brain on the right way round that there are a number of problems to be dealt with and it needs people of exceptional quality to deal with them. Not politicians, skilled people who can work together regardless of background or wealth. I offer myself up as a business woman prepared to put herself on the line for the electorate to decide if I possess those skills. I hope others will follow and we can build a government of brains instead of card carrying club members.'

'Surely you must have some political views, some agenda?' Adam pressed her further.

'Of course I have ideas and issues that should be raised, and they will become apparent as the campaign progresses. The most important thing is that I encourage as many people, like me, to stand for elections throughout the land and break this party political monopoly. Let's debate real issues, not party ideology.'

'How does your agenda fit with the riots here in Leeds? How would you solve this problem?'

'Firstly, these people need to work to solve their own problems and take some responsibility for what they are doing. People have to make their own minds up to stop the violence. Our job, as politicians, is to take on the issues of the day with fairness and honesty commanding the respect of people, regardless of their background or whether they agree with you or not. This kind of situation is directly linked to a lack of honesty in politics and an inability to face the facts of the day. Politicians seem to spend more time avoiding difficult topics. What people want is someone who will admit what's wrong or perhaps they individually have got things wrong and then provide the direction of how to move the organisation, city or country, forward.'

'With respect, you just ignored that last question, with another political statement. I don't see anything different.'

'Ok fair point. I was simply attempting to give my campaign context. If you want a practical answer then this is the way I see it. If I see things going wrong in my business, then instead of sticking my head in the sand and pretending it's not happening, I call each of the people involved and get them together in one room until they sort it out. Obviously, I can't put hundreds of people in one room, but we could manage a certain amount of representation from all sides. The closer people are together in conversation the more likely they are to be able to see others' points of view. Communication is always the answer and the only way to get to a mutually satisfactory solution. I'd be happy to facilitate that or even lead the discussions.'

'Would that do anything? I mean there are some pretty violent thugs out there.'

'Criminal acts are for the police to deal with on an individual case by case basis. Whilst there are clearly some bad elements that may or not be controlling the violence or even enjoying it, most reasonable people get involved in this kind of thing because they are desperate and believe no one is listening to them. If we can get to those reasonable elements and show them we are listening then the violent malicious ones will be left isolated with little respect in the community.'

'That sounds pretty light weight. What is your feeling about the BFB's hard line suggestion for immediate deportation of any Asian involved in the riots and immediate custodial sentence for any violence?'

'The BFB live in cloud cuckoo land. For a start, you can't deport people who were born in this country and have a British Passport. 99% of those rioting will be from here. They have as much right as you or I. And as for chucking the other thugs into prison, they seem to think we've acres of space to put these people. The other point, is that a good proportion of these thugs are card-carrying BFB supporters and if anyone can stop them rioting, the BFB can. The truth is that the BFB are enjoying this chaos as it plays right into the hands of those who would want to divide this country.'

'What do you make of the article this morning in the courier about John Pilkington getting the sack from the Health Service because of his political views?' Adam asked, trying to put her on the spot, not realising the interest Anna already had in the case.

'If you ask me whether his political beliefs are compatible with the equal opportunities ideals of an employer like the hospital, then I think they are untenable, and most people would see that. Whether they were right to dismiss him or not comes down to the detail of employment contracts and procedures at the hospital, something that we can't get into in this discussion. But the fact that he is using this as a flag to wave for BFB openness is about as ridiculous as you can get and quite offensive to all people and businesses that have benefited from the competence based approach equal opportunities has brought us. Do you think I'd be here having this conversation with you if we hadn't had the cultural change in the country brought about by equal opportunities legislation?'

The presenter was satisfied with her answer and moved on to her opinions on other candidates. Anna kept it clean with no specific accusations about her competitors. She kept her criticisms general and tried to make more of a play of her ideas. After seemingly no time at all, Adam cut her short.

'OK Anna we've run out of time now, perhaps you can come back and talk to us again as nearer the bi-election.'

She thanked him as he quickly moved onto his next topic and she left the studio.

As she stepped out into the foyer, Rachel gave her a short round of applause. 'The campaign is officially started. Let's go onwards to the next interview,' Rachel said as she patted her on the back.


One hour later, Lucy Sayers was shivering in her thin coat outside the same BBC Radio Leeds studios, Fortunately, she didn't have to wait too long as the car arrived to take her to her next meeting. As she opened the door happy to get out of the cold, her phone rang.

It was Patrick Barclay.

'Up two percent in the polls, things are looking up.'

'Just a sec Patrick,' she said, pausing to smile for a photographer who'd spotted her. She had no idea where the photographer had come from but she knew at this stage any publicity was good publicity. The shot was taken then she jumped in the car driven by John Pilkington.

'Thanks John,' Lucy said as she got in the car.

'It's cool, Patrick told me to look after you. Make sure you got around.'

'Sorry Patrick. It was a bit difficult to talk out there,' she said into the phone as John pulled away.

'How did the interview go?' Patrick asked.

'You mean you didn't listen to it?' she said teasing him.

'I can't listen to all your interviews.'

'Which way are you going?' Lucy said to John, who was driving down towards Sheepscar.

'We are going up to Beckton aren't we, to the community centre?' John asked looking confused.

'Yeah sure, I just thought we'd have gone up York Road,' she turned back to the phone, 'well anyway that businesswoman Anna

Stockton had been in before me and she'd given him a few bricks to chuck my way. I handled them, no worries.'

'The polls are looking good, and John's piece in the courier looks good, although that reporter friend of yours tried to put in as much shit as he could to make it look like it was all bullshit.'

'He is not my friend or my lover. I told you,' Lucy said getting pissed off with his constant sexualising of her relationships. John Pilkington hearing her comment jumped in with his own view.

'Yeah well there's plenty think the same, maybe you should drop round and see him again; get him sorted.'

'Listen both of you,' she said to the phone and to John Pilkington next to her.' I'm not flashing my tits just to get his attention. I don't need to and you know it,' Lucy replied. She'd tell them to fuck off in a minute but then she knew he was just winding her up. It was like John told her; this is what everyone was thinking. She was a good looking woman and people would automatically make the assumption that she used her body, either notionally or actively. The problem was that she was quite prepared to use her body, hence Andrew Bebbington; she just didn't like others to think of her in such a one dimensional way.

'Ok Ok,' Patrick said filling the silence, 'don't worry about it. What's the agenda for the rest of the day?'

'We are off to Beckton right now, to talk to people in the community. See what we can do to help. Then I'm attending the press conference with the police. We are supposed to be appealing for calm, although to be honest things already seem to be calmer this week. According to the news, incidents are isolated now rather than orchestrated.'

'Remember not to let those journos wind you up. Keep it along the party lines.'

'You know me better than that Patrick. Anyway what are you doing for the cause today?'

'I have a teleconference with Kevin Inkerman shortly; he wants to know how things are going. Then I'm preparing for the fundraiser tonight at the Printers. You coming down? I would be good for you to show your face?'

'Yeah, I'll be there. Although to be honest I'd rather stick pins in my eyes.'

'Ha, ha,' he laughed, 'I know that they are not the most charming lot but they are putting their hands in their pockets. So we should attempt to seem grateful.'

'Ok, talk to you later Patrick,' Lucy said as she closed her phone. She nervously pushed her hair back behind her ears. She was beginning to feel the pressure of the constant attention and performance.

# CHAPTER SIXTEEN

Sarah Brownlee parked her Audi A3 in a lay-by in Ackton, a large council estate in northern Preston. She looked at Joe Barker sat next to her.

'Is it ok to leave it here?' Sarah asked.

'It's either that or we leave it outside the estate and walk in. I think I fancy that even less.'

They looked around the estate and the house they were due to visit. It was just like any run-down council estate in any town or city in the UK. This one looked like a throwback to the seventies with boarded windows everywhere and garbage strewn around the streets. If any investment had gone into this street it was not obvious from the outside.

They had found the address quite easily with a bit of luck and common sense. Using the Lancashire Evening Post archive website, they had searched around the time that the disappearance of Adrian Cullen had been reported by his mother, Mrs A Cullen of Ackton. A remarkably easy call to directory enquiries provided the phone number and address. Obviously Mrs Cullen had not moved from the area in all the time since Adrian's disappearance.

'Are we sure this is the right house? I thought that there might be some other reporters here?' Sarah asked, 'I wouldn't want to get the wrong one.'

'For the third time yes it's the right one. I guess we are one step ahead here. Are you coming in with me?' Joe asked oblivious to how she was feeling.

Sarah knew he didn't mean anything by it but his all-knowing tone had been annoying her this morning.

'Of course I'm coming in. Dont patronise me,' Sarah replied.

Men can be so superior she thought. She was feeling nervous but she wasn't going to miss this for one moment. Maybe she wouldn't have done this on her own and she was most definitely out of her comfort zone, but that was no reason to be pushed aside.

'Mrs Cullen, it's Joe Barker. I called earlier,' Joe said as he knocked at the door. They'd phoned earlier and as they suspected she wasn't keen to talk to him, just as she was reluctant to answer the door now. It had taken some persuading and it was only because Joe said he may have seen something back when Adrian was taken, that she'd agreed to see them. She told him that if she suspected he was lying she'd kick him out there and then.

They listened for a moment, hearing nothing. Joe was just about to knock again when the door opened slightly with the chain still applied.

'Any ID?' A voice came from the gap. They could just make out the shape of a large old woman in a housecoat but couldn't see her face. Joe pushed his press card round the door and after a pause for a few seconds, the door closed again and the chain was removed.

She didn't say anything as they entered the living room. An old style gas fire was on full and it was boiling in the room. Mrs Cullen sat in an armchair close to the fire and a small black and white cat sat next to her. The cat offered a momentary glance to Joe and Sarah but settled back down to its sleep with that superior look that only a cat can give.

Mrs Cullen was most likely in her seventies, but it was really impossible to tell. The room was relatively clean, which was a sign of reasonable mobility.

Staring round the dated décor of the room, Sarah could see pictures and ornaments filling every surface including a number of pictures of a young boy, which Sarah assumed must have been Adrian. There was no sign of a man around. Mrs Cullen gestured towards the small reasonably smart red cloth sofa for them to sit down.

'If you want a drink you can make yourselves one,' she said, 'I'm not much up to entertaining these days.'

Joe got up and said he'd do it.

Sarah was a bit surprised, assuming that perhaps he would have expected her to make the tea. Maybe he'd more faith in her than she gave him credit for, or more likely he wanted a nosy in the back.

She hadn't noticed it at first, but as she watched Joe go to the kitchen she saw the back of the room contained a full bookcase. She couldn't make out most of the titles but one or two famous ones that stood out. The top shelf appeared to be all thrillers she recognised and then further down there were a lot of travel books. There was also a whole section of Readers Digest atlases for various regions of the world. Sarah had seen many of these mail-order book offers from Readers Digest over the years but had never known anyone who paid money for them.

'I like to read a lot,' Mrs Cullen said as if knowing what was on Sarah's mind, 'I can see what you're thinking, little old woman in her council house, nothing between the ears,' she said, 'don't reckon you know me. I won't be messed about, and don't think I won't kick you right back out that door if you deserve it.'

'I wouldn't dream of it Mrs Cullen, we are just very pleased to talk to you,' Sarah said thinking quickly of ways to keep her on-side.

'Impressive set of books,' she added to flatter her.

'Yes, collected a lot over the years and read them all, just hard to read so much these days with my eyes, but I still do, you know,' the old lady replied determined to assert her capability to Sarah.

'Where is Mr Cullen?' Sarah asked.

She seemed to sniff with mild disgust at the question, the gesture not intended for Sarah.

'I haven't heard hide nor hair from him for twenty years now. He buggered off years ago, couldn't handle life round here without Adrian.'

'Oh, I'm sorry. I didn't realise that. Did you have any other children?'

'Oh, don't worry about him... and no there wasn't any others. He was a waste of space anyway. No, that was the problem, see. Without Adrian we only had each other to deal with. It wasn't long before he'd had enough of that.'

'That's a long time to live alone.'

'Happy enough on my own. I've got my books and Cherry keeps me company,' she said as she stroked the cat next to her. Cherry purred in grateful agreement.

Joe returned with three cups of tea and some sugar.

'I hope this is ok for you,' he said putting the cups down on the small table by the sofa.

'That's fine, I'm sure it will taste better, given I didn't make it,' she said, smiling at her own joke.

'I was surprised to hear that you had kept Adrian's DNA for the police,' Joe said, immediately getting to the point of why they were here.

'I always knew he would turn up someday probably dead, so when I heard about this DNA thing I went to see my solicitor to see what he could do. At least then I'd know what happened to him.'

'You had a solicitor?' Joe asked.

Sarah was astounded at Joe's patronising tone; fortunately Mrs Cullen was equal to it.

'Don't assume just because I live in this estate that I don't know how things work, you know. This may not be paradise but it's my home and it will stay that way until they carry me out in a box. For your information, and I'd have thought it was obvious, when Adrian went missing I needed someone to handle the search for me. We found it too difficult to deal with everything, and most of the time the police didn't want to know. Edgars, in Main Street, helped us out a lot with keeping things moving and asking questions. It cost us, but I had some money come from a small inheritance. Spent some of it on holidays but mostly I didn't have much use for it, so using it on Adrian was right enough for me.'

'So tell me what happened when he disappeared?' Joe asked, 'if you don't mind.'

'I told this to the police the other day but I'll say it again. It's not something I'll ever forget.' Mrs Cullen said looking tearful as she started to talk, her bravado of earlier diminishing.

'It was a Wednesday evening and Adrian had been home from school as normal. He told me he was to go to the church that evening as the priest wanted him to do some more practice. It seemed he'd made some mistakes at the service, the previous weekend. He left here at five and I expected him back about six thirty. He never came home.'

'Who was the priest? Did he say anything?' Joe asked.

'His name was Father Doohan.' Joe and Sarah looked each other as the name registered. It was the same name on the justice website from the Maltshaw parish.

'I didn't like him much,' Mrs Cullen continued, 'he liked the drink too much for my liking, always stunk of whisky. He said that Adrian left the house at six. There were no witnesses though and the housekeeper wasn't around at the time. No witnesses came forward and no one said they'd seen him walking home. I don't know what happened but from the moment Adrian left the sacristy, no one saw him.'

'Did you believe Doohan?'

'Of course I did, he were a priest. He wouldn't lie.'

'Twenty years on, what do you think now?'

'These days I don't know what to think. Anything could have happened I suppose. At the time I took him at his word. But you hear so much these days you don't know what to think.'

'Did Adrian enjoy going there?'

'He did at first and then he started to treat it like a chore. He quite liked the church and all that. We used to go as a family. John, my husband, was quite faithful in them days. After a while Adrian seemed not to like working the altar. I asked him if he wanted to give it up. He just told me I didn't know what I was talking about and that he simply had to go.'

'Was he the only one who used to go? Did he have friends who went with him?'

'Oh yes. There were some other boys from the school,' Mrs Cullen replied.

'Were they with him that night?'

'His friends told the police they hadn't been to the sacristy that night. So nobody knew anything.'

'Do you remember the names?'

Sarah was conscious that Joe was pushing the old lady quite hard but she seemed ok with it. She was wondering whether to tell him to cool it but Mrs Cullen continued on, so she said nothing.

'I have a photo of them, but I gave it to the Police. They did say they'd give it back to me. Never forgotten the names …David McGhee, Ian Hamilton, Stephen Gorton and Roy Hunter…that's them.'

Joe had his notebook out taking a note of the names. He asked if she knew anything of the other boys now and she said not. She didn't even know where they lived at the time, except that they lived around the estate. Happy that this would have been just a bonus, as they were unlikely to still be there, Joe prepared to leave.

They now knew the connection with the church and with Peters. What they still didn't know was why Jenny was frightened and the key piece of information she had found. After all, she hadn't been to Preston as far as they knew, so how did she find out what had happened?


'So, tell me the truth?' Anna asked turning to Rachel in the passenger seat as she pulled up at the lights on the loop road approaching The Calls.

'What chance have I got next week?'

Rachel said nothing for a moment, thinking about a tactful response. They had not spoken since they left the last newspaper interview. Previously they had been at a lunch time reception at the Chamber of Commerce, conveniently put together by Anna's friend who was the Chairman. The silence was broken with Anna's question and all morning it had been the elephant in the room. Was she wasting her time?

Anna took her foot off the brake as the lights changed. She drove past the cathedral and into The Calls. Rachel considered her response as she stared out the window noting the expensive restaurants and exclusive clubs as she always did when going through here. As they moved closer to the centre, she saw a bar on the left, burnt out, and wondered whether that had been a victim of the recent violence.

'I have to admit it's hard to see how you could win this. And that is not a comment on your campaign or what you have to say. But let's face it; this by-election is about a battle between the Tories and BFB. Labour is losing ground by the day with their incompetent handling of the riots and with their general unpopularity. It's a case of who is going to pick up those disillusioned Labour voters. Normally you would just expect them to switch to the Tories but Lucy Sayers is doing a very good job of filling the void. Rightly or wrongly she's the one you have to take on.'

'Find anything interesting in your search?' Anna asked.

'Nothing useful really. She is what she says on the tin: a normal working married woman with her 2.2 kids. She's worked for the council for all her career, been a member of the nationalist movement in one form or another for six years. She joined after the death of her parents in a car crash caused by an Asian driver. It's hard to tell whether it was an overnight revelation as the politics of race have always been confused in the working classes. Her father had been a staunch labour man before his death but who knows if he was the protectionist type hating immigrants or if he was an "*each to their own*" type of happy-clappy socialist. It doesn't really matter which, I think the crash probably provided its own motivation.'

'I didn't know that… Interesting,' Anna said thoughtfully.

'It doesn't really matter what started her off down this avenue, what is for sure, is that she's intelligent, driven and seemingly formidable,' Rachel said.

'She'll have a weakness somewhere. Everybody does, even me.'

'Ha ha, yes. I know yours,' Rachel said laughing, 'you like that red wine too much.'

'Not that; you know what I mean,' Anna said reaching over to slap her lightly on the arm, 'she'll have done something that she doesn't want anyone to know about.'

'I've had a dig around and talked to a few people. If she has any secrets they are well hidden. That's often the problem with people who are forthright in their views. What you see is what you get.'

They pulled into Anna's allocated parking space outside the office and walked into the Stockton's office. In reception Rachel saw a familiar face in the comfortable chairs to the left.

'Rachel. I need to talk to you,' said Patrycja Wladek, the nurse from the hospital.

'I'll leave you to it,' Anna said as she tapped the security code into the door behind the reception desk.

'You've got to do something about that bastard Pilkington,' Pat demanded.

'Come with me,' Rachel said, 'let's go get a coffee.'

They walked back out of reception and twenty metres down the road to Joan's coffee shop.

A lot of people from the offices around used Joan's for decent coffee and a reasonable sandwich without costing too much.

They finally sat down and Rachel asked what the problem was.

'Have you seen the papers today?' Patrycja asked, 'that bastard has pasted himself all over the Courier; how they were wrong to sack him; how he was hard-done-by because he was a member of the BFB. He is a mad, fucking rapist racist. He should be locked up, never mind be in a position of responsibility.'

Rachel nearly choked on her coffee.

'That was quite a mouthful,' she said laughing, 'a rapist racist,' seeing Patrycja was not laughing, Rachel decided she better be serious.

'Sorry,' she said, 'it just sounded funny. You know I'm no lover of him myself.'

Pat still didn't look like she was playing.

'Well, he fucking well is one,' Pat complained, 'he didn't do anything to me but there's definitely talk around the hospital that he raped an African woman. I reckon he is well capable of it.'

'Whatever you think, that is quite an accusation. A very dangerous one to make, so you better be careful,' Rachel said, trying to get her to calm down.

'He can't just go around presenting himself as Lord high and mighty. He is at the least a liar and a bigot.'

'Look, I agree with you. I even tried to do something about stopping it myself. I talked to the reporter who wrote the article. No one would come forward and put their name to anything. He couldn't print anything that suggested what you said without any proof. In this environment he would be in court before the newspaper hit the shops. And you would be there with him.'

'I can't believe it…I'm so angry,' she said looking defeated.

'There is a way to deal with this,' Rachel said as she took another sip of her coffee.

Patrycja looked up at her with fear in her face, she started to anticipate Rachel's words, but Rachel reassured her before she could speak.

'It's ok we won't use your name, we can't go to print in name as we discussed, but strength in numbers may get us somewhere.'

'How do we do that if nobody will come forward?' she asked.

'The internet,' Rachel said.

Patrycja looked confused.

'On the internet, you can be truly anonymous. No one knows who you are and you can say what you like. Yes, he might get an injunction to close the site down where you make the accusations but by that time it may have had its affect.'

'They can still trace me via the internet though, they have allsorts of stuff for that these days like they do with those paedophiles,' she said not at all convinced.

'Not if we are clever they won't find you,' she said reassuring her, and I know how it can be done.'

'So I go on the internet and say what I know about him? But how will anyone know where it is to see it?'

'We go to other gossip, networking and political sites. We reference the site and people will follow the link to the web page. The thing is, once the accusations are in the public domain a reporter can comment on them as long as he doesn't repeat the accusations.'

'Ok but I don't know how to set up a site like this.' Patrycja asked, still not really getting it.

'Leave that bit with me, I've a friend who can set it up. All you need to do is set up an anonymous email account, hotmail or something like that. Do not use your real name. Only ever use it from an internet café and never use a card to pay for it. Leave me your mobile number. When the site is set up I'll text you the details. Then tell anyone you talk to at the hospital that this site exists and let's see what happens.'

'Do you think it will work? Could we get in trouble for this?' Pat asked sounding apprehensive.

'This is why anonymity is the key. Once real numbers of people get involved then the momentum will take hold and you can back off. It will take on a life of its own.'

'What about the person who sets up the site? Won't they get in trouble?'

'That's the wonder of the internet. Site proprietors can be hidden quite easily.'

'So that means you can start up a campaign about anybody on the internet? That's crazy. I'm surprised it doesn't happen more often.'

'To make anything like this work, as I said before, it needs numbers of people. If enough people agree with you and know who he is, then a site like this will generate a lot of entries. People might not want to go to court, but if they have an axe to grind with our mate Pilkington, then you can be sure they won't mind voicing it, via the precious anonymity of the internet.'

Patrycja thanked Rachel, feeling a lot better and left to get the bus back home. Rachel walked back to the office. She was happy to be doing something and cursed herself for not thinking of it earlier. She'd done this many times before when waging some of her campaigns. But those had been business. This felt more personal given what he was.

She would call Ravi, her geek computer mate. She'd met him when dealing with a wrongful arrest case for him. She'd got him compensation and he said that if she ever needed anything from the net then to let him know, legal or illegal. She knew he didn't do these jobs himself, he wasn't that clever, but he did know a lot of people through his chat rooms and he had never let her down so far. She didn't ask too many questions and he always gave her something useful. Perhaps at the same time he could do a bit of digging on Lucy Sayers. She had to be careful about what she asked him for though. He'd told her before that there was a certain morality to the on line community. They didn't really mind what tactics they used to find information, looking in virtual dustbins and stealing data, but they just liked to think they were doing it for a just cause.

Rachel sat back down at the desk and made the call. She thought about whether there would be any comeback from this. After all the trouble she'd had in the last few weeks was she inviting more her way? In the end there was only once choice as Pat had said. He shouldn't be allowed to get away with it.


Alex sat at his desk in the Courier office and read the email correspondence he'd received following the article last night on the sacking of John Pilkington. Everyday, since the bombing, the level of correspondence had gone through the roof. Everybody had an opinion. He had to sift through the mails and hand over a selection of the best to the letters editor. It was a chore in many ways but at the same time it was good to gauge the reaction to anything you had written.

Today's correspondence was split down the middle. Half of them thinking that Pilkington was a victim of political correctness gone mad, the other half believing he was a fascist bastard in a fascist party and deserved all he got. In some ways it was good to see a polarising of opinion because that usually meant the article had reasonable balance. If it was all one sided then he'd probably fucked up.

Rachel Lancaster had phoned to tell him that she was going to set up a website with a hate campaign on him. Alex had told her she was crazy and was wasting her time. This was dangerous, because, whether it was or wasn't true, if it was traced back to her she could be in serious trouble.

Judging by some of the emails, though, there was maybe something in it, a few specifically saying they had heard rumours about him. He decided he would give it a few days and see what she turned up, if there was something concrete to work with then all well and good.

He generally trusted Rachel's instincts and those instincts had led him to spend the day rethinking the BFB angle. As well as the Pilkington stuff she believed there was more to find out about what was going on inside the BFB. For all Alex liked the way that Lucy Sayers operated and understood her message, he couldn't deny Rachel was right. The mob he came across two weeks previously was a definite reminder of the roots of nationalism in the UK. Yet they were winning support outside the mob and things were happening.

He remembered that Joe Barker was looking into party set up to see if there was something interesting behind the surge in membership and cash. He dug out his number and called him.

'Sarah's driving. We are just on our way back from Preston,' Joe explained briefly as they connected.

'I hope you get something useful out of it,' Alex said wanting to move onto his own issue, 'listen Joe, did you get anything from your digging on the BFB? You said you would see what you could find out.'

'Shit mate, I'm sorry. I asked one of the guys in the office to do some digging but I haven't been back to chase him up. I'll give him a call and get back to you. What are you thinking? Sounds like something is bugging you?'

'Nothing specific, I just want to know whether there is anything going on there below the surface. You know that by-election is coming up and I reckon the BFB is doing well. There could be some major repercussions if they win and I want to be on top of it. You know what I mean?' Alex said, not sure he knew himself where he was going with it.

They ended the call with Joe agreeing to follow it up. Alex wondered if there was some way he could speed up the information on this and get his own story. The phone ringing interrupted his thoughts. It was his editor.

'Get down to Police HQ now. There's an announcement on the bombing.'

Alex had his coat on before he'd put the phone down.

# CHAPTER SEVENTEEN

The atmosphere at Eastside Police Station, in the centre of Leeds, was electric. All anyone had been told was that there had been a major development in the bombing case.

The room for the press conference was heaving as it had been the first day after the bombing, TV, radio, tabloids and broadsheets were all there. Alex had made his way straight across town in a taxi, not wanting to waste time having to find somewhere to park.

Dead on three o'clock, the Chief Constable and the Detective Chief Inspector in charge of the case walked out to the desk. They settled in their chairs and the Chief Constable spoke.

'Welcome everyone, thanks for coming down today. At eleven this morning two men were arrested for the bombing of Old Street Mosque in Beckton. One is a nineteen-year-old white male from Turkham in Wakefield, the other an eighteen-year-old white male from Boulton in South Leeds. Both males are currently helping police with their enquiries. These arrests are the result of intensive and patient police work by my officers. Detective Chief Inspector Holding will now give you details of how the arrests were made...Following the publication of CCTV pictures of the surrounding area on the day of the bombings, a number of calls from the public led us to identify these two males as potential suspects. We didn't publicise the names at the time because we didn't want to alert them and therefore give them reason to go on the run. We subsequently observed the two males and arrested them when we were sure that we had the right suspects.'

There was a lot of shouting of questions in the room, but the first question of any clarity came from a TV reporter at the front.

'Have they been charged?'

'At this stage these two males are helping with our enquiries. Investigations are ongoing?'

Another question came over the commotion.

'Are you likely to be making any other arrests?'

'As you'd expect I cannot comment on that. I will say, however, that our investigation does not end here.'

'Do you think this was organised and planned by someone else? Are these two just the fall guys?' Alex managed to get a question heard over the commotion

'Once again I will not comment. Investigations are ongoing.'

'In previous press conferences, it has been indicated you believed this to be an organised terrorist operation. Do you still believe that?' Another TV reporter asked picking up on Alex's question.

'I cannot say any more at this stage. As you know this is a major investigation and there are many lines of enquiry that have yet to be followed up. We still intend to investigate all angles of this case.'

The questions went on but there wasn't anything more to learn. Alex made vigorous notes ready to put together his report. Two young white guys had been arrested. One thing was absolutely certain. These two couldn't possibly have put this together themselves. Someone else was behind this and it was clear from the tone of the police that they knew it as well.


Lucy Sayers, Patrick Barclay and John Pilkington stood together watching the live streaming of the press conference on BBC news from the BFB office. They happened to be in the office doing a debriefing of the day's campaigning. The news was on TV in the hall as they kept up to date.

'Would you believe it? Two little white boy thugs did it,' said John Pilkington, 'you wouldn't have thought anybody off that estate would have had the intelligence to do something like that?'

'Of course they haven't got the intelligence to do it. Two toe-rags like that couldn't have put together something as well executed as that. Let's face it, they can't have been too bright otherwise they wouldn't have got caught.' Patrick said looking at Lucy and John, 'someone else did this and we need to know who.'

'What do you mean?' Lucy asked staring at Patrick, 'you think we had to something to do with it?'

'No I didn't mean that,' he said, 'when it comes out who was behind that bombing, and it soon will, I don't think these two will stand too much asking of questions. We don't want to be anywhere near it.'

'People already think it was us anyway,' Pilkington said, 'people are pointing the finger all the time.'

'Exactly why we will need to deflect the blame somewhere else, meanwhile, if I find anyone in this party was connected, I'll personally go down to the police station and shop them myself.'

'Look, I don't know who was behind this, but I know for sure that none of us were,' Lucy said defensively.

'I wasn't accusing you; I'm just fed up with this. We've spent so much effort trying to clean up our image and present an intellectual straightforward argument and we get constantly undermined by stuff like this.'

'I know...tell me about it', Lucy said in agreement, 'everywhere I go I get it, constantly on the defensive. Having said that, as much as people think we might have had something to do with it, there are many that think the Muslims had it coming and will vote for us because of it.'

'John, can you prepare a press release, right away. I want everyone to think we are in full support of the Police investigation,' Patrick said looking over at John.

Lucy's phone vibrated in her pocket. She quickly informed them she was going to the Ladies and left the room. There were only two toilets in the office, one each for men and women. Fortunately Diane wasn't in there as she dived into the small bathroom.

'Sorry I couldn't answer then,' Lucy said as the call connected.

'You saw the news then?' it was the familiar American accent of Andrew Bebbington.

'Yeah sure. Not good,' Lucy said.

'Too right, it's not good. I thought we were clear at this end with no comebacks.' The anger in his voice was obvious.

'We are. There's no way they can link back to us,' Lucy said, defending herself for the second time within a few minutes.

'If those two blab then we are in big trouble.'

'Even if they blab they don't know who we are.'

'Look, they know who your pet copper is and who told them what to do and if they grass, then they can include you and the rest of us on their roll call of suspects. You need to get them out of there. What ever way you can, you or that copper need to get them out,' Bebbington said raising his voice at Lucy now.

The tone of his voice worried her. She knew the stakes were high in this game but he'd never spoken like that to her before.

'Ok I'll deal with it,' she said quietly and hung up, immediately dialling another number. It was a test now to see if she was up to it. Could she manage a crisis and win? It was time to get hard-faced and start to take some of the credit due. Her mind was talking tough but her hand was shaking as the call connected.

Joe Barker sat in his hotel room writing up his own version of events in Leeds. He'd quite mixed feelings about the whole situation, on the one hand wanting to be in Lancashire helping Sarah out, but really his job and career would suggest being in Leeds. He decided that he needed to follow the big story and he'd go there tomorrow.

Fortunately, now he had Alex as a contact in Leeds, he had a ready store of information already which had allowed him to get a decent story together with enough details that the Agency had paid him.

Having completed that task, he went back over what they'd found in Preston. Between him and Sarah, he believed they'd already discovered quite a bit of information about what might have happened, certainly enough to start to speculate. It appeared that Adrian Cullen was killed in the company of or by the priest Doohan. Then the priest had called Peters and, with two of Adrian's friends arranged for the body to be dumped. A wall of silence had done the rest of the job.

What they needed to do now was to trace those boys and find out who wanted to keep that wall of silence in place. That was a lot easier said than done as they would probably now be married, or separated; in their mid-forties, hardly recognisable. They could have left the country or be dead.

They'd got back to Bury and Sarah had dropped him at the hotel as usual. She was going to pick Jane up from school and said she would meet him later if she got the chance. That was ok with him because it gave him time to think and to put together his notes.

He knew he owed Alex for these notes but then he also knew that he wasn't a direct competitor to a regional newspaper like the Courier so it wasn't a big deal. Also, these things worked both ways and there was plenty that Joe could give Alex.

The first pay back would be finding more information on the BFB funding and it was with this purpose he called Fletch at the office in London.

They exchanged pleasantries and eventually Fletch asked Joe what he really wanted to know.

'Remember we spoke last week about the funding of the BFB and BCA. Did you find anything interesting?'

'Well yes and no,' Fletch said, 'I went on the electoral donor register for the BFB and there was no major single fund provider for them. But what was interesting was that they'd numerous single donors all paying in the region of one to two thousand pounds. The key thing about it is that the donations received since the party was formed have gone up over three hundred percent from the previous incarnations of any of these nationalist parties. They'd funding of over two hundred thousand just in the last year. There were of course numerous unlisted members who are just ordinary members amounting to about sixty thousand. I know the party have rebranded, but that is a serious increase in funding. I didn't call you back because I talked to Heather Lockhart about it. You know Heather; she does a lot of politics stories for us?'

'Yeah I know who you mean. I haven't spoken to her for ages. How is she doing?'

'She was cool last week when I spoke to her, but the thing is… she never rang me back. I hadn't chased her because to be honest with all this riot stuff on the news I've been pretty pushed digging out stuff for you guys.'

'Why did you call Heather? Am I missing something?' Joe was curious as to why his stories were spreading far and wide. There was a lot of competition for stories at the agency and he naturally liked to keep things tight to his chest.'

'It's ok, I wasn't selling you out, don't worry. It's just that she knows a lot about this funding stuff, and to be honest she'd asked me to look at it before. You see, she reckoned that the BFB were creating artificial donors. She asked me to check some addresses in London, but I couldn't get any information on them.'

'You mean they were false addresses?'

'No, no they existed all right. But I couldn't find the people at the addresses. The names were on the electoral roll but not listed at that address. That was a few months ago. I told her what I found and she thanked me. She said for me to leave it for now and she'd think about what to do next. I called her last week to see if she'd got any further with it.'

'What did she say?' This was interesting stuff, definitely what he was hoping to hear.

'She told me something, but not a lot. She said that she suspected that someone was spreading donations through false donors to remain anonymous and hadn't yet discovered who it was, but she had enough to prove at least that there were illegal donors. If not, who was providing the money?'

'Why hadn't she reported them?' Joe asked Fletch.

'I guess she wanted the holy-grail. She wanted that name.'

'Did she give you any details, anything to go on?'

'She said she'd go back to it and give me what she had. She knew you wanted the details and she said she'd call you about it. To be honest that's why I didn't come back to you. I thought she'd call you.'

'Have you heard anything from her at all?' Joe asked.

'Nothing, in fact, I haven't seen her for a week.'

'OK see what you can find out, I'll try her myself.'

'What about the BCA?'

'They are not actually a political party, but technically a club or society, so they don't have to publish donors. They just have to provide annual accounts. Because they have not gone through a first year, there are no published accounts. I spoke to the Harrison guy you gave me and he just said that there was a mixture of individual members and some corporate donations. I asked who the corporate donors were and he said that those who wanted their sponsorship to be available were detailed on the website. Others would remain confidential for now. I checked the corporate donations and there were four of them. SAS Holdings Ltd, who are a the holding company based on London who own mainly SAS security, who I'm sure you've heard of, and some other operations, I can check them out if you like?'

Joe had heard of SAS security. Their vans were everywhere providing cash deliveries and private security to businesses and citizens who could afford it.

'The next one was Crocker Developments some kind of property development company, and the next was a Faithisus.Com; a religious supplies website selling anything from music and books, to travel packages, trinkets and other various religious tat. Finally AT&I Health Services who seem to be a private clinic for various therapies, the link on the site only referred to US operations so I didn't go too far with it.'

'Ok I'll go on the website for that stuff. Do you know any of the names behind the companies?' Joe asked.

'A guy called Peter Brown is the Chairman of SAS Holdings. I don't know about the others. I'll get them for you.'

'Ok thanks. Let me know if you talk to Heather. I'll try her myself now.'

Joe thanked Fletch for the information and finished the call. He then searched his phone book and found Heather's number. He tried her but just got voicemail. He left a message, wondering whether he should be worried.


Rachel Lancaster took a sip of her beloved white wine and as the cool liquid floated around her mouth she began to relax. It had been such a big day, starting with Anna's interviews and campaign, dealing with Patrycja and then the news of the arrests.

The news was on the TV in her kitchen as she prepared some dinner. She quite often cooked stir fry because it was easy to do for one, but tonight she was cooking for two as Alan was on the sofa reading the Courier. The Yorkshire news was coming from outside the Eastside Police station where not only was there a mob of media waiting for news on the arrests, but numerous protestors who were being held at bay by a line of police in full riot gear. The crowd, mostly made up of Asian faces, were noisy but didn't appear to be violent. There were some placards demanding death to the murderers and similar messages, but the mood was one of waiting for news rather than any excitement. Rachel assumed that Alex would be among the media crowd somewhere.

The next item on the news pricked her ears as she didn't recall hearing anything quite so outrageous being suggested on a British news channel. It was a report from a University where a speaker, representing the British Christian Association, had been proposing that the rise in crime and social disorder was conclusively linked to the decline in Christian religious education in schools. It went on to say that the rise in other religious teachings, that had become part of the broader religious curriculum, had undermined God's message and confused children to the extent they turned away from the church rather than towards it. The reporter went on to say, the speaker had moved into more controversial territory, saying Christian education needed to learn from other faiths in non-secular societies where religious teaching went through all education and not just one short hour a week. This meant that religion should be taught alongside science and the arts; that way children understood that society, history, and science all came back to God.

Incredulous at what she was hearing, she shouted through to the other room where her boyfriend Alan sat.

'Have you heard this dickhead on the TV? You wonder why we've all these riots and stuff when we get this sort of rubbish in the world. I thought this kind of shit was limited to the Neanderthal states of America.'

There was a reply from the lounge but she didn't quite hear what it was. She assumed agreement, and continued with the cooking; adding the marinated chicken and then fast frying the remaining vegetables. The smell was making her very hungry. Alan had started staying regularly with her now. She hadn't planned on developing this type of relationship but it had grown organically, seemingly no expectation or pressure on each side. It was just the way she liked it and she was reasonably comfortable in referring to him as her boyfriend.

She poured the sizzling food on to the steaming rice and took the plates into the living room. She passed Alan his food and went back to get her wine.

'Smells good,' Alan said as Rachel returned with the wine. She topped up his glass and settled down to eat her dinner.

'You heard what I was saying about the news, that religious nutter?' she asked him.

'Yeah, I heard you, I could see it on the TV here as well,' he replied pausing to take a mouthful of food, 'he has a point though.'

Rachel stared at him aghast.

'Don't get me wrong, I'm not agreeing with him, I'm just making a point. If you're going to be part of a religion, well it's kind of all or nothing. To me, if you believe in something, you can't believe in it for just one hour a week or Sunday morning when you're sat in the pew. It's all day, everyday. That's what this guy is saying. Allowing people to hear different messages whether it's alternative histories, teaching of other faiths or hardcore science. It all undermines the message of that faith.'

'That's because it's all bollocks right. You don't believe in that shite do you?' Rachel was seriously beginning to doubt her boyfriend's intelligence.

'No,' he said in defence, 'you're not hearing me. I'm just explaining the purist position.'

'I don't believe there's such a thing as a purist, people always have different opinions. The purist is just the one with the power to tell people what to think.'

'God you really are a cynic.'

'Tell me this isn't what you believe?' she asked still trying to get her head around him. Was he just playing devil's advocate or was he speaking his mind?

'I can't believe how little trust you have in people sometimes,' he said, sounding a little tetchy with her questions, 'if you ask me, the truth is I don't know what to believe, I was brought up as Church of England and did Sunday school and all that. I found it all fairly interesting, but my family didn't take it too seriously and neither did I. As I sit here, I can still profess an interest in it, but I can't say I understand it or know which side of the fence I sit on. Quite honestly I don't spend hours of my day caring about it.'

'That's a relief then, I didn't see you as Father Alan of Leeds preaching from the bible of religious claptrap,' Rachel laughed lightening the mood.

Alan looked relieved that he was no longer at the back end of Rachel's cynicism.

'Let's change the subject,' he said in the end, 'something more cheerful.'

'Ok, if you insist. Was there any excitement today at the council?' Rachel asked. She took a mouthful of food in anticipation of a reply.

'I thought I said something more cheerful,' Alan laughed, 'nothing remotely cheerful about that. Anyway, as you insist on asking, there was nothing new. The only thing everyone is still talking about is the news.'

They'd caught up earlier on the day's events and what had happened.

'What do you think will happen now?' Rachel asked.

'I don't know, you're the one who seems to have the contacts. Your mate Alex seems to be the guy with all the information.'

'I don't think the arrest of these two will be the end of it. There will be more to know than they are saying.'

'What does your boss say?'

'Anna is ever the pragmatist. She sees everything like a business meeting,' Rachel laughed, 'she thinks as long as everyone talks, you can negotiate your way out of it.'

'She's right in some ways. I guess they should just talk to each other.'

'Ha ha, life is not that simple, or I imagine someone might have tried it once or twice before,' Rachel said teasing him.

'What else are you working on right now?' It was strange; as much as she liked Alan she'd never felt close enough to tell him everything that she did. Some of it was confidential of course, so she'd be in big trouble with Anna if she talked about that stuff. But she'd generally told him that she did research on clients. She just didn't tell him which clients or what they were doing. She wondered about telling him about Pilkington, given he wasn't a client anymore, but in the end decided not to. It didn't feel right. She hoped by now he'd already be beginning to accept her ways.

'This and that, nothing exciting,' was her bland reply, hoping that would satisfy him. He said nothing and carried on eating so she thought the matter was dropped.

They both ate whilst watching the TV and things were relaxed, the silence comfortable. After sometime Alan spoke, making it clear to her that accepting her ways was the last thing on his mind and she'd misread him totally.

'Why don't you talk about your work much?' Alan asked. It was a simple question but Rachel knew it was loaded with meaning.

She paused for a moment looking at him before speaking. In the three weeks she had been out with him, he had never made a comment like that. Admittedly, that was not a long time but this was way out of character in their relationship. She took a sip of wine continuing the pause.

'I told you before,' she said eventually deciding to try to play down its importance, in the hope that it was not as big a deal as she feared. 'There's not much I can talk about. It's not that interesting anyway.'

'I get the feeling you don't trust me enough to tell me anything,' he continued, keeping the spotlight on her, 'I won't tell anybody you know?'

She decided to take the professional line about her work, expecting him to see the sense in that.

'Don't you see? It's not about you. Anna's business is built on confidentiality. It's a secretive business and I'm so used to not discussing anything about it that I just don't talk about anything, that way I don't slip up.'

'Yes, but you talk to Alex Thompson about stuff, I've seen you do it.'

'Is that what this is about, jealousy?' Rachel asked, this conversation was definitely beginning to annoy her, and petty jealousy was not a trait she was prepared to put up with.

'I'm not jealous, but it's obvious you talk to him about stuff. So you trust him and not me. Then there's the business before about religion. You're quite happy to dish out the questions and the mistrust, but you don't like it when it turns on you.'

'Fucking hell, Alan,' she said, frustration beginning to show through in her tone. She self-consciously took another drink trying not to react more than she wanted to.

'I like Alex, don't get me wrong, but our conversations are purely business. We share certain information, quid pro quo. I give him stuff, he gives me stuff. That doesn't mean I tell him what I'm working on. I have to have contacts to get information, given that paying for information is not an easy activity we do it on a shared basis. So there's nothing to be jealous of.'

'So you can tell me what you tell him. Obviously that information is not so confidential or you wouldn't give it to Alex.'

Rachel nearly choked on her wine. Anything she might have thought about sharing before she definitely was not going to now. Obviously Alan hadn't worked out how contrary she could be. The more someone demanded she do something, the less likely she was to do it.

'Look, what is this about? My work is not that interesting that you really want to know about it.'

Alan took another drink and thought about his reply.

'You don't trust me enough to tell me, and that concerns me.'

'I hardly know you and I don't see it's that important. You've never been like this before,' she said, surprised that her anger was beginning to be tinged with emotion.

'If we are going to go out, we have to trust each other, which I see includes being open about your work. I tell you about planning applications which are supposedly confidential,' Alan demanded.

'That's up to you. I just don't work the same way. I like to keep some things private no matter who I'm with. You have to know that about me.'

'I can't be with someone who doesn't trust me.'

'Alan, can't you see it's not about trust?' As she said it, she knew it was absolutely about trust but that wasn't the message she wanted to give out. 'It's about me keeping my work separate from my home life. It's just the way things are. And the more you keep going on about it, the less likely I'll feel comfortable talking about it.'

'I think I better go then. I'm not getting through to you.' It appeared his frustration with Rachel's replies had wound him up equally.

'Don't let me stop you,' Rachel said, not caring. Her evening was ruined anyway. She was not sure who she was more angry with; him because of his lack of trust or her because she kept losing boyfriends for the exact same reason.

He took his coat and walked into the pouring November rain. Rachel looked out the window and watched him drive away. The dark night and the rain reflected her darkening mood. She satisfied herself that at least he hadn't had much wine and his escape was a quick one. The thought of him being around any longer waiting for a taxi would have just been impossible.


Lucy Sayers was at home having just put her kids to bed when she received the call from Alan Farmer.

'I can't get anything from her. She won't tell me anything,' he told her.

'God, why is everyone so shit around here?' Lucy said furious with the day's events.

'I walked out. I couldn't hack it anymore.'

'What do you mean you can't hack it? Get back in there and sort it out. You were supposed to find out everything she was doing, and you got nothing.'

'I'm not sure she'll let me back. She was pretty pissed off with me'

'Well use what little charm you have and apologise. Buy her a fucking ring for all I care but get back in that house and find out what she's up to. That woman is fucking dangerous and I want to know everything she does.'

She slammed the phone down and kicked the door.

'Men, they are such useless wankers,' she said to herself.

# CHAPTER EIGHTEEN

*Friday*

Breakfast was a chaotic affair in the Stockton household. Anna always felt that it didn't matter how much of a start she gave herself, she never had enough time. This morning she'd been up since six. She'd showered and got herself ready in time to take in the breakfast news, whilst she ate. She watched the TV for five minutes until she could stand no more. The presenter, with her supercilious, superior smile, was discussing the latest health scare and asking an expert a series of questions. The interview lasted three minutes in which she learned that the health scare meant absolutely nothing and it was nothing out of the ordinary. The presenter asked questions designed to sound controversial and pressing but actually sounded silly given the common sense answers that the expert provided. Just as Anna felt the presenter was finally getting the point, the expert was informed that there was no further time.

This would have been marginally less infuriating if the headlines, read out moments later, didn't just return to the same story, ignoring the rational explanation provided by the expert.

Infuriated, she switched off the TV news and put the radio on instead.

She wondered whether there was really enough news going on in the world to justify twenty-four hour news channels. These channels lived for the smell of a big story that could fill those hours with excitement and constant revelations. But it rarely came and meant they had to squeeze as much juice as possible from the most mundane or unlikely story. In that way celebrities, politicians or scientists who made the most outrageous claims could find their story examined to the smallest detail and have the luxury of watching everyone from the Prime Minister to the street cleaner being asked what they thought of it.

She wondered how brave it would be for a channel to put up a test card saying *we've all gone home because there's fuck all happening in the world*. Maybe that should be one of her policy announcements.

The radio news headlines came round with the same regularity as the TV but to her they seemed fresher, more balanced. The headlines listed the quietening of the situation on the streets as Police seemed finally to be getting a hold on things. There was some further reaction from various spokesmen on the BCA education campaign, and then reference to the same health scare she'd seen on TV.

Just after seven o'clock, James appeared with her children, Robert and Michelle, following down soon afterwards. Breakfast became a competition between the radio, conversation and argument around the table, the chomping of food in between sentences or not in some cases. There was also the modern addition of text messages demonstrating the social convention of stopping mid-conversation and checking a mobile phone. It was probably the same in every family household in the morning as it prepared for the day ahead.

As the others finished breakfast she went into her home office and thought about plans for the day ahead. She'd planned a number of media events, hoping to raise more interest in her campaign and possibly gain a bit of cash for it as well.

Her first appointment was at nine when she was going to attend the Women's Institute meeting in Otley. Following that she'd scheduled an interview with the Courier back in Leeds. She'd spent the last few days organising her campaign literature and was clear about her strategy. It was based around a practical common sense approach using inclusive communication.

She didn't know whether this was really enough to get elected, but hoped at least to make a dent in the debate, if nothing else.

Anna was ready to leave at eight and was checking her handbag to see that she had everything she needed for the day when she heard her mobile phone ring.

It was Rachel.

'Have you seen the news?' she said straightaway.

'No, what's wrong? I saw it earlier. There was nothing much going on so I didn't pay much attention,' Anna replied sounding uninterested.

'Switch it on now. They've released the two blokes they got for the bombing.'

Anna walked in the kitchen and put the TV on. The cameras were outside Eastside Police Station and the reporter was explaining with some excitement, the decision to release the two suspects. The reporter said that the Police press release had stated that evidence had come to light that meant the suspects could not have been involved. Consequently, they'd been released immediately.

'What's going on Rachel?' Anna said eventually.

'I don't know. I tried to call Alex at the Courier but he didn't reply. I know he was there so he'll have heard before anyone else.

This doesn't sound good. For the police to be sure they'd got the right people and then to release them within hours, is either a major cock up or someone is covering for them.'

'You really believe that?' Anna asked, switching the TV off and returning to the hall to get her papers together.

'Think about it. I know I'm the cynic here. If you believe that those two were not capable of doing this on their own, then you can easily believe that whoever it was directing them would not want those two to spill the beans. Who knows how far their influence reaches? But I'd put money down that someone is giving them a cast iron alibi. The more I think about it, the more serious it gets. For the police to take an alibi that seriously the person must be someone in authority. Anna, this means that the plan to blow up that mosque was organised by someone the police believe and trust. If we find out who that is, we can blow the whole thing apart.'

'Rachel you're making some pretty dangerous claims there. You be careful about this. This is not a bit of petty mischief. This is serious.'

'I know, I know. I'm going to talk to Alex. I want to see if he believes the same thing as I do.'

'Fair enough, but I've got to go now. I have to get to this meeting at nine. You need to be careful Rachel, I know you hate this kind of injustice, but shooting your mouth off is not your style and it may get you in serious trouble.'

As Rachel walked from her car to the office she felt the miserable atmosphere of the day surround her. The sky was dark as if daylight had decided to stay under the duvet. Winter was approaching and the last warmth of the year had gone.

The wind was pushing her around like a bully. Rain showers formed a coat of misery around her in the same way as the unpleasant feelings she'd had about the world in general. She hadn't slept much after the argument with Alan, and her search for a conspiracy in the morning's events had made her feel worse.

As she continued the battling walk into the office, her mind drifted back to her anger at Alan. She still hadn't decided whether she was angry at herself or him.

To try and sort it out in her head, told herself that she'd over reacted. Not that it worked, she still couldn't get it into balance. Yes, she was secretive and intensely private over some things which could be frustrating to a partner, but that didn't make it right that Alan should react in that way.

Realising she was getting nowhere and it was a waste of effort, she turned her mind back to business, focussing on what was going on at Eastgate.

The Police had let them go. Why was she so angry? It had nothing to do with her. When it came down to it she hated the idea of people getting away with things but there was nothing she could do about it right now, so she told herself to get back to her own issues and support her boss in trying to get something out of the election.

Rachel eventually got to the office door and smiled at Sharon as she entered the building. She was really looking forward to that first coffee.

She walked to the stairs and Sharon shouted her back.

'Rachel, I've got something for you,' she said, 'it seems you have an admirer.'

Sharon handed her a large bouquet of flowers.

Rachel said nothing as she handed them over.

She thanked her, and although Sharon was dying to ask, Rachel just smiled as she took them upstairs.

When she got to her office she put the flowers directly in the bin. She hated flowers and it was another example of Alan not having a clue about her. Flowers, as a gift, had always represented lies to her. They were an apology and compensation for deeds done and as such she preferred people to be straight about what they'd done, rather than trying to patch it up with flowers.

She wanted coffee before she opened the envelope.

She came back two minutes later with a drink in hand. She sat down and stared at the envelope. Should she tear it up and forget about him? Or should she open it, accept the predictable apology that was coming.

In the end she opened it to find one simple word, 'sorry.'

Straightforward and simple at least, she thought. Maybe he deserved some credit for not dressing it up with excuses.

She thought about him as her email box opened. The first email on the list was from Patrycja Wladek with 'Love the website' in the subject box. She followed the link in the mail. She hadn't forgotten about the new website set up by Ravi, but she hadn't thought much about it either. The link opened up a new page headed. *Iamalyingracistrapist.net./johnpilkington*

The name made her laugh and she loved how they had left the flexibility to use for any other suitable nominees that came to their attention. The website header made it clear that this website accused the nominee Mr John Pilkington of Leeds of being a rapist and a racist, and that he'd threatened, attacked and abused numerous women in the Leeds area, and was getting away with it. The site was created so those women who didn't feel able to go to the Police could vent their fury in a safe environment. Comments could be left by anyone registering on the site either in defence or in support of the accusation. A further comment, in smaller print, warned contributors that protecting their anonymity should be foremost in their mind.

In the first few hours there had been two major contributions with numerous comments. She quickly read through them. The first she recognised as Patrycja calling herself the "blonde demon", with a few comments in support of her and some saying she was a stupid bitch who shouldn't have led him on. From the comments it seemed that a Facebook group had been created on a similar basis which had been circulated around Patrycja's friends. The later comments indicated that the group had been taken down but not before the link to the site had gained its own momentum.

This led to a second major contribution which was from someone with the alias "afro-star". She was a cleaner who said she'd been touched-up in a toilet by Pilkington. He had threatened her saying he was mates with her boss and she'd lose her job if she said anything. "Afro-star" said she didn't work there anymore so she didn't have to worry about saying anything now. She reckoned there were other girls who had been abused in the same way because you could see it in their faces when he was around them.

This was just what she wanted to see and if this was the response after one day, then within a few days there would be some serious pressure for it to be taken seriously. Surely Alex could do something with this now.

Joe Barker had his phone glued to his ear all morning in the car as the events of the morning took hold, although he decided now to give up on it as the Pennine hills were approaching. He was so glad to have Sarah with him as she continued to provide a personal chauffeur service. This allowed him to concentrate on his work, whilst she worried about where they were going.

Joe had spoken to Alex Thompson in Leeds as soon as the news broke and arranged to meet him at lunch time for a catch up. He'd spend the day and perhaps a bit longer in Leeds whilst the story developed there and then head home to London.

Sarah had said she would drive Joe today, for a few reasons really, but mainly because she wanted to be with him. Fortunately

Jane, her daughter, was going to see a friend after school and wouldn't be back till later that night. That meant she was free to go, so she told Connor that she was going on a shopping trip to which he grunted some response. She chose to ignore his complaint and hadn't elaborated on where she was going.

As it was, Sarah did need to do some shopping, but she could do it just as well in Leeds. She could spend some time with him and then, as he was busy in the afternoon, she would do the bits she needed to do and head back when the time was right.

It was for this reason that Sarah was now heading into the Pennine hills along the M62, driving up the long hill from the metropolis of Greater Manchester towards the summit of the motorway and the bleakness of Rishworth Moor. Within five miles the world changed from residential areas, factories, offices and cityscapes, to moor-land, sheep and heather. Whilst conditions sometimes could be poor up here, often with fog, wind or snow, Joe still enjoyed the journey into Yorkshire.

The road cut through the hills like a river, finding its path naturally as it followed the contours of the moor. The high concrete bridge overhead was like a gothic monument as you passed down into the windy gap towards Scammonenden Reservoir. The colour of the landscape was unique to the Pennines, not green, not yellow, not brown, but a combination of all of them. The landscape was at times above as you looked at the hills surrounding the high point at Rishworth Moor, and then suddenly below coming into Ainley Top, where you could see the whole of Calderdale five hundred feet below. The luxury of being the passenger was that you got to take all of this in, instead of having to concentrate on keeping the car in a forward direction as the wind picked up.

In the meantime the radio carried on with the news debating once again the battle of faith, race and society across the country from any and every point of view.

A guy came on the phone saying that he agreed with the BCA stance on education and that the violence came from the religious apathy of the masses. Joe cursed the idiot.

Looking at Sarah, at the same time, he saw a curious look in her eyes.

'Why do you hate them so much Joe?' she asked him, 'you're one of the nicest people I've ever met but these fundamentalists bring out such nastiness, suspicion and pure hatred in you.'

Joe thought about what she'd said, unaware how deep his views were. She was right. They did have that effect on him.

'I guess it's because they've screwed with both of our lives in one way or another. I thought you would feel the same, we both had similar upbringings with our minds twisted by exuberant religious fools.'

'To be honest it's never been that important to me on a day-to-day basis, it really hasn't. I got over my upbringing as soon as I left home and started living life. Maybe you're over-compensating as a guilt ridden white male?' she asked with a smile.

He laughed at her joke but then his tone became more firm as he explained his point.

'I learned through Liza about the seriousness of religious doctrine and the blatant division of society. I didn't like it but accepted it in a foreign country that I had no control over. The US has never shaken off religious influence in politics, unlike the UK, and it's become stronger among the white middle classes instead of the opposite in this country. I would hate to see it take hold here. That's why I fear them. The Muslim fundamentalists are one problem but they have little power and influence on society here. The differences with the type of Christian religious fundamentalism that comes out of the US, just like this guy on the radio, is that it comes from the moneyed middle classes and do you know what the most dangerous thing about that is?'

'No,' Sarah replied impatiently.

'As a society we are more likely to listen. If an Asian or African face comes on the TV speaking the exact same words we would hardly listen, thinking them to be foreign deluded idiots. If a white English voice says those same words we are more likely to listen as they are the same as us. In fact we are just a stone's throw from being him. That makes these people far more dangerous. They have the money and the influence to make things happen and if we are not careful they'll gather more and more power.'

'Wow,' Sarah laughed at him, 'you really do go for it. No compromises Barker I think. Fly the flag of freedom.'

Joe laughed, aware of his own pomposity. The trouble was he could rationalise perhaps a bit more but felt this deep down in this bones.

They were getting towards Bradford so he decided to pick up his phone again. The phone signal was ok over the top but it could cut out quite easily whilst on the move. He was about to make a call when he saw that it was already ringing.

'Joe its Fletch,' the caller said as he answered.

Joe greeted him and asked him what was happening.

'You know we were talking about Heather yesterday? You're not going to believe this,' Fletch paused, 'she's dead. I'm sorry.'

'Dead?' Joe said stunned. As he said the words Sarah's head turned to him with a look of fear in her face. Joe put a hand up to calm her down before she reacted. He turned back to his call, 'how can she be? I mean what happened?'

'I managed to speak to her boyfriend yesterday. She was knocked off her bike by a large wagon. The driver didn't stop so it's being treated as a hit and run, although it's not clear from the Police whether the driver genuinely didn't know he'd hit her.'

'Shit, when was this?' Joe asked, still trying to process what had happened.

'Wednesday. Her boyfriend only just got round to formally informing people late yesterday. Apparently the boss knew about it last night. He'd planned to tell us today. Shocking, right?'

'Right,' Joe said his head processing thoughts as quickly as his heart was beating, 'Fletch, did they find the driver?' This sounded very convenient and very suspicious to Joe. Cycling accidents were common in London but hit and runs much less so.

'I don't know, I didn't ask. I was too shocked. Why, are you suspicious or something?'

'I don't know but the cameras must have picked up the wagon and therefore the police must be trying to trace it. It would be interesting to know what happened if nothing else. Any chance you can suss it out?'

'Yeah no problem,' Fletch replied, 'anyway, it means I haven't got much else for you, I emailed some stuff on those companies I mentioned.'

'Fair enough, maybe we can pay a visit to her boyfriend when the dust has settled. Perhaps he'll let us onto her computer.'

'Might be a bit insensitive.'

'Yeah, maybe,' Joe thought for a second, 'she was a journalist. The boyfriend would know that if she had some good stories, Heather would not have wanted them to die with her.'

'That sounds a bit melodramatic Joe,' Fletch said sombrely, 'surely we should be thinking about Heather right now, not what she was working on.'

'Look, of course I care about her and what happened, this is terrible. But if whatever she was working on contributed to her death then we can't sit back and pretend it didn't happen. We should be raising the rooftops.'

'Do you really think this has something to do with the accident? That is a bit of a leap.'

'Yeah well, we are journalists, paid to be cynics and not to trust anything that is said. I need your help with this Fletch.'

'Yeah, of course. No problem. I get you,' Fletch replied.

Joe finished the call and told Sarah the story.

'Someone else, with key information is dead,' was all that she said.

Joe couldn't help but agree.


The phone on Rachel's desk rang, and she picked it up seeing it was Sharon's extension.

'I've just had the guy from the car park on the phone. He suggested you get down there. Your alarm is going off and someone has vandalised your car.'

Rachel swore and was out of the door in seconds. She grabbed her coat but hadn't fastened it properly so was fighting with it as she ran towards the car park through the wind. She got there relieved to reach the protection of the concrete structure. Her car was on the ground floor in its usual space. She almost cried when she saw it, not believing the damage. Every window was smashed and tyre slashed. She flicked off the alarm as she got closer, observing that every other car in the car park was perfectly fine.

Walking round the side she could saw the reason only her car was damaged. There was a roughly painted message on the door, written with her in mind.

SCARED YET?

Not hearing anything in the last two weeks, she thought the whole thing had gone away but there it was again. They had found her at home and now at work. There was no doubt about it, she was scared, but she wouldn't back down. She needed to be careful but she wasn't about to give in, whoever it was.


Patrick Barclay sat in his office in Leeds, yesterday's frustration added to by the release of the suspects. Today was fast turning into a nightmare. The phone had been ringing all morning, for him, for John or for Lucy. Every caller wanted a comment.

This was bad news for the party and he'd sent Lucy and John to find out as much as they could. He called the Chief Constable himself although he hadn't got a reply, and didn't think he would. He knew him well from various community projects he'd been involved in over the years and thought he might get a line into him to find out more, but he knew that the Chief probably had far bigger issues to deal with than him.

More and more, the people were looking for a connection to the BFB and he needed to find ammunition to separate them from the story. Fortunately nothing had been released that linked these youths to any factions or nationalist groups, and as far as he knew nobody had informed him otherwise. In the end, it might not make any real difference. They were always going to be guilty by association with two white youths in the media spotlight.

He thought about what the consequences might be. The election was less than a week away and they'd invested significant time and effort into preparing a *clean* Lucy Sayers. They really didn't need any dirt surfacing now. Patrick considered the connections that might be made, like a meeting being seen in a pub by someone who recognised a party face. It was tenuous but it could be enough for a journalist to turn into something.

Whilst the bombing had usefully strengthened public opinion into more extreme camps, with one side firmly in support of what the BFB had to say even when they might not actively vote for the party. If they were somehow to be presented as the political wing of a violent faction, in the same way as the various parties in Northern Ireland, it would be disastrous and would undermine any confidence the public had in them as a serious political force.

Nothing had surfaced so far, but he was nervous. He didn't believe he'd seen the end of the story yet, and he had no idea what might happen next.

# CHAPTER NINETEEN

It was probably not the best location to choose for a coffee at lunchtime, as it seemed many others had the same plan, but the Costa Coffee on Boar Lane had two distinct advantages, the coffee was reasonably sound, and it was easy to find.

Alex wanted somewhere convenient because Joe said he was coming over from Manchester. Rachel also said she wanted to see him and this would be handy for all of them.

He hadn't stopped since last night, staying late outside the police station waiting for something to happen but nothing had. He decided at midnight to give up and returned to the same spot at six this morning waiting for what he expected to be a formal announcement of charges and the naming of the suspects.

One of the hacks on the news desk had been down to the estate where one of the boys had come from. From talking to kids there, with no doubt a few ten pound notes to encourage gossip, he already had a name. He just wasn't allowed to print it. The name he'd been given was Paul Evans and the others wouldn't take long.

What he hadn't expected was Evans and the other guy to be released and it had a provoked an exciting reaction among the journalists outside. There were numerous conspiracy theories and conclusions jumped to, but absolutely no facts.

He'd written up his notes earlier and sent in his report, happy to take a break following Rachel's call from. She'd been calling him all morning and he finally answered around eleven. He agreed to meet her here after filing his story but he already knew she was pissed off, some problem with her car.

Alex sat down with his coffee, took out his laptop and started searching through all the other online sources to see if anyone had found something he hadn't. After fifteen minutes of reading he satisfied himself that although there were numerous theories around, no one knew anymore than he did.

Looking at his empty coffee cup he decided he ought to consider replacing his drink before he started to get looks from the staff and other customers hovering over his table. As he looked towards the counter, he saw Rachel come through the door looking around the bar for him. Nice timing, he thought. Eventually she spotted him and came over to his table.

'Were you intending to leave me standing like that for your entertainment?' she said looking less than amused with life.

'You were providing amusement for everyone, I didn't like to interrupt.'

'I was going to get you a drink but I'm having second thoughts now,' Rachel made a pretence of laughing but it didn't work, he knew she was not in the mood for banter. She went to the counter to order a drink for them both.

'So tell me, and get it off your chest. What was the problem with the car?' Alex asked when she was back, 'it's clearly eating you up.'

Rachel explained what had happened.

'I had a feeling you were treading on some toes.'

'Don't start Alex, to be honest I wasn't going to tell you. I really don't need a lecture, but this really upset me. I don't like it.'

'I can see that. Maybe you should start to consider your own safety. We know already that we are dealing with some particularly dodgy characters and it seems someone knows who you are,' he said.

'I'll think about it, but it's not the only thing that's annoying me,' she said as they caught up about the other events of the day.' What do you think is going on here with these releases?'

Alex told her what he'd learnt that morning.

'There's evidence that Evans and his mate, couldn't have done it. From what I can gather, the police found these two from witnesses who identified them from the CCTV pictures. It's conceivable that the witnesses were wrong isn't it? These two could be perfectly innocent.'

'Yeah, right,' Rachel replied sarcastically, 'look, maybe I'm seeing something that's not there but it doesn't feel right to me. If the police went after those two it was because they thought they had enough on them to arrest them. They would have known the media clamour over the arrests and would have had to be sure they were right.'

'Perhaps you're giving the cops more credit than they deserve?' Alex said in response. He agreed that it was possible, but believed the more likely scenario was that the police had fucked up.

'Maybe you're right,' she said, 'but I wouldn't put money on it.'

'I still think you should be taking care of yourself, perhaps lying low or going to stay somewhere else.'

'Alex, how well do you know me?' she asked watching his response which said that he knew that his last sentence was wasted breath, 'anyway I've got a gig tonight and I'd really like to do it. It was so nice to be back singing again. I'll think about it after then,' she said, and then smiled, '...I'll tell you what, you're the journalist, you find out what's going on.'

Alex raised his eyebrows in mock horror as he heard a different voice join the conversation.

'She's right you know, your job is to find out what's going on here.'

It was a voice from behind him.

He felt two big hands on his shoulders and turned to see the familiar face of Joe Barker.

With Joe, was a tall blond woman of similar age who he assumed must be Sarah. He turned to Rachel and put on his broadest Lancashire accent. 'Look we've got visitors from t'other side of t' hills.'

Joe laughed and began the round of introductions and coffee orders.

'You're early,' Alex said after everyone had sat down with drinks, 'I wasn't expecting you yet.'

'No, we got here a bit quicker than expected and decided to come and have a coffee anyway. So what's happening?'

Alex filled Joe in on the morning events, and Rachel threw in her comments about the cover up.

'If I was going to jump one way or another I'd tend to go with Rachel's view,' Joe said in response to them, 'but then I'm the old cynic.'

'And there are a few other things going on that would tend to make me think there's more to all this,' Sarah said joining in the conversation. 'They might be totally unrelated, but I've heard of two suspicious deaths recently, including my sister. They were both people who had information that may have been harmful to somebody.'

'I was sorry to hear about your sister, Joe told me about it,' Alex said with sincerity, 'whose was the other you referred to?'

'Actually, we don't really know much about either one, but we are suspicious,' Joe jumped in before Sarah could answer.

Then Sarah spoke for herself. 'Thanks Alex for the thought,' she said quietly still finding mention of it hard to handle. She filled Alex in and what they'd heard about Heather, and for Rachel's benefit a summary of her sister's death.

'I'm so sorry to hear about that,' Rachel said. Alex could see Rachel was quite moved hearing the story from Sarah, 'you must be feeling terrible. Gosh, I can't imagine it. Then you both got together after that, how lovely.'

Alex stared at Rachel for fear that she was stepping into inappropriate territory, but was relieved to see that she'd restrained her natural instinct to want to know more.

Sarah leaned into Joe as if to soak up the grief that was gripping her again.

'So, what was this Heather going to be able to tell you?' Alex asked Joe releasing the cloud of depression.

'I don't know, exactly, but I know she was into political scandals, and somewhat of an expert in party funding. She could tell you anything you wanted to know about various political donors and she probably knew more than the party administrators themselves. She'd also been known to do a bit of moonlighting with some administrators seeking her out to check whether certain donors were operating within the rules.'

'She sounds an interesting character and someone useful to know,' Rachel added.

'I didn't know her that well in the end, but she was popular around the office. I had asked one of the guys to do some digging on the BCA and BFB and he'd gone to her with some information. Apparently she'd taken an interest in what I'd given them and she said she'd come back to him. She never did. I'm going to try and see her boyfriend. Maybe he'll let me have access to what she was doing.'

'We really have arrived in the land of paranoia here,' Alex said, 'I think there are some interesting coincidences but I don't see a connection right now.'

'I know what else I meant to tell you,' Rachel jumped in, 'Pilkington's website is up and running, there are already some interesting contributions. Are you going to have a look and maybe put together a story about it?'

'I'll have a look and see whether there's anything interesting on it,' Alex said sighing, 'do you really think anyone will take it seriously?'

'If you read some of the things written on that site you'll see that some women are taking it very seriously.'

'What's this?' Joe asked.

Rachel explained what she'd done.

'Hey, Alex, I'm damn sure going to write about it and I don't even know this guy. But the idea of a website dedicated to building a hate campaign against someone who has been getting away with abuse and rape for years, now that's news. This is an article all about how the internet can bring its own form of justice. Justice that people cannot get through the law. This is dynamite.'

Rachel eyes opened wide with pleasure; finally someone was taking her seriously.

'Don't you think there are some legal issues here, reporting it I mean?' Alex asked, refusing to get excited about this, 'I have to show my face round here when all of this mud is being chucked around.'

'You really have to be brave Alex, that's the beauty of this kind of thing. As long as you don't repeat any specific allegation in print, you can argue that you're just reporting someone else's campaign. This kind of thing grows and grows. It starts with an internet site, and then someone picks it up in one newspaper. If the person is high profile or someone of interest like a celebrity or politician then this could become very bad for them. It sounds like your guy Pilkington may not be high profile, but the nature of these allegations on their own, with the back drop of the political landscape this guy belongs to is well worthy of a story.'

The conversation continued in the same vain, until Rachel said she had to leave. She got up making her apologies; Anna needed her help this afternoon. Joe dug out a business card and passed it to her, explaining that if she got bored of feeding Alex stories then he'd be glad to hear from her. Rachel seemed to enjoy the dig at Alex.

Alex chose to ignore Joe and thanked Rachel for coming down saying he'd take what she said seriously and see what he could do. He'd really wanted to stick to his guns, but had to concede there was a pattern. Abuse of power, murder, violence, politics and religion, it had been done before, so why couldn't it be done again here in Leeds.

Rachel walked towards the door but never made it. Breaking glass pierced the atmosphere. Rachel instinctively ducked down as a red brick flew into the cafe. There was an initial look of shock around the café and then a reaction as everyone looked to the window to see a mob of masked Asians chanting and throwing missiles as they ran down Boar Lane. Quickly Alex and Joe raced from their seats, past a stunned Rachel, and into the street. Simultaneously they produced cameras and started taking pictures and of the action. Alex stayed back a bit nervous of the last time he got involved in a scuffle.

A moment later a mass of police appeared from down the side street and started laying into the mob. There was no pretence of trying to maintain order this time. These were all out blows on both sides.

Initially the protestors were up for the fight and happy to battle one to one with the police, but as police numbers grew and their force was unrelenting, the rioters quickly spread looking for places to run and hide. It seemed as quickly as it had started this clash was over.

Alex's heart was beating at full pelt watching what was happening. The reaction to the releases had begun and once again the streets of Leeds were running with blood.

# CHAPTER TWENTY

As she finished the last note of the last song Rachel's eyes were closed in concentration. She opened them and acknowledged the applause of the small crowd. Looking round the room, she spotted Alan Farmer near the bar.

She acknowledged him, and collected her thoughts as she switched off the microphone and the amps. She hadn't been surprised to see him. After the flowers this morning she expected he would turn up at some point. The question was whether she was pleased to see him? She put off the answer as she walked over to the bar.

'Hi,' he said, 'I got you a drink.'

He'd ordered her a glass of white wine, which slightly annoyed her. She didn't like that he knew her likes and dislikes and that she was becoming predictable. She smiled though, offering her thanks, telling herself not to be a misery.

'Thought I might see you here,' she said.

'I'm sorry,' he said.

'What for?' she asked deciding she wasn't going to make this easy.

He thought about it for a moment.

'Ok, I'm sorry for being selfish and untrusting. I just wanted to know more about you and thought you were holding out on me,' he said finally.

'What does that tell you about me?' she asked continuing to push him.

'I guess it tells me you're quite protective of your privacy and you don't like people prying.'

'Hmmm, I wouldn't put it so bluntly, but if that's what you think you understand about me, are you prepared to accept it?'

'Yes, that's why I'm here. I like you and I don't want to throw this away. I'll just have to accept that's the way you are and live with it.'

'You will,' Rachel said firmly, 'this is how I am, and I'll tell you this. If you push against me then I'll just push back. I'm contrary like that. Ok?'

'Ok I get it,' he had his hands up in defence.

She smiled and took a welcome sip of the wine. She then leant over and kissed him.

'Thanks,' she said, 'I'm glad you came.'

'So am I. So am I,' Alan said, with a relieved smile.

'I needed to get out and sing tonight, get today out of my system,' she said.

'Why what happened?' he asked showing the necessary interest.

She went onto explain about the brick thrown at her and how her car had been vandalised. She explained that she'd dropped her car at the garage and hired one in the meantime. She feared if she said anymore he would start to ask too many questions and be right back at square one.


'This doesn't look good for us, you know,' Patrick Barclay said to Lucy Sayers as he took a drink of whisky. They were in the lounge at the Printers with other members of the party. Lucy's husband Pete also had come along complaining that he never got to see Lucy since she'd agreed to stand in the election. Although since he came he'd seemed bored with the conversation and found one of his old mates to chat to at the bar

'I don't know. It's not all bad. Every minute those Muslims are out on the street smacking hell out of anything that gets in the way, it's another vote in our camp,' she said gleefully.

Patrick looked at her concerned about her tone.

'Of course I'm not going to say that out loud,' she said, knowing what he was thinking before he said it.

'I told you before be careful. Even if you have the most amusing thought in your head, stop before it makes it way to your mouth. Even private conversations can be heard.'

'Now you're being paranoid,' she said, bored by Patrick's nagging.

'You're a star now, tabloid fodder and fair game for any hack wanting a story. You can be sure that if you or anyone of us is associated with a remotely racist comment then it will be all over the next day's paper,' he said, catching the eye of everyone including Andrew Bebbington.

'Hey, we all know the game,' Andrew jumped in, 'you're not the only one who has been here before.'

'I know, sorry. I just think we're doing really well at the moment, but one slip and we could be right back in the shit with the no-hopers. If we want to win this week, then we have to be squeaky clean.'

'So what happened to that honesty we promised the public?' Andrew asked, seemingly winding up Patrick.

'You know exactly what I mean.'

'I know what you mean, and believe me I've seen it all before. You just have to remember that for everyone who wants us to sit on the fence and be polite to these people, there's another wants us just to say they are all a bunch of Paki bastards and should get out of here. Maybe we would get more votes with some real honesty.'

'I know you're taking the piss now.' Patrick decided he wasn't taking Andrew's bait anymore.

Lucy and John were laughing now. Patrick looked at Lucy not aware of the shared glances between Andrew and her. He had no idea that he wasn't in control of what was happening.

Rachel went back to Alan's flat in Meanwood after the gig. They had taken their separate cars, and although Rachel thought about staying, she didn't feel in the mood, too distracted after the day. She was relieved to have the flexibility of the hire car.

'Do you want another wine or would you prefer a coffee?' Alan asked.

'Coffee's fine thanks. I need to get back home later. I've a lot to do in the morning.' She added a sorry for not staying the night and sealing their kiss-and-make-up session.

'You sound like you have things to do?' Alan went on.

'I guess so, plenty to think about. Mostly I need to help Anna with her campaign. It isn't going very well at the moment.'

'No one knows who she is,' Alan said, adding his own explanation.

'I know, and with all this rioting and other parties dominating the agenda, it's hard to get exposure. It's almost as if unless she does something outrageous, like run naked down the centre of Leeds, then she isn't going to get that attention.'

'And you get to be her campaign manager. Lucky you.' Alan put his hands on her shoulders and kissed her forehead. She put her arms around him.

A buzzing sound could be heard as they embraced and it took a second or two for Rachel to realise it was her phone. She quickly broke the embrace and picked up her phone.

She saw on the display it was Lee Potter the young copper on Mark Davies team. Alan was watching her intently. She was surprised to see it was Lee but she didn't want to give any impression of that to Alan as it would only lead to questions.

'Sorry,' she said, 'I just need to answer this. I'll only be a second.'

'Hi,' she said, deliberately not saying the name and walking back out to the hall to find some privacy.

'Hi Rachel, I need to talk to you.'

'Did you get the recording?' she asked.

'No, I haven't been able to do it, I haven't had the opportunity. Look something's happening and I need to talk to you about it. I don't think it's right. I think its all bullshit.'

'What are you talking about?' she said in a tense whisper.

'You saw the news today, you know what happened?'

'Yes, but I'm not getting it. Why is it all bullshit?' Rachel asked.

'Davies was the one who got them off and it stinks. Someone needs to know about it.'

Rachel nearly dropped the phone. She recovered herself.

'Can you meet me tomorrow?'

'Same place at one, I'll be wanting a pint after my football game in the morning.'

Rachel finished the call and paused a moment before returning to the kitchen. She felt rude taking a private call at Alan's but it was important and she had to be discreet. Alan would wonder who was on the phone; it was clearly his nature, so she needed to make something up. She'd just explain it was something to do with a sensitive case they had and stop at that. He didn't need to know anymore.


She was unaware that Alan Farmer had heard every word. He knew she was meeting someone tomorrow and he was going to be there as well.

A few minutes later after Rachel had left, he'd called Lucy Sayers.

'Make sure you find out who she's meeting and call me when you know.'

That was all she had said. She was a cold bitch but he knew she was right. He only reacted to her tone because he was guilty at his inability to turn his shadowing Rachel into anything useful.

Even Mark Davies's attacks hadn't encouraged her to open up. This was probably his last chance to turn it around.

So far she was unwilling to share anything and he knew she lied about the call tonight. Whilst he quite liked her and he'd certainly been happy to share her bed, if she knew what was really going on in his head, what his real attitude was, she would run a mile. She was due for a real shock when she found out what was going on under her nose.

Joe Barker told Alex that he'd had enough at ten thirty. The night had been quiet and he was disappointed to have stayed in Leeds. He should have gone to London as planned but the prospect of more rioting in the evening would have been worth hanging round for.

After the initial panic of the riot in the afternoon, Alex and Joe had decided to follow the crowds into the estates where they were likely to have come from.

He'd spoken to Sarah first who had said it was cool. She said she would go do some of the things she had planned and head back to Manchester anyway. He decided to stay at the Premier Inn near the station and now found himself in his corporate indigo strewn room as he typed up his notes from the day.

In the end there hadn't been much to type up although he had enough for a decent submission. An advantage of the internet agency was that they were structured to take news more immediately than newspapers.

They had headed up to Beckton expecting to see some signs of trouble if not full blown rioting. But there hadn't been anything more than what probably occurred on an estate like this everyday. In fact there were probably more journalists than people. It was weird he couldn't understand how such an immediate semi-organised outbreak of violent anger could disperse as quickly as it had arisen. Maybe that was a deliberate tactic of the gang. Hit quickly and disperse thereby splitting the police pursuit and making the risk of arrest much smaller. It was a major hint as to the cynical nature of the violence.

He knew from the news and what Alex had said, that the tension outside Eastside police station had been growing with more and more dissatisfaction in the crowd. Whether the violence was an extension of that, or a more targeted response, wasn't clear.

Experience had taught Joe that generally mob violence was never random, there was always an instigator. It needed someone to be brave and wind up the troops. Most people were too apathetic. They certainly would never react as an individual and only the safety of a crowd could rouse them to such hysterical levels.

The day hadn't been a total waste though. He'd found Rachel an interesting character. He'd asked Alex a lot about her and it was clear she fascinated him as well. Rachel had the measure of Alex; a nice guy, with a lot of enthusiasm but a bit wet behind the ears. Too ready to believe what people said.

He would learn, Joe concluded. He had the right idea in taking a gamble to chase the story and seeing who the people to follow were, but he had to be more challenging, particularly with politicians. He should look for as much what there didn't say as what they were.

That was the thing he'd seen in Rachel, here was a woman who took nothing at face value and questioned everything. She would have been a great journalist but had clearly found her talents elsewhere.

Joe had taken her phone number as a useful contact. There was also the story about her boss Anna standing as an independent. Maybe he would do a piece on her. She certainly had no profile outside of the region, yet she'd something to say that was worthy of debate.

It might be a cliché, but it was useful to be reminded that there was a big world outside London full of interesting characters and stories. As someone from the North he should have known that as well as anyone.

He checked his watch; it was coming up to eleven. Sarah would probably ring soon so he put the small room kettle on to make some tea. Flicking on the TV, he waited for it to boil. She'd said she would call at a discreet moment. He hoped it was soon as he wanted to get an early night and head back on the first train in the morning. He still needed to find out what happened to Heather Lockhart.


Qamar lay in his bed, lights out with everything dark. The adrenaline was still running through him as he replayed the excitement of what he'd done. Never in all his life did he think he was capable of such a thing but it was the first time he felt positive about something for as long as he could remember.

The feel of the missile in his hand, just a brick, that was all. To him though it was the frustration of everything that had happened wrapped in one small heavy packet. It was Alice's dad, kicking him out of the house on Wednesday when he'd taken some cash for her after Tuesday's job. It was the feeling of hatred as the man had called him a useless Paki bastard. It was the look in Alice's eyes of pity as she watched her father humiliate him.

It was the news today of them releasing the murderous bastards who'd killed his friends, it was the police conspiracy to make it alright for Asians to be brutalised on the streets of Britain. It was the words of hate for them on every news channel and in every newspaper. That brick felt heavy as he hurled it into the shop window, the breaking glass shattering the frustrations in every nerve of his body.

He wanted so much to be a part of the world he was destroying, but they had made it clear the world didn't want him, so what choice did he have? He had to fight for self-respect; that was what everyone was saying on the street. It was no longer time for standing on the sidelines, it was time to raise the flag and fight back. He truly belonged to something now, not even caring where it led. Every word spoken to him, through his mates, through the TV, through the people who abused him, made him stand taller and stronger. He didn't think about Alice anymore or of his dream, he just saw the fight before him.

# CHAPTER TWENTY ONE

*Saturday*

Hidden away in the cocoon that was her bedroom, Sarah Brownlee sat up in bed with her laptop in front of her. She had been downstairs already, made some breakfast and returned. She had no idea where Connor was and Jane would probably still be fast asleep.

This was her quiet time and this morning she decided that she was going to find out what happened to Adrian Cullen. Sarah knew that if she could uncover his story then she'd likely know why her sister died.

She'd hoped that Joe could do it for her but also realised that he couldn't be everywhere at once and had to earn a living. First and foremost he had to find stories to keep the money come in. Chasing around after this potential wild goose chase was not going to put much food on the table, at least based on what they knew already.

Joe had said that he'd be looking into what Heather knew but he suspected that was more to do with the potential of that story in itself rather than any sure knowledge of any link back to their problems. She was fine with that and she was certainly interested to hear what happened, but she knew if she was going to get anywhere with Adrian Cullen she was going have to do the digging herself.

She had the weekend free and would dedicate her time to finding the answer, starting with the facts she already knew.

Adrian Cullen disappeared from Ackton after meeting Father James Doohan one evening in September 1981. Four other boys knew about that meeting or were there; David McGhee, Ian Hamilton, Stephen Gorton and Roy Hunter.

Adrian's body turned up in Carlton probably a few days later. Joe and Jenny witnessed the burying of the body and a short time after saw Father Peters in the street nearby.

Doohan was involved in a child abuse scandal in Maltshaw some years later. He was protected by Father Peters from the same parish where the body turned up.

It was reasonable to assume that Peters was connected to the burying of the body. This was the only explanation. Given Doohan's record he must have contacted Peters who gave him somewhere to dispose of the body. In those days, no one would have believed a priest to be involved in the death of a child, so the cover up was easy. Peters and Doohan were now dead, so the story should have died with them.

But it hadn't. There were at least two other people who knew what happened that night, perhaps all of them on the list that Mrs Cullen had provided. She wished she'd been able to get the photograph. That might have given her more to go on.

She started the search.


Joe parked his car outside Heather Lockhart's apartment in docklands and thought about how he would approach this conversation.

He had called her boyfriend Paul earlier, before setting out across the city. It hadn't taken long to get started after arriving back from Leeds by ten o'clock. He'd dropped his bag at home and got straight down to business. An hour later he was parked outside the apartment block ready to go in. Comparing the time it took to drive around London, with the train from Leeds, Joe wondered why he bothered with the car. But parts of docklands were not that easy on the tube or DLR so he resorted to his hire car. He found Paul and Heather's apartment on the Isle of Dogs looking over the river.

He'd told Paul on the phone that he was very sorry about Heather but he'd some questions about what she was working on that were very important to Heather and he wanted to see if he could help.

Finally ready with his strategy Joe set off to the door and rang the bell labelled with the name *Lockhart and Spencer*, showing his face to the video camera.

Paul was waiting, once Joe had reached the third floor in the lift.

'What do you want?' Paul asked. He didn't say anything else in greeting Joe which Joe didn't think was too abnormal in the circumstances. Looking at the guy he didn't look like he was ready for lengthy open conversation, in fact he looked more like a man who'd any sense of life and vigour removed. Joe guessed this told him more than anything else about what Heather had meant to him, recalling the same look on Sarah's face two weeks ago.

'Look Paul, I wont beat about the bush here, I don't want to set any hares running with you, and I don't want to upset you, but you look like you don't want me to waste your time either.' Joe said the words thinking how he'd react himself and he was tempted to think he might just tell himself to fuck off out of here. Fortunately Paul accepted what he said.

'What do you want to know?' Paul said without displaying a single emotion or reaction.

'What happened to Heather?'

'You heard the news right?' Again spoken in that flat tone

'Yes of course.'

'Well, go fucking read the news again and quit bothering me with it.' His eyes flickered with anger.

'You know as well as I do, that what's in the news is bullshit,' Joe said, deciding there was no point pussy-footing around him.

'If you know so much what are you doing here?' Again the cold angry reaction.

'I can only say that I think Heather was taken out by something or someone. Something she was working on hit a nerve. She was silenced and I'm pretty sure you think that as well.'

Paul didn't say anything for a while. He stood up and walked into the kitchen and returned with a drink of water. Joe wasn't sure why he did it; maybe he was collecting his thoughts. It was a strange reaction.

'Who the fuck are you?'

Joe was surprised by the aggression. He'd that Paul might not welcome this intrusion because he was grieving but he hadn't figured that he might be scared someone would come after him as well.

'Look Paul, I'm a friend here. I know we've never met but I was a friend and colleague of Heather's. I'm only here because I think Heather would want whoever did this, to be exposed.'

'I'm not buying that line, whatever it is that you're here for it certainly isn't for Heather. You came here because you want to know, so don't pretend it's some glory mission.'

'Ok fair cop,' Joe held his hands up, and before he had a chance to explain further, Paul jumped back in.

'Tell me how you know Heather? When did you last speak to her? What did you discuss? If you're really a friend of hers then I'll know.'

Joe accepted this and explained how they worked at the agency. He was honest about not knowing Heather well, as he worked out that Paul would suss him fairly quickly if he pretended otherwise. Joe then moved to why he was here, why Fletch had called Heather.

Paul said nothing and Joe assumed he was deciding whether he believed it or not.

'You're right,' he said finally. 'I think something's not right with her death. It's not that I believe Heather was superwoman and nothing could possibly happen to her. I'm much more of a realist. I just think it's too convenient. Heather comes upon the biggest story of her career and suddenly she has a fatal accident. At first, my reaction was shock and perhaps anger at the useless lorry driver who hit her and drove off. After the police had gone, it struck me. I thought about what Heather had been saying to me all week, and it was a shame that her big moment was never going to come. I realised that whatever it was, someone was going to suffer by that story and might go to some lengths to make sure it didn't happen. When I thought about it, in those terms, it wasn't hard to believe that a random hit and run was really murder. It gets worse when you hear that the Police can't trace the driver or the wagon. Now you're here with the same feeling, I know there's something in this.'

'I take it she didn't tell you what it was?' Joe asked. It felt like a weight had been lifted in the room. Paul wanted the answer to this as much as he did.

'No. She would never tell me anything until after she'd finished. It was almost a superstition thing with her. If she spoke about it too soon, then it would come to nothing. If she kept it to herself and protected the secret, nurturing until it was ready to be revealed, then everything would be perfect.'

Joe watched Paul catch himself, as he re-lived a moment with her.

'I did have a look through her stuff,' he said, sounding a little guilty, 'to be honest, I looked at a couple of things but I just couldn't do it. It ripped me apart thinking about it all. She was so excited this week. It was like she'd found the answer to a question she'd been looking at for months.'

'Do you want to know what it was all about?' Joe asked directly.

'Of course I want to know. The only issue for me is whether you're the person I think can find it?' he said directly with no hint of empathy.

'I can't answer that for you. All I can say is that I have my own reasons for finding the answer and isn't about money for a story.

'It could be dangerous for us,' Paul said with a hint of fear.

'You said it before though didn't you, whoever is behind this is not going to stop with killing Heather. They are going to come looking for the evidence she had. I think we have no choice.'

Paul didn't say anything. Striding with purpose, he went to another room in the apartment, returning with a briefcase and a laptop.

'You have what you need, go find them.'


Never in her worst nightmares did Rachel Lancaster ever expect to be knocking on doors asking people for their vote. These were people she would have crossed the road to avoid normally, but today she had to smile sweetly as she listened to them telling her where she could shove it.

The only consolation was that it took her mind off the pressure of the last few days and the unwanted attention. Anna had asked for her help and she felt she could only agree. She may not have agreed with Anna's delusions of election success but she and Anna had been a team for so long it seemed petty to let her down on a basic need like this. So she decided to grin and bear it, although as Anna had commented many times, Rachel hadn't done much grinning at all.

'Who are you?' The forty-something woman dressed in smart trousers and blouse, asked at the next door. This was the most common response from the houses they had visited so far. That was those who didn't just shut the door in their faces. This was a decent neighbourhood; God knows what kind of response they'd have received on the worst estates. They had deliberately decided to avoid those places, hoping to get more response from her target audience in the middle classes.

Anna started with her same enthusiastic speech. Rachel could not deny she was a natural politician.

'My name is Anna Stockton and I'm standing in the Leeds North by-election as an Independent candidate. Perhaps I can leave a leaflet explaining why I'm standing and ask if you would consider voting for me?'

The lady looked them up and down. Seeming to think them worthy of attention, she took Anna's leaflet and had a quick glance, 'I'm not really sure who I'll vote for,' she said, 'they're all as bad as each other.'

Anna waded in like a salesman into an open door. The woman was going to get the full Anna effect now that she advertised herself as exactly the type of person Anna was trying to attract.

'Well madam, I think exactly the same as you do. That is why I'm here as an Independent, I'm not affiliated to any party or any particular viewpoint, I'm just standing as an experienced successful business woman who believes she can make better decisions than career politicians. I don't have any restrictions or any agenda holding me back, just good sense and good experience.'

Rachel could see the woman was beginning to regret not shutting the door on them as Anna continued. Surprisingly she didn't turn on them as Rachel thought she was going to, but said she liked what Anna had said and would read her leaflet. She didn't hang around for any more discussion though as she encouraged them away from the door.

'Caught one,' Anna cheered as they walked down the drive.

'I think you're being optimistic there, she was just humouring you so she could get you out the door. That leaflet will be in the bin by now for sure,' Rachel said more than happy to burst Anna's balloon.

But Anna's balloon was not for bursting as she enthusiastically headed down the next driveway. No reply there, onto the next.

A few doors down another door opened, and Anna started with the same speech to the thirty-something white man, dressed in white t-shirt, Bermuda shorts and trainers, sporting a tattoo across his arms and gelled hair. Rachel cringed as she watched Anna appeal to his better nature.

'I'm voting BFB, missus, so don't come round here with your liberal do-gooder bullshit. Get rid of the foreigners smashing our streets up and the country will be a better place.' The door was quickly closed again. Whether he had a better nature or not, Anna certainly hadn't appealed to it.

'Another quality individual,' Rachel said as they made their way to the next door.

'God you're a snob Rachel Lancaster, why don't you just enjoy the challenge?' Anna complained.

'Me? A snob? Anna, normally you wouldn't let these people within the same street as you, never mind the same building, unless of course they were paying customers. You never had a problem taking money off them.'

'You're in a mood today. I know things have been a bit dire lately but come on, I need you on form here.'

'Ok Ok,' Rachel conceded.

The next doorway offered an older lady, who politely asked them in for a cup of tea. Given it was the first generous offer they'd had that morning, they both took the opportunity for a break and a chat with this woman, who seemed glad of the company.

Rachel put on her best smile as she was happy to eat up the time they'd set aside for the canvassing. She was even less convinced that Anna had a snowball's chance in hell of getting any votes next week and the less doors she had to knock on to confirm it, was fine by her.

If Rachel thought she was in a dark mood this morning it was nothing compared to the thoughts brewing in John Pilkington's mind as realised that he might not be able to show his face round here for a long time to come.

'I don't know what you've done but someone's pissed off with you.' The voice on the end of the phone said as he once again tried to plead his innocence, 'is this you or what?'

'Look Chris, it ain't me. So fuck off and go bother someone else. Someone is going to pay for this shit,' he replied cursing the caller. This was the third call this morning about that site.

If his mates had been calling him about this, then news was spreading fast. He'd been on the site himself and couldn't believe what he saw. Yeah he'd done some things he wasn't proud of, but hadn't everyone? There was also a lot of stuff on there that wasn't him, but people were going to think it was now. It seemed every black bitch who had a grudge against him had been on and made out that he'd done all kinds of shit.

He had to stop this, but how? He knew he was in deep trouble. He'd been straight onto the solicitor, Dave Millington at Stockton's, who handled his last case, to see what could be done about taking the site down and secondly about suing the bastard who set it up. Of course it was the weekend, so no fucker was going to be there today.

He tried to ring up his internet provider to get some advice, but ended up arguing with some foreign twat who insisted that there was nothing they could do other than remove it from their server, which given the content they'd do. But he'd advised he couldn't do anything about the others. They'd checked the IP address though and it turned out to be registered to some island in the frigging Pacific. He realised that this line of attack was going to be fruitless.

He thought about going to the cops but what would they do? He would have to keep his head down until this was sorted. There was no way he was going to tell Patrick Barclay about it. He'd be out of a job before he could get the words out. All he'd heard for the last few weeks was make sure no shit sticks to our door. If this shit got out then there was going to be one almighty turd nailed to the door, and just at this moment in time he didn't give a fuck about them pretending to be all friends to everyone. They were a bunch of racist fucks just like him at heart and no amount of bullshit could hide it. Lucy Sayers could fall in a crate of her own vomit as far as he was concerned, given the self righteous bullshit she spouted. She would drop him like a stone just like Barclay. They would not back him on this.

He'd been along for the ride for sure, he and his mates had been happy to support any party that kept England for the whites. Things were different now. He was back where he was when they kicked him out of the hospital. He had his own ass to look after now and intended to do just that.


Alan Farmer sat in his car outside The Wellington. It was just coming up to one o'clock and he'd just watched Rachel go in. He was already pissed off, after a morning trying to discreetly follow her around the streets of North Leeds. Eventually she had packed in and come here.

The problem was, he couldn't go in. Rachel would see him for sure, he couldn't risk that. Having watched two or three people go in the pub, he realised he wouldn't be able to guess who she was meeting. He called Lucy telling her it hadn't worked.

'I can't go in there,' he said.

'You're going to have to. Make up some story about being jealous or something like that. I don't care. I just want to know who she's talking to,' Lucy replied, clearly in a no frills mood.

'This will blow everything. There's no way she'll have anything to do with me after this.'

'It's a risk worth taking. Once we find out who she's talking to then we can decide what to do next about her.'

'What does that mean?' Alan asked a bit concerned about her tone.

'It means what I said. We'll have to decide what to do about her,' she ended the call.


'How was the football?' Rachel asked as Lee sat down with his pint of John Smiths.

'A lot better now,' he replied smiling, 'Although I took a kick on the shin's for my troubles which is going to bother me all week.'

'You won't get any sympathy from me,' Rachel laughed, 'is it a police team?'

'Yeah we have a police team, keeps us fit. Trouble is doing overtime gets in the way of any decent training, although it usually means I get Saturday morning off, so I can play. That's one good thing going on at the moment.'

Rachel smiled, for the first time relaxing today. She was feeling shattered after spending the morning walking the streets and the chance to relax with a drink was more than welcome, even if the topic of conversation was likely to still be as tough as before.

'So, what was the thing you were going to tell me?' she asked Lee, 'you told me that Mark Davies provided the alibi.'

'That's the thing isn't it? You can't say it was me who told you this. If he finds out then I'm dead. The word is everywhere about this.'

'Ok, I'm listening,' she said.

'The Sarge apparently told the head of the bombing investigation team that he'd collared the two suspects in Beeston trying to break into a car. He was coming back from a call and he saw them hanging around this BMW 5 Series. He had a word and took their names; he even had it in his notebook. He didn't pursue it because they hadn't actually got into the car and he was coming off shift.'

'How do you know all this? Was he on his own?'

'That's the thing, I know this because Rob, off my team, was in the car with him, and he told me. In fact I know he wanted it put around, which is why he told me. He wanted everyone to know that this one was tight and covered between him and the Sarge.'

'Why so public? Did they want to embarrass the arrest team or something? Why would Davies put his head above the parapet for this? I mean this is pretty brave stuff,' Rachel asked, her brain racing at a hundred miles an hour.

'That's the bullshit thing. I think they are lying and the best way to make a lie work is to front it out.'

'Why do you think it's a lie?'

'It just doesn't sound right to me, that's all. It's too convenient given all that's happened. I just know it, especially the way the word is being put about. Like everyone needs to know that Mark Davies is the only one who knows what is going on around here. That's why I'm talking to you about it. You know how to deal with this stuff.'

Rachel had stopped listening for a moment. Her mind was working too quickly.

'What time was the bombing? Wasn't it about four in the afternoon? Is that the time Davies said he saw them?'

Rachel thought for a moment. She hadn't realised this before, but now it dawned on her. Alarm bells rang through her head.

'Yeah of course, he'd need to match the time up,' Lee answered.

'Yeah, well you know you said you thought he was lying?' Rachel asked, '…I can prove that he was.'

'What? How? What do you mean?' Lee asked nearly dropping his beer.

'Because I saw him at four o'clock, nowhere near Beeston. I know that for a fact because I took his picture at that precise time.'

'Shit. I knew it…fucking hell…this is seriously bad. You better be sure Davies doesn't find out you know this.' The words were coming out of his mouth so quickly. 'Rachel this is –'

'Stop, say nothing,' Rachel stopped Lee speaking as she looked over towards the bar. He hadn't spotted her yet but she'd seen Alan Farmer standing at the bar clearly looking for her. Fortunately she was just outside of the eye-line of the bar and she was behind Lee, which made her difficult to spot immediately.

She immediately stood up with her bag, 'You're not with me. I'll call you sometime.'

She left Lee behind as she approached the bar. In the corner of her eye she saw Lee head to the gents.

'Rachel –,' Alan started to say as he saw her approach.

'I don't want to hear it, Alan. You followed me here. I don't care why, don't call me again,' she said unsure whether to scream at him or just walk out the door. In the end she stood her ground for a moment in order to see his face.

'I just wanted to know who you were seeing. I was jealous that's all.'

She thought about the words to say, but in her building anger they stuck in her throat. She just shook her head and walked out. She had far more important stuff on her mind than worry about a stupid idiot boyfriend who wasn't worthy of her breath. Never again she swore to herself. Her ex-husband had given her enough scars of jealousy over the years and she would not take on another one.


'Done,' Alex Thompson said turning to his girlfriend Tina who was sat on the bed reading.

'Finally! Are we going to go out now then?' Tina said putting her book down and jumping off the bed.

'Yeah, no problem. I just needed to get that article finished,' Alex explained.

'Have you got the wording right?' she asked, 'let me see what you've done.'

She looked over his shoulder and read the introduction.

BFB Official Hate Campaign on the Net.

*A BFB official recently sacked from the hospital for being a BFB member is now the subject of a campaign launched by women making a string of allegations that this newspaper is not prepared to repeat.*

She read on, noting his caveats as well as his carefully worded insinuations.

'Yeah that's ok. There are enough caveats in there and you haven't repeated any specific allegations,' Tina said.

'I'll see what the boss thinks tomorrow when he puts Monday's paper together.' Alex said.

'I can't believe what those women have said. This guy must be a real creep.'

'Rachel really doesn't like him. I've met him a few times at Elland Road and he seemed relatively all right to me. But Rachel is usually a far better judge of character than I am.'

Tina laughed.

'I can't argue with her on this occasion.'

'I'm going to send this off to the boss. I just need to try Lucy Sayers again as she wasn't answering her phone before. I want to see if I can get a quote from her.'

'Ok, Ok. I'll go back to my book,' she said disappointed with another delay.

'Lucy Sayers,' the voice on the phone said promptly.

'Hi Lucy, this is Alex Thompson from the Courier.'

'Hi Alex, how can I help you?'

'I wanted to ask you for your response to the hate campaign against your colleague John Pilkington.'

There was silence on the line.

'I don't know what you're talking about,' she said flatly.

'You mean you're not aware of a website, making accusations of rape and sexual assault, and overt racism?'

'I better not see that written in the Courier or you'll pay for it. You clearly have no proof of any of this or you wouldn't be asking me about it,' Alex reckoned from her reaction that she wasn't aware of it, as she was missing the point totally.

'Lucy, I'm not accusing him of anything, all I'm saying is that there are a number of people making accusations. I'm just reporting that the campaign exists. That's a legitimate story. Can you tell me what your official response is?'

'Ok, well officially, let me tell you that I'm sure these allegations are false and we will seek to prove it.'

'And unofficially?' Alex pushed.

'I don't know anything about it. Give me twenty four hours before you print anything whilst I find out what's going on?'

'I'll call you this time tomorrow, but it will be in Monday's paper anyway,' Alex said pleased that he was getting her attention.

'Actually, I like the fresh air on a Sunday afternoon. I'll be walking my dog in Temple Newsam Park with my kids. Come and find me there at two. Don't talk to anyone else until you speak to me. Are we right?'

'Agreed,' he confirmed.

Lucy didn't reply and the call was ended.

He was just about to speak to Tina when he felt his phone start to vibrate. He looked at the display. It was Rachel.

'Rachel, make it a quick one.'

'I need to see you.'

'Rachel it's Saturday, I'm tired and want to take it easy today. What is it?'

'I can expose this whole sham at Eastside. I know who got the bombers off. Alex I can break that alibi,' Rachel was almost shouting down the phone at him.

'I can't deal with this now. I've got something I need to do. Drop round my place later, but Rachel, you'd better be sure about this,' Alex warned her, pissed off that his Saturday was getting overtaken.

'Oh, I know I'm right about this, and if you don't want this information I can take it elsewhere,' Rachel shot back at him, 'forgive me for wanting to give you the biggest story of your career on a plate.'

'Don't get antsy with me. I don't doubt you,' he ended the call and indicated to Tina he was ready to go out, but his mind was already elsewhere.

Everything was going crazy he thought as he digested what Rachel had said. If it was true about that Rachel was able to blow the alibi on the bombers, it was enormous. Perhaps this was the biggest story of his career and he should start getting on top of it.

# CHAPTER TWENTY TWO

Lucy Sayers didn't take a breath between putting down the phone from Alex Thompson and calling John Pilkington.

She summarised the conversation she'd just had with Alex Thompson and ended with a sharp question. 'Did you know about this?'

'I heard about it this morning,' he replied.

'When exactly did you think you might mention it to me?' she said sharply.

'I thought it would go away, just people taking the opportunity to pay me back, disgruntled employees,' he tried to explain.

'Is it true?'

'No of course not Lucy, what do you think I am. It's just some people I've pissed off in the past. I don't even know who they are.'

She didn't like his arrogant response at all and was beginning to lose patience.

'Sounds like a lot of trouble to go to, to piss you off.' Lucy said, 'I want you in the office tomorrow morning. This is going to hit the papers on Monday and we need an answer to it. We need to make this go away John. This is your responsibility. If one word of this is true I'm going to slap your face with a brick for every woman you hit. I'm giving you the benefit of the doubt here, but if I find out otherwise you better start running now. Clear?'

'Yeah cool!' he replied.

She had to get home and check this site out. This could seriously fuck things up, just as everything was getting close. She tried not to think too much about the future but the feeling of excitement and anticipation of what could happen if she won this seat overwhelmed her. She would not let anybody screw it up for her, yet there was risk all round her and some things she seemingly couldn't control.

Lucy always knew that John Pilkington was a bit of a jack-the-lad. He certainly mixed with a fair amount of lowlife, but he'd always seemed capable of professional pretence and intelligence. He had to have done something right to get that job in the hospital and the qualifications that went with it, although the way he always looked at her arse, she wondered how he ever got through the door of an HR department. Perhaps underneath he was just the dangerous perverted thug that her instincts had always told her he was.

She had this to deal with and then Alan Farmer. She was waiting for Mark Davies to call after his shift. Farmer had sent her a photograph of the guy that he thought he saw with Rachel Lancaster, which she forwarded to him. He might've been the one leaking stuff to her about Mark's practices. She pitied the guy if it was one of his team, he didn't take kindly to disloyalty.


It had taken a few hours of digging but Sarah Brownlee had found two of the names on the list. The first she was sure about, the second was a good start. She hadn't done much else. She had her laptop, a regular supply of coffee and the radio to keep her company.

After a while, she turned the radio to music. For a time she'd been interested in the stories coming out of Leeds and the race for the by-election. There had been so much news the day before and she was listening for any new information or an update, but really most of it had been a repeat of the day before.

The thing that had annoyed her more than anything else was a spokesman for the BCA who seemed to be everywhere now, in some speech to a university or college she couldn't remember, condemning violence but in particular condemning Muslim leaders for failing to stop the cycle of violence in their communities. This had sparked a whole new debate on the radio which she found too annoying to listen to. When would people learn that this increase in antagonistic rhetoric was not going to solve anything? Maybe Joe was right about the agenda of the BCA; they had certainly ramped up their news agenda with new announcements each day, attempting to get everyone talking about them. Controversy appeared to be their tactic, the more controversial the statement, the more likely to get the attention.

In the end she got fed up with it and slipped on her ipod player to play the new album by Florence and the Machine that Joe had bought her. It had her singing along and fired her up so much after the depression on the radio, that she had played it again straight after.

The music was a much better tool for concentration and she quickly got results. Ian Hamilton, it appeared, had been happy to display his whole history on 'Friendsreunited'. She'd known the school they had all attended in 1981 from Mrs Cullen, so just had to search the school for that year, and then find the name. Once she found him, a whole lot more information, came with it. He'd attended Preston Technical College, and seemed to have a few dead years before turning up at Manchester Polytechnic on a part time business degree. Since then he'd been managing an independent book store, Everyman Books in Bolton High Street, which he'd conveniently advertised with a link from his profile. He obviously thought drumming up a bit of business from old friends was a useful marketing tool. Perhaps he didn't realise that he had provided a nice link from the past to the future.

The next name she had some success with was Stephen Gorton who had put himself on the school site, but there was no photograph and no information post school days. She tried Facebook and there were a few names the same but nothing that stood out or gave a clue to the area. Instinct told her he was still in the Preston area because he hadn't put down a university or a fancy job. Most people with successful careers or university degrees loved to advertise the fact on these sites, if nothing else to tell everyone, who knew them, how well they'd done. The fact that Gorton had thought to put his name on the site but nothing about his post school life led her to believe that there was nothing dramatic or interesting to say.

The other two had not been helpful at all. Roy Hunter had not put his name anywhere and searching for the name Hunter was impossible, there were so many of them and there was no starting place with school records. She would have to think some more about that one.

David McGhee had been equally elusive. Firstly the exact spelling of the name was not useful as search engines would come back with many variations. Again there was no mention on his school site.

Still, it was no problem; she was making progress. She'd start with Ian Hamilton tomorrow, she just had to check the shop was open on Sunday and then she'd go along for a visit. Joe had asked her not to, but she said she was only going to a book shop, nothing could happen to her. He'd been on Messenger all day whilst working on Heather Lockhart's computer.

She was really excited to have found Hamilton's name so easily. She imagined the police were well ahead of her, but she had her own questions to ask and he might welcome her a bit more than the police. Gorton would be a task for Monday. The library would be a good start with a phone book. There couldn't be that many Gorton's in the Preston area.


Joe Barker had spent much of the day with Heather's

Heather hadn't made it easy for anyone to find anything. She'd left some stuff which he knew was neither secret nor particular sensitive to anyone. There was a lot about the MP's expenses scandal but now that was out in the open and publicly available it offered nothing of any interest to anyone. There was so much of it and it had taken him a long time to sift through.

Once he'd got past the files and articles on the expenses scandal he found some previous articles on Labour and Conservative political funding, the debate over state funding of parties and election campaigns. The only mention of the BFB or anything to do with minor parties was in reflection of the share of the funding they'd receive under such a scheme. It was all very interesting but not worth killing someone for.

He found some personal files, her C.V., some attempts at a blog. He read one or two of them which were reasonably amusing satires on the political classes but again nothing out of the ordinary.

He began to think there was nothing useful on this computer until he went through the directories as a last gasp attempt to find hidden files. He then realised his mistake as he found a whole set of folders among the program files rather than in the document directories. The directory just had a number which didn't appear to be a date. At first he tried to guess what the number meant but it didn't appear to be important.

Thinking about it he realised that this was good and bad news. These folders were encrypted and he would need a password key to undo them, but the fact that they were hidden meant there must be something to hide.

He tried a few obvious things, her name, Paul's, combined names with numbers. After a few attempts he knew that Heather was not going to make the password that obvious and it would certainly not be widely known information, otherwise why encrypt it at all?

Joe called Paul to see if he could help. The range of possibilities extended to family names and pets, still nothing came up.

In the end he concluded he needed to talk to Fletch back in the office. He would know what to do. Joe could go on guessing for a week and still get nowhere.


John Pilkington was on his fifth pint since lunch time. He was already beginning to sway as the alcohol dulled his senses. He didn't know why he'd come here but it was the most natural place for him to go to sort his head out. He was back in the Kings Arms amongst his mates, he definitely didn't want to go anywhere near The Printers. The last thing he needed was another lecture from any of that lot.

He ordered another drink…he needed to forget about things for a while. Be with his mates… he told himself.

The Kings Arms was where a bloke could go and be a bloke. You could slag off the women in your life. You could say anything you wanted to about anybody you wanted, because this was a place full of people just like him. In his mind all blokes were like this instinctively sexist, racist, tribal, competitive, aggressive and above all looking to escape any responsibility that women, jobs and life had thrown at them. That's why pubs were invented centuries before and although some blokes might like to take a more sophisticated view of it by going to a golf club, rugby match or something like that, they still wanted to get away.

Football was on one TV, Racing on the other. There was the smell of stale beer in the air as well as piss if you got too near the bogs at the back. The smoking ban had got rid of one problem smell but uncovered a whole set of other unpleasant ones. The most significant smell in this place though was man. It was a man's pub and man's place.

Another drink… he needed not to care… listen to the guys… forget about everything. 'Terry what are you drinking?' he asked back in the mood now, he could say anything to his mates, 'how is that slapper I saw you with last week, fucked her yet?' Yeah, he didn't care.

He was never judged in here although people always took the piss, especially when he'd gone to college and got himself a qualification and a suit. They really took the piss then, said he might dress himself in a suit but he still came out of the same sewer they had and he'd always have the same smell as them. They'd been right and the proof was that year after year he was still with the same beer-drinking time-wasters wallowing in the smell of working class Britain. He was fully aware that he'd never been able to leave this behind but as he got older he realised he didn't want to. This was his security blanket. It was the place he could be the same as he was as an eighteen-year-old.

His mind wandered on as thoughts become more and more confused. Anger mixed with laughter, mixed with banter, all crossing swords in his mind swilling with alcohol. Fuck Lucy Sayers he thought as his mind continued to twist itself, random thoughts spinning out. Smart-mouthed bitch…she'd had it coming. She's the same as the rest of us but thinks she's better. Just a tart in a skirt… same as the rest of us… smart-mouthed bitch.

He needed not to care.

He took another drink, listening to Davey Tindall slagging off his wife because she'd had a go at him for slapping all the meter money on the horses again this week. He needed not to care...another mouthful of beer...it wasn't working... fucking hell, Davey get a grip.

His mates had been winding him up all the time he had been there. He couldn't handle what they were saying anymore, it was too much. Every word that came out of their mouths, whether they were slagging off their wives, moaning about immigration, talking about a sexy bit of stuff they'd seen, was a like a gong booming in his head. Their words, words he used himself all the time, hit him like the slap that Lucy Sayers had promised him.

Another mouthful... shit nearly finished this one. He needed another. He needed to forget... Lucy Sayers...God he hated her... wanted her... needed to give her a seeing to. She was one smart-mouthed bitch he said to himself as his thoughts became more and more confused, the beer taking its full effect.

'Sod off Terry, a man can drink if he wants to,' he said taking another mouthful, 'you having one or what?'

He'd done these things they accused him of, right enough, but every one of them had been begging for it. They'd known, each of them, how to manipulate a man and played to his weakest point, a look here and there, a slight touch, a smile. He'd read them all like a book, seeing what they really wanted. But then he got angry with himself, that he'd let them win. They had seen his weak spot and drawn him to their flame and he wasn't having that. So he lashed out, he hit them, he fought them, he abused them because they had to know that they were not the ones in control.

Once again though, they were in his head taking back that control. He took another drink.

Fuck Lucy Sayers... she was one smart-mouthed bitch in a fancy skirt. He was going to have to do something... can't go on like this... another drink... going to have to do something. Putting his fist through Lucy Sayers smart mouth was all he could think about.


'Lee Potter, that's who the little twat is,' Mark Davies said when Lucy Sayers answered her phone.

It was the call she'd been waiting for all afternoon.

'I knew it. I knew it was one of your lot,' Lucy said, 'what do you think he knows?'

'He knows enough to be dangerous, but in truth only what we wanted out there and that's that these two were covered by me.'

'Are you sure you can handle this?' she asked, not concerned for a moment about his welfare but more about damage limitation.

'That's the beauty of it. The media are going to be so set on the story of why they arrested two people who were clearly innocent, they'll forget about what they were supposed to have done. It shifts the focus. The extra pleasure is seeing that tosser of a DCI sitting like he has a poker shoved up his ass, squirming his way out it.'

'Your alibi is unbreakable right?' Lucy pushed him.

'Course it is, only me, you and Rob know I wasn't there that day and of course those two knob-for-brains, and they aren't likely to say much, are they?' Mark bragged confidently.

'Good, good.' Lucy relaxed a little, 'I'd love to know what those two were discussing today. Alan Farmer was useless in finding out.'

'I told you we should have off-loaded her weeks ago when she was first onto me.'

'As I told you, we didn't want the connection made, and you can bet she has kept records. No, she's too dodgy to touch yet we need to think about it more.'

'Still going to give Potter a doing, and then maybe that slut as well.'

'Hold off for the moment. I need to think about it,' she said thoughtfully

'I'd rather give out a good kicking.' Mark said not prepared to waste time trying to catch them out.

'No. There are things we can do that will make you the folk hero of West Yorkshire police. After this, no one will touch you.' Lucy said, contemplating her idea, 'I just need to think about it. Don't do anything until I'm ready.'

'Ok, I'll be here,' he replied, 'better be worth it though, I can't be arsed poncing about with this much longer.'


'Start at the beginning Rachel and tell me slowly what you found out,' Alex said trying to calm Rachel down. She had called him numerous times that afternoon trying to find out when he'd be home. She had been waiting outside and followed him in with Tina.

They stood in the kitchen with cups of tea whilst Rachel told them what she knew.

Tina decided to stay and listen, she knew this was going to be interesting and was clearly important as Alex had been chewing it over all the time they'd been out.

Rachel updated him on her contact with Lee, and finally got to the lunchtime meeting.

'The heart of it is that I know Mark Davies lied to provide an alibi for those two blokes who were arrested. I know he lied because I saw him talking to Lucy Sayers at the exact time he claims to have been in Beeston.'

'And there's no mistake, about this? You know exactly what time it was? You know it was him? How can you be sure?' Alex asked firmly as if he needed convincing himself before he'd repeat it again.'

'Because, as you know Alex, I've been watching him for weeks, I could recognise him if he put a dress, a wig and a gorilla mask on. I would still know it was him, because he has a walk, a manner, a swagger, if you like. He is unmistakable. Plus I took a photo on my mobile phone with a time and date on it.'

Rachel took out her phone and showed him the photo. She explained that she knew the time stamp wasn't evidence but it was proof that she'd remembered it correctly.

Alex tried to take it all in but she was talking too quickly, adrenaline running through her.

'I know what time it was because that particular afternoon, that particular day was one of the most memorable days in the recent history of this country. I also heard that bomb like everyone else did in Leeds and it shook everyone of us to our heart and soul, including you. Now, ask me again if I know where I was that afternoon and what I saw?'

'Ok I get you,' Alex said, 'what was it you said about Alan?'

'Nothing much, he turned up at the pub, checking up on me. I didn't want to be seen with Lee so we split up before Alan could see us.'

'Alan turned up... what has that got to do with anything?'

Rachel explained about him being a jealous bastard.

'Sounds like you're well shot of him,' Alex added.

'So getting back to the point, I tried to ring Lee later on, but he wasn't answering his phone. He has gone on shift tonight so I don't think he'll answer now.'

'What you're telling me is, that not only did Davies overtly lie to his police colleagues to get two supposed bombers off, Lucy Sayers is likely fully aware of this because if she was speaking to Davies that afternoon, she likely knows that he's providing that alibi, and that it's false. This means, by default, she's in on it. Fucking hell, what a cow. What a fucking lying two-faced cow,' Alex fumed.

Alex walked up and down the kitchen for a moment staring a Tina, looking for the words to say.

'So who knows you know about this?' Alex asked Rachel, trying to get past his anger and onto thinking about what to do next.

'Lee, you and Tina now,' she said looking over at a silent Tina. She was listening intently to the conversation, realising that this was far more interesting than the hour she'd been about to spend sat in front of the TV.

'First things first. We tell no one about this until we are ready to go with the story,' Alex said looking at Rachel and Tina in turn. They both nodded.

'This is big, you're right,' Alex's heart was beating so fast he thought he'd explode. This was way beyond his comprehension.

'It's what I've been trying to tell you for days. This was never right. This whole thing has been put together to start a war in this country, and she wants to be commander-in-chief.'

Alex paused not really listening to Rachel, his mind on what to do next.

'Right,' he said finally, 'are you prepared to provide a sworn affidavit? Tina are you prepared to witness it?'

'Too right I am. I always thought she was just a tart and was playing you. I'm in for this,' Tina said, sounding nothing like as confident as she wanted to.

'Wait,' Rachel said, 'you can't just drag Tina into this. Alex this is dangerous. I know what I'm getting myself into here. Tina doesn't.'

'Of course, I know what this is,' Tina replied indignantly, 'I might only be a receptionist but I ain't dim.'

'I never said you were. What I mean is...' Rachel seemed to be thinking of the words to explain and then realised it was pointless, 'what I mean is, that it's dangerous. I'm sorry I didn't mean to patronise you. Just want you to consider your own safety first before jumping in.'

Tina accepted Rachel's apology, which was a relief to Alex as he didn't need an argument right now.

'If I can get a statement from that copper that would be even better. My editor will really go for it then.'

The adrenalin was running, working out the implications of each thought as it ran at him.

'You definitely can't get hold of Lee.'

'I told you, I tried this afternoon; I think he's gone on shift.'

'Fuck, I don't want him blabbing about this.'

'Believe me,' Rachel said, 'he isn't going to say a word. If anyone at the station even gets a sniff that he knows something more about that alibi, then he is in big trouble. According to Lee, everyone there is talking about it and already thinks those two were bang to rights and that Davies is lying. If they find out Lee can prove it, he'll be at the centre of this within seconds, and he'll be in big shit. This could blow his career, and like everyone else it may not end there,' Rachel sounded grim. You know already what these people are capable of.

'Do you really think they'd go that far?' Alex said

'Alex, get real. They blew a fucking mosque up. Do you think they'll give two shits about chucking any of us on the bonfire?'

He didn't know what to think, and Rachel was probably right. Getting this story out was the important thing so they could break the news. As long as what they knew didn't leak out before Monday they should be safe. He realised that the adrenalin in him wasn't just excitement. It was a stone cold fear that if he got this wrong they all could be dead.

Staring at the computer all day had begun to drive him mad so Joe Barker decided to switch off for a while and relax.

He walked down to the Chinese take away around the corner from home and waited whilst they prepared something for him. He could have ordered on the phone and they would have delivered, but he felt he needed the walk and some fresh air.

The past had been good to him in a number ways but also had laid some demons at his door. He wondered how much this new chapter would affect him. In his own mind he knew this whole thing was leading somewhere and that place was not good. He didn't understand it yet but there were too many connections and coincidences for there not to be something more coordinated happening.

And then there was Sarah, Joe really didn't know how this was going to pan out. They had such different lives and both had their baggage to deal with, could they really make a go of a relationship? He supposed by the time anyone reached his age, then by default, they would have developed a lifetime of baggage and there was always going to be some complication with anyone new. Sarah was lovely and he really wanted to develop something with her. They would need to talk more about it but the agenda of chasing around finding out about Adrian Cullen and the riots in Leeds had kept them both so busy they really hadn't had much of a focus on their own relationship.

The TV was on in the corner and he realised he hadn't watched it all day having been so busy working.

Whether it was good timing or not, he was pleased to see it was the news coming on and it gave him a chance to do what he was supposed to do as a job which was keeping up with the world around him. The news offered nothing new, pretty much the same as yesterday so he was content to switch off until it came to one of the lower agenda items. The next news item caught his attention.

A new clinic had been unveiled in rural Berkshire where you could get Sexual Reorientation as they called it. The company running the clinic had a number of places in the US and had now set one up here. The company AT&I Health Services named after the proprietors of three evangelical churches in the US specialised in dealing with health and welfare issues based on Christian teachings. The clinic in the UK was aimed at initially offering a service to families with gay children who they claimed they could cure.

Joe immediately caught the name of the company, as one of the BCA sponsors that Fletch had given him. The news item went on to detail protests from gay pressure groups who were rightly outraged at such a move. Then a BCA spokesman came on, outlining his support and what he felt was everybody's responsibility to support the new venture. The spokesman, he recognised as Martin Atkinson from the BCA rally two weeks ago, who went on to say that it was clear the only relationship model that God had intended was heterosexual and that we should consider anything else to be sinful. Under questioning from the reporter he said he couldn't deny homosexuality existed but society needed to accept, as all the major faiths did, that it was wrong and people should have the chance to seek help for it.

Joe made a mental note to look up more about this company, to see what else they got up to in the US. He could just picture parents dragging little Johnny down to the clinic ready to sign over thousands of pounds in cash for drugs and mind-warping because he'd been taking a bit too long over his hair in the bathroom or putting boy band pictures on his wall. It made him sick to think about how twisted these people were.

He was glad his food was ready and he could get out in the fresh air again.

Premila Premdas waited near the bus stop on Albion Street. She was waiting for her husband who was late. She had been working all day at the Jones Shoe Shop and the boss had kept her and some of the other girls behind to do some stock checks. She was tired and hungry and was just thinking about going home.

The wind was blowing through her thin jacket and scarf and she was already beginning to wish she had brought her winter coat. It always took some time each year before she realised that protection from the cold was more important than looking and feeling smart. Still, she couldn't complain she'd had a good day, her boss had praised her for some good sales work on the shoes and she'd even shifted some extras which the boss loved because of the extraordinary mark up on them. She even caught him checking her out a couple of times which made her smile. The tight skinny jeans and the extra eye make-up had clearly had an affect.

She would never do anything about it, of course, but knowing that the boss liked her made her feel good. Her husband would never let her back in the place if he knew, but she wasn't going to tell him.

'Where was he?' she wondered. He said he would be here ten minutes ago. She kept watching up the street. The bus came and a few people got on. She couldn't see up the road now and hoped that her husband didn't miss her because of the bus. She stepped back out of the way of the people getting on and inadvertently bumped into a guy with his hood up over his head sheltering from the breeze. He seemed to stagger a little and then fall.

Premila immediately apologised and went over to him holding her hands out in admission of her fault. She tried to help him up and it was then that she realised he was drunk and incapable of standing up himself. He smelt of alcohol and had dirt on his trousers looking like this wasn't the first time he'd fallen over. She stepped back from him, realising that the state he was in had nothing to with her and she needed to get back to looking out for her husband.

As she moved away he grabbed her leg, and she found herself being dragged down the alley by the side of the precinct. She tried to resist but the look of doziness on his face had changed to a look of dark determination. She thought she had screamed but as she desperately looked around nobody seemed to hear or see her and then his hand was over her mouth. She was thrown against the wall, his eyes inches from hers, the smell of his rancid beer breath sneaking between the gaps of his dirty fingers held over her nose and mouth.

Then he spoke and out of his mouth came pure hatred and anger.

'I reckon you owe me bitch. You fucking pushed me over. What right you got to do that? You don't even belong here. Yeah, you owe me,' as the words came out of his mouth, his other hand was everywhere, over her chest, squeezing her between the legs. He used his weight to overpower her tiny frame and she found herself unable to move as he tried to get his hand under her clothes.

Her fear grew with the realisation of what was about to happen. He let his hands go for a moment and she thought maybe he had backed down until that hand appeared as a solid fist into her right eye.

'Stay still bitch and this will be more fun for both of us.' The next fist was into her gut. She was winded and couldn't get her breath.

His weight and strength were everywhere like he'd four pairs of hands. She couldn't do anything. She closed her eyes praying it would stop.

Then suddenly the weight was lifted, there was nothing. She opened her eyes and he was on the floor being kicked by two men. Premila could hear the hollow sound of the kicks as they struck the drunk. She stood staring for a moment horrified by the violence she was witnessing and at the same time wanting to join in. She couldn't handle this, she had to get out. She ran out of the alley into the street, saw her husband in the car in the lay-by anxiously looking for her. She opened the car door and almost dived in. Her husband looked horrified at her bleeding nose and eye. Premila just screamed for him to drive.

As the car drove away she could still hear the kicks that her rescuers had rained down on the drunk. She felt the connection of each kick like an electric charge through her. Premila recognised the feeling inside her that she had read in so many magazines over the years, that feeling of shame, betrayal and sheer horror at herself for somehow letting it happen to her. She couldn't look at her husband as she broke down, the shock finally taking her over.

The BCA spokesman earlier that day might not have known the impact of his words, but maybe he did. Whether it was intended or not, it had an affect. The sound of sirens screaming through the streets of Leeds was no rarity on a Saturday night, but the fact that it was fire engines racing to the rescue of three churches one Catholic and two Anglican was something new. The churches had been targeted and firebombed and the fire service were working all out to save them

The violence had a new catalyst now and Leeds was paying the price.

# CHAPTER TWENTY THREE

*Sunday*

Rachel woke, not really sure where she was as she felt the unfamiliar bed sheets and the unfamiliar smell of the room. It didn't take too long for the night before to come back to her and to remember why she came here. She had gone round to see Anna last night for dinner explaining that she could do with lying low for a few days and could use her spare room.

Anna had asked what was going on, but Rachel told her it was better she didn't know, except that she'd discovered things that some people might find a little unacceptable, and until it was out in the open she had better keep out of the way.

Anna hadn't taken her too seriously at first.

'So you thought that staying at the house of a potential MP was low profile?'

'No,' she'd replied, 'I'm staying at the house of a woman with delusions of being an MP but given the current response to her campaign, she's got about as much chance of being the next MP for Leeds North as Rosemary West. This is about as low profile as it gets.'

The banter hid Anna's real concern for what was going on, but Rachel avoided saying much. She didn't like keeping things from her but it was really for the best that she didn't know. Anna had a way of wanting to solve everything in her own style and this was far too dangerous a situation for such tactics. Rachel didn't even know herself how to approach it; she was just determined to see it through.

She had to decide what she was going to do with the day, knowing she had to stay out of the spotlight. It didn't mean doing nothing though, there were a number of things she thought about doing. Anna had wanted her to go door knocking with her again, but that was the last thing on her mind so she told Anna that she should take her daughter Michelle. She sweetened the pill by suggesting she might get more attention as a family woman and perhaps less abuse than last time.

She took a long shower and then went down to face the day.

Lucy Sayers returned from another long Sunday run, trying to get the frustrations of the week out of her. This was her greatest escape. It was one of the only things she got to do on her own and pleasure in the challenge as she pushed the pace. Over the fifty minutes she took to do 10km she could go through a whole range of feelings, initial escapism as the wind blew her hair, the pain of the first ten minutes until her pace and her heart settled down. Into twenty minutes when the adrenalin was pumping and her body was in rhythm with the run. It was a natural high like a drug. It was the time she could feel like anything was possible. As she hit the half hour point, the exhilaration of the last ten minutes would begin to wear as she fought tiredness to maintain the pace. This was the time when she always attacked the run. Tiredness had to be countered with more adrenalin, so she increased the pace for a minute and then slowed it again to the previous pace, now comfortable again. The last ten minutes were the climax and the time to bring it all to a head. She knew in her body it was the way home, a chance to burn every last bit of charged tense energy, so she pushed harder and harder again. When she had the vision of the last two hundred metres she began to sprint. Piling any outstanding energy into that last stretch, her mind was completely free of worry and distraction.

Finally it was the release of tension and energy as her body relaxed and recovered. Her chest wheezed and heaved gasping for air. Within a few moments she was back to normal taking in a pint of water as she stretched her legs.

The house was quiet as Pete had taken the kids swimming. More time to herself, she thought as she made the mistake of picking up her mobile phone.

It was a missed call from Mark Davies. At least it was under the pseudonym of Genghis she kept in her phone to indicate his number.

Fuck, what did he want this morning? It must be important, he wouldn't ring her otherwise. He knew he had to keep minimal contact with her and this anonymous Pay As You Go mobile phone was the agreed mechanism.

She rang him back.

'That fool Pilkington got arrested last night by one of the night crews,' he said without introduction.

'Bloody idiot,' she cursed, 'what was he doing?'

'Apparently he was having the shit kicked out of him by two big guys. A couple of our guys pulled them off before they could do him any serious damage, more's the pity. They apparently claim to have pulled him off some Indian girl whom he was giving a serious going over.'

'You mean he was trying to rape her? Is she going to press charges?' Lucy couldn't believe what she was hearing. Any release that her run had given her was gone now.

'Apparently yes, her husband brought her in later on to make a statement and to get her checked out. It's unusual with the Asians; they'd rather pretend it didn't happen than bring one of their wives down to a cop shop. This one was different. He said he wanted that guy, meaning Pilkington, done for what he'd done to his wife.'

'This is crap; this is going to ruin us,' she said thinking out loud, 'we drop him. I'm calling Patrick now. We doing nothing for him, he is damaged goods. We need distance from this. Try and keep a lid on it at your end.'

'Not sure how much I can keep a lid on this. He hasn't been charged yet but as soon as it gets out that we've a card carrying BFB employee in the nick for attempted rape of an Asian woman, we are going to have every brownie in the country outside this door.'

'Do what you can. You're being looked after very well in this enterprise and if any part of this gets fucked up we are all in the shit,' she said, 'and what about that kid on your squad? Have you seen him yet?'

'No, I'm on shift with him tonight. We're going to have a little fun together,' he said with the sound of a big grin across his face.

'Just don't let him know you're on to him yet. We need to think it through before we start to deal with those two.'


Sarah Brownlee found the bookshop without any problem. It wasn't big but it did seem to be a proper traditional store rather than a novelty place selling cookbooks and calendars.

She stood outside for a moment, going over her already well-rehearsed approach. When she talked to Joe this morning they discussed some questions and she wondered whether she'd remember all of them. She decided she'd be happy if he just actually spoke to her and didn't kick her out of the shop.

She walked up to the cashier desk and asked the young girl behind the counter if Mr Hamilton was in. It crossed her mind as she asked, that he might not actually be in the shop today in which case it would have been a wasted journey. In truth she had thought about it, but she so much wanted to make this trip today; she hadn't allowed the thought that it wouldn't work out to enter her mind.

'I'll just call him. He is in the office,' she said politely, 'can I ask who is asking and what it's in connection with?'

She said her name with a big sigh of relief.

'I'd prefer to discuss it with Mr Hamilton. It's a personal matter from some time ago.'

The girl gave her a curious look but made the call anyway. They spoke for a moment and she eventually turned back to her.

'He'll be down in a few minutes.'

She thanked the girl and went to browse the books whilst she waited.

When he did come down she'd become quite engrossed in checking out the latest releases and was taken a bit by surprise as he said her name.

She turned to see a very tall dark-haired man in a well-worn grey suit. She introduced herself and got ready for her rehearsed lines.

'Many thanks for seeing me,' she took a breath, 'perhaps it'd be better to discuss this over a coffee somewhere more private, but basically I want to talk to you about Adrian Cullen's disappearance. You may have heard that his body was found recently.'

He thought for a moment.

'Who are you? I spoke to the police a few days ago about this. Are you a journalist? I really don't have anything to say,' he was polite but she could tell he was not up for negotiating this.

'No I'm not a journalist, but I won't deny I've a very definite interest in the story, otherwise I wouldn't be here,' she let that statement settle with him and then for the first time she realised how hard it was to talk about this to a stranger... 'My sister may have witnessed the disposing of Adrian's body and I'm keen to find out more about what happened.'

'Well maybe you should discuss it with your sister. I'm not sure I can help,' he said ready to dismiss her.

She was ready for this and whilst she didn't want to use her sister in this way, it was her ace card.

'I'd love to discuss it with my sister. Nothing would make me happier right now. Only she died recently and I'm convinced that there's a connection between her recent death and what happened to Adrian. Can you help me?'

The look of shock on his face and his subsequent sympathy showed her that she'd won. He turned to the girl behind the counter.

'Sophie, I'm going to go out. Could you keep things going for a little while?'


In London, Joe Barker was doing his own research into Heather Lockhart's files but still hadn't got anywhere.

He was in the Agency offices, playing away with the passwords for the encryption but he was waiting for Fletch to arrive and knew no matter how much he guessed he was not going to break it. Fletch had groaned about coming in on a Sunday but Joe had promised a cut of the story and gave him an incentive to put down the play station and get his backside into the office.

Eventually at two thirty he arrived, looking like he wasn't long out of bed.

'Given up washing on a Sunday?' he said to Fletch, teasing him.

'Yeah well, there's normally no need of such indulgences,' he said not willing to let Joe wind him up, 'what am I doing here?'

Joe explained the set up of the files, the numbered folders and the encryption password.

'I think I have it,' he said within one minute of checking the files.

'What? How can you do that? You haven't even tried anything,' he said.

'What is the best way to remember a complicated encryption key?' he asked Joe.

'Write it down I suppose. But she hasn't left it anywhere obvious.'

'Yes, she has,' he said smiling.

'Where?' he was about to ask then the penny dropped, 'you mean those numbers. Surely that's too obvious?'

'I'm not saying that is the whole answer. But she'll use something she knows well to combine with those numbers. That will be her encryption key. Let's try the boyfriend's name. He placed 'PAUL' in front of one of the number sequences… failed. Then he placed it after. And the directory opened with a whole set of photographs.

'Fantastic, I knew you'd sort it. I could have tried for the rest of the year and not guessed it.'

'That's the thing about passwords. You always need to be thinking laterally, one step ahead of the hacker.'

'It obviously wasn't that clever, you spotted it,' Joe said.

'Yeah, but I'm brilliant,' Fletch said laughing, 'can I go home now? My sofa's calling me.'

'Yeah sure, get lost. I'm going to have a fun this afternoon going over this lot.'

Joe immediately opened up the other directories using the same method and was happy to see them all open as he hoped. He went to get a coffee from the machine then sat down to read.

It wasn't a bad afternoon in Temple Newsam Park. There was a breeze and it certainly wasn't like a summer's day, but it was ok for walking around with a warm jacket. Alex parked his car at the House and walked onto the open field around the back. He looked out across the view of South Leeds, now split by the M1 ruining the almost rural outlook. He continued down the hill towards the farm seeking out Lucy Sayers. He figured most people, here with their families, would be around the farm or the gardens.

He couldn't spot her around the Farm so he wandered down through the Rose Garden and found her down at the lake with her son. She was feeding the ducks. There was a guy a little way from her with another child looking at some flowers. He assumed they must be her husband and Lucy's daughter.

He didn't immediately approach. He watched for a moment seeing the contradiction between this seemingly dedicated family woman and her apparent political intolerance. After a few minutes he stepped into her view and allowed her to decide whether to come to him. She saw him, took her son over to her husband, said something, and then came over to Alex. Her husband looked at him but said nothing. This was clearly something he was used to.

'So you found me?' she said.

'Yes it wasn't that hard,' Alex said leaving her to make the running. She'd asked him to come.

'Let's walk,' she said, turning away to walk back up the hill towards the house, not waiting for his agreement. He strode after her.

'So, what's your quote on John Pilkington? Has it changed since yesterday?'

Lucy said nothing for a moment and appeared to be thinking about her response.

'John Pilkington is no longer a member of this party. We do not represent him or support him in any way. The allegations made against him are abhorrent and not something we want to be associated with,' she said firmly and with a hint of venom, 'is that clear enough for you?'

'My God, you think it's true don't you? You've found something out?' Alex said as what she was saying clicked.

'You have your quote. I'm not going to say anything more about it.'

Alex leapt on it now.

'You know this is big and dirty and you don't want him littering your campaign. You're dumping him,' Alex said with a look that said, 'I've got you'.

'Look, Alex, you don't know anything.'

She stopped walking and turned to him.

'You still got your tape recorder?' she asked with her hand out.

Alex took it out of his pocket. He handed it to her. She took out the tape. Gave it him back and put the tape in her pocket.

'Have you another? You better not have.'

Alex shook his head, hoping the physical action would not to give away the lie.

He had wound her up a bit with his last comment and wondered how far he could push her. Maybe it would uncover the real Lucy Sayers. Before he could say anything she started speaking again

'I like you, so I don't want to fall out over this. So let me make it absolutely clear. I've given you pretty good access to me. I've taken your calls, I've given you quotes, and you've reported them honestly and fairly. But now you're getting ahead of yourself. You print one word that misconstrues my statements, twists it out of context and turns it into the usual biased rhetoric written about me and my party, you'll never get a word out of me again. I'll make sure that no one in my party will touch you with a bargepole.'

'You think you'll still win with all this kind of shit going on? What about the rioting? That's proving that your plans are not working.'

'Have you looked at the polls? We are getting more votes everyday. People are seeing through the media bullshit and seeing that we are the only alternative. Britain for British.'

'Do you really want to see riots spread to everywhere in the country, so they are part of everyday life for people?' Alex asked pushing her as far as he could.

'You just don't get it do you? This is what it needs. There needs to be an uprising, an English revolution where we stand up for ourselves and say what we want. Never mind pandering to minority interests. If they don't like it they can go home.'

'But this is their home, isn't it?'

'For some maybe; for many others no,' she said forcefully annoyed that he wasn't get the message, but Alex had got the message loud and clear. 'Those who claim this country is their home should start to treat it like their home. Have some respect for the institutions and their neighbours.'

'Like those bombers you mean?' Alex threw this one in. He didn't want to give away what he knew about her, but at the same time he was dying to get a reaction from her. He had lost any respect for her, spouting this shit and at the same time trying to engineer a war herself.

'That was nothing to do with us and you know it.'

Why would we do that? It would turn everyone against us,' she fired back at him.

'But it hasn't, has it? You said yourself look at the polls. You've played on everyone's fears, and you're winning by creating fear.'

Alex could see the anger in her eyes. She was under pressure and this was her weak point. Pilkington was just an inconvenience, this was her real fear. Once someone pegged her and the party for the bombing, they were doomed.

'This is the end Alex; it's in your hands. You print one word that links me or anyone else in the party, to that bomb, and we will ruin you. You haven't got the slightest bit of evidence to suggest it. The only thing that is happening is that people are waking up to the only party than can lead this country out of the mess that immigration and multi-culturalism has created. You make anything more of it and we are finished.'

Lucy turned to walk away from him.

'What if we did have evidence?' he asked her. The words seem to linger in the air and cause Lucy to pause for a moment.

She turned to him with a look of fury, unable to decide what to say.

'I think I made myself clear,' she said, dismissing him as she continued on her way.

'Gotcha!' Alex said quietly to himself.

Rachel stood at the other side of the field a good distance away and watched Lucy Sayers leave. She had witnessed the whole scene and was relieved to see that apart from a few cross words and apparent tension, nothing out of the ordinary had occurred.

She had come, not because she didn't trust Alex, but because she didn't trust Lucy Sayers. She wanted to be sure that she hadn't set a trap for him. Rachel knew they were treading a thin line with what they knew and that if Alex continued to prod Sayers with a stick, eventually she would react.

She wanted to make sure that they had everything ready before then. Tomorrow Alex would hit the newspapers with two major scandals that would blow the BFB apart.

First the denouncement of Pilkington the rapist, but that would get lost behind the news that they could link Lucy Sayers to the cover up of Police evidence and then by association, the bombing of Beckton mosque.

They had to make this story stick.

# CHAPTER TWENTY FOUR

'So you think I might be able to reveal some insight into what happened to Adrian?' Ian Hamilton asked after they had settled down with coffee.

'Of course, that would be great, but perhaps too much to expect you to know exactly what happened, otherwise I'm sure you'd have gone to the Police many years ago.'

'Yes I suppose,' he said thoughtfully, '...well, you're right I don't think I'm going to provide any great insight for you. But yes I knew Adrian and knew him reasonably well as anyone knows another at that age.'

'Can you tell me what happened from your point of view?' Sarah asked, pleased to see that he wanted to talk, 'you're the first person I've spoken to who was actually there.'

'One day he was there, the next he wasn't. In some ways it was simple as that. There was no prediction of it, no sign that it was coming, nothing spectacularly different at that time. We were just normal teenage boys.'

'Were you involved in the church with him?'

'Oh yes, that's why we were friends. We were all involved in the church at some point. We used to work on the altar and the offertory collections. We earned a bit of money between us. Some of us even sang in the choir for weddings and stuff like that, but Adrian and I couldn't sing a note so we didn't get involved in that.'

'Were you with him the night he disappeared?'

'No, I wasn't, so I couldn't help much. The police interviewed us all at the time but we really didn't know anything. It was an awful time. I can't remember much now about it as I wasn't there. It's all a bit vague to be honest. We weren't always together. Maybe my parents had wanted me home for some reason, or I was sick.'

'Were any other of your friends there that night?' She mentioned the names of the others in the photograph and he nodded in acknowledgement.

'I can't remember exactly who was there. You'd have to ask them directly for what they knew. I don't remember discussing it with the others much.'

'How do you mean?' Sarah asked.

'We speculated on what had happened, but we couldn't deal with the thought of it. Do you see what I mean?'

'Yes, of course. It must have been awful,' she said aware of how it must have felt for one of your school mates to just disappear, 'what about the priest? Did he say anything about it?'

'Not that I know of, and he wouldn't have. We all hated him. Looking back now I guess you have to say he was probably one of those priests you hear about nowadays, creepy child abusers, I mean,' he paused for a second as if to clear his thoughts, 'it wasn't that he abused us physically so much, at least he never touched me and none of the others said anything like that. It was just that we didn't like him. One minute he would be trying to be our best friend, asking about girlfriends, football, our parents, stuff like that. The next he would be telling us off for the slightest thing.'

'That's hardly evidence for a paedophile, is it?'

'I know what you mean, but it was little touches here and there, the way he was always in the room with us. Adrian and Roy were always his favourites. He used to take it in turns to ask them to help him to clean the sacristy, always on their own. He never asked me and I don't know why to this day. We used to tease them about being favourites, but in those days we didn't understand abuse in that way, and we certainly didn't imagine a priest could be like that. For all our teasing Roy and Adrian never said a word about it.'

'So you think he was abusing them?'

'As I said, I don't know anything for sure. But on reflection, if I heard that about him, then it wouldn't surprise me in the slightest.'

'Do you think this potential abuse could have been anything to do with the disappearance?' Sarah asked, watching the cogs whirl in his head.

'I didn't at the time, that's for sure. I suppose it would be a fair assumption knowing what we do now, and knowing that priests are capable of some fairly extreme things.'

'What about the other kids, Stephen, David, and Roy? Do you think they'd have the same opinion as you?'

'I guess you'd have to ask them. To be honest I've no idea. Like I said we didn't discuss it much, and then we lost touch,' he said quietly. Sarah could see that he was realising what could have been going on in front of him all those years ago and he'd had no idea.

'Do you know what happened to the others? I'd like to see if I could find them.'

'David McGhee, I've no idea. Roy Hunter went off to University. Manchester I think, never heard of him since. Stephen Gorton was in Preston still, although it's years since I knew him. You might be able to find him though. He was a tiler. I only know that because he did some work on the offices I was working in once, and I recognised him. We spoke a little but he was a bit strange. I mean he was always a bit weird anyway but it was like he didn't want to know me. He'd only mutter acknowledgement when he saw me and he'd look to his brother who was effectively his boss, all the time to tell him what to do. I think he was a little insecure and perhaps depressed.'

'So you think if I looked in Yellow Pages, I might find him?'

'It's an idea isn't it?' he said pointedly.

'I suppose so,' Sarah said.

They talked some more as they continued to drink coffee, and Ian asked her some questions about Jenny and what had happened. She found herself opening up and talking freely, somehow it felt natural to talk about it. Maybe this whole thing was turning out to be the perfect therapy for her sister's tragic death, or maybe she hadn't considered that talking about it was about to take her into the same trap Jenny had found.


In the 24Seven News Agency offices, Joe Barker had spent much of the afternoon trying to interpret what he had found. There was a mass of information on party donors and very little in the way of summary.

Where she'd got all this information from, God only knew.

The crux of it was a list of addresses of party donations. She had started to go down the list and attempt to contact each of the donors. She had indicated, for each one of them, where the person was known or not known at the address. There were a couple of pages of names.

This was fine, he knew this already from what Fletch had told him. This information could get the BFB into major trouble over electoral fraud but they could at least claim that they weren't aware of this. This was why Heather hadn't gone public with it. She was after the person behind the fraud. That was the story, who and why would someone want to control a political party in such an underhand way?

There was a file, notes from EC. He opened it and immediately everything clicked. This was Electoral Commission and not European Community as he'd thought. It appeared that Heather had a contact there so it was no wonder she was getting this information. It was being leaked to her.

Heather's contact, just listed as TT on the notes, had done a routine audit on the party and as such had been able to request evidence of payment information. The commission was suspicious of the party funding increase and consequently had done its own audit. The information had been supplied in full cooperation which meant that either the BFB had felt they were bullet proof on this, or the administrators at head office were unaware of any scam. Joe supposed either could be true. If there was a funding scam going on then it would have been known only to those who needed to know.

He read further down the notes, comments on persons not known at the address from which they donated or whether they were listed on the electoral roll. It seemed that TT had requested bank statements to trace selected payments as part of the audit to ensure that they were valid contributions. This was inconclusive because the statements indicated that the payment had come from a bank account with the same name as the donor.

TT had commented in the notes on the clear contradiction between someone that effectively didn't exist at the specified address but had a bank account. This had left TT with a problem, as to be able to investigate further she would have had to involve the police to get a court order to sequester the bank accounts of the named individuals. To do that would have meant that she had to have a rock solid case as the resulting publicity would be highly politicised. Her boss hadn't backed her without more definite evidence because of the relatively low contributions. Perhaps this was the reason TT had leaked it.

It was clear from the notes that TT hadn't got anywhere. So what did Heather do to get herself killed?

He looked through more files but nothing took him further. Whatever she had gone to last week must have been significant because that's what changed the game and made her a target. Taking that onboard, he searched by date bringing him to a set of downloaded company accounts.

Why had she gone on to these? And then saw what she'd been looking at. These were party sponsors. He didn't know much about the rules but understood party sponsorship was different. Donors had to be private individuals who were eligible to vote, but sponsorship rules were different.

Under sponsorship rules a business could provide funding for specific events which would work for both party and business. Perhaps there would be a certain amount of mutual compatibility. He wondered how a business could find any benefit from linking itself to a nationalist party. He looked at the businesses listed and didn't know any of them, certainly there were no household names.

A PR company named as Corporate Credibility. The company brochure in with the accounts was straightforward, specialising in PR for companies with a poor publicity record. The brochure seemed quite clear about that, and the BFB was ironically a prime candidate for some of this "Corporate Credibility".

Next was a small engineering company, Coopers Tools, making tooling components for larger manufacturers. He read the brochure again and saw the sense of their potential interest in the BFB as it referred to being committed to investing in Britain and British jobs. It looked like a firm that would no doubt benefit from protectionism; overseas competition was so much more difficult to defend against in manufacturing these days.

He saw a security company selling CCTV equipment under the name of CC Secure. These were relatively small businesses, certainly nothing spectacular. Although it reminded him that it was the second security company he'd seen linked to the BFB.

The final one was some kind of bank. It was called Social Equities Ltd. The brochure talked about providing social investments, long term funding of projects of social benefit. Returns were expected on a long term basis and projects could apply for funding at a fair interest rate with no demand for immediate returns. It all seemed fair but he didn't see why this company would want to limit its market by associating with the BFB or perhaps they were quite selective about the social projects they supported. He then noticed that this company was a wholly owned subsidiary of Social Equities Inc, a US business. Interesting again, he thought, another US business.

So what was the link here? Had Heather decided that this was where the answer was? Did she think that someone connected with these businesses was the provider? Seemed logical, although he would have thought if they 'd that much personal interest in the party they'd have been up front about their donations as well as the business interest.

Joe scratched his head. Whatever was going in these documents wasn't clear to him. There was too much general information and nothing specific. He sensed he was close and that whatever it was would come to a head soon, possibly before the election on Thursday.

He decided to call Sarah and give it some further thought over night.

'Are you absolutely convinced you can stand this one up?' Andrew Quinn, news editor of the Courier said to Alex as he explained what he had.

'I've emailed the story in and the number of lines. I can stand it up, no problem,' Alex said. He had spent the last three hours putting together the words and now he had to get this past the boss. He wouldn't let this one go.

'I want to see what back up you've got and that this is water tight. I might need to go to the lawyers,' he pushed Alex.

'I'm not going to come in with the name of my witness, enough to say I can back it up. You're going to have to trust me with this. I have the sworn affidavit. But I can't let anyone see the names as yet. You've got to agree that this is pretty dangerous for those people if this gets out.'

'I'm not going to print the names. You can be sure I'll protect your source, but, I can't take a risk on this kind of thing without seeing it for myself. I'll print the Pilkington one, no problem as that is out there in the public domain, but I'm not going with the allegations against Lucy Sayers without seeing the paperwork.'

Alex knew he was losing this.

'Look Alex. It's not that I don't trust you, it's just that my neck is on the line here.'

'Ok, Ok. You can have it. Make sure you get the page together. I'll meet you at ten tonight before the deadline.'

'Alex make sure you're there or I'll pull it! Don't let me down on this.'

The November darkness had descended on Leeds like of veil of misery. The dark sky, howling wind and squally showers that had started in the afternoon did nothing to brighten Lucy Sayers' mood as she sat in her car listening to the radio, waiting. Even the continuous debate on the news about the riots and the potential result of the election did nothing to make her feel better. She turned it off trying to focus her mind and get a grip of what was happening.

She had driven out of town in her VW Gold on the old Pontefract Road through Cross Green. The road had finally been rebuilt ten years after the new M1 link and was now the main route east out of the city. She kept an eye out to see if she was followed, knowing the press were everywhere. She was high on their list of targets, one for whom a story was always waiting to be written as soon as she made a mistake. She was lucky no one had been outside her house that evening and was able to get here unnoticed. On a Sunday evening the road was fairly quiet and parking in a dark lay-by would attract minimal attention. If nothing else someone would only suspect she was shagging in the car and leave her alone. She'd been here ten minutes and had only seen one car. Then she saw bright headlights approaching in her mirror.

The car door opened and Mark Davies climbed in.

Lucy didn't react in the slightest. She just spoke sharply.

'You're late.'

'Yeah, well, I'm here now,' he replied, 'so what's the score? I thought you were going to leave it to me?'

'Yeah well, things have changed,' she said staring into the night.

'Look, my balls are about to squashed in a vice, so this better be worth it.'

'Exactly…it's time for direct action. Too much is at stake,' she said still staring straight out of the window, 'Alex Thompson knows something. He came over far too cocky today, and whatever it is, I reckon we are going to see it in the paper tomorrow. Whatever he knows I'm sure he got it from Rachel Lancaster.'

'I'm listening,' he replied.


Alex picked up his phone as he sat reading his story for the tenth time. It was Rachel returning his call.

'Do you have to use my name? I don't have a big problem with it but I've had enough trouble with unwanted attention recently,' she asked.

'It's only for the editor he won't sign off on it without seeing the affidavit.'

'OK, as long as it stays there. Have you written everything down?' Rachel asked.

'Of course,' Alex said, 'I just can't stop correcting it and touching it up.'

'Can you email it to me? I don't want this to get lost.'

'What could possible happen? I know this is hot stuff but I've got approval from the editor. It will be printed.'

'Alex, they are not going to just let us print this. You said yourself that Lucy Sayers threatened you. We have to be careful.'

'You worry too much,' he said to her with the confidence of someone who had no idea what might be round the corner, 'it will be in tomorrow's paper.'

'Excuse me sir, would you mind stepping out of the vehicle?' The officer said to Andrew Quinn, 'perhaps you could join me and my colleague in the car here.'

He walked to the police car and climbed in the back seat as the officer opened the rear door.

'I observed you driving along York Road just now. Did you notice that Pelican Crossing?' the officer asked.

'Yes, I did. And I drove through it. I wasn't speeding,' he said.

'Indeed, sir. Have you any idea why we've stopped you?'

'Frankly, no. I don't believe I was driving incorrectly.'

'What is your name?' The officer asked.

'Andrew Quinn'

'Mr Quinn, are you in a rush?'

'No I'm just travelling to the office, I work for the Courier. We are about to prepare tomorrow's paper,' he said.

The officer seemed uninterested in his explanation.

'So Mr Quinn if you were not in a rush, why did you feel it necessary not to stop at the red stop light on the crossing? You do understand what a red light means?'

'Of course I do. There was no red light and there was no need to stop.'

Andrew was beginning to comprehend what was happening here. He had no doubt that he hadn't missed a red light.

'Are you saying that you didn't see a red light, Mr Quinn?'

'I'm absolutely saying that, I didn't miss a red light.'

'Have you been drinking sir?'

'No I haven't. What is going on here?' Andrew knew what was coming next.

The officer advised him that he suspected he'd been drinking and produced a breathalyser kit.'

'This is ridiculous,' he said, 'I haven't been drinking and I haven't missed a red light.'

'Sir, I'd like to ask you blow into this and we can clear the matter up.'

He took the breathalyser and breathed into it as instructed. He just hoped this would be the end of it and he could get on with the night's work.

The officer took the breathalyser and consulted it. He turned back to Andrew.

He shouldn't have been surprised, but he was in shock when the officer explained the test was positive and that he was being arrested. Whether the reading was faulty or had been fudged he had no idea, but he did know he hadn't been drinking. As he thought about the scheduled front page that night he wondered how far someone would go to make sure that story didn't go out. In twenty years of working on the paper no one had ever done this to him.


Alex Thompson took his usual walk from his apartment to the Courier Office. It was only five minutes and it was route he knew well.

He stepped out of the doorway and walked along the road. His mind was buzzing with the story. Revision after revision had been done and finally it was as good as he could get it. He knew that the boss would look at it and make some more changes. He wasn't sure whether it was because there was something he genuinely saw in it or just wanted to justify that he was the boss.

The dark weather had no affect on his mood and he ignored it as he progressed towards the Aire Bridge. The street was quiet as was typical of a Sunday night with hardly any traffic around

He sensed movement behind him which made him jump. Turning he saw two men approach him and braced himself to get out of the way. His instinctive fear was right as they grabbed him and bundled him to the floor.

Strong hands lifted him and forced him over the wall. He dropped rapidly, his laptop still attached round his neck, then hit the freezing water of the River Aire. The panic rose almost immediately as he fought for air and struggled with the current of the water. He found it impossible to breathe. More and more water invaded his lungs. It wasn't a conscious thought, that he might be dying, nor did he reflect on what happened; he was focussed on fighting for his life. Slowly, his energy ebbed away and he slipped under the water to nothing.

# Part 3

# Revolution

*"The more there are riots, the more repressive action will take place, and the more we face the danger of a right-wing takeover and eventually a fascist society."*
**- Martin Luther King**

# CHAPTER TWENTY FIVE

*Monday*

Monday morning had crept round and once Sarah Brownlee's morning routine of getting her daughter to school was completed she was able to get back to her search for Adrian Cullen's friend.

'Is this Gorton Tiling?' she asked, having found the number on the internet Yellow Pages site.

'Yes, what can I do for you?'

'Are you Stephen Gorton?' she asked hoping that this would be the next part of the puzzle slotting in.

'No, I'm Danny Gorton, his brother,' the voice said tentatively, '…can I ask who you are…this is not exactly a good time?'

Sarah briefly explained that she was looking for Stephen, a friend from the past and she'd been told that he was a Tiler.

'I'm afraid you wasted your time, Stephen died four weeks ago.'

The news hit Sarah like an earthquake.

'I'm sorry to hear that,' she said instinctively, but her mind was spinning round searching for questions and answers that she couldn't find.

She was glad she was at home, sat down already, or she may have collapsed in the street. Another person connected to Peters dying, this couldn't be a coincidence.

'Do you mind if I ask what happened?' she asked, trying to be as diplomatic as possible, 'I realise this is a difficult time.'

'He killed himself at the community home where he was resident,'

'Community Home…what sort of community home?'

'Look, who are you? I'm damn sure you're not some long lost friend…Stephen didn't have friends, and certainly not female ones.'

His hostility was not surprising and she realised that if she was going to get anywhere with this conversation she had to be honest. So she explained about her sister and how she thought Stephen might have had the answer.

'You're sister was Jenny?' he asked and Sarah's heart leapt as she realised Jenny must have spoken to him.

'Yes. Did you speak to her?'

'She phoned just like you are, and I think she went to see him. It was a couple of days afterwards that he did it. Look, this sounds a bit weird, what's going on here?'

'I know, I know…I'm sorry…I don't know either. That's why I'm calling. I'm trying to find out what happened to Jenny. Can you tell me about Stephen, Perhaps we can piece it together?'

'I can tell you about his history, not what was wrong with him. You'll have to contact the unit for that. Look, I'm busy working right now, can I call you later when I've had chance to think about it.'

Sarah was relieved in some ways it would give her chance to digest the situation and think about where to go from here.


Rachel Lancaster read the Courier from start to finish for the third time that day. Yes there was a whole spread on John Pilkington being arrested, and the local radio had picked it up, but nothing on the false alibi provided by Mark Davies and nothing about Lucy Sayers. If anything it was quite the opposite. The BFB were getting positive write up's everywhere.

One or two comments had been made to link Pilkington with the party philosophy but most seemed to see him as a fool on his own. Comments, interviews and party statements all clearly distanced themselves from Pilkington and with the general escalation of violence; all the rhetoric in the media was that the BFB predictions had been correct. Things were only going to get worse, and this was the inevitable result of uncontrolled immigration.

She'd rung Alex's mobile, numerous times that day and each time got a voice mail message. Getting worried, she had tried the newspaper offices and Tina on reception. She said he hadn't been home the night before and she was worried sick. Tina had been to the Police but they didn't think that there was anything to worry about. A twenty-seven year old journalist disappearing for a night was not in the least bit surprising to them. Tina told Rachel they had suggested he would turn up when he found what he was looking for.

Tina and Rachel both knew that something was not right and he wouldn't have run off without getting this story out. It was the biggest story of his career and he'd been determined to get it out. Tina had said she'd been to see Andrew Quinn the editor, but he hadn't been in that morning either. The sub-editor had said that he wouldn't print anything as controversial as Alex's story without his boss's approval.

Her next call was to Joe Barker; finding his card in her handbag earlier. They seemed good friends and there was a chance he might know something.

'Hi Joe, this is Rachel Lancaster here...we met on Friday in London.'

He remembered her, and Rachel explained to him that nobody had seen or heard from Alex since yesterday. She asked if he knew anything that would help.

'I haven't heard from him at all,' he said. It didn't surprise Rachel, just confirmed that wherever Alex was, he couldn't contact any of his friends.

'Perhaps he went off on a fishing mission somewhere and wasn't able to call.'

'Joe, I don't know Alex that well and I guess neither do you, but I know one thing about him. He wasn't that brave. He would have told someone what he was doing, I'm sure of it, especially given the story he was about to print.'

'From a journalist point of view, I'd have said the opposite was true, but I take your point, Alex isn't that kind of guy,' Joe replied. 'What was this story he had on the go?'

Not sure whether she totally trusted Joe, she decided to be vague about it. She thought he was probably sound but needed to play safe for the moment.

'He uncovered something about the BFB. It was pretty damning apparently.'

'Look, if I can do anything let me know, and call me again if he hasn't turned up tomorrow,' he said, '...and if you feel you want to share any of the story with me I'd be glad to take on the BFB. For the moment this is Alex's baby and I can understand you don't want to give it away.'

Whilst she was happy that he didn't pick up that she didn't trust him, she was also concerned that he thought she was holding back because she was protecting Alex's story. Not sure there was a better explanation of the situation; she let it go at that.

If it came to it that Alex was missing, she might need him on her side. She would have to trust him then.

Rachel tried to think about what else she could usefully do. Certainly there was plenty to do for Anna, but whilst everything else seemed trivial right now, there was little she could do either.

Joe put the phone down after talking to Rachel. The fact that Alex had gone missing was worrying, but could be explained easily as well.

He wondered whether he should be taking it seriously especially given what happened to Rachel last week, but in truth unless Rachel shared what he was working on there was little Joe could do about it. He decided that if Alex was still missing tomorrow then he would push Rachel for the story.

Fletch brought over a coffee.

'Thought you might need this?' he said to Joe.

'Too right,' he said, 'this documentation of Heather's is a nightmare to work through.'

'We are pretty sure, are we not that one of these companies must be involved or connected to the electoral fraud?' Fletch asked.

'I can't see it coming from anywhere else right now, unless there's some invisible organisation out there, these are the only names that have associated themselves with the party.'

'And whatever is going on with that funding, it has got to come from a high level, hasn't it?' A company is not going to align itself with a controversial party like the BFB if they don't have some history or investment in the outcomes of their policies.'

'Yep, I agree about that.'

'Let's go through each one of the boards, write down each name and do some digging on the key people. See what falls out of that. It has to be easier than trying to find holes in annual accounting and bank statements.'

'Ok, then,' he said, resigned to the task. Wherever the answer to the electoral scam was, it was not proving easy to find.


Her mobile rang and she immediately thought it was Joe calling.

She quickly scrabbled to pick it up and dived into the kitchen away from Connor and Jane who were watching the early evening TV. She was conscious that it looked suspicious but with everything happening she didn't want to miss a call.

She recognised the number as being the one she called that morning.

'Is that Sarah?' Danny Gorton asked as she answered.

She asked him to wait for a minute deciding she needed somewhere quiet, well away from the distractions of a nosy daughter. She made her way up to her bedroom.

As she settled down Danny told her the story.

'Stephen voluntarily sectioned himself a few years ago following a history of depression and anxiety. He worked with me for years but struggled to find a way to live with himself. I never knew what Stephen's problem was, as he wouldn't talk to me. I just knew that he couldn't cope with himself. I did my best to look after him and give him a job but there was too much going on for me to deal with.'

Danny carried on talking openly about his brother. He was clearly proud of Stephen's attempts to manage his illness and try to live a normal life but in the end it had been too much for Stephen.

'Whatever was going on with him, I blame the church. When he left school he was never away from the place, doing jobs round the church, helping the Priest, obsessively praying, carrying rosary beads or the bible round with him. For years his whole life had been about religion. It gave him structure and helped with his depression but I think it was too much.'

Alarm bells began to ring in Sarah's head as soon as Danny mentioned the church.

'Did something happen to make Stephen section himself? Did he suddenly become ill?' she asked

'He was a witness at a trial. It was some kind of priest abuse case and they had called Stephen because he knew the Priest from the parish and could say that he hadn't had any problems. I thought at the time it was an odd thing for him to be involved in. I mean I knew the guy, I always thought he was a bit weird but given I never had interest in the church, they were all weird to me.'

'What happened with the case?' Sarah asked, excited to discover a connection to what she and Joe had found before.

'He got off of course,' he replied, 'I didn't follow the case much myself, it was only the fact that Stephen had been there, that interested me. Stephen told me he was innocent and the allegations were shown to be without foundation or some bollocks like that. It was only a few weeks after that I noticed Stephen returning to his bible and saying prayers. It was a bit scary to be honest and I was glad when he went to get help about it.'

'Do you reckon that the Priest abused him, and it was all a cover up?'

Danny went silent for a minute as he thought about a response.

'If it was a cover up, it was a damn good one, but I guess if you look at Stephen's response that could explain a lot. Truth is, I've no idea, but he definitely had a screw loose and I reckon the church had something to do with it.'

She asked some more questions but there wasn't much more to learn. It was a heartbreaking story and left both of them quite upset.

He was clearly quite raw about it which added to Sarah's own still real feelings of grief.

She got the address of the Home where he was living in Preston and decided to visit tomorrow to see if they could tell her anymore about him. She felt this was only the start of uncovering this whole story.


The Stockton kitchen was busy that evening as Rachel helped Anna prepare dinner. This was the third night she had stayed and consequently beginning to miss home.

Anna had pushed her on a few occasions to tell her what was happening, but much as she'd said to Joe earlier, she explained that she and Alex had uncovered something about the BFB, and she was waiting for Alex to print it. Until the story was out, she wanted to lie low for her own safety.

Knowing that Rachel's car had been smashed up on the Friday before, Anna had agreed completely that she should stay with her. Like all things with Anna, she was able to make light of a situation, no matter how serious, and keep positive. Rachel found this spirit admirable and annoying at the same time.

'I sent Josie home early, too many people in the kitchen otherwise,' Anna explained, 'thought it would be fun making some dinner ourselves.'

'And I thought you were busy with your campaign?' Rachel said, 'clearly you've given it up as a bad job.'

'Don't be ridiculous, nothing of the sort,' she replied, 'just taking a well earned break to have some fun with my favourite colleague.'

'You mean, you want me to go leafleting tomorrow and you think by getting me drunk, I'm more likely to agree to it.'

'Never even crossed my mind...now you come to mention it, though, you could open that bottle in the fridge.'

Rachel happily went along with Anna's request and poured them both a drink.

'Ok, let's look at this recipe again; fish pie can't be that hard...can it?' Anna said laughing.

'It seems there's a reason why you employ a maid and cook.'

'Cheeky sod, I can cook, just get on with peeling the spuds and shut up.'

They carried on chatting, until their attention was drawn to the TV.

The local news presenter was announcing that the BFB candidate would be in the studio to answer questions on the bi-election campaign and the recent escalation of race related violence.

They both said nothing, their humour stunted, as the issues dominating their lives was played on the TV in front of them.

Rachel knew she was not going to enjoy watching this.

Once the headlines were out of the way Lucy Sayers and Patrick Barclay appeared in the studio.

Immediately Patrick Barclay went on the attack when asked if the party had anything to do with the bombings.

'I've answered these questions on numerous occasions over the last few weeks and I fail to see why the media keep returning to it. There's not one piece of evidence that has been put before me or anyone else in the party to suggest this is the case, and I cannot see any logic where we'd even consider such a disgusting and violent act, especially when, as is happening here, you would point the finger right back at us. This party is winning this campaign, in spite of a biased media agenda. You cannot accept the fact that we've presented an honest straightforward argument and that people out there, as proved by the polls, agree with us.'

Rachel stopped peeling, unable to contain her frustration.

'What is it Rachel…what is going on with you?' Anna asked her, 'I've never seen you this angry.'

Rachel ignored her and continued to stare at the screen.

Turning to Lucy Sayers, the interviewer asked if she thought the BFB would win on Thursday.

'I cannot say what will happen,' she said smiling with an air of false humility, 'we are in the hands of the electorate. But I'll say we have a chance, and would have a better chance if we got a fair hearing in the media.'

'You're here,' the presenter stated, 'I don't see any agenda in this studio.'

Lucy didn't let it go there.

'How can you say that when the first question you asked us, virtually accuses the party of blowing up a mosque? This is not a political interview but an exercise in slandering our good name. We are a party that stands for the man in the street…that feels that it's right for people to say no to immigration, no to foreigners taking our jobs and driving down wages, no to their houses and streets being attacked by people who have no right to be here. The more everyone keeps attacking us the more people will recognise that it's not just the BFB you're slandering but the people on the street who share our beliefs.'

Anna turned off the TV and turned to Rachel.

'You have got to tell me what's going on; I can see it in your face.'

'That lying fascist bitch sits there like butter wouldn't melt in her mouth, but I know for a fact that she knows who planted that bomb, and I think she may have killed or done something to Alex Thomson from the Courier. He had a story ready to go today that would have wiped that smug, self-deluding smile, right off her face.'

'You need to go the Police,' Anna said, but she could see in Rachel's eyes she was not thinking the same thing at all. 'Rachel if you know something, you must.'

'How can I go to the Police, when there's a good chance that one of them is involved, and is likely to come looking for me? You know already what they've done to my car. The only answer is to get that story out there and tomorrow that is just what I'm going to do. This has gone on too long.'

# CHAPTER TWENTY SIX

*Tuesday*

There was an air of satisfaction oozing through the offices of the Britain for British party meeting that morning.

The TV interview the night before had played well in the party offices and the election committee members were happily replaying moments from it. Coupled with the weekend poll results, the team really thought they sensed change coming their way. There was a real sense of opportunity.

Even attempts by the interviewer to link John Pilkington's arrest to party philosophy had not succeeded as Patrick and Lucy continued to disown him. Lucy was extremely vocal in her disgust at his behaviour and empathised with all women who were victims of such violence. It was a powerful performance by her and had won the respect of everyone at the BFB meeting, even those who believed she wasn't the right candidate.

They worked through the poll details. The spread of votes was split three ways between the BFB, Labour and Conservatives. The Liberals, independents, and other parties were nowhere to be seen. The Conservatives were in the lead by a few points but nothing that a bit of momentum wouldn't overturn.

The Conservative candidate, a wealthy white businessman from Bingley, had tried to secure his lead using the same rhetoric as the BFB but presented his argument from the context of a party of reason and fairness and not racism. In the end he was constrained by his party from overtly coming out on the side of any group and that left his argument too weak. His party wanted to be seen as inclusive to all communities as it was essential for national government. The BFB however, had no such constraints and therefore people could vote for them knowing exactly whose side they were on.

Labour had equally difficult issues in trying to appeal to all sides especially with the nomination of Muslim candidate. Whilst it was clear that he was a decent family man who didn't use his religion or background in his politics. He even spoke with a Yorkshire accent and raised numerous issues that affected every working class local resident, but his religion and race were still a handicap in gaining wide appeal in a community that was struggling with its attitudes to immigration.

The platform was set to take the campaign on to the big day and this meeting was the rallying call for the party to get their message out there.

The tone of the meeting was different from previous weeks in the sense of unity and optimism around the table. The usual arguments about taking a softer line had dissipated with the rise of Lucy's star. It was clear now that their only hope for winning this seat was to get behind her.

That made life easy for Patrick to get through the agenda, get agreement for actions and have everybody walking out with their heads held high. Lucy couldn't believe the change in attitude since the debacle of the rally last month. They had recovered their core balance in terms of what they were about and had managed to get the political agenda on their terms with fair and foul means. As she left the meeting Lucy was euphoric, happy to put behind her feelings of guilt and insecurity at what she'd done. She was ready to ride the wave of power.

As the members dissipated and left the room Andrew Bebbington had managed to get to speak to Lucy in a corner on her own out of earshot of the rest.

'It seems it's all coming together now. Are you sure there's nothing out there linking us to the bombers' release?' the American asked her.

'Yeah well you've seen the papers. It's all over that the police fucked up,' she said, 'there's no link back to the party and we are in the clear.'

'Do you reckon Alex Thompson really did know something or was he just trying his luck to get something out of you?'

'Like you said, we couldn't take that risk,' Lucy replied not quite looking him in the eye. There was no doubt she liked Alex and accepted the need for what happened. She hadn't however fully taken on board what it made her. 'What did you do anyway; or should I not ask?'

'No, you don't want to know. Let's just say we got to him before he could do anything,' Andrew replied.

Lucy smiled thinly, putting it out of her mind.

'What about the other one, the woman who was feeding him all this stuff?' Andrew asked.

'We've got something planned to shut her up for good. I don't think she knows anything for sure otherwise she would have come out with it already. But just in case, this will be enough to convince her that if she tries to use it, she'll be humiliated.'

'Good news then. I won't call the dogs off her yet though?' he said.

'Must be costing a fortune keeping tabs on her,' Lucy observed.

'Yes, but it's worth it. She's hiding out at her boss's place and we can't touch her there.'

'At least we know what she's up to and who she's talking to.'

'Yes and so far it seems not a lot, she seems lost without her little reporter lap dog,' Andrew said laughing at his own joke, 'our investors are very happy with you, you know? This is the start of good things. You should be proud.'

'It feels good,' Lucy said trying to feeling as good about herself as Bebbington wanted her to. She could say the words and fight the fight and she knew that her conscience would come along with her in the end. That was enough for now as the words flowed easily from her.

'I can really feel it now, so close. We are going to do it this time.'

'Two days to go, we are going to do it,' Andrew said feeding off her words. 'Don't suppose we can sneak a meeting tonight?'

'You're joking aren't you? You know we can't risk it this week,' Lucy replied. The sex hadn't been that good, that she would risk exposure.

'Yeah, I know, it was worth a thought.'

'Just think next week when it's all over, you'll have the pleasure of bedding the next Member of Parliament for Leeds North.'

'Well I hope you win it then because I don't want to be shagging Ken Greenwood,' Bebbington laughed as he dreamed of what might be just around the corner.


Sarah Brownlee walked out of Foxton Community Residential Unit in South Preston, making her way slowly back to her car desperately sad at what she'd learnt about Stephen Gorton's death. She also had no doubt about the link between Jenny and Stephen as he committed suicide two days after her visit.

The unit was a community mental health residential centre where the residents lived as close to the community as was practical; the modern practice for managing and rehabilitating patients who previously would have been in larger hospitals.

Stephen had been admitted following voluntary treatment for depression. He'd been in the unit now for quite a few years, his symptoms becoming worse rather than reducing as he grew older.

The nurse on the unit had explained that Jenny had been to see Stephen a month earlier. The nurse hadn't forgotten, not because of anything about Jenny but because of the impact her visit had on Stephen. He explained that the day after, a Priest had been to see him and it had been too much for him to take.

The priest's visit made Sarah think there was something suspicious about the suicide but it was more than possible that he wanted to give his confession before he did himself in. The visitor's book had the priest's name assuming it was real, as Father Williams. It could have been made up easily and no one would have checked his ID. It was hard to know if he was connected or not.

More information and few answers left Sarah confused and frustrated. It was time to call Joe and see what he had to say.

Joe was at his desk in the 24Seven News Agency offices in London working on his own research. It didn't take long for him to be cynical as Sarah relayed the story.

'So all in all, we reckon Stephen Gorton was abused by the same priest as Adrian Cullen,' he said. 'Someone filled Stephen's head full of guilt making him do penance and he committed himself to the church in order to come to terms with what had happened. Obviously seeing the trial news had brought it all back to him and he couldn't handle it.'

'That's a fair assumption,' Sarah added, 'do you think he was one of the boys you saw that night?'

'I've no idea but it wouldn't surprise me. He could just have been traumatised by abuse but secretly burying the dead body of a mate, would probably add a whole truck full of guilt on his shoulders. It's no wonder he turned to the church to bear the weight for him.'

'What do I do now?' Sarah asked.

'You've done pretty well so far. Maybe you should be doing my job,' Joe laughed. 'We need to find the other two, and I think I might just be ahead of you on that one. I talked to Fletch earlier and he gave me a list of names for those companies I was looking into. Well on two of the BCA sponsored companies, there was a non executive director in common. Guess who the name was?'

'Joe I'm not in the mood for games, just tell me,' she replied impatiently.

'Sorry didn't mean to sound so excited about it, but the name was David McGhee.'

Sarah went silent for a moment.

'The same David McGhee who was a friend of Adrian Cullen, surely not?' she said not quite able to believe what she'd just heard.

'If it's not the same one, it's a hell of a coincidence don't you think?'

'I suppose so, how will we know for sure?' she asked.

'I'll go and ask him,' Joe said, 'I found out he lives and works in the North. He has a big place out near Ilkley. I looked it up on the net and it's next to a monastery on the moor there, religion seems to be a very common theme here.'

'So now we've a potentially abused altar boy from thirty years ago running two companies which coincidently are sponsoring a religious pressure group. Then we've a different abused boy who was racked with guilt for what he knew and ended it all,' Sarah said flatly, amazed that she was even having this conversation. How had she become so accepting of conspiracy and death as if was an everyday occurrence.

'It's not a happy conclusion, but it's becoming a more real one as we speak.'

'Are you sure it's wise to go and see McGhee, he might not take too kindly to you turning up with this kind of accusation?' Sarah asked him.

'I'll be ok. I'm more worried about you to be honest up there in Preston.'

Sarah felt herself shiver at the thought of other people seeing her as a target. She looked around the car and the car park and was slightly relieved that she couldn't see anyone. The only thing of note was a tired old red Astra with a smashed headlight, which just made her think that whoever was driving that around was crazy with winter coming along.

'Joe I'm getting a bit scared,' she said, her mind coming back to what she was doing, 'I keep thinking that Jenny was here and then what happened to her.'

'I know, perhaps it's time you stopped doing this. Maybe it's too dangerous,' he replied.

'Stop it now. I have to drive back to Manchester now and you're not helping me at all.'

'I know, I'm sorry, I'll shut up now. Just take care driving and call me when you get home.'

'By the way did your mate Alex turn up?'

'No, and I got a phone call already from Rachel Lancaster this morning.'

'Yes of course. Did she say anything?' The anxious edge in Sarah's voice had risen again knowing that Alex was still missing.

'Rachel is really worried about him. That doesn't sound good to me. She's emailing me the story. She wants me to run it.'

'Oh my God Joe, I'm not happy about this. I really hope Alex is alright, he was such a nice lad.'

'It's all a bit crazy, I can't deny. There are a lot of coincidences and whilst I haven't found any connections, it doesn't feel good.'

'Will you run the story?' Sarah asked, knowing the answer before she finished the question.

'I need to have a look at it first and check it out. But if it's what she says it is then I don't have a choice. With that and what I'm getting from Heather Lockhart's stuff, this is massive.'

'Joe I can't believe you, this is dangerous you said it yourself and there you are waving a big flag to whoever is behind this to come and get you. You go on about seeing people and printing stories that have got other people killed. How can you be so bullish about it?' Sarah complained. Her frustration, at not being able to restrain him, showed.

'You know as well as I do that we have to do this, as no one else is going to. From what we can see the police are not even sure a crime has been committed. If we drop it now, nothing will happen and I just can't do that Sarah,' he replied, 'all this, in my view, has been about suppressing the story and they've succeeded in keeping it quiet. For the moment I don't think they know Rachel has this story otherwise she would have been a target. They certainly don't know who I am. Maybe once this is out in the open then there's no mileage in getting rid of us. There would be nothing to gain whilst they would be suspect number one. I think if we can get the story out then the whole picture changes.'

'I hope so Joe. I really hope so.'


Sarah last words sat with Joe a moment before he could move back to what he was doing.

The implications of the situation were weighing heavily on him. He had knocked down many doors in his time as a journalist and certainly pissed a few people off. It went with the territory. This was different though. People were disappearing or dying around him and he didn't know how to handle it. The only thing was to keep going and find the truth. It was what he did and he couldn't imagine walking away from that responsibility.

Time to focus he said to himself and picked up his notes on the party sponsorship. He'd spent all day Monday on the internet researching each of the companies. He'd traced back the ownership and the history of each company looking for any political motivations, anything that would link them to corruption or a nationalist background. Whoever had started this political donation scam had to have some kind of history.

He hadn't found anything of use other than a list of chairmen and chief executives including McGhee. He'd left Fletch to do more work on that as he was more patient. His time now would be best spent looking at what Rachel had sent.

He opened up his email and started to read.

Five minutes later he walked over to Fletch.

'I have to head back up north to deal with something.'

'Where are you going?' Fletch asked.

'Leeds...a friend of mine has gone missing and I've just seen the likely reason for it. I need to check some things out, but if what I've just seen is true, there's going to be an almighty storm.'

'I thought you'd be going to that BCA day of action tomorrow after you said you were looking into their activities,' Fletch said.

'When's that?' Joe asked, '...you didn't tell me about that.'

'Sorry, I thought you knew, they've organised a day of action where they've listed a target in each city and want to organise a protest for each one. In London they've picked Soho fairly predictably, a couple of abortion clinics, Manchester's gay district, a new mosque in Birmingham and a casino somewhere I can't remember.'

'That seems a bit mad, better to focus on one thing at a time you would have thought.'

'Maybe they think there's something for everyone in that selection,' Fletch laughed.

'If I have time I might see if there's one in Leeds otherwise I'll pick up something from other sources,' Joe replied, frustrated at how little time he had.

'Not like you to miss out on something like this.'

'No, I know, but this story could be way bigger than a few God-Botherers causing a nuisance, that's what worries me,' he said. He put his laptop in his bag and grabbed his coat shouting back to Fletch, 'send me that stuff, soon as you can.'

Joe left the office and headed towards Kings Cross. Thirty minutes later he was on the train. Once the train cleared the London area, and his phone was working, he called Rachel Lancaster.


In Leeds, Rachel was at her desk as the phone rang.

She was pleased to see it was Joe Barker.

'I'm sorry I didn't send the story yesterday,' she said after they exchanged pleasantries. 'To be honest I don't really know who to trust but I know Alex trusted you so I thought I would too.'

'No problem Rachel I'm glad you did,' he replied, 'look, I'm on the train coming north. Where are you at the moment?'

'I'm in the office, why?' Rachel asked.

'After reading this, I think the fact that he's missing is not a coincidence as I'm sure you do too. Maybe you should be looking out for yourself right now.'

'They don't know I have this information though. They don't know I can blow their alibi,' Rachel said feeling the immense pressure of holding onto this information. She was relieved to have someone to talk to about it.

'They know you've talked to Alex and they know he was about to print the story about the alibi. They probably suspect he had something else and we can assume that they think you have it as well. That makes you dangerous to them.'

'Yes I'm aware of that, but what can I do? I'm staying with my boss, who is also standing for the election. I know there's no way they'll touch me whilst I'm with her. It's too risky for them.'

'I can see your point I suppose, it's as safe as anywhere… I'm on my way to Leeds to see you, if you don't mind. We can talk some more when I get there. I just need to re-hash this story a bit.'

'Is something wrong with it?' Rachel asked, 'Alex did a lot of work on it.'

'No, just needs a bit of sharpening up I think with what has happened since,' Joe replied, 'how can I find you?'

Rachel explained what to do and where the office was. He agreed to be there in two to three hours.

She put the phone down and went to get another drink, her head buzzing with confusion, which frustrated her. She was not normally so indecisive.

With still no word from Alex this morning she'd called Tina. She hadn't heard anything but managed to speak to his editor Andrew Quinn. He'd said that there was a problem with the police on Sunday night and he was detained overnight due to a faulty drink driving sample. It was cleared up by the morning when his blood tests proved negative and he was released. The news desk put the paper out on Monday with what they had already but as she already knew they didn't file Alex's story. Quinn apparently wanted to run the story but in Alex's absence he hadn't been able to follow up on the source.

If she hadn't already decided to follow up with Joe she would have gone down to the Courier herself, but having spoken to Joe yesterday she felt she could trust him a whole lot more than Alex's editor. Knowing that Joe was coming to see her made her feel a whole lot better, hoping that something could finally be done to derail Lucy Sayers.

First though she needed to talk to Anna again. She hadn't done anything about Purnell with all of this going on and Anna needed her to get the Purnell to drop the case. Perhaps they were both losing focus on the business, too busy playing games they should have stayed well away from.

Anna's election campaign had gone from bad to worse and Rachel was seriously thinking about asking her to drop it. It seemed though that Anna was determined to get to Election Day and take her chances. The doorstep campaign had resulted in lots of people agreeing with her but few wanted to vote for her. It wasn't a negative thing so much as people didn't believe she could win and therefore voting for her was a pointless action.

She went through to her office to see if Anna was free, happy to be discussing something that didn't make her feel worse than she already did.

'Hello dear,' Mrs Cullen said as she answered the door, 'I didn't expect to see you here again.'

'I was in the area so I thought I'd pop in to see how you were,' Sarah said with a smile. She wasn't sure why she'd come back. She hadn't planned to, but on a whim, had decided to pay her a visit before leaving Preston.

Mrs Cullen invited her in and Sarah was ordered to make the tea and get the biscuits as Joe had done last week. Mrs Cullen waited patiently sat in her armchair with Cherry the cat next to her; both appeared to enjoy Sarah waiting on them.

'Where is the chap who was with you?' she asked as Sarah returned with the drinks.'

'He is away working, back in London,' Sarah explained.

'I bet you're missing him, you seem such a lovely couple.'

Sarah was about to correct her, but decided to leave it. It wasn't important and it made her feel really cosy to think of being part of a romantic couple again.

'Thank you Mrs Cullen. Has anyone else been to see you since our last visit? I hope it's not too much bother for you?'

'Oh, I had a few reporters round and on the phone but I said that I wasn't speaking to anyone. I didn't have anything to say,' she explained. 'They didn't like it but they soon gave up when they realised they were not getting anywhere. I can be quite stubborn you know. I only spoke to you because of your connection to what happened otherwise I might not have bothered with it.

'Well thank you again. We did learn more about what might have happened.'

'Did you find those boys I mentioned to you? I guess they won't be boys anymore. You know what I mean though.'

'We found some of them, but haven't learnt too much really,' Sarah not wanting to say too much more. She didn't want to upset her.

'I forgot to tell you, the police returned the photograph, would you like to see it?'

'Yes please,' Sarah replied, feeling pleased that her trip wasn't wasted.

Mrs Cullen reached over to a brown envelope on the mantelpiece and passed it to Sarah. Sarah stared at it for a few moments. She recognised Ian Hamilton, his features obvious and standing out from her recent meeting. Adrian Cullen was obvious from the other pictures in the room. The other three faces seemed so distinct and anonymous at the same time. They showed individuality and personality that must have been apparent to those who knew them, but to anyone else they could have been anybody. There was simply nothing special about them. They all appeared familiar in their way.

Sarah asked if she could take a copy to a local photo store and bring it back. Mrs Cullen agreed on the promise that Sarah wouldn't ever print the photo or sell it on.

They went on to pass a further thirty minutes chatting, but once she had the photograph Sarah was only half interested in the conversation. The photograph had taken over her thinking as she kept returning to stare at the faces, convinced that one of them murdered her sister.

# CHAPTER TWENTY SEVEN

Arriving in Leeds at Central Station, Joe walked out of the front entrance and into City Square. Rachel had told him it was as quick to walk to the office as it was to get a taxi, and he probably would have been grunted at by a taxi driver, who having just queued for an hour for a fare, gets to go five hundred metres for nothing.

As he entered the Square there was a large crowd of people and a lot of noise. In the centre was a small platform with a microphone and a number of people milling around who appeared to be taking turns to speak. There must have been only twenty or thirty people as most of the passers-by were ignoring them, instead trying to get on with their shopping. The platform had a number of chunky looking bouncers protecting it. He couldn't hear the speakers for a number of reasons. Firstly he was across the square and perhaps the sound didn't carry, particularly when the voices were competing with the noise of buses and general traffic. The other reason was the counter chanting that came from another gathering in the square.

As he got a closer view of the platform it all became perfectly clear. It was surrounded by posters for the BFB and Union Jacks. The main poster at the back invited people to join the BFB Free Speech Open Mike.

Unbelievably the BFB had set up in the square inviting people to stand up and say anything they liked under the definition of free speech. Joe thought this was a major publicity stunt designed to get maximum exposure because there was only one way something like this could end. The chanting of the gathering was only the start and would soon turn into confrontation. He couldn't imagine, the groups peacefully backing down. Although any resulting violence might be blamed on the BFB they had offer the simple defence of free speech and individuals saying what they wanted to say. It was neither an organised incitement to violence or racial hatred. It was simply people speaking their mind.

Joe was not sure how long it had been going on for but he reckoned the police would be here before long. Seeing a good opportunity for another story, he took out his camera and made his way to the platform. He would try to catch what he could of the speeches and maybe get some opinions from those around about it. Rachel would have to wait for the moment.

Patrick Barclay and Lucy Sayers stood across the square from the platform watching the show.

'This was an inspired idea, Lucy,' Patrick said as he watched the people who felt inspired to say something when presented with a microphone and an audience happy to hear anything.

'Thanks, it's going even better than I expected,' Lucy replied, 'to be honest I thought we might get trouble from the start but most people, at least those who were sober, have been quite articulate.'

They watched another white male stand up and say how he was fed up of people who were not from round here taking jobs from those that belonged here.

There was a queue of five to six people at a time, all wanting to say something. Patrick was quite frustrated that a number must have fallen out the pub relatively recently as some of them were just talking rubbish.

The crowd of jeerers decided it was time to speak. A young Asian dressed in jeans, scarf and a white jumper stepped forward into the queue. He seemed to be full of the bravado of the crowd he'd found himself in and appeared happy to be the centre of attention for the moment. The atmosphere was tense and everybody sensed this was the crucial point of the whole occasion.

Patrick watched the crowd and expected a negative reaction from the other people in the queue, but maybe everyone saw this as a bit of sport and waited to hear what he had to say.

This would be interesting, Patrick thought. He was pleased to see an Asian stand up as this would balance any argument about free speech. He wondered how the crowd would react; he was hoping that the occasion could proceed without any confrontation.

Finally the queue diminished and the Asian youngster made it to the platform. He stood for a moment nervously watching the opposing crowds in front of him. One side aggressively told him to get on with it, the other wanted him to produce some words of wisdom that would win the battle of verbal justice being fought over in front of them.

'Look man, I heard it all right. I heard all of you, I heard it today and I heard it everyday.'

The man paused to get his breath and get over his nervous energy.

'Listen man, I can't argue with you here. It'd be the same if this was the other way around, we'd complain about immigrants and foreigners, right? I see it. But you got to see it from the other side as well. We are people, right? You don't know about us, you don't know what happened to us and why we came here. You don't know what we think and what our religion is so don't come up here and tell us what you know. You don't know nothing.'

He paused again probably realising he was repeating himself.

'All I want is say is, I was born here, I'm British, Yeah I'm Asian but it doesn't make me evil. I just want to work hard and live a decent life like everyone without being called a Paki everyday. Not much to ask. It's the same for all of us. I know there are some nutters around. But don't speak to us like we are shit. Because one day we might decide we can't take it anymore. You know what I mean.'

The jeers from the immediate crowd were getting louder. Patrick had been so intent on watching the guy speak he hadn't noticed the police arrive and start to take over the situation. They immediately surrounded the platform. The Asian man realised no one was listening anymore and he stepped down as the police pulled the microphone cable. The crowd started to disperse.

Patrick was a little relieved to see the police. The platform had achieved what it had set out to do and there was no resulting violence. It was another victory for the BFB, at least in his mind.


Qamar, his heart racing with nervous energy, stepped down from the platform cheered by those around him. Everyone was giving him a big pat, high fives or touching fists. He loved being the centre of attention.

He smiled at the lads, enjoying the banter, as the police started to push them all away.

They found themselves back in the centre of Leeds early that afternoon, looking around for the next thing to do. They had got into a habit of meeting up in selected places deciding where the next action would be, today had been outside the town hall but one of the guys had spotted the open mike session going on, and they figured this was a chance for a bit of action.

He didn't know what made him step up there. He didn't normally step out from the crowd like that, seeing himself as quite shy really. These days he knew he was becoming a different person. Something was driving him, anger or frustration, he didn't know. One thing was for sure it felt good to be this new person, and that confidence had led him to make that stand today. Standing up and speaking for everyone all his friends, not spouting religion, just telling people how it felt to be him.

Of course nobody listened, well maybe his mates did, but that didn't matter. The words were one thing, action was another. People were going to start taking notice soon. He could see the BFB and the others playing little politics in Leeds, but his mates had found a much bigger game to play.


The arrival of the police put an end to the show before anything really got started and that appeared to be a relief to all concerned. Joe was pleased just to have been at the right place at the right time to see it and he'd be getting a few pounds in the bank for that.

He decided it was time to move on and find Rachel's office. He followed her instructions and found the café she'd referred to. He took a seat, and called her. Five minutes later she sat opposite him.

'Thanks for coming up,' she said once they had both got a drink. Joe also picked up a sandwich as he hadn't had chance to eat yet.

'I was beginning to go out of mind with all this. You wouldn't believe how hard it has been just waiting for something to happen. I'm also really worried about Alex. This is not like him.'

'I agree, but I'm not sure how we would go about finding him. Have the police said anything to you yet?' Joe asked.

'I spoke to his girlfriend, Tina, today and she said she keeps calling them. They acknowledge her concern but they don't have anything to go on.'

'Typical police, especially where guys are concerned. Slow to respond unless they know for sure there's a problem.'

'What did you think of the story,' Rachel asked, not wanting to dwell on the situation with Alex.

Joe opened his laptop and showed her what he'd written, 'see what you think of this now.'

Rachel quickly read the report seeing that he'd re-written much of what Alex had done to his own style and was impressed how he'd phrased it more pointedly; particularly how he'd been braver in his criticism of the police's inability to deal with obvious racism in the ranks. He had also added a paragraph and a separate page detailing how Alex as a journalist about to break this story had disappeared and the police weren't taking it seriously.

'This is strong stuff,' Rachel said eventually.

'I can be a bit more direct than Alex. Working on the internet you're not part of the local community angle. I don't have to keep in with the local police for sources of good information and relationships. The Courier is part of the community and Alex doesn't have the luxury of all-out attack on a local public service. Whereas, to a certain extent, I can say what I like as long as I don't libel anyone.'

'I see,' Rachel said, 'when will it be posted online?'

'If you let me use your email it can be online later today. As you see I haven't named you in the article but if he sues me then you'll have to stand up and be counted. I need that sworn affidavit you gave Alex for my protection. I can protect you for so long but I think when we publish we should both go down to the police station with what we know and you should make a statement. This will start a ball rolling and who knows what will happen next? We both have to be prepared for that,' Joe said looking to Rachel to accept the reality of the game they were in.

'I think I'm happy to stand up and be counted but I was just not sure about the timing. '

'I think going to the police to make that statement is what's going to keep us alive. I know that sounds a bit melodramatic but Alex's disappearance should be seen as a warning. Once we've been to the police, there's nothing to gain by getting rid of us. They might seek to discredit us in someway but as the information is out in the public domain it would attract too much negative attention if we disappeared now.'

'I can't get past what happened to Alex,' Rachel said, 'I'm sure that Lucy Sayers knows something about it, she was the last person he spoke to before he disappeared.'

I've seen what's going on in Lucy Sayers eyes which tells me she's a woman who will do what's necessary to get what she wants, but…' Joe paused.

'But what?' Rachel asked.

'But she's a practical woman; she's not going to do anything she can't get away with. If there's a chance we can point a finger at her she'll run like the wind. She's a chameleon and she'll change colour faster than the TV. She wants to win this election and she'll find any way to do it. The police turning up on her doorstep is the last thing she needs. If we stay on her tail she knows we'll get enough evidence to link it back to her. If she arranges for us to be killed then she will be chief suspect and has no chance. She's the one who will be more scared than we are right now.'

'Maybe that means she's more dangerous, a desperate woman,' Rachel said, 'God this is crazy, I don't know what to do.'

'That's why we are talking. We need to make a plan to get out of this, without any of us getting hurt.'

Life returned to normal for Sarah Brownlee as she arrived back from school with her daughter, and it was surprising how easily she slipped into it.

Jane had a particularly difficult fall out with her friend Jennifer and was complaining to her mother about the situation, relaying in intimate detail how she had no right to say what she did. It was something to do with the new skirt she'd shown her, that Jennifer said had made her look like a slag and she'd only got it so she could steal her boyfriend. Jane had continued to complain about how she wouldn't go near Jennifer's boyfriend as he smelt like a dog.

It was wasted on Sarah, as every word went in one ear and out the other side.

In some ways she was happy to indulge in the normality of life because it stopped her thinking about things.

'Mum, you're not listening,' Jane said.

'I am,' Sarah protested, 'I'm just a bit distracted at the moment.'

'Yeah well I know what it is,' she said teasing her mum.

Sarah turned sharply to her daughter. 'What do you mean?'

'Don't look at me in that scary way, I just mean you're in love with that guy. I can see it in your eyes,' she said, 'I haven't seen you like that before.'

Sarah smiled with relief; she thought Jane had got hold of everything else that was going on, although she couldn't think how.

'Hmm, I'm saying nothing, but no it's not just that. I'm a little upset about your Auntie Jenny, I still think about her a lot,' she said.

Jane came over and gave her a hug, which Sarah accepted fully, not just because of the emotional cushion that her daughter was providing but because she almost never did it. The lack of intimacy and emotion between her and Connor resulted in a similar deficiency in the house generally, even with a hormonal teenager around.

'I miss seeing Holly and Beth, can we go around and see them sometime?' she asked.

'I'll talk to your Uncle Russ soon. He wasn't very well last time I spoke to him. I thought we should give him some time.' It was the best explanation Sarah could give her.

Jane seemed to accept that and returned to what she was doing. It gave Sarah a moment to think about what things might be like if she got together with Joe and left Connor. Jane would have to come with her but how would she feel about Joe? Leaving Connor was no problem; she'd left him in her head so many years ago. That was the easiest bit. She had so many questions in her mind, it was about time she started to answer some of them.

'Oh and mum?' Jane said, ready to tell her something.

'Yes, love?' Sarah said, wondering where this was going.

'I can tell you've been smoking again,' she said, 'it's so not cool and you stink.'

Sarah wasn't sure how to respond.

'I know you're right, honey, but I've been a bit stressed, I'll give up again. I promise.'

'You better had before Dad susses you out; he'll go mad.'

With that, she poured herself some orange juice and took off up the stairs.

Sarah was alone again so made a drink and went to sit in the back room with her laptop, trying not to think about the cigarette she desperately wanted. She would have been ok if Jane hadn't just mentioned it. Instead she picked up a pen and started chewing that as she thought about what to do next. She was confident that the clues were probably there for her if she could find them.


It was six o'clock in the evening when Joe Barker and Rachel Lancaster walked into Eastside police station stating to the officer at the desk they had information about the bombing of Beckton Mosque.

They took a seat and waited. It reminded Joe of the visit to Bury Police with Sarah last week. He wondered why he was one step ahead of the police in all this, but he supposed that he saw things from a different point of view and perhaps could work a little more freely.

A few minutes later they were asked to come through the security door and into an interview room. He looked at Rachel who appeared incredibly nervous. She obviously felt highly vulnerable here and Joe would need to take the lead.

He was introduced to the two officers in the room, one a female detective sergeant called Gilhead the other a male constable he didn't get the name of. They were offered a drink. The officers were as courteous as they could be, faced with the stark atmosphere of the interview room.

'I understand you have information for us?'

'My name is Joseph Barker and this is Rachel Lancaster. I'm a journalist for 24Seven News Agency. I've just published a story where Ms Lancaster claims that the alibi provided by one of your officers for the two bombers arrested last week is false. Ms Lancaster saw the officer, at the time he claimed to be with the suspects, at a different location. Here's a print out of the article that is now published on the net and a photograph showing the meeting. Note the time and date taken. Ms Lancaster would like to make a full statement explaining what she witnessed.'

The two officers looked at each other. This was clearly not what they had come into the room expecting to hear.

'Wait there,' Gilhead said as both officers got up from the table and left the room.

'You ok?' Joe asked Rachel.

'Not really,' she replied, 'I feel under a lot of pressure here. If they don't take us seriously then I think we could be in trouble. We've nowhere to go after this.'

'It'll be ok. I'm sure,' Joe said, not sure he believed it himself as he spoke.

Five minutes later the constable was replaced by the officer Joe recognised as DCI Holding from the TV press conferences the week before. DS Gilhead followed behind him.

'Right let's get down to it,' he started aggressively, 'how do you know this and why did you only come forward now?'

The question was directed at Rachel but Joe answered for her.

'Firstly, I'm not going to answer the question about how we know this. That is journalistic privilege, but I don't think that is the important thing in this situation. It's well known that a police officer provided that alibi and it's not hard to know who that officer was. The most important issue here is that Ms Lancaster can deny that alibi, which means that you let the bomber go, on the word of one your officers.'

Holding was fuming and it was clear he was just about keeping it together.

'I'll decide what I want to know,' was his first response, 'I'll ask what I like. Ms Lancaster, can you tell me why you didn't come forward earlier with this information? And I'd prefer it if Mr Barker here would keep his mouth shut for a moment or I'll ask him to leave the room.'

'I didn't know myself until two days ago when I learnt who had given that alibi and that I had seen Sergeant Davies at that exact moment.'

'How can you be sure it was him?'

'I know who he is. I've no doubt about it,' Rachel replied.

'How come you know him so well you can have no doubt?'

'Let's just say I've come across him in a professional capacity.'

'What exactly is your profession, Ms Lancaster?'

'She doesn't need to answer that, it's not important here,' Joe jumped in before Rachel could speak.

'Mr Barker, I've warned you to keep quiet.'

'Ms Lancaster is entitled to have someone here. I can always get a solicitor here and I could remind you that we came here voluntarily.'

'Yes, and I might just make your situation involuntary if I arrest you for withholding information about a known suspect.'

'Look, can we get on with this?' It was Rachel who spoke this time, 'I'm a researcher for a legal firm. Sergeant Davies was the subject of a number of cases that came my way. Therefore I was familiar with him.'

'Thank you,' the DCI replied, 'why did you not come forward earlier? Were you just waiting to sell your story to the highest bidder?'

'Quite frankly, I work for a legal firm that has a specific interest in only working with the police on the basis of need. I came across this information in a professional capacity by accident. I think you can understand that I might not have come here straight away especially given who this was about. I first raised this issue with another journalist you may be familiar with, Alex Thompson. He is a good friend of mine and we often work together,' the DCI nodded at the mention of his name, 'you may or may not be aware that Mr Thompson has been missing since Sunday, not long after we had the same conversation about Sergeant Davies. I think it's therefore reasonable to assume that advertising my knowledge of what happened may not be good for my health. What do you think?'

'You're here now, so you obviously decided that it wasn't that much of a problem to you?' he replied.

'Yes, you're right,' Rachel said.

Joe was watching and knew that she'd got over her nervousness and she was matching Holding's aggression with her own. Joe was at the disadvantage here and he had no control over what Rachel would say. He just had to wait and see where this confrontation went.

'We discussed this and decided that it may be wiser to go to the police with the information. Safety in numbers I suppose.

'I see, so in the meantime you thought you'd share it with the rest of the world before me,' he said staring at Joe.

'I'm journalist. I have no obligation to share anything with you,' Joe replied by way of a challenge, 'it was you who released the suspects, not me, so don't blame me if stories come out about you that undermine your actions.'

Holding looked at Rachel for a more positive response.

'Joe, I mean Mr Barker, advised me to come here. Otherwise I'd probably not be here. So please stop complaining about him,' Rachel said.

This time he seemed to accept the situation without reaction and his anger with them receded.

'Detective Sergeant Gilhead will take a statement from you both,' he said finally. He got up to leave the room.

'Is that it?' Joe asked.

He ignored Joe and continued on his way.

'I didn't expect to hear from you today,' Andrew Bebbington said at the other end of the line.

'I just had a call from Davies at Eastside. He says his contact on the Mosque bombing has just had a visit from Rachel Lancaster. She can crush Davies's alibi because she has a photograph of me with Davies at the same time,' Lucy explained.

'How the fuck did she get that?' Andrew Bebbington asked, 'Were you with him then?'

'I was there with him at The Printers although fuck knows how she saw us. He came round The Printers that afternoon to tell me that everything was going down. I had no idea we had been seen. She must have been following me.'

There was silence on the end of the line.

'Andrew, are you there?'

'Yes I'm here,' he said angrily, 'I'm thinking. Was she alone? Has she spoken to anyone else? This must have been what Alex Thompson was cooing about on Sunday.'

'Apparently she was with some journalist called Barker. I don't know him though. That nosy bitch, I knew she was trouble. We should have got rid of her at the same time as Thompson. I thought Davies had warned her off but she obviously didn't take the hint.'

All the guilt and second thoughts she'd had earlier were gone now as she grasped how exposed she was. She had discounted Rachel Lancaster as a nosey inconvenience and not a serious threat, but here she was offering the one piece of evidence that could lose Lucy everything.

'If she was with a journalist it must mean that it's going to press. It's also likely the police are going to come knocking. Lucy, just deny everything, what ever you do, don't give an inch on this.'

'It's ok I'm not about to admit to anything. Trouble is, if she's going to keep chucking mud some of it's going to stick soon.'

'Yeah, well, maybe it's time we silenced her as well.'

'We can't do that. Everyone will know it's us. You sound like some amateur gangster Andrew, this is not the US. We can't keep popping people off.'

'Come on Lucy, grow up, you're in a serious game here. We are going to have to play hard ball with her, get her to drop the whole thing, get her to tell the police she was mistaken, the day was wrong or something. If we don't stop her she'll sure as hell stop us.'

'How are we going to do it?' Lucy asked.

'Do you really need me to go into that?'

'No not really, you're right. I don't want to know, just make sure you get her off my back.'

Lucy ended the call and swore again. She couldn't believe how close that woman was to fucking up everything. She didn't want another death on her conscience, but she refused to feel guilty over a stupid woman who couldn't resist putting her hand in the fire.

The phone vibrated in her hand just as she was about to put it away. It was Patrick Barclay.

'I just had a call from the Courier,' he said, 'what's going on Lucy?'

Fucking hell she thought impatiently, it was like having her conscience phone her everyday and scold her for what she was doing.

'What did they ask?' she replied with a disinterested tone knowing what was coming.

'Apparently there's a story doing the rounds on the internet that you and Davies were together at the time that Davies gave his alibi for the mosque bombers. Is this true? They want me to comment on this?'

'Patrick, of course it's not true and I'll deny the whole thing.'

'Are you sure? Because I've had a look at it on the internet news site 24Seven where it started and it looks pretty clear to me, there's a photograph of you and that copper.'

'The woman behind this is delusional; she's obsessive and has a thing about us. She's been making up stories about us for weeks and telling anyone who listens.'

'Well that photograph is quite clear,' he said accusing her of lying, which wound Lucy up more.

'I didn't say I hadn't ever met him. The time and date can easily be altered.'

She bit her lip trying to resist saying more.

'Yes well doctored or not, there are plenty of people who are going to listen, especially after John's arrest.'

'Yeah I get that, but she's nothing. She can't stop us now,' Lucy replied emphatically.

'I hope so Lucy. We've got the party leadership turning up tomorrow. This is the last thing we need.'

'Patrick, don't be nervous. We knew this was going to be a rocky road. You've seen how popular we are on the streets today, you know how it is. We are nearly there now. I'll deal with it.'

She ended the call perhaps reassuring Patrick, but not herself. She knew that it was only a matter of time before the Police turned up at the door and she was going to have to fight like mad to stay ahead of this one.


'So, what do you think?' Rachel asked Joe. They were in the bar at the Marriott Hotel just off Boar Lane. Joe had decided to return here for more comfort and managed to get a decent last minute rate for a change.

'I think we are awaiting the storm,' he said, 'we are yet to see the BFB's reaction and the more I think about it, I'm pretty sure they are not going to accept this easily as we thought.'

'What makes you think that?' she asked, 'I mean I don't disagree but I'm interested in what you think.'

'Holding's reaction made me think he was more worried about how it looks for him than our welfare. He may not do what we expected him to.'

'I don't know what to think, to be honest. I'm normally not the sheepish type but I'm pretty scared right now.'

'It's out there now and the calls will be coming. The boss was dancing a jig earlier from the hits he was getting.'

'Your boss might be happy but it isn't going to help me sleep at night.'

'I know. Sarah says I've a tendency to get carried away with my stories without worrying about the consequences sometimes. But trust me, I've not forgotten about the situation. Something clicked with me tonight when I was listening to you with Holding, there's more going on here than just this election, although I still can't get at the real story. I haven't shared all that's been happening with you or even Alex. There's a bigger picture here somewhere.'

'Ok I'm listening,' Rachel said beginning to get pissed off with him, 'perhaps it's about time you told me what barrel of shit you've just dropped me into.'

'First of all on the BFB side, there's someone secretly bank-rolling the new party. They are using numerous false names and addresses to get small donations under the wire. With internet banking it's easy to set this up on a mass scale and hard to track back legally, as the banks don't like sharing information backwards through a transaction. You need a court order to do it, and that requires some real suspicion of fraud based on evidence rather than just supposition. A colleague of mine was killed when she discovered who it was.'

'Ok, that's intriguing,' Rachel said.

'And the second thing, you know that my friend Sarah was looking into the death of her sister?'

'Oh yes, I remember your married friend Sarah,' she said amazing herself of the emphasis she put on married, maybe she was scoring a low point with him because he'd pissed her off.

Fortunately Joe ignored it, typical man she thought, doesn't even know when he is being got at.

'I think there's a connection but I can't make it for sure. The real reason I suspect a connection is simply because there are people dying which appears accidental but could just as easy be deliberate. Also, there's a similar political angle, although the politics is of religion and not nationalism. In my book, though the two things are not that different. Nationality, race and religion are linked.'

Joe went on to explain some of the details of the cover up of abuse by catholic priests through to the set up and funding of the BCA.

'The common element of this is deniability and corruption, that to me is an unhealthy coincidence but I cannot prove anything as yet.'

'I can see why you think that,' Rachel replied trying not to show how annoyed she was, not only with Joe but herself. She'd totally underestimated this whole story and realised she was in way over her depth. 'I wish I had known this all earlier, I might not have been so eager to put my head above the parapet. These people are bastards.'

Joe nodded in agreement

'So, given I'm right in the middle of your national conspiracy, you'd better tell me everything you're thinking,' she said sounding more calm now, 'where do you think this by-election fits into the whole picture?'

'It's obvious isn't it?' Joe replied. 'Think about it. What would be the implications of a nationalist party getting a foot into the House of Commons?'

'I guess it would give them legitimacy and a platform.'

'Exactly, it would escalate them from a minor party to a party with MP's and a seat at the big table. This would start a rollercoaster that might be difficult to stop. What has happened in Leeds would spread all over the country. The North of England is the power base of the Nationalists. This is where it would need to start. If they can get a foothold here, then it will spread across the North and eventually through all the inner cities.'

'I never saw it that way before, but I can't disagree with you.'

'It's so important for them to win this. They'll do anything to get over this hurdle as you're already beginning to witness.'

Rachel continued to take in what Joe was saying as the conversation went on. She needed to get away and warn Anna. Did Anna understand what she was battling against?

Looking at her watch, she told Joe that she needed to get back to Anna. She finished her drink, went up to the reception desk and spoke to the receptionist, who had a foreign accent, to organise a taxi for her. Rachel was so distracted that she made no attempt to even guess the accent.

Five minutes later the receptionist informed her that the car was waiting.

She said goodbye to Joe and walked out. She saw the typical Leeds black and white cab waiting for her and spoke to the driver telling her where she wanted to go. She got in the back looking forward to getting back to Anna's.

Rachel hadn't seen the man who came in to the hotel earlier to see the receptionist and explain that he was the woman's husband and she was to call when him she wanted a taxi. She didn't see the receptionist take the one hundred pounds passed across the desk. Rachel was unaware that the receptionist, the very same day, had been threatened with eviction by her landlord because she didn't have enough money to pay her rent. She had no idea how readily the receptionist took the money offered without asking questions.

She didn't see the front seat was occupied until the occupant turned round to her to announce his presence, by then it was too late to run.

'Evening Rachel,' said a smiling Alan Farmer.

She immediately tried the door but it was locked. The driver took his seat, started the car and pulled away. Fear, anger and panic rose all at once as she realised she'd been played for a total fool for the last few weeks and now walked straight into a trap.

# CHAPTER TWENTY EIGHT

The wine bottle dwindled down as the evening progressed. Sarah hadn't planned to drink a lot but the argument with Connor hadn't helped. He'd confronted her about Joe, although he had no real idea who exactly he was. He just knew she was seeing someone.

The argument took the form of all marital confrontations. The kitchen was the required location and although there were the to and fro of accusations it was amazingly devoid of emotion. It was almost as if it was something they had to get out of the way but actually neither was seeking a positive outcome. It was more about finding the level ground on which to move forward.

Connor wanted to know who Joe was and what she was up to. In response, Sarah hadn't wanted to get into who Joe was, as to her it was not important. She got more than enough satisfaction from informing Connor of his poor record as a husband and that she could have been sleeping with every guy in the street for all he cared about her.

The counter arguments flew back about her being the one who was not interested and since Jane was born she hadn't wanted anything to do with him.

There was just no heart in it and finally they agreed to do absolutely nothing, which is exactly what they'd been doing for at least the last five years. Neither wanted to disrupt things for Jane and neither had anywhere else to go. Sarah knew there was a fair chance that she could set up home with Joe but she didn't want to put that pressure on their relationship. One crap relationship was enough for a lifetime and she didn't want to rush into another. She agreed to keep her affair with Joe away from home and away from Jane for the moment and life would continue to trickle on just as it had done before.

Sarah couldn't resist sticking in a few digs about his continual late arrivals home and whether he was using this free time to satisfy the needs that Sarah wasn't fulfilling at home. There was a stern denial, which she shouldn't have been surprised at, probably playing safe for the inevitable lawyers at some later date. She made a mental note that she might have to do some of her own homework on her husband before that day came about, if she was going to get anywhere with a settlement.

So after all the excitement she got Connor back to the subject that had started this whole confrontation. She wanted to know where the court records for Lancashire cases were kept and asked if it was Burnley. As he worked as a barrister for the County Court he could access previous cases and he would know where to get them.

Naturally Connor wanted to know why, so she explained that she thought that was where Jenny might have been that day. She got away with a brief explanation which was a relief to her.

Connor confirmed that that the records would likely be in the Court office in Burnley. That was enough for Sarah to be sure that's where Jenny had been on the day she died.

The visit to Stephen Gorton had given her a lead that she'd followed up, but somewhere between there and the courts record office Jenny had set off an alarm bell to someone.

Joe said he would call when he got back but he hadn't yet. As she took another drink she looked again at her phone. She wasn't sure whether her stomached ached with desperation to hear from him, or whether it was because she'd barely eaten all day

Joe had returned to his room after Rachel left. At that moment he thought about ringing Sarah but the local news on TV took his attention away. They were talking about the body of a man in his twenties being fished out of the river at Goole. It looked as if the body had been in the water for a few days and most likely came from further up the river. Police were investigating all likely missing persons fitting the description.

Joe knew with no doubt that the body was Alex Thompson. He felt sick as he picked up the phone to call Eastside police station. If they hadn't taking him seriously before, they would have to now as he confirmed that Alex Thompson was murdered.

The news continued as he waited for a reply to his call. *'The investigation into the bombing of the Mosque has been officially linked with the terrible attack on a Muslim soldier three weeks earlier. The soldier was still in a coma and hasn't been able to speak to officers as yet. The police, however, have found identical DNA on the soldier's clothes to the DNA of the two suspected Mosque bombers who were released last week. The police are seeking the re-arrest of the two suspects and asked anyone with information on their whereabouts to inform the police immediately.'*

Joe turned the TV off, the call to the station still not answered. He grabbed his coat and headed for the door; there was no point waiting.

Across the city on an anonymous council estate was an equally anonymous block of flats, the same type that appeared in every cityscape in England. Like many others, this block was due for demolition but in the meantime provided suitable accommodation for people who could not be placed elsewhere. Most coming into this category were asylum seekers who fell well below the level of caring about their standard of living. Most people were of the opinion that if you were really seeking asylum then this had to be better than where you came from and if you were conning the system in order to get into the country then people would have been quite happy to offer them the way home as an alternative.

The problem was that these immigrants had become the untouchables of society along with the homeless littering the streets. The masses were happy to turn the other way as long as the problem didn't affect them. They chose not to see it and reassured themselves that the immigrants could get out of their situation if they really wanted. All this deliberate ignorance didn't solve the problem and left those in the middle of it little choice but to turn to crime and begging as the only ways to survive creating a further social problem for the city to manage.

Whilst Rachel Lancaster lay tied to a damp smelly mattress in the top floor of one of these decrepit apartment blocks the desperation and the poverty that these people lived in did cross her mind but only by way of trying to think about something else other than the mess she found herself in.

She was torn between irritation at herself for getting into this situation and anger at being kidnapped in the middle of fucking Leeds. It was just unbelievable that it could happen, but it had, and it happened to her.

She was such a controlling person normally and she'd lost control. This was worse than the pain where she'd been hit in the face and the bruises on her arms and body from the beating they gave her. That was superficial and meant to keep her quiet after the volley of abuse she gave them when they dragged her from the car into the flats.

The real horror was looking across at Lee Potter. He was hardly recognisable from the blood, bruising and swelling in his face. His uniform lay in rags around him. He was sleeping now and they'd left him alone since she'd been brought in. Lee wasn't important now; she was the one with the higher value.

Rachel had been dragged upstairs by two large blokes, if she wasn't mistaken they were the two of the guys she had seen with John Pilkington, but she couldn't swear to it. She was placed in this flat on the third floor of the block. She wasn't sure where exactly she was as it was an area of town she didn't know. It didn't matter, there was little she'd be able to do about it. It didn't matter how much noise she made, nobody in this building would complain to the police. The irony was of course that there was a certain body of police who knew exactly where she was.

Rachel had found Lee dumped in the corner already beaten. She'd gone to comfort him, feeling guilty that she was the reason he was here, but she was dragged back to her own mattress and restrained there. She'd tried to call Lee since she saw him at the weekend but he hadn't replied. She had assumed he was either working or couldn't return her calls. She felt so much anger as well as shame as she looked at him now.

She sat up against the wall, feeling the cloth ties cut into her wrist and ankles and tried to breathe to get control of her anger. She had to think, had to find her way out of this before it went a way she didn't want to contemplate. She looked at what she could see of the mattress and floor not wanting to know what had caused the stains and marks all over the large room she was in. It was like a scene from a horror film but that would make it seem too fake, too false... this was all too real. She recalled in the early days of the band, living out of bed-sits and the back of vans and remembered some pretty smelly and horrible places, but she would have taken any one of those places instead right now.

The most sickening thing of everything that had happened in the last hour, the thing that cut her right through the heart of her, was seeing Alan Farmer, her ex-boyfriend, someone she'd shared a bed with, was one of them. All the time she'd been keeping tabs on Pilkington and Davies they'd been keeping tabs on her. All the things that had happened had been designed to warn her off and she'd kept on walking into it. They didn't know exactly what she was up to hence the reason for sending Farmer in to her, but they knew who she was and what she'd been doing. She had never been in control and this was proof. She conned herself that she was better than them and she could fly under the radar. Now here was a smug Alan Farmer screaming in her face about how much of a stupid bitch she'd been. She couldn't help but agree.

'You didn't have a fucking clue, did you?' he said to her, 'you got all precious about keeping things private and that I should trust you. All you were really protecting was your dirty little snooping business.'

She said nothing resigned to his continued ranting.

'The signs were all around you. All the warnings and you wouldn't leave it alone. This was your own fault,' he ranted on mocking her, 'and then you see to it that my good friend John Pilkington goes off the rails. I'm sure he'd enjoy being here tonight.'

That was meant to scare her giving the clue that Farmer knew what Pilkington was capable of. But Pilkington wasn't here and she'd been lucky that being touched up during the scuffle was all the sexual assault she had to deal with. Small mercies, she thought to herself that Farmer wasn't that type but he seemed ruthless in plenty of other ways. She tried fighting back verbally but that just wound him up. Lee told her to be quiet, as she would get nowhere.

Eventually she asked Farmer what he intended to do.

'That's easy,' he replied, 'we are going to sit here and work out how you're going to withdraw that statement you made to the police.'

'You're joking aren't you?' she replied defiantly.

He then slapped her hard across the face. Her already bruised face stung even more.

'Deadly serious I think, we've got all night,' he said with real menace, 'between me, you and Lee over there, with a little help from our friends who brought you here, we are going to work it out.'

They left her alone for the moment but she knew they'd be back. She didn't know how long she could hold out or whether she should even try. Like most people the prospect of torture had not been something she ever been faced with in her life. She felt her bruises and tried to get some comfort on the smelly mattress thinking about what was going to happen.

Her thinking time didn't last long as the door swung open and Farmer walked in.


The sick feeling in his stomach grew as he returned the hotel. The hour at the police station hadn't done anything to make him feel better.

The confirmation of Alex's death was crippling him with anger and fear. He felt as if he'd been hit with a heavy weight punch in the gut. He'd totally underestimated the threat and the lengths they would go to protect themselves. Whilst there was no body he'd tried to reassure himself that Alex was safe somewhere, and that made him feel worse, two days had gone past with none of them doing anything about it.

This was the final nail in the coffin in any theory of coincidence. Joe was now sure that Jenny and Heather had stumbled on something that would have exposed somebody or something about this story. Whoever was behind this had taken steps to stop this exposure and murdered them, doing it in a way that offered no clue and no connection. It was only the luck or bad luck of his involvement and his chance meeting of Alex that meant they had a picture of what was going on.

He needed to call Rachel and Sarah and warn them, although looking at his watch it was fairly late now, nearly midnight.

The bar was still open so he decided to have a drink. He ordered a large Laphroag, a quality and distinctive single malt, from the top shelf and sat down at a table.

He took a sip of whisky and let the fiery smoky liquid swim around the back of his mouth. The burn had the desired effect of soothing the heavy ache in his stomach. As the burn subsided the smooth character of the whisky came through.

As its effect seeped into his body he focussed on what he needed to do next.

He called Rachel first knowing that it didn't matter what time it was, she needed to know that they had to stay safe, maybe Holding would give her some protection. He was frustrated to hear the call went to voice mail, so he left a message, surprised that Rachel would have turned her phone off.

Hopefully that meant she was safe at Anna's, so he tried Sarah next.

He was relieved to hear her voice as she answered it.

'Joe, where have you been? I've been waiting up to hear back from you,' she said to him.

'I'm sorry. I went back to the police station,' he explained the news about Alex.

'God, Joe, I'm so sorry.'

'I know, Sarah, I'm gutted too. I'll have to go and see Tina tomorrow at some point. This is awful. Alex was such a good kid.'

'Joe we have to stop this now, I can't imagine losing you the same way,' she pleaded.

'Sarah let's not go there, I don't think I can stop this now even if I walked away from it.' He was hoping that she would see they had no other choice now. 'My name is all over this now.'

They talked some more, Sarah explaining the conversation between her and Connor.

'I know it's not the time for making promises and I really don't want to put pressure on you, but I just want you to know that I need you Joe and I love you so much,' she said tearfully, 'I know I'm being emotional and probably pushing you too much but I need something to hold onto Joe, and I think you're it right now.'

'Don't worry Sarah I feel the same, I understand about your domestic situation and we can take our time to work it out,' he said, taking a mouthful of whisky to stop his voice from breaking. He hoped he'd reassured her.

'I just need you to stay in Carlton and look after yourself.'

'I'll go and see Russ tomorrow that's all. I need to talk to him about the girls for Jane's sake. I also want to mention those names to him and see if he has any clue about it. Jenny might have said something about them.'

'You might get thrown out of the house again,' he said.

'I might but I'm hoping he is a little less emotional than he was last week,' she explained, 'also I need to for Jane's sake, we can't let our differences come between the girls.'

They said their goodbyes for the night, promising to take care and that Joe would call in the morning before he went to see David McGhee.

Looking round the bar he wondered how much time he still had here. There were only one or two left now and he would soon start getting stared at by the barman.

He took out his laptop and found what he needed to see; an email from Fletch. The key to this would be found by connecting all the dots. As he'd hoped, a few more dots had been provided by Fletch and he wondered whether there was enough to paint the complete picture.

Fletch's mail was short and brief. There were the ten names, of which, Fletch had said six were not significant. The mail explained that of the four names left, one of them had interests in more than one of the companies and each one of them had links back to one place, Columbia in North Carolina, on the East Coast of the US.

'You can find the detail in the enclosures. I don't know if this is significant or not, but all of the four at some time in the eighties attended the "University of Columbia College for Catholic Education".'

Joe's eyes widened with excitement. This was it, the answer. He would dig through it further but it was obvious really. Where would you find religious fundamentalism mixed with racial superiority.

Naturally it was in the heartlands of the US where religious obsession was the norm and racial tension was integral to everything.

He looked at the four names he had from these companies. Terence J Rimmington, Henry van Leitjen, Carter Tate and Bill Roy.

He opened up the pages and started to look through the enclosures, focusing on the four names.

Henry Van Leitjen originally from the Netherlands, who now lived in the Dutch Antilles most of the time was the first name he checked. He was Chief Executive of Starling Holdings, which owned two of the businesses listed on the BFB website. It was an Investment Company taking shareholding in other businesses it considered strategically useful or 'Cash Cows' from which it could make money. He was also a non executive member of the board of the SAS Security that was managed by Carter Tate. Terence Rimmington was the owner of the Social Investment Company. Tate and Rimmington were both Americans. That left Bill Roy who appeared not to be in a controlling position in any company but was on the board of each of them. That must mean something in terms of overall influence as he was the common factor.

He didn't see David McGhee on the significant list which he found a bit odd, given his previous reading on him. He decided to come back to McGhee, moving on the personal profile of Roy. Focussing initially on his picture, he wondered whether it would give an indication of what he was about. He studied it, just a small face shot. He got the feeling that he knew this guy and had come across him before.

Reading the profile that Fletch dug up, he immediately noticed that the guy was English but had been based in the US for many years. He had many business interests in the UK and Europe but his base was the US. The profile didn't give any further details about his English origins but he was convinced that he knew him.

He spent some time looking through the company details and another name struck a bell; Professor Andrew Bebbington, a professor of American History from Louisiana originally. Checking out further details he found that he lived in the UK and not only in the UK but in the North of England. He was said to be one of the richest guys living in the UK with numerous business interests coupled with his academic interests.

He was no longer working academically, apparently retired from the university and now performed an honorary role. According to Google, Bebbington had published numerous papers on the social history of white America and how ethnic integration was undermining the American way of life. It seemed, from the general gossip on the internet, his position in the US had become untenable and he was seen as openly racist and anti immigration. Bebbington had denied all of this, but had left the US preferring to settle down with a less public profile. Joe remembered where he'd seen the name. Alex had mentioned him in the notes on the party operation. He apparently provided some much needed intellectual bulk to party policy. Of course he wouldn't have been able to make donations as he wasn't a UK citizen. Was it his money flooding the party illegally?

Joe summarised on his notepad what this told him overall.

There was a group of wealthy businessmen with connections to the UK; they were strongly linked to a fundamentalist Christian College with an interest in white supremacy. Was it too much of a leap to believe that this group of people were trying to manipulate and buy an election in the North of England to suit their own political aims? Well, why not? The North of England and the East End of London where the working class were numerous and frustrated by minority ethnic groups dominating the political agenda were hotbeds of English Nationalism. This large population of traditional Labour supporters disappointed in a Labour government that had done nothing for them, were ripe for exploiting. If you wanted to transform the nationalist movement from a bunch of no-hopers into a dominant political force this is exactly where you would start.

So Joe now knew the motivation, and he also knew what they were capable of. He even had a good idea who the people were behind it. This didn't constitute any kind of proof but he wondered whether he actually needed it. The BFB had achieved so much on the basis of deniability. There was the Mosque bombing, the murders, all of which were done without any direct links to party members or specific individuals. Therefore like Rachel had done with Pilkington he could put out a story about the party making any allegation he liked as long as it could not be linked to any individual.

He started to write the story that he hoped would not only undermine the BFB, but break the whole story wide open in the press.

# CHAPTER TWENTY NINE

*Wednesday*

The phone call on Wednesday morning didn't come as a surprise and she was grateful that it was a remarkably civil conversation.

'Mrs Sayers, as you may be aware from the press this morning, an allegation has been made that you deliberately withheld information from the police. We'd like to ask you some questions about this matter,' the inspector explained. 'However as we don't want this to be a media circus it would be better if you could come to the police station this morning at a time convenient to you.'

'I did have a busy morning planned, I'm standing for election tomorrow you know that,' she replied playing out her role showing her expected self importance.

'Mrs Sayers, we are well aware of that which is why we are doing you the courtesy of allowing you to come here of your own accord in your own time. Would you prefer I sent a car to your house right now as I would normally do in this situation?'

Lucy looked out of the window at the mass of media. She hadn't even been able to go out for a run this morning. Personally she would love to have had the attention of going to the police station with a very public denial of the whole thing, but Pete wouldn't thank her for it and it wouldn't be good for the kids.

'I'll be there at ten,' she told the Inspector and the call was ended. She would have her media circus but it would be outside the Police Station and not her home.

As she discussed with Andrew this morning, until anyone had any concrete evidence to charge her with something, she would deny it and stay on the attack. Andrew had told her that the allegations would go away, as he fully expected Rachel Lancaster's statement to be withdrawn.

She returned to the newspapers and to the TV news, enjoying the fact that she and her party were headline news. Yes the publicity wasn't exactly positive but they'd been there many times before and it really didn't affect their hardcore supporters. Lucy knew that one person would still be panicking and therefore the next phone call was not a surprise either.

'Lucy, why have I got five police officers searching the premises?' Patrick Barclay asked her, 'I also see that Joe Barker has gone with a whole piece on allegations of electoral fraud and illegal funding.'

'I didn't know about the electoral fraud stuff but the rest is all over the newspapers. They haven't got anything I'm sure if it,' Lucy replied sounding tired of him already.

'Is it true?' he asked.

'Does it matter Patrick?' she replied.

'Of course it matters; we've been over this so many times,' Patrick said to her in a tone so superior she wanted to scream how insignificant he was in the pecking order.

'We cannot be seen to be going back to our old methods or we will never win this election,' he said, sounding more agitated now, 'what about this new stuff, it says that our funding is not legitimate and that there are numerous false addresses given for donations? They reckon our sponsors are funding the party illegally.'

'It's got nothing to do with me. How the hell would I know about that stuff? Anyway, I'm going down to Eastside later this morning to make a statement, they won't find anything and we should be able to turn a negative into a positive just like we did with John Pilkington.'

'Lucy, I really hope there's nothing to find, because if there is, you're on your own.'

'Patrick, I haven't done anything,' she lied, 'and thanks for the faith in me, by the way. Nice to know who your friends are when your back is to the wall.'

The self-righteous tone worked wonders as he backed down.

'You know I'm right behind you, so don't get so defensive.'

Satisfied she'd shut him up, she moved the conversation on.

'You'll have to do the meet and greet with the boss when he gets here.'

'Yes, no problem, I've made all the arrangements,' Patrick said, 'I spoke to Kevin last night, he is bringing some of the sponsors to show them how well we are doing. If you're out of the station in time for the teleconference, maybe you can make a statement then, denying everything, and turning it back on the media.

'Great idea,' she said, 'we could really sling some mud then.'

She finished the call on a high ready to make the performance of her life. Lying had become natural to her in the last few weeks as she grew into the role. The key to a successful lie was to never compromise on it. The lie had to become the unassailable truth and this was how she'd play out the day. There could be no question that she was in the wrong, and by default that meant everyone else was.

Patrick would never see that, but then he'd already admitted right at the start of this process that he could never win. They both agreed about that, but what Patrick couldn't possibly understand was that a campaign like this would never be won with just a great candidate. As Andrew Bebbington explained to her, it needed a wholesale change in the mindset of the people. A revolution in thinking that would see the country return to itself. The pattern would repeat across Western Europe as white indigenous populations would learn that it was ok to be racist, it was ok to demand that your country was not undermined by people who didn't respect your way of life.

Her election to the Leeds North seat would be the signal that the revolution had started.


Sarah stood outside the front door of her brother-in-law's house not sure of the welcome she would receive but she felt there was no choice. The door opened a few seconds after her sharp knock.

'Sarah, what are you doing here?' he asked, surprised, but not uncivil. That was a relief for Sarah.

'Russ, I know you said not to come, but I need to talk to you about something,' she said.

'It's ok. To be honest I wanted to talk to you anyway. Come in and see the girls.'

Russ smiled and opened the door for her to walk in. Sarah was visibly relieved and actually quite shocked that he wasn't still angry with her. It was almost as if the previous conversations hadn't happened. She walked through the hall towards the kitchen almost on air.

'I'm sorry about what I said to you, it was just the stress of what happened. I hope you can forgive me.'

'Yes of course,' she replied still amazed, she'd never heard such gracious words from Russ in all the years she'd known him.

As she opened the kitchen door she was welcomed by two girls running to her, so pleased to see their Auntie Sarah.

She sat and talked to them for a few moments until told them to get ready for school. Sarah promised to come back and see them later, with Jane, checking with Russ who was nodding in agreement.

After the girls had gone he asked what she wanted to ask him.

'I don't want to stir the pot again,' she said, 'but I would like to show you a picture and see if you recognise anyone that Jenny may have known.'

'I thought we had been over this,' Russ said.

Sarah went back to her speech, knowing she still had to tread carefully.

'I know, I know, trust me I don't want to upset you or cause any issue. But there's something going on and I think Jenny may have known. Please bear with me, I promise if this comes to nothing then I wont ask you another thing about it.'

'Ok, let's get it over with.'

Sarah showed him the picture she got from Mrs Cullen with the five boys. Sarah explained that the one on the left was Adrian Cullen, the boy found in the grave that Jenny witnessed thirty years ago.

'How did you get this picture?' he asked.

'From his mother, I visited her because of what I found. Do you recognise anyone?'

He seemed to think about what she said, taking it in, deciding whether to challenge her. Finding nothing wrong in it, he answered her.

'Sort of, but to be honest could be anyone. Who are they?'

'They are five boys who were Altar Boys at a church in Preston. There's evidence that some, if not all of them, were abused by the priest whose care they were in.'

'That's terrible,' he said in complete surprise, 'you think that this young lad was killed because of that abuse, maybe because he talked?'

'I don't know to be honest, but something like that happened, and there's a good chance that one or more of these boys knew what happened and may even have colluded.'

'Have you been to the police with this?' Russ asked

'I've talked to them a couple of times and they told me they were following up their enquiries, but they are not connecting anything to Jenny.'

'But you are?'

'It depends on whether my theory is right and that Jenny knew who one of them was.'

'If the police don't think there is anything to it, then why should you know anything better?'

'Because she was my sister and I know her. Which I know doesn't mean anything really but does mean that I see things from a different point of view…her point of view.'

'Who are they?' Russ asked intrigued himself now.

'This one is Ian Hamilton, pointing to the first face, I've met him and he said he didn't know anything, this one is Stephen Gorton, he died a few weeks ago not long after Jenny visited him in hospital. He was definitely abused by the priest, which resulted in him spending a number of years in mental institutions. The next one is David McGhee who we think is a company directory very much involved with the church.'

She didn't mention the BCA link as she didn't want to arouse any defensive reaction from him. She thought she saw Russ's eyebrows rise in surprise as Sarah mentioned McGhee's name, but maybe not. 'This one I haven't been able to trace and goes by the name of Roy Hunter.'

'I haven't heard of David McGhee,' Russ said. The lack of reaction in Russ was beginning to disappoint Sarah; she really had though that he might know one of them. Then he spoke again. 'I do know someone called Hunter.'

'Roy Hunter?' Sarah jumped in.

'Did he have any other names?' he asked.

'Not sure why?' she held her breath waiting to hear the confirmation.

'Let me look at the picture again.'

He stared at the picture hard for a moment.

'It could be him, although a lot younger than I ever knew him.'

'I know someone very well who I know as William Hunter. I know his middle name was Roy as when we found out about it, we used to call it him a lot to tease him. He said he used to get called that a lot at home and he didn't like the name.'

'Shit, I know who you mean. I don't know why I didn't spot it before. He was at the funeral, you introduced me to him.'

'But this guy couldn't have anything to do with Jenny's death. I mean he's been our friend for years, we met him at university. He was part of our group of friends back then.'

'So it's definitely him?' Sarah asked, not listening to Russ for a moment.

'Roy is a deeply religious person and a successful business man. It was him who got me involved in the BCA. He couldn't possibly have been involved in this. I know him.'

'Did Jenny mention him, in connection with this?'

'Jenny did ask me once about William, but to be honest I put it clean out of my mind,' Russ said to Sarah's relief. He was actually opening up to her now which, showed not only did he trust her, but that he had nothing to do with it.

'She asked me if I knew whether William had said anything about abuse from a priest when he was younger, I told her it was ridiculous, but perhaps it wasn't I even asked William about it afterwards when I saw him a few days later at a faith meeting I went to.'

'You spoke to William about this?' Sarah didn't want to say the words as the penny dropped and she knew what led William Hunter to kill her sister.

Sarah wasn't sure what to say, she didn't want to upset him anymore but she was already convinced that her theory was right. She decided to be diplomatic.

'Maybe he did or maybe he didn't know anything, but there's no denying that is Roy Hunter your friend. He may well have known what happened to Adrian Cullen and may still be able to help the police clear up the situation. Do you know where he might be now?'

'I told you he runs an investment business, not really sure of the details, he never discussed it with me and I never felt the need to check it all out. He is not often in the UK so it was just by luck he was around for Jenny's funeral.' Russ continued to scratch his head, 'you're not going to the police with this are you?'

'I think I should. Maybe he can help, maybe he doesn't even know that he could help with the investigation if he is out of the country.'

'I don't think you should go to the police without talking to him first, it could all be very embarrassing for us and for him,' Russ said, as he checked his watch. 'Look, I've to go to work soon. Promise me you won't do anything about this until we talk about it more.'

'OK,' Sarah agreed, not sure at all that this was a promise she was going to keep.

She fired some more questions whilst she had his attention, wanting to find out as much as she could.

In the end, Russ insisted he had to get ready for work and she left, happy that not only was she back on terms with him, but she knew what happened to Jenny. As she got to her car she noticed the car across the road from her had a broken headlight. Her mind racing quickly as the recognition came back to her that this was the same car she'd seen yesterday in Preston. It was an Astra with a broken headlight. There was no doubt. The person at the wheel was deliberately looking down at a newspaper so she couldn't see his face.

Her heart was pounding with excitement and fear. She was being followed and had only just realised. She memorised the number plate, before getting into her car and driving away. She dug out Sergeant Timm's card then drove to Bury Police Station. This time she wasn't taking any chance, whatever was going on; it was time to make sure her family were safe.

The lane up to the house at Ilkley was a long one, the owner clearly enjoying the privacy the road provided. Joe Barker felt quite tired after the longer than expected journey getting around Leeds. The combination of a minimal sleep and an early start hadn't helped his energy levels but he put it out of his mind as he approached David McGhee's house.

It was a large stone house at the back of the monastery buildings although, still part of the same complex. The house, an old stone cottage, was backed by large trees with open views at the front over the Wharfe valley towards Ilkley. It was a beautiful, peaceful and magnificent setting as the noise of the traffic and city life kept its distance on the other this side of the valley.

He walked to the large wooden door and knocked. A large middle aged woman with heavy make-up and a business suit answered the door.

'Joe Barker,' he said to introduce himself, 'I phoned yesterday to arrange to see Mr McGhee. I'm sorry I'm a bit late, it took a bit longer than I expected to get here.'

'Oh yes, it's no problem, Mr McGhee can still see you. Life is fairly relaxed here and we don't run tight timetables,' she explained politely, 'please come in.'

She followed him into the old house. They wandered through a narrow doorway, then dodging a low ceiling before entering a comfortable room with French windows looking over a small private garden. An open fire provided welcome warmth from the cold blustery day. A large cross alongside a number of religious themed icons and pictures lined the light coloured walls, telling the story of the man's faith. David McGhee sat in an armchair reading a newspaper. As he looked up and acknowledged his presence Joe tried to sense whether he saw someone who could be coordinating all this trouble and in truth he couldn't see a single hint.

He was a similar age to Joe yet he could have been ten years older from his dress and his manner. The blue blazer, cravat and starched shirt belonged to a different generation. He was completely bald wearing thin glasses that just didn't look right. Where most people of his age were seeking fashion thick framed small glasses this guy had gone the opposite way.

'This is Mr Barker, the journalist who called yesterday,' the woman said to McGhee.

'Hello, David McGhee,' he said as he collapsed his newspaper to stand up, politely.

'Nice to meet you,' Joe said as he reached out his hand.

He asked Joe to take a seat offered him a drink which he gladly took.

'How can I help you?' McGhee asked.

Joe settled down and recalled his prepared opening.

'I've been looking into a story that happened sometime ago in Lancashire when you were at school. It involved the disappearance of a boy called Adrian Cullen,' Joe looked at McGhee for some acknowledgement of the name but he didn't give anything anyway. Maybe that was this guy's business acumen because he didn't show it any other way.

'I understand from Adrian's mother that a David McGhee was a close friend of Adrian, along with three other boys and I'm speculating that you're the same David McGhee.' Joe listed the names of the other boys as he knew them.

McGhee listened carefully to Joe's statement acknowledging the words. He paused before responding whilst he thought further.

'What is your interest in this?' he asked, telling Joe that he had come to the right place.

'I'll be honest with you Mr McGhee,' Joe went on, 'I was witness to Adrian's make shift burial all those years ago although I had no idea at the time what I saw. You may or may not know that the body was discovered recently and this has uncovered a shocking story about what happened to Adrian. I'm here because I believe you were aware of what happened and I wanted to find out more about it. Am I right?'

Again McGhee lapsed into silence before he spoke again.

'Adrian has never left my conscience in all the time since he passed away. It's eternally sad what happened, and I've prayed for him every day since.'

He must have caught Joe's less than sympathetic look as he turned on him.

'You may look at me like I'm stupid but believe me I'm nothing of the sort. If you're just going to sit there believing me a misguided fool then you may as well leave now and write your story. Nothing I say will change your mind.'

'I'm sorry I didn't mean to give that impression, please go on,' Joe said by way of an apology.

'I didn't go that night before you ask, so I wasn't with him when he died. But I was always fully aware of what happened. Stephen told me soon afterwards as we both shared a disgusting secret at the hands of Father Doohan. We helped each other through it. You see we both had suffered abuse, details of which, I would rather not share with you. Suffice to say he took advantage of our vulnerability and used the good book to scare us. Fortunately both Stephen and I sought solace in each other and found true peace in the Lord.'

'Were you aware that Stephen died recently?'

'No I wasn't. I haven't been back to that area for many years and quite frankly I spent many years trying to put this to the back of my mind in order to focus on doing some good in the world. It may sound a bit simplistic to say that but it's true. I chose to spend my success paying the Lord back for being my guiding light throughout my life.'

'Stephen unfortunately never quite succeeded as well,' Joe explained the circumstances of his death.

'That is tragic,' Joe saw genuine emotion in his face, 'Stephen was never as strong as I was. As I left for university he struggled with his exams and seemed to lack confidence. We lost touch after that.'

'If Stephen told you what happened that night perhaps you could explain it to me if you wouldn't mind.'

'Stephen swore me to secrecy and I kept that secret to this day. Stephen was so scared and it seemed the right thing back then, although of course I would see it very differently had it happened now. From what I understand it was an accident but not a pure one, if you consider that the circumstances should never have occurred. Stephen and Adrian were together with Father Doohan, as he always liked them to be, after the service. They were his favourites I think. For some reason Adrian resisted him that night, Stephen never knew why but I guess for all of us there comes a time when we can't take anymore. Adrian struggled and Father Doohan lashed out at him in frustration, Stephen went to protect him but only managed to knock Adrian over. He hit his head on the stone fireplace and died immediately. It seemed Father Doohan panicked and called a different priest to help sort the problem. Stephen had gone home that night scared about the whole thing and was told not to say anything for fear of damnation. You see Doohan made out that it was Stephen's fault and that particular trick was extremely useful in keeping a young boy's mouth shut.'

'What happened next?' Joe asked.

'Stephen said they called him back early the next day on the premise that he had extra services to do. That was when they took the body to be buried. I didn't know it was in Bury and neither did Stephen, it could have been anywhere.'

'You said that you were not the one who went with Stephen that night, does that mean the other boy was Roy Hunter?' Joe asked.

'Yes exactly, Roy was another one of the group but he seemed more devout, more loyal, than the rest of us. I wouldn't say he enjoyed the experiences but he somehow accepted what happened as if it was the price to be paid for being favoured at the church. Doohan would have chosen Stephen and Roy for the simple reason that Stephen could be scared into keeping quiet and Roy would just see it as his duty to do it.'

'Did you know the priest they asked to help?'

'No, not at all but Stephen said he scared him even more than Father Doohan,' McGhee explained.

'Do you know where Roy is now? I haven't been able to trace him,' Joe asked.

McGhee seemed to snigger a little to himself as if he was enjoying a private joke.

'Roy was very clever, he seemed rather sensitive about his past so adapted his name over the years. He dropped the name Roy after leaving school and preferred to be called William or Bill. Roy was just his nickname at school which they used to distinguish him from another William in the class. Everyone knew him as Roy in the end and then after university it was always Bill. In later years, as he went into business, he was even more protective of his past and dropped the Hunter, and referring to himself with both his previous nick names, Bill Roy. Imaginative don't you think?'

Joe nearly dropped his cup from his hand in shock. It was so obvious and yet it wasn't. William Roy Hunter had become Bill Roy severing any connection with his past. The next question leapt from his mouth.

'If he was so worried about the past how come you knew all about it?' he asked.

'As you know we have been in business together. We stayed connected through our faiths and naturally we were both successful so shared certain paths.'

'Talking more broadly, you are aware that some of these businesses are supporting the new Christian Association I assume?'

'Yes of course, it was my proposal. I saw it as a positive move for the country and for the church, anything that brings more people to the church is a good thing in my view.'

Joe found himself believing what he said. Throughout the whole interview he'd been remarkably frank and sincere. He'd keep pushing though.

'Are you aware of the BFB and that some of your friend Bill Roy's business's are supporting that party?'

'Not entirely, but it doesn't surprise me. And you refer to Bill as my friend. I'm sorry but we never really were friends, more acquaintances. When Bill went to the US and started to grow his businesses I'm afraid he developed some more extreme views that I would never profess to understand. The university he went to in the North Carolina rather nurtured an unpleasant obsession with race that I couldn't get to grips with.'

'Ok I understand what you're saying,' Joe said. 'Are you absolutely sure you were not aware of Stephen's death and the discovery of Adrian's body?' he asked, finding an easy question needing time to think about where all this took him.

'I really had left that life behind and I think you can see what the focus of my life is now. I am, though, extremely sad to hear what you've had to tell me today and that is the only reason I felt compelled to tell you more about it. I have to say I wasn't sure I welcomed your tone to start with.'

'I'm sorry about that, but there's more to this than I have let on. I'm afraid at least four people have died in the last few weeks who all knew something to do with this story and I'm desperate to find the person behind it so that no one else dies. I'm sorry if that sounds melodramatic and my tone with you more challenging than you might like, but it's the truth.'

'That's terrible,' he said, 'do I take it by deduction that you believed myself or Bill Roy to have something to do with all of these deaths? If that is the case then I have to tell you that I hope you can see that I had nothing to do with it and perhaps that points you in the direction you need to go.'

Joe heard the words and took it all in. This last half hour had completed the picture of what this was about. The BCA was not connected to this conspiracy at all. That was just a coincidence. This was about one person protecting his past so that he could control the future. The one gap left he needed to work out was what Jenny knew that had got her killed. That was the last piece of the puzzle that would lead him to Bill Roy.

# CHAPTER THIRTY

Cold, damp, smelly, sore, humiliated, frustrated, ashamed, angry, Rachel wasn't sure which one was worse, but she felt each of them in a continuous cycle throughout the night. She'd flittered between consciousness and fitful sleep as the hours had passed until the morning came and the awareness that her humiliation would be complete when she made that call.

Unless some miracle came charging through the door, she would have to do it. She didn't see any white knight charging in. Just like Alex, no one knew she was even missing yet, perhaps they wouldn't decide until tomorrow when she didn't turn up or maybe if she was lucky Anna might get suspicious today after she wasn't at work but she may just have thought she'd gone back home last night. She would be annoyed with Rachel for not telling her but that would be all. Rachel hadn't told her everything that was going on so she had no idea of the risk she was under. Joe Barker may have tried to contact her but he would have no more sense of whether she was missing or not, all he would know was that she didn't answer his phone calls.

No, this was all down to her obsession with trying to deal with things on her own.

She looked across the room at the unconscious Lee. Despite the fact that she'd begged them to stop, they still used the baseball bat on him for a good while afterwards. That was their tactic; they had come to the conclusion that beating a woman, other than a few slaps and fists wasn't much sport. The mental torture of watching them beat Lee much more productive.

She couldn't stand to see Lee hurt on her behalf, but they had done it anyway just to be sure any resistance was completely broken.

It was all about her agreeing to call the police this morning and withdraw her statement. They had also pushed her to reveal who she was with in the hotel so she told them about, but only said that he'd wanted to interview her about Alex's disappearance. They'd pushed her for more but they hadn't connected him yet to the article in the press about the party. That had been a relief.

The two animals, beating Lee, seemed to take so much pleasure in it, which had sickened her more than anything. There was no humanity in their eyes.

Farmer had to pull them off in the end as he told them Lee was no good dead. Rachel held on to that throughout the night. They were no good dead. She had no doubt that was the final solution but for the moment they needed Rachel to withdraw that statement and Lee was the leverage. She would ring the police but as she informed Farmer when he was in her face screaming at her, the police would only allow her to properly retract the statement if she went down to the station in person.

This had stopped them in their tracks and caused an argument. From that moment on the dynamic had changed. They knew they could persuade her to make the phone call, that was the easy bit, but how could they control her going to the station and withdrawing that statement?

Then she realised they'd hold Lee over her, it was quite simple, unless she made that statement, they would kill Lee. They could withdraw it later but who said this would be the end of it?


The taxi pulled up outside Eastside Police Station where a barrage of reporters and photographers were waiting for her.

She climbed out with her solicitor, provided by the party management, and was immediately surrounded by the reporters with cameras and recorders shoved in her face. She managed to edge her way to the steps and strategically turned round as if listening for the one question she wanted to answer. Her solicitor stood quietly by, like a loyal servant. He started to speak over the shouts.

'Ladies and Gentlemen, my client would like to just say one thing and won't be taking questions at this moment.'

The noise died down allowing Lucy to begin her statement.

'I will fully cooperate with the police in their investigations and I will make it clear that the article in the press is not only false but libellous. My colleague here is already taking steps to have the original claims refuted and a full apology printed. I will make a full statement at the scheduled press conference later.'

She turned and they both walked into the reception, it was five minutes to ten. Just as she planned, she thought to herself. She spoke to the officer on reception and was asked to take a seat.

Ten minutes later an officer in a scruffy suit and loose tie introduced himself as DCI Holding and apologised for keeping her waiting. She suspected he wasn't sorry at all, but she kept her polite manner and they followed him through to the interview room.

'Mrs Sayers, thank you for coming so promptly,' he said as they settled down in the chairs. He switched on the tape recorders and formally introduced himself and the female Detective Sergeant, Gilhead, who sat next to him silently. Her look said everything about her view of Lucy.

'Please state your full name for the tape.'

She did as instructed saying nothing else. Her solicitor Malcolm Greenhalgh also introduced himself.

'Mrs Sayers, can you tell me where you were on the afternoon of Sunday 18th October 2009?'

'I imagine you have a very good idea of where I was on that afternoon,' she said firmly.

'Please can you confirm it for the tape,' he replied.

'I attended the BFB party rally in City Square that afternoon. After that finished my colleagues and I went to have a drink in the Printers Arms in South Leeds.'

'What time were you at the Printers Arms?'

'I was there from approximately three until five o'clock.'

'Do you know a police officer by the name of Mark Davies?' he asked continuing to linger around the point.

'I do know him in a professional capacity, he's helped to organise some security for our meetings. As you know our meetings seem to attract unwelcome attention,' she said with a wry smile on her face.

She could see that already the DCI wanted to say something other than what he could. He continued his questions.

'Did you know him in any other capacity?'

'I'm not sure how that is relevant Detective Chief Inspector but given I've nothing to hide and I'm sure Mark doesn't either, we got on well. I wouldn't say we were close friends but we were well acquainted.'

'Did he assist you in any party matters?'

'Again I'm not sure this is relevant and I know where you're going with this, so let me make one thing clear before we continue any further with this charade, Mark Davies is not a member of the Britain for British party and has never been. Is that clear for you Detective Chief Inspector?' she asked with supreme assurance rising in her voice.

Holding carried on ignoring her sarcasm.

'In the time you were at the Printers Arms that afternoon did you speak to or see police sergeant Mark Davies?'

'No I didn't.'

'Did you at anytime step out to the street and speak to any officer in a police car?'

'No I didn't,' she said even more firmly.

'Did anyone else with you mention that they'd seen or spoken to him that afternoon?'

'Not that I'm aware of.'

Holding stopped speaking for a moment.

She was enjoying this, especially watching a tense Holding look for another way around the questions. The only sound in the room was Malcolm Greenhalgh busily taking notes. Whilst she was enjoying the tension, she wasn't aware that for each of the lies she told, her hand was continually placing her hair behind her ear. A body language expert would have known she was lying, and whilst Holding wasn't an expert he definitely suspected she wasn't telling him everything.

'When was the last time you spoke to Mark Davies?'

Lucy wasn't expecting that question. She gave it a second whilst she tried to recall the last legitimate conversation they had. Most of their conversations were on Pay as You Go mobiles so there was no trace of a link between them.

'I spoke to Mark at the weekend to ask him if he could tell us what was happening with the police investigation into the Mosque bombing. We were naturally concerned that the rumour mill continued to link the two young adults you had in custody to our party.'

'Was it in fact true that those two young adults were linked to your party?'

Malcolm Greenhalgh was about to speak but she beat him to it.

'I'm not even going to respect that question with a response. You have no basis to ask that,' she answered with a pretence of anger. She knew the allegation would come and had prepared her response. She was happy he was getting to the real point of the exercise.

'I can ask whatever questions I like,' he said angrily, 'Mrs Sayers as you are well aware a substantial allegation has been made to us that you met with police sergeant Mark Davies on the afternoon of 18th October 2010 at the Printers Arms, at a time he stated he was with the two young adults mentioned previously. In my mind that constitutes a link with you and your party. May I make it clear that it's a criminal offence to knowingly withhold information from the police and I have enough here to hold you under the Prevention of Terrorism Act.'

She laughed, but her hand went up to her ear as usual.

'Don't lecture me about withholding evidence and corrupt actions. You let go your suspects and from what I hear on the news they were the same two who brutally attacked that soldier. Now you're trying to find another scapegoat for your incompetence.'

Holding ignored her and seemed furious that he wasn't getting anywhere.

She went for the kill, 'I think I've made myself absolutely clear. I'm well aware of who gave you this information and I should warn you not to pay too much attention to a woman who has nothing better to do than spy on members of my party and fantasize about fantastic conspiracy stories. It's bad enough that the media take her seriously but now she's managed to convince the police. Have you finished with your questions because I really have better things to do than listen to any more based on the fantasies of a lonely mentally ill woman?' she reached for her coat regardless of what Holding was saying.

'I have no further questions, but I may want to ask you more at another time,' he stated trying to engineer control to the end of the meeting, but it was too late. She was already at the door and stared at him as she left noting that Holding knew he'd made a mistake dropping the terrorism act in. There was no evidence and other than Rachel Lancaster he had nothing else. He was in a leaky boat in a sea of bullshit.

Lucy walked out of the interview room and then out of the police station with Malcolm Greenhalgh following behind like a pointless accessory.


Leeds rarely was the centre of UK news and politics, but the political temperature of the nation was due to be tested today and was everyone's last opportunity to stake their claim on the landscape. The news focus on the racial tension in the city and the approaching by-election day had set all eyes on Leeds, as this week would dictate the future of politics.

The conservatives were looking to turn a long running poll lead into seats in the next parliament. This would be a key test to see if they could win potential swing seats in a constituency with a decent labour majority and fearing the challenge from the split political make up they had sent the big wigs to try and pull out some media interest. The labour government, fearing an embarrassing defeat, had put every minister they could through the seat in the last week.

None of this attention from the party leaderships changed anything. All media eyes were focussed on only one aspect of the election; the effect the Mosque Bombing would have and whether this would be a win for the BFB. The political columnists and news editors were in absolute panic about the potential consequences of such a win fearing the same reaction in the general election with the BFB gaining more seats in the North on the back of this. It was said the people of Northern towns such as Halifax, Burnley and Oldham where the BFB already had a large following, would be watching the outcome closely.

It was this same political focus that the new Christian pressure group the BCA decided to take advantage of as a key part of their Day of Action, hoping to use the opportunity to spotlight their own agenda in a city where the world was watching.

A few hundred protesters had assembled, with the permission of the Police, in Millennium Square. The new large open space in front of the civic hall was an easy place to bring together a large amount of people and judging by the crowd it was a successful strategy.

Only a small number of police and community support officers turned up as they hadn't expected much trouble from a protest with an average age over forty. It appeared that the population mix was a sound guess and the police took a relaxed view, happy to leave them to it.

The crowd, holding a large number of varied banners, started their chants with one or two cheerleaders at the front with fog horns. Someone had brought a large speaker and a music player which encouraged the BCA supporters to sing upbeat hymns in an attempt to excite the crowd. The banners though were the main amusement for passers by watching, with every religious cause of recent years highlighted, *ban gays*, *ban abortion*, *ban stem cell research*, plus those claiming there only to be *One God*, others prayed for the *damned to be saved*. It was a real collection of disparate, confused messages that were intended to attract attention of the media, as well as the candidates of the election.

The weakness of the message and the little hope of getting any attention from the media quickly became very apparent as not one journalist could be seen in the square. In other circumstances, in other by-elections, this may have worked but today, the BFB were controlling the agenda and all the media had gone to the other side of the city centre to await Lucy Sayers' press conference.


One hour after leaving Ilkley, Joe Barker was in front of a furious DCI Holding again. As soon as he'd left McGhee in Ilkley he'd picked up the message to come back to Eastside as soon as possible. That was after the first message from his boss back at the Agency telling him he better have something to back up that article he put online last night otherwise they'd drop it. The lawyers had clearly started their day's work.

This time when he arrived at reception there was no waiting around. He was herded straight into an interview room.

'Do you have any idea how much I can charge you with for wasting police time?' Holding fumed.

'What are you talking about?' Joe shot back.

'I'm talking about your fantasist girlfriend you rolled in here yesterday, you know the one who sat in front of me, with you goading her on, talking the biggest pile of bullshit I've heard in years.'

'That was not bullshit and you know it; every word of it's true,' Joe said, very confused. Something had happened.

'What's going on?' he asked.

'I had a phone call not so long ago from your friend Rachel Lancaster. She said and I quote, 'I'm sorry to have wasted your time but I was really upset at my friend going missing and wanted somebody to blame. I decided to make up the story about Lucy Sayers and Mark Davies because I believed they were involved together. I now know this is not true and it was wrong to do it. I want to withdraw my statement.'

Joe said nothing at first and then before Holding could start speaking again he jumped in quickly to get control of what would happen next.

'This is bullshit and you know it. Rachel Lancaster is no fantasist. Somebody has got to her, I tried calling her last night and she didn't answer her phone. Somebody has taken her and told her to do this.'

'Do I have to listen to this?' Holding shot back at him.

'You can't be taking this seriously, after everything that has happened?'

'Mr Barker I wasn't born yesterday, so don't take me for a fool. I've had so many people come in here making every claim under the sun, and then the next day walk straight back here and withdraw those wild claims. Some are fantasists, some have been got at, some might have numerous other reasons but the fact of the matter is that if she comes in here and signs a statement retracting yesterday's one, we've nothing to go on and this investigation is over.'

'So she hasn't been here to sign it, it was just a phone call?' Joe asked.

'No not as yet.' The DCI replied.

'Then please do me a favour, don't take it seriously until she walks in here and signs that statement herself. I'm telling you this is not right.'

Holding just laughed dismissively and walked out the door.

'Am I free to go?' he asked the DS as she followed.

She nodded at him.


Rachel was still in the same place an hour later after making the call. Farmer had gone somewhere and she was left with Bill and Ben in the next room. Lee hadn't said anything when she tried to speak to him but she could hear him breathing, which was reassuring.

It was only a temporary relief because she believed that they both would end up dead in the end, whatever way it played out. They'd seen too much for the BFB to simply let them walk back to normal life as if nothing had happened. They would play this game as long as it took for those polls to close tomorrow, after that everything could be denied and the publicity gained from winning the seat would bypass anything that Joe could throw at them. He could sling as much mud as possible without any decent back up from witnesses he would have nothing.

She came to the conclusion she would have to look after herself and leave Lee for the moment. She couldn't deal with him as well right now. He wasn't going anywhere. If she could work out a way to get out then there was a chance that she could get the police to raid the place before he suffered anymore. That was a big if for the moment and short of jumping out of the window still tied to the mattress she didn't have much of a clue how to escape.

She'd been trying to listen to what was being said in the other room where they'd been talking. There were numerous calls in and out and they hadn't taken much interest in her and Lee. She couldn't make anything out though. She resigned herself to the fact it made no difference what was said, the outcome would be the same. Fed up of doing nothing she resolved that whatever was going on she would start taking some gambles and try to determine her own destiny.

Over the next few minutes she put her mind to trying something. Firstly she needed to get free of the mattress. Her hands were tied behind her using torn up sheets tied to the loops on the mattress. It meant she could move around on the mattress quite freely but she couldn't lie comfortably because one arm was always lying awkwardly under her body. If she could get free of the mattress then she figured she could make a run for the door. Getting to the door would be high risk but she thought it was better than lying here. Her chances of making it were less than fifty-fifty but there wasn't an alternative.

She smiled as she realised what she could do.

In her handbag she had a pocket pen knife in the inside pocket and she figured that if she could find a good reason for them to bring her bag over then she could sneak it out. For a change, there was one advantage to being a woman and it was the one thing men could never deal with. Periods. She could claim it was her period and she needed the pads from her bag. That would give her access to her bag and a man would never go routing to find tampons or towels.

She didn't act on it immediately but spent the time thinking it through, what she would do and the risks involved. It kept her mind sharp and positive. She went over it again and again, the repeated patterns of what they did and who was coming and going.

It was just a question of whether she had the bottle to do it.


Qamar Akthar and a small number of his friends gathered at the top of Corporation Street,. They came into the centre once again looking for trouble. Over the last few days the election had become a focus for their actions. Previously it had just been a laugh, but as Qamar got more and more involved and encouraged by his mates, it began to put pressure on him to respond.

He still saw himself as different from them believing he had more ambition and potential than many of the lads he knew. He saw himself as someone who had a clue about things. The rest were like sheep, doing what their bosses said, thinking they were clever because they were in with the crew. Qamar had been the same at first, just fitting in, but he'd quickly found his own voice. Now it was him they were listening to, it was him they were supporting and encouraging.

The only reason that he didn't succeed at stuff before was that people didn't listen; they were too quick to dismiss him, not to trust him. Nobody gave him the chance to prove himself until now. This whole business had showed him how he could affect things. He saw it on the news each night with the reports, the words of disgust at what he did. Qamar didn't feel any shame about that, taking immense pride in his rebellion against those people who had pushed him away.

Even one the gang leaders had spoken to him last night, telling him he was a cool guy with a big future.

Qamar had watched the others respecting the leader as he gave out instructions. He saw the plans they were making knowing this was about more than just the Mosque bombing.

The election was now the focus because they understood that this was where the big stories were at. People were so precious about voting and inclusiveness here, so much bullshit he figured. He didn't care about that, never had, he'd just wanted his dream and it was taken away from him. He could see now how these precious these elections worked, supposed proof of civilisation, proof that they were better than everyone else. Qamar could see a way to bring down their delusions and to see how fair and civilised society was when your skin and religion were different.

As he watched the Christian protesters in the square he told his mates that they could scare the shit out of them, but no violence. This was just about getting in their faces.

As he got them all together, he smiled looking forward to showing them how it felt to be intimidated.


'Lucy, finally we meet,' the voice belonging to a large hand reaching out to her, 'I've heard so much about you and looked forward to this moment for a long time.'

'Thank you,' Lucy Sayers replied, 'it's very nice to meet you also. I've heard plenty about you too.'

The polite wordy response belied Lucy's nervousness.

She stared at the man who she knew had prepared her for this moment and tried to take in his stature. It was not that he was tall or wide, he just seemed to have a presence and charisma that meant his personality filled the room. Everyone was immediately drawn to him. His accent, a combination of broad Lancashire mixed with an American twang, and vocabulary that made for a unique sound. His bright, staring eyes stood out from his strong face and fading grey hair.

Next to the man, were Andrew Bebbington and Kevin Inkerman. They both stood nodding in unison, Andrew smiling directly at Lucy as he spoke.

Patrick Barclay hovered by her side. She noted in see his face that he was desperate for an introduction to the chief.

'This is my colleague Patrick Barclay,' she said, 'Patrick has been a major factor in the strengthening of the party in this area and building the public profile. Patrick this is Bill Roy.'

'Hi Patrick, yes I'm aware who you are and the good work you've done, from Kevin and Andrew. I want to offer you a big thank you for getting us to this point.' He put his giant hand out. Patrick responded with an enthusiastic handshake.

'It's a bit unfortunate about all the negative news flying around today. I'm really sorry you had to arrive in the middle of this,' Patrick said. Lucy could see he was trying to play down the significance of what was happening. He wasn't expecting the response he got.

'Patrick, one thing you have to understand is that not only is this not a problem, it is in fact exactly what we wanted to see. Winning elections is all about creating a following and a passion for change. This kind of passion only comes from necessity and adversity. This country's politics is full of apathy and disenfranchisement. People will only come out to vote for change when they see something they believe in being beaten into the ground. What you see here is national identity being threatened and anyone who speaks up is abused. The good people of this area recognise this is happening and are turning to us in droves. The more distance we can put between those people teetering on the edge of supporting us and the middle ground, the more we appear as the only alternative. The more we fight the more we create gaps between the national psyche and the liberal wets.'

'You mean to say this was all meant to happen?' Patrick asked aghast as his party thinking and planning was being undermined by this enigma in front of him.

'I didn't say that as such, now did I?' Bill replied patronising Patrick, 'I just said that this situation was actually quite positive and I'm looking forward to Lucy standing up there in a moment and giving a statement to our friends in the press that will put another thousand ticks on that ballot paper.'

Patrick didn't respond. He knew this was an argument he wasn't going to win. This guy was way out of his league. Lucy watched him retreat into the background to find an ally. He averted his eyes from Lucy unable to face her. She could see from his reaction that he knew he was not needed here and that she was in fact the only star on the Bill Roy's horizon.


Joe Barker was furious when he left the police station, but he wasn't sure who to be furious with. He couldn't blame Holding although he appeared to take a reasonable amount of pleasure in pissing Joe off. His one hope was that Holding hadn't dismissed what he said. That told him that Holding also believed something wasn't right and that might buy him some time. He tried Rachel again and got no answer which confirmed that she was still missing as far as he was concerned. Knowing Rachel the small bit he did, he had to believe she wasn't flaky and she was being forced to do this.

He wasn't sure where to go to next and in the end decided on the BFB press conference. He heard about the arrest on the news in the car and that there was to be a press conference afterwards.

He made his way round to the City Varieties club where it was being held arriving in time to see Lucy Sayers taking the microphone.

Initially he recognised a few faces from the rally last month, but not every one had taken their seats so it was hard to see who was who.

The assembled media suddenly stopped muttering and focussed on Lucy Sayers as she began to speak.


'I want my handbag as need to go to the toilet,' Rachel said to the bull dog as he came through the door in response to her continual banging on the wall.

'You went this morning; you can hang on for now,' he replied, 'besides you didn't need your bag before why do you need it now?'

'Because I'm a woman you stupid ass, why do you think women need their bags when they go to the loo?' she replied angrily at him. He looked confused as if he didn't understand the question.

'Bloody hell I knew you were ugly but I didn't realise you were that fucking stupid as well,' she shouted at him, 'I have my period dodo, and unless you want smelly blood swimming around in here then I suggest you give me my bag so I can change my pads. Now is that too much to ask or can your tiny little brain not understand?'

His face flushed as Rachel's rant had its effect.

'Ok ok, I'll get it, but you try anything and I'll slap your mouth so hard you'll be sucking on soup for the rest of your life,' he said turning away.

A moment later he returned giving her bag a quick check over to see if there was anything she could use. Luckily Rachel kept her penknife in an inside pocket so she always knew where it was when she needed it.

'You can take out what you need in front of me and take it with you. I'm not letting you take the bag.'

She was expecting that but hoping he might not. She had to go with plan B which was a sleight of hand. Rachel wondered how sharp he really was. The good thing was that he didn't try to get her towels himself. Most men seemed to treat tampax and sanitary towels as if they'd catch a disease touching them.

Her hands were shaking as he undid the mattress ties. She was desperate to pull this off. When she was free he handed her the bag at arms length, as if it wasn't his business to know the goings on of a woman's handbag.

Consequently he wasn't watching closely as she delved in the bag. It gave her that necessary moment to slip the penknife out and into her hand wrapped in some towels.

In that second she thought about rushing him with the knife but she didn't know if she could do it. He was just so big and she would likely come off worse so she stuck with the first idea.

'Ok you got what you wanted. Go and do what you need to do,' he said aggressively but she began to think it was a bit of an act as his heart wasn't really in hitting her. Somewhere at sometime a woman had attempted to civilise him and that was perhaps the bit of luck that was going to get her out of here. She walked into smelly horrible bathroom. Normally she would never entertain such a disgusting toilet but this was her one chance to prepare her escape and she didn't want to lose it.


'Ladies and Gentlemen,' Lucy Sayers began, 'thank you for coming this morning. 'I'd like to use this opportunity to explain what has been happening and put our side of the story. So often we find ourselves forced to put up with the spurious allegations, myths and rumours that circulate around. We are just a political party like any other political party who just want to stand up and speak honestly and positively for the people of Britain. This week it seems I've been branded a racist, a Nazi and now it's capped off with conspiracy to murder.'

There was a lot of murmuring and noise in the room in reaction to the Lucy's bold uncompromising statement.

'I will not answer specific questions about what happened, I will just say that I've cooperated fully with the police and I'm completely innocent of the allegations made. I believe the person making these allegations saw something she wanted to see and was seeking attention for her own peculiar aim. This is part of a concerted attempt to discredit our honourable party.'

Joe Barker seethed at the back of the hall. He wanted to jump on the stage and beat that confident smirk off her face but he knew he couldn't say a word.

He had to think about what could have happened to Rachel. They clearly hadn't killed her otherwise the statement couldn't be signed. That's it; they were holding her somewhere until they could force her to make that statement. She'd been kidnapped, she must have been. Otherwise he couldn't see anyway she would have conceded the situation. They were holding something to make her do it. His mind went round and round thinking about how it could have happened, but he had no idea what. He continued watching the stage, his mind working overtime.

All the time the press conference continued half his brain was thinking while the other half stared at the other reporters to see their reaction to the vile lies that were spouting from Lucy Sayers's mouth. To the side of the stage her allies stood smiling and lapping up every word. Camera's flashed everywhere. He was looking at the local girl, made superstar.

Joe went through each face one by one trying to remember their names and profiles. He put his hand in his briefcase matching their faces to the stuff from Fletch that he printed off earlier.

He saw Kevin Inkerman, the party leader, but he knew him already from the TV. He saw Andrew Bebbington, the university professor. There was James Worthing, the TV chef who had the appearance of a scruffy bulldog. The next face jumped out at him like a firework. He recognised him instantly, and knew that not only did he know who it was but he'd even met him.

The papers he'd read last night had a familiar photograph but with the different context and names he hadn't made the connection. This was Bill Roy, the same guy Russell Bowes had introduced to him three weeks ago as William Hunter. The situation with Rachel slipped away as new bells and connections raced through his mind. He swore as he realised how everything had happened. He needed to speak to Sarah straightaway.

He stepped outside the hall and made a call.

No reply, damn where was she? He cursed himself for not thinking about her earlier and now he didn't know where she was. She had left a message earlier for him to call but he hadn't had the chance before.

Just as he turned to go back into the hall, his phone rang.

The scene in Millennium Square was fast turning into chaos. Twenty or so Asian intruders made their way into the crowd of BCA protestors. It didn't take long for panic to spread. The BCA realised quickly that conciliation was not on the Asians agenda and they started to scatter in fear.

The relaxed police presence had been slow to do anything. It took some loud screams from the crowd to make them move, and then with no actual violence going on, just a lot of argument and noise there was little they could do. They eventually attempted to separate the groups but with the panicking crowd it was becoming more and more difficult to manage.

Radios were crackling appealing for support which became more frantic when they saw a new gang of white faces approaching from Great George Street. Everyone's attention turned to the hundred or so amassed white men not carrying banners or making a protest, but carrying baseball bats and clubs of any shape or size available. Dressed in the uniform of well known sports brands, each face was covered with plain scarves, football scarves, towels anything to disguise their identity and increase their menace.

The BCA protesters ran in panic in the opposite direction, shell shocked that their meagre protest would end this way. The Asians looked at each other, trying to decide what to do. Should they stay and fight or was that a folly given they were so outnumbered? It was clear they faced an ambush. For days the Asians youths had been turning up in groups in the city centre, targeting various sites and it was only a matter of time before one of the gangs came looking for them.

The gang started to run at the crowds, their menace complete and intention clear. The police on location had no chance to stop this and were totally outnumbered. Their radios crackled with messages to organise reinforcements. Faced with the same choice as the Asians they'd come to control, they had to turn and run themselves.


Rachel leaned back on the mattress waiting for the moment. She knew that she only had one chance and she had to get it right.

Farmer hadn't returned so far this morning leaving only the two goons standing guard including the one who had given her the bag. She wondered if Farmer had gone to work, something as mundane as his day job continuing whilst this was going on was crazy.

Once she returned from the disgusting bathroom she allowed him to re-tie her wrists already having hidden the knife under the mattress. She decided to wait a few minutes after he'd gone so that he would settle back down and not suspect anything.

There was a TV in the kitchen and her trip to the bathroom had confirmed that this was where they were sat. As she walked past, she observed that the door was slightly ajar. She could see there were two plastic chairs in the room and not enough space for them with the door open. Even if they had their back to her, there would still be a reasonable gap in the doorway through which they could potentially see her sneak past.

She had racked her brain over this because she knew it was highly risky, but short of jumping out the window and killing herself, she didn't see any other option.

She needed to pull together every single element of her body and mind so she could do this. Simple as the plan seemed, it was going to be difficult to pull off. Could she really just walk out of the door with no one noticing?

The answer was yes, in theory. Providing they were looking the other way; if they didn't see her and if she made no noise. Were there too many 'ifs'? Once through that door, she had a chance. It was the chance to break free and run. They might chase her and she would have to run for her life but she had a chance and she was not going to miss it.

Now was the time. Rachel felt for the knife, deftly opening the blade as she'd rehearsed earlier.

She started to cut.

There was no going back now.


Joe Barker was back in the police station a few minutes after Holding's call. A car had picked him up outside the City Varieties and using sirens had raced round the east side of the city.

He was sat in the interview room again only this time he was looking at a laptop with a casually dressed Sergeant Mark Davies telling a story that had to be seen to be believed. It appeared for all his nationalist sympathies Mark Davies didn't trust his allies as much as he didn't trust his colleagues in the police force.

The video showed him in his room, dressed casually in jeans and tee shirt wearing what seemed to be a trade mark arrogant smile.

*'If you're watching this, then it's clear I didn't get out of town quick enough. Let's get the simple stuff out of the way so I can get on with telling you how you stitch these bastards up. I had a feeling that once that nosy bitch Rachel Lancaster had seen me that night this would all start falling apart. I also know that they would look to make me the fall guy. Fair enough, I knew that was the game and they'd want to protect themselves, but they also knew that once I was*

*named and shamed, I might decide to share the load and starting
naming names.*

*I knew they wouldn't risk that and the time had come to take
myself out of the equation. I wasn't going to stay around to be turned
over by my so called mates in the force or in the BFB. If you're
watching this then it's more than likely that I was right and they
were going to take me out.*

*Just in case you're giving Tog a hard time over me he doesn't
know anything. I chose to leave this with him because he was outside
the loop on this. I aint going to name anyone on the force so don't go
trying to turn this on any of them. You know as well as I do, plenty of
the guys have the same views as I do, just not all of them were
prepared to take action like me, they are too shit-scared of the
political correct brigade to say anything that would let people know
the real truth of what goes on, on our streets.*

Joe watched with mixed feelings, it was good to get some of
Rachel's suspicions confirmed but at the same time here was an
obnoxious racist cop almost able to generate sympathy due to the
fact that he ended up on the wrong end of all this. He would make
sure anything he wrote about this and made the distinction and that
this guy deserved everything that came to him.

*So getting to the real reason I'm sat here like a fat turkey
blurting away waiting for the cleaver. You need to get that two faced
bitch Lucy Sayers down the nick and let her tell you about how she's
playing the princess one minute and arranging her own little mafia
racket the next. I was just one of her tools for making things happen,
making witnesses disappear. But don't make the mistake of thinking
she's the brains behind the outfit. She likes the smell of money and
power and she's quite happy to suck any cock to get it. Also as you
can see, she'll tread on any fucker she thinks is in her way. This is
one hard faced bitch. She came from a bucket of shit and I reckon
she'll end up with her face back in that bucket before too long.*

*She's done well I'll credit her, but if I'm going down for this then
she's coming with me.*

*In this package with this video you'll find records of mobile
phone calls, emails and meetings between me and her. Also
conversations I've had with people she put in touch with me,
especially the goons from SAS security who she sent round a few
times needing a bit of local knowledge. Isn't it fantastic to have a
political party with its own private boot boys, bit like having the IRA
running round the streets, but just because they have a badge and
pay cheque they are perfectly legal. You want to pay them a visit*

*because whilst I might have covered for those little fuckers who blew up the towel heads, it was them who arranged the whole gig. It won't stop there by the way.*

*So that's it, nothing more to say. Do what you like with this because I'm already fucked.*

Joe got the impression that Davies wanted to say more and wanted to find some final words that would have some meaning but in the end realised that it was pointless as whoever was watching didn't really give a shit what Mark Davies' view of the world was, and this video had one purpose and one purpose only; revenge.

Joe watched Holding throughout and could see a tinge of sympathy as if he were watching the last words of a friend.

'There it is, on a plate,' said DCI Holding flatly.

'How long has he been missing?' Joe asked.

'Since the end of his Monday night shift. He didn't come back in last night as expected.'

'How did you get the tape?'

'I spoke to a few officers who knew him. One of the sergeants came in once it became clear he was missing. He'd left this package with him a few days ago saying that if anything happened to him then he should give it to me. 'Don't get me wrong Davies was a bastard and he made me look a fool over those arrests, but this is gold dust.'

He went on showing his grudging respect for Davies.

Joe decided not to get into an argument over this.

'What next?' he asked, 'this is far more than I gave you, what about Rachel?'

'We are preparing the papers for the arrest of Lucy Sayers and a warrant to search her house, BFB Offices and SAS security.'

'Do you believe me now that Rachel was being harassed into retracting that statement?' Joe asked.

'Seems fair, but we've no idea where she is or who she's with.'

Joe pleaded with him that she was in danger and likely kidnapped. He acknowledged what Joe said and gave it some thought.

'I'll put out a bulletin for her but at the moment we don't have anywhere to start looking. I will need all my team on the Sayers arrest.'

'That's the worst thing you could do. If they know that Sayers has been arrested and the whole thing is blown they are going to run for cover. Do you think they are going to leave any witnesses?'

'I've got no choice. I cannot sit on this evidence. I cannot allow a situation to occur where I have firm evidence against murderers and

I don't take immediate action. Can you imagine the reaction if someone else gets killed today because I didn't move quickly?'

'You said it,' Joe screamed back, 'you said it, you'll have another death on your hands if you do this, and you know it. You make those arrests then you're going to kill her as much as if you put your own hands around her throat.'

Holding eventually gave in to Joe's rant.

'You've got an hour; Lucy Sayers is not going anywhere. I'll use the time to prepare the warrants. You can have two of my officers to help, but if you can't find her or any sign of her in that time then I have no choice. You've seen yourself there's a war starting out there and this one thing will likely stop it. I can't hold back on that much longer.'

'One hour?' Joe asked.

'One hour.' He replied.

# CHAPTER THIRTY ONE

Rachel stood in the hallway waiting and listening. She could see the door to the flat a few metres ahead of her, and she could hear them talking in the kitchen. Her heart was racing and she was absolutely terrified. She turned round to see Lee still lying on the other mattress, sleeping again, which was a relief. She was sure he would tell her to sit back down but she needed to get out. She couldn't wait any longer, and the longer she stared at the door the more likely she would get caught. One turn of the weak lock and she would be out.

She made the first step which felt like the first step on a bed of nails. She didn't dare put pressure on her foot, not for fear of the nails but for fear that once she did, she would need to make a second.

'Come on Rachel,' she said in her head. This time she moved to the second step knowing she couldn't stop now, she had to go. She didn't turn her head as she passed the kitchen. She didn't know whether they saw her or not and now it didn't matter, she just had to get through that door.

A chair scraped on the wooden floor, feeling like a hook dragging her back, but it pushed her that much quicker.

She was at the door, quickly turned the lock and was out into the open landing. The smell of piss and stale garbage rushed into her nose but she didn't care. The door slammed behind and now she was not even considering whether they were behind her. She just had to keep moving. Down the first flight of stairs, down the second, no sound behind her yet. She kept going, feeling the concrete steps tearing at her stocking feet. She had to keep moving. The last staircase and the street beckoned.

She turned on the last landing.

It was something she hadn't planned on, but momentum was with her, as she balled her fist and slammed it into the face of Alan Farmer. She felt something break on contact as blood spurted from his face. She wondered whether that large stone ring on her finger had done some serious damage. God she hoped so.

Alan Farmer had been as surprised as she was to see her flying down the stairs and had quickly made a grab for her. Whether it was strength, determination or just momentum that got Rachel past him she didn't care. She just kept going.

It was then she heard the first sound of the goons from the flat as they realised she had run. Rachel looked over her shoulder as she ran out into the street seeing them pass Farmer and follow her. Apart from the odd car the street was deserted. There was no sanctuary here she just had to run.

'Finally I found you,' Sarah screamed down the phone, 'What's going on Joe?'

'I can't explain everything right now. Have you seen the TV Sarah?' Joe explained relieved also that she was ok. She hadn't responded to his earlier messages and he was desperate she didn't end up the same way as her sister. He was in the front seat of an unmarked police car looking for potential locations around the streets of East Leeds where it was believed they were keeping Rachel. A quick trace of the mobile phone call Rachel had made earlier that morning to the police station, had given them the clue.

'I saw it yes, why? What's going on?'

'I've just seen Bill Roy the guy funding the BFB, and I know exactly who he is and how Jenny knew him. He is the guy we met with Russ at Jenny's funeral, William Hunter.'

'I know I've been trying to call you all morning to tell you that Roy Hunter was at Jenny's funeral. I talked to Russ this morning,' she shouted at him.

'You mean Russ knew this guy well?' Joe asked shocked at another revelation.

'Yes they were friends at University. She quickly explained what Russ had told her. All this time you were looking for connections on websites, but it was as simple as Jenny finding out that Stephen Gorton was a witness at a Father Peters' trial and going to see him as the only one who knew anything about Peters' history. Stephen told her everything and Jenny had asked Russ whether he knew anything about Williams's connections to Peters. Russ must have called Hunter to talk to him about what Jenny said. That is why he put the frighteners on her. He knew who she was all along. Hunter had been watching Jenny since she had been at school, the one link to his past.'

'Why didn't he tail me?'

'I don't know, Joe, but maybe he didn't know who you were, maybe it was Peters who told him about Jenny, and he saw her as the weak link. It doesn't matter, she was going to Burnley to get the court records of Doohan's latest abuse case where Stephen was the witness and she was probably going to go to the police with it, Joe that's why they killed her.'

'Yes and a guy like Bill Roy had a lot to lose if his name came up in this. He also had the money to make it happen.' The circle was complete.

'Look Joe it didn't end there. The nurse at the unit was arrested this morning for Stephen Gorton's murder. She explained how he'd followed her since yesterday recognising the broken headlight. Hunter had been paying him a retainer to keep an eye on Stephen Gorton and to report all visitors. When Sarah had followed in her sister's footsteps he'd been ordered to see what she did.'

'You're safe now?' Joe asked.

'Yes I'm back home now, I feel safe now the police have arrested him, what about you?'

'I haven't got time to explain right now but I have to find Rachel. It's not over yet.'

Joe ended the call and went back to working out how he was going to find Rachel in the forty or so minutes he had left. He'd been given two detective constables to work with, an older bloke he didn't know and the woman Detective Sergeant Gilhead who had sat in the interviews with Holding.

Time was running out.


Rachel managed to lose them for a moment running through some passage ways and into the park. She had doubled back into the estate and so far they hadn't spotted her. Still she had no idea where to go. Then she saw something that she never thought she would ever use again. They used to be the lifebelt of the community until the age of the mobile phone. Only now, desperately running round the streets with no money and no phone, did a telephone box provide the rescue she was so desperate to find.

She sprinted to it desperately hoping it worked.


They continued searching East Leeds. It trace had been from a phone in this area and given there was no shortage of abandoned, run-down housing in this estate then it was not difficult to think that this would be a good place to hide her. They had driven up and down numerous streets but nothing had jumped out at them, although he had to wonder what he really expected to see.

The police radio burst into life.

CHARLIETWO just had a 999 come in from a telephone box on James Street in your vicinity. Caller says she has escaped from kidnappers, name of Rachel Lancaster.

Gilhead picked up the radio.

'That's the one,' she shouted into the radio, 'on our way. Say again James Street? How long ago did the call come in?'

'Confirm James Street, telephone box three minutes ago.'

'OK we are on it,' she replied.

Joe started to believe that this was going to work.

The radio continued on and the words snuffed out that moment of hope.

'CHARLIETWO the caller didn't complete the call, we told her to wait but she never replied.'

The tyres screeched as the car turned heading straight under the fly over and back into the estate.


She was bouncing round in the back of the car where they'd shoved her. Blood was pouring from her head where she had banged it on the roof of the car.

Rachel was furious for allowing herself to be caught again. She had stopped in an obvious place and they had found her too easily. She should have run or hidden from them for longer. She wouldn't give up. She would try again. This wasn't going to end without a fight.

As she bounced around the back seat of the car, she swore she could hear sirens.


Within seconds it seemed police cars were everywhere on the estate.

They were at James Street within a minute.

She had to be nearby; she couldn't have run that far.

The radio was constantly screeching with noise of failed chases and sightings. But also with some other major incident in the centre of Leeds. Joe couldn't make anything out and wondered how anyone understood it.

Then he caught something he did get, 'A woman is being dragged by two blokes into Carson Flats.'

Once again the tyres screeched as the car was turned round.

They hit her hard this time, and it hurt. She fought and fought, kicking, lashing out at anything so they couldn't get her out of the car.

She knew they could and eventually they did overpower her, but not before wasting a valuable thirty seconds or a minute stopping the thugs getting her. Once they dragged her out, the bald headed one hit her hard.

She could taste blood in her mouth and her face felt swollen, the pain from the night before screaming through her again. She continued to struggle and put up a fight but she didn't have the strength to keep holding them off. In the end they dragged her, her feet and knees scraping on the road.

It was then she heard the sound of sirens screeching into the close where the flats were. Instinctively the thugs turned to see what was happening and that one moment of distraction was enough for her. She struggled and got free. She started to run again, she wouldn't get far she knew that, but this time there was some where to run to.

# CHAPTER THIRTY TWO

Five minutes later everything had changed. Rachel Lancaster sat in the back of an ambulance with Joe Barker holding her hand, whilst a paramedic cleaned up her wounds.

The Close had filled with police cars within minutes and the kidnappers arrested. An ambulance was called and Lee Potter was to hospital. Rachel wanted to go with Lee, but Joe insisted that she get treated properly for her own injuries.

Joe called DCI Holding and explained the situation.

'You gave me an hour and we got her out. You can do what you need to do now.'

'Yeah I got all that from Gilhead. We're on it now.'

'You want me to come with you?' Joe asked, 'I want to see the face of Lucy Sayers when you pick her up.'

There was a pause on the line as Holding thought about his response.

'OK jump in with Gilhead, she's coming back in now.'

'I'm coming too,' Rachel said, suddenly pushing herself out of the chair, 'I wouldn't miss this for the world.'


Qamar Akhtar lay in the back of an ambulance himself, not by choice, but because he couldn't move. The pain in his back where the baseball bat had repeatedly struck was searing through him. The bruises from the police batons the week before had almost healed but it all came back again with the beating he took.

They had no chance, once the whites started to run at everybody, they were forced to seek cover. They were overrun in seconds and their plan of winding up the Christian protestors seemed such a stupid and pointless idea that he cringed thinking about it.

He didn't see what happened to the others, with everyone splitting and spreading there was no way to know who got away and who didn't. The noise of sirens, and screams from the attackers, the police and everyone else, all blended into one noise.

As he lay on the floor in the centre of the square he could just see feet shuffling and interchanging with flying blood. He lost all sense of what was happening. Then it all stopped and calm returned as ambulance and police staff seemed to be the only ones in view.

He hadn't wanted to be taken as the ambulance would mean Police and questions. Trouble would be on its way. It wasn't the worst thing on his mind though, the pain took care of that. To push it away, he tried to think about other things. The thought of revenge was the one thing which drove him on.

Joe and Rachel managed to arrive ahead of Holding at the Marriott Hotel ten minutes later. He updated them on the riot that occurred in Millennium Square, and the city now was going into lock down as every copper in Leeds was on the streets. Neither had believed that anything like this could be happening on the streets of Leeds, and he wondered whether Lucy Sayers had any sense of what she had done. Joe would love to ask her but Holding had given them strict instructions to wait outside until he arrived as he wanted to make sure every thing was together.

From what he picked up after the press conference the BFB party members had all headed to the Marriot for a reception for the party leadership and sponsors.

Joe jumped out of the car as they arrived ignoring the request to wait. Gilhead shouted at him as he left the car so he ran round to her door.

'It's ok I'm not going to give the game away, I just want to get in position to see what's happening', he said, not stopping to get a reply, I have a room here so it won't be suspicious.'

He ran into reception and noted on the reception board the room for the BFB meeting.

He headed down the corridor to the private room that had been booked and hung around outside trying to work out what was happening. The door was open and a waiter came out.

I'm not sitting here like a spare part, thought Rachel, as she followed DS Gilhead into the hotel.

The DS had decided to follow Joe, not wanting him doing anything that Holding wouldn't have liked. She must have known that she would get the blame. Left alone in the car she decided to go as well. Her head was still hurting and her feet were sore, but she wasn't going to sit it out.

She found DS Gilhead in reception looking for Joe, but he was nowhere to be seen.

'He'll have gone to the Millennium Room, that's where they are,' she said to Rachel as she began to march down the corridor. 'You should go back to the car; you're in no state to be in here.'

'No way, I'm not sitting out there and missing this,' Rachel insisted.

'Gilhead seemed to relent at seeing the determination on her face and perhaps was glad of another pair of hands, even in Rachel's state.

They went together along the corridor to the conference room where they found Joe Barker standing in the doorway staring into the room. Inside, a number of people were milling around with drinks. The meeting hadn't yet started.

'I can't see Lucy Sayers,' Joe said to DS Gilhead.

'That's because I'm here.'

They all turned to see Lucy Sayers stood behind them.

Before any of them could speak, Lucy got there first.

'I don't know what you think you're doing here, but you're not welcome. This is a private…'

She didn't get to finish the sentence as Rachel grabbed her and pushed against the wall.

'You fucking evil bitch, you're finished,' Rachel screamed in anger at her.

She didn't get to land the punch that was coming as she was pulled off.

'You need to get that woman away from me,' Lucy screamed back, trying to retain some dignity, whilst she worked out how Rachel could be in front of her.

'Lucy Sayers, I'm arresting you on suspicion of perverting the cause of justice,' Gilhead said, placing handcuffs on her in a surprising efficient movement.

The noise of the confrontation brought the party members out of the room.

Lucy wasn't going to keep quiet now.

'You're stupid if you think you can make this arrest stick. I told your Chief Inspector this morning that you didn't have a shred of evidence.'

The Sergeant, who'd heard it all before, ignored her anger.

'You're going down for murder,' Rachel screamed at her, 'I'll make sure every one of your evil actions is uncovered.'

'You're fucking delusional, if you think I'm going down for anything,' Lucy replied losing any last shred of dignity she had left.

'What the fuck is going on here?'

It was DCI Holding as he arrived at the crowd with a posse of other officers. At the same time other protests were going on around them. The scene was becoming chaotic.

Joe pulled Rachel away for her own good.

He couldn't deny she had guts, but she looked like a mad woman, her hair and clothes torn, dried blood everywhere and screaming like a banshee.

'Come on, they've got her. It's him we want now,' he said pointing down the corridor at Bill Roy escaping in the melee, 'he is the one who is really behind it all.'

'Who is he?' Rachel asked as they followed him out to reception and out to the front of the hotel.

'That is Bill Roy; remember I told you yesterday about my national conspiracy as you called it. He is the conspiracy and the bastard is getting away again.'

They watched him climb in the back of a Black BMW, which tore out of the complex onto Boar Lane.

'What the fuck are we going to do now?' Joe said, as he watched in frustration.

Rachel held her hand out dangling a set of keys.

'Gilhead left them in the car when she followed you,' she said smiling.

Joe grabbed them, not stopping to think.

'You coming or what?' he shouted as he got to the car.

'I suppose I've come this far,' Rachel said, not sure this was such a good idea.

The next moment he was in the car and it was moving.

'How mad do you think Holding is going to be right now?' he asked laughing, almost proud of his own rebellion in stealing a police car.

'Not as mad as if we actually manage to keep tabs on him,'

'Which way do you think he'll have gone? He can't have got that far in the Leeds traffic.'

'I think he would have to go down towards the railway because of the one way. My guess is he'll run for the motorway, with millennium square closed off I bet you can't get round the city loop,' she said as they turned south out of the city.

Fortunately the lane opened up for them and as the lights changed they passed under the railway bridge.

They took the road out to the M621 junction. One hundred metres ahead, stuck at the next lights was what looked like a black BMW, 'I think that's it, but I can't tell from here.'

As the traffic moved ahead, the lights changed to red, two cars in front of them in the queue. Joe banged his hand on the wheel in frustration and then in a moment of madness pulled out round the traffic onto the opposite side of the road, and tore across the junction just as the traffic from the side road began to pull out. Horns blasted but he made it across and round to the motorway junction.

'May as well get done for reckless driving as for stealing a police car hadn't I?' he said, shrugging his shoulders.

Rachel said nothing. She didn't know what to say but like Joe she didn't want this guy to get away. For all that, she wasn't at all sure what they would do when they caught up with him.

Looking at her again and the mess she was in, Joe asked whether she was ok.

'I'll live,' she said, 'I got away with a lot more than I probably deserved she said smiling. The relief of escape had started to come but she was still shaking with shock. The fast movements of the car didn't help as it felt as if she had bruises in every place on her body. She shouldn't be here she knew, she should be getting treatment but somehow with Joe, this felt safer. This felt like doing something positive for a change.

Joe reached into his pocket and chucked his phone at Rachel.

'Last number called is Holding,' he said, 'ring him and tell him what we are doing.'

As the road spread into three lanes the traffic thinned out and they were able to get a closer to the cars ahead by pulling along the nearside.

The final set of lights turned to green and they watched the BMW head towards onto the M621 south, they followed making sure they were not too close. Once again Rachel thought about where this was taking them and what they'd do when they got there.

She called Holding.


Forty minutes later there was no doubt where they were going.

They'd been driving down the M62 at what felt like record speeds towards the East Coast and now they were on the John Sullivan Way into Hull.

Joe had no idea whether Hunter knew he was being followed or not. He had kept his speed at close to one hundred miles per hour throughout the journey, only slowing for traffic, he was definitely keen to get where he was going.

Working hard to keep up, the Police Vectra was sluggish and difficult to handle. He kept the BMW in his sight but was still almost four or five hundred metres behind. Any closer and he was sure Hunter would have spotted him.

Holding had been furious and he could hear his voice even with Rachel holding the phone to her ear. He'd demanded that they return to Leeds immediately and that even if they got to Hunter, there wasn't enough to arrest him until they had gone over the rest of the evidence. In fact, from what Rachel told him, the only person going to get arrested was Joe for theft of a police vehicle.

Between Joe and Rachel they both agreed that they weren't going to give up on Hunter. They didn't know what they could or would do but they wanted to confront him with everything that had happened.

As they drove along they caught up on everything that had happened. They made the connections between Hunter and Jenny Bowes, Hunter and the BFB leadership, between SAS security and the Mosque Bombing and the connections between Mark Davies and SAS security and Lucy Sayers' role in effect as local section chief. It all fitted together as an enormous conspiracy to manufacture an election win and create an angry paranoid nationalist power base in the North of England which could spread throughout the land. Nationalism grew exponentially when fear was at its maximum and this was exactly what had been planned.

This was a revolution growing out of Bible Belt America, where religion wasn't just religion but a political power base. The arrogance of white middle class American belief had grown into a doctrine of its own. It was self perpetuating, funded by commercial success. This had generated universities and academics intent on dismissing science and rationalism, replacing it with generous bible interpretations of known and sometimes mythological elements of history. The inevitable consequence of religious fundamentalism was to provide conflict with opposing religious dogmas whether in more moderate Christian elements or other faiths. The effect was the same, more conflict, argument, paranoia and reinforcement of existing beliefs.

Joe felt that religious conflict often translated to an issue of race and even though a massive element of Christian fundamentalist views came from black people in the US, the power came from the white middle class population as they'd greater resources. The class debate in America was also a race debate and even sharing the same religion didn't mean they shared the same class.

Somehow Hunter had tapped into this during his time in the US. From what Sarah had gained from her heart-to-heart with Russ, she learnt that Hunter had always been the stronger faith-wise at University than any of their other friends. He'd always been the leader and the instigator of debate in the groups, keeping them all from straying away from the central message.

Russ recalled he had gone to the US for a year on a sponsored trip provided by the Bishop. They had wanted to support his theological studies and felt that a period of time in the US Catholic College would help his research. Russ had no idea how it had come about, but Joe suspected that it was arranged by Father Peters who must have retained long term links with Hunter. It was no coincidence that he went to the same university as Jenny and was probably the reason why Jenny had remained with such a strong faith which she shared with Russ.

Peters must have had such a hold over Hunter, and Joe knew himself what a powerful presence he had. He must have nurtured Hunter after the cover up of the burial, ensuring he stayed within the faith, although Peters was not the nurturing type preferring to threaten hell and damnation to keep people in line. Whatever he did, Hunter must have been so wrapped up by him. He must have tried the same with Stephen Gorton but instead drove him to depression. Peters must surely not have imagined what he created by sending him to the US. For all Peters was a scary and manipulative priest he can't have wanted to create such an uncompromising murdering monster.

Hunter would have known that the two witnesses to the burial of Adrian Cullen were Jenny and Joe, because Peters saw them. So keeping tabs on one of them was essential and Jenny would have been the easiest to target given the hold her father had over her. She feared her father and the church, whereas Joe was more likely to be difficult to manipulate. With Jenny in the fold of the church she was unlikely to speak against a priest or any aspect of the church. In that case no matter what Joe discovered or spoke about that night no one would listen to him at least whilst Jenny didn't back him up.

What Hunter hadn't bargained for is that twenty-eight years later Jenny was not the same person as the innocent sixteen-year-old and was more than capable of raising questions that Hunter didn't want asking. The discovery of the body had blown his comfortable hidden past, and he had to act.

Jenny had stumbled on that site whilst looking into Peters' history. She'd found the website on Justice and tried to talk to the

Altar Boys listed as witnesses including, Stephen Gorton and Roy Hunter. She would have only found Stephen Gorton because he was probably described in the article as a tiler. Roy Hunter may have been described but he didn't exist under that name. She went to see Stephen Gorton after speaking to his brother and set the alarm off to Hunter about what she was doing.

Joe laughed ironically as he explained to Rachel, that the timing must have been crippling for Hunter. He most definitely wouldn't have wanted a scandal identifying him and linking him to his present persona at the same time as the opportunity had arisen in Leeds for his new party to begin the battle for Britain.

That was why he'd arranged for Jenny to have an accident, and he was determined that Hunter acknowledged it, although he considered that possibly he never would.

Passing under the Humber Bridge, Joe focussed on the drive. He wondered why he hadn't been stopped by police. One call from Holding to the Humberside Police would have stopped him by now. Perhaps, Holding had decided to let things take their course, after all Rachel and he hadn't done a bad job so far. For all his bluff and bluster, Holding was a reasonable guy. If Joe was able to keep tabs on Hunter then it was a convenient arrangement.

They moved through the city thinking about whether Hunter had some pre-arranged means of transport out of there. It certainly would be a stretch to think that Hunter had planned anything in advance. He surely would not have expected to have to get out of the country this quick otherwise he would never have come back. So if he was meeting a boat then it had to be someone he knew who could get him offshore straightaway.

It should have clicked with Joe earlier but it registered now as they turned into the marina. The BMW pulled up ahead of them. Joe continued past the car pretending not to notice Hunter getting out and heading for the quay. He pulled up as soon as he could find a space along the road.

'You're not going to go after him?' Rachel said shaking her head.

'What else do you suggest?' Joe replied. 'I mean, he's not exactly going to volunteer for a chat.'

'What are you going to do? Stop him getting on his boat?' she said, 'you can't do anything, Joe.'

'I don't know what I'm going to do except keep following him, if he leaves the country, we lose the whole thing.'

Without another word Joe jumped out of the car and headed after Hunter. Rachel immediately picked up the phone and called Holding. She couldn't let Joe do this.

Joe ran down the Quay looking for the boat Hunter intended to use. He could see him about fifty metres ahead of him, carrying a large brief case, probably at minimum, containing a laptop.

He watched Hunter turn right and step onto a gang plank. Joe slowed his run so he wouldn't be noticed approaching the boat. Fortunately there were other people wandering around the marina so he didn't stand out. Hunter hadn't expected to be followed and if he knew Joe was behind him, he gave no impression of it.

The boat was impressive, although he shouldn't have been surprised. Hunter was a multi-millionaire at least and a hundred-foot luxury cruiser was well within his means, including a crew to run it.

The engines were running as Joe checked out the cruiser. Clearly Hunter was not hanging around to admire the local night life. The ramp to get on the boat had been withdrawn and he saw his chance gone. Hunter was on his way out of the country and he likely wouldn't be back until the dust settled.

'Fuck it,' Joe thought. He took a running jump and leapt onto the boat as it pulled away. Getting to his feet, he got his composure back and climbed up the steps onto the rear deck of the boat.

This was probably the stupidest thing he'd ever done. He didn't even have his mobile as he'd left it with Rachel.

The boat pulled out of the marina and Joe ducked down. Hunter must have had approval from the Harbour Lock Keeper as the gate opened and the boat left the marina and out into the Humber. Joe got up from his hiding place and wrapped his coat tightly around him sheltering from the cold wind.

There was no choice. He didn't want to stay outside all night and freeze to death, waiting to find out where they might turn up. It was time to confront Hunter and face the consequences of his stupidity.

# CHAPTER THIRTY THREE

Standing on the Quay, Rachel watched with horror as the boat left. She struggled from the car after Joe had left, her body stiff and sore from running earlier, and tried to see what would happen.

With no shoes she couldn't run that fast to stop him and in the end she was just able to watch him leap onto the boat. She stood staring at the boat as it headed for the harbour lock. What did Joe think he was doing? He hadn't only leapt into the lion's den but closed the door shut.

'I guess I shouldn't be surprised to see you,' William Hunter said to Joe as he stood facing him.

'I couldn't let you leave without talking to you face to face.' Joe replied nervously.

William Hunter laughed. He stood in the large luxurious inner deck area. It was like being in a modern apartment with seemingly every gadget and indulgence catered for. The gamble of announcing his presence was that Hunter couldn't actually do anything to him as people would know that he was on the boat. Whilst killing him might be something Hunter wanted to do, in effect it wouldn't achieve anything.

'Sorry I'm being rude,' Hunter said, 'let me introduce my friend and colleague here, Henry Van Leitjen. It's his boat that you saw fit to trespass on.' Joe had seen the guy sat on the stool at the bar. He'd wondered how it was that Hunter had known to come here and recognised the name from one of the lists Fletch had given him. Maybe van Leitjen had regular reason to be in the UK and used his boat as transport, and Hunter had conveniently found his way out of town.

'If I was Henry I'd be very pissed off with you,' Hunter went on.

'I think I'm well beyond caring about what you, or he, thinks,' Joe responded as he tried to face down Hunter, 'I came here to ask you whether you killed Jenny Bowes?'

'What makes you think I even know what you're talking about or why I should tell a nobody like you?'

'Who is this guy?' van Leitjen asked Hunter, in a loud vulgar Dutch American accent, 'what the fuck is he talking about?'

'This, Henry, is Joe Barker. A pain in the ass journalist who has been making up some nasty stories about me, and it's largely the reason we are making this journey.'

'OK, so that's who he is,' he went on, 'why have we not thrown him in the drink. This is a waste of time.' Turning to Joe, van Leitjen got up and walked up to him.

'Who do you think you are already, James fucking Bond? You come on here like a big hero, what are you going to do, eh? Beat the fuck out of everyone on this boat and drive it back into Hull with a big fat hero flag?'

'I just want to know what he did,' Joe pointed at Hunter, his face flushed with anger and adrenalin.

'Well, fuck that, you're nothing, and I wouldn't piss on you if you were burning like a firework on this boat of mine. This is where you find your bullshit hero adventure has badly failed and you get to go swimming.'

'The problem is, my friend, that this nobody is not stupid,' Hunter took over, 'he didn't come here without people knowing where he is. He is a butt covering journo and if we dump him, then there's trouble round the corner. At the moment nobody knows anything for sure, even he doesn't. He's been chasing round after us for weeks now but he still doesn't have any facts, only rumour, innuendo and coincidence. If we dump him in the Humber, then everyone will know it was us and that may be more difficult to defend.'

'We should just dump him further out then, nobody will find him then,' van Leitjen went on still staring angrily at Joe.

'Let's think about it, we need a better way out of this one,' Hunter said thoughtfully.

'You killed Jenny Bowes didn't you?' Joe decided to get back to what he came for. 'She recognised you and you know and I know that I saw you back in 1981 burying Adrian Cullen.'

'If you're so clever; what are you doing here? Why should I tell you anything?' Hunter said angrily.

'Because you want to, you want everyone to know how clever you are, how you conspired to screw up Jenny Bowes. You ruined lives, how does that fit with your wonderful catholic beliefs?'

'Don't start lecturing me about our good Lord. I learnt a long time from the late great James Peters that belief in God wasn't just about worship but protecting the church from those that would destroy us. You should have learnt that lesson a long time ago I'd have thought. The wrath of the Lord is not something you should wish to contend with.'

'Threatening me with a hell and damnation, didn't work when I was sixteen, it certainly isn't going to work now,' Joe said defiantly.

'You think that's what I'm talking about? You've seen hell on earth before from what I hear. Do you know how easy it is to bring it on once again? You might think that somehow you can walk out of this alive, but taking a few chunks out of you would be boring. I think Hell works so much better when I inflict it on those close to you.'

Joe couldn't believe what he was hearing, was he referring to Liza?

'How about your new girlfriend...or her daughter?' he went on, '...makes a change from the Muslim whore you had before. What was that like, by the way...you really don't know what you've walked into, do you?'

'You're evil, this has got nothing to do with God, you're just an evil bastard,' Joe screamed.

'Enough of this crap,' van Leitjen spoke up, 'I think we should let the boys play with him for a while. It wouldn't get us anywhere but it would be a lot of fun to wipe that smug moral superiority off his face.'

'You're right, I'm bored already,' Hunter said, reaching for his intercom.

As he was about to speak a voice came out of the speaker.

'Mr van Leitjen we've just received an order from the coast guard to return to harbour.' The voice said, 'do I comply?'

'What is the reason?' van Leitjen asked.

'They have rescinded our permit to leave. They have reason to believe that you have someone on board that the police want to talk to.'

Relief flowed through Joe as Hunter and van Leitjen looked at each other. He couldn't read their thoughts but surely they had no choice. Did they?

# CHAPTER THIRTY FOUR

Leeds Town Hall was full of noise and bustle for the final election declaration late on Thursday morning or early on Friday morning depending how it was viewed. Everyone was exhausted from the long day previously but nobody wanted to leave until the announcement was done.

Rachel had wanted to stand as close to Anna as she could in the last day of her campaign, feeling a little guilty that with her own distractions, she'd let her boss down badly. She knew quite confidently though that although she hadn't been there for Anna whatever she would have done to help, she wouldn't have changed the outcome of the days voting. She could influence many things but elections were a little beyond her abilities.

As she watched everyone around her organising the room for the final declaration she smiled at the group of close friends she'd found through the nightmare of the last few days. The bruises on her face were obvious for everyone to see, a black eye, damaged nose, fat lip. The bruises on her body and legs were naturally covered and she would fight like hell to ensure the bruising inside would never show. After all she'd been through she intended not let it get her down. She would force herself to see past it and get back to normal life as soon as it was possible.

She satisfied herself that there were still cases to follow up, Purnell's court case was approaching and Anna, much as she'd like to think she might succeed tonight, was more than likely going to be available to manage the show as usual.

Admiring her boss for her blind optimism, she watched her chat to the other candidates and the dignitaries around, confident and assured as always. James stood by them with the kids, allowed to stay up late and see the democratic process in action. Rachel had talked to them a little earlier as they couldn't stop asking questions about her injuries and her face in the newspapers.

'Did it really happen like that?' they'd asked excitedly, of course Rachel managed to not answer and turn the chat back to them, sussing out the latest teenage challenges they wouldn't dare tell their mother.

James initially had been a bit loathe to let the kids talk to Rachel, he wasn't all together happy with the attention that Rachel had attracted with her abduction, but Anna had cut through all that as usual with her straightforward manner, and told him not to be ridiculous.

Joe and Sarah stood talking to each other for the most part, spectators in something that now didn't affect them, but had felt obliged to be here to see out the final act of the last four weeks. Rachel thought there was work to be done there in terms of them both dealing with what had happened but they were good people and she was confident they would work it out. Rachel and probably later Sarah, had screamed at Joe for his stupidity about going on that boat, but in the end they'd been lucky that the coast guard had reacted quickly to Holding's call. It seemed van Leitjen had the sense not to run, both of them believing they could argue their way out of it on land with some expensive lawyers on board. Running would have meant they were both on the run from the UK and that didn't make business sense for either of them.

The final part of the group had been Tina who had also come to see out the final part of the story that Alex had been so integral to. Rachel had been to see her with Joe earlier today and been surprised when Tina said she would come. Rachel had always liked her and these last few days they'd bonded well. She and Alex hadn't been bound to marry, but they were a steady couple who hadn't deserved to have their lives split apart this way.

Joe's return from the Humber Estuary after the halting of van Leitjen's boat by the coast guard, had started a whole barrage of further questions from Holding and the others. Lucy Sayers though had turned whistle blower due to a deal of some sort, as Rachel suspected she would. She was someone who looked out for number one and would find a way of talking her way out of any shit. She was clever, manipulative and she wouldn't be surprised to see her back in some other capacity.

For the moment Rachel was just happy to see the election go ahead without the nationalist party present, withdrawn from the ballot whilst electoral fraud was investigated. The others were still being held by the police including Lucy Sayers and the chief executive of SAS security, Peter Brown under the Prevention of Terrorism Act. Bill Roy and Andrew Bebbington had waved US passports but so far that this hadn't got them out of the police cells. Everyone else connected to the events at the BFB including Patrick Barclay were currently officially helping police with their enquiries but unofficially were as shocked as everyone else about what had occurred.

The last two victims had ironically been the two people who had started the whole scandal: the two bombers from South Leeds. They were found in a burnt out car on the moors near Penistone. They were identified through dental records. Mark Davies hadn't been the only one they intended to clean up.

The bell went to signal the declaration was ready.


Ten minutes later after the congratulations and commiserations were complete; everybody left the stage and made their way out of the building. Joe and Sarah offered their commiserations to Anna Stockton. She had managed a triumphant one thousand or so votes, which she appeared more than happy with.

'Respectably showing,' was all she said to everyone, almost happy just to have taken part. She was joyfully berating anyone who would listen that nothing would change with the Tories winning.

Joe turned to Rachel to say his goodbyes. He was feeling quite sad about leaving her but she just made light of it as usual, telling him that she would be in touch. Now Alex was not here she needed a contact in the press. Joe accepted the light-hearted goodbye seeing Rachel didn't want to dwell on it. There was far too much pain for her under the surface to want to touch it just yet.

Joe and Sarah moved out of the hall together, Sarah with her arm looped through Joe's as the crowd followed all around them. As they stepped out from between the large pillars at the front of the building they felt the bitterness of the dark autumn night.

They, along with the police watching the front of the building would not have been aware of the transit van pulled into the side of the Town Hall. They wouldn't have noticed Qamar Akhtar and his friend, the dark faced occupants, running away. They only would have known something was wrong when the flash of light exploded from the van followed by an ear splitting sound that could be heard right across the sleeping city of Leeds.

Lightning Source UK Ltd.
Milton Keynes UK
173613UK00001B/1/P